THE HUSBAND . . .
Edward Goad – a self-made millionaire devoted
to his miles of jute fields, to his estate, York House,
to the preservation of British rule. Mary was
grateful to him, but she could never love him.

THE LOVER . . .
Tiger Flemyng – a military aide to the Governor
of Bengal, a professsional soldier tired of all the
killing but still capable of torture and even
murder in behalf of His Majesty, the King-
Emperor. Mary knew he loved her, but she would
never be his wife.

The Raj

Donald H. Robinson

CORONET BOOKS
Hodder Fawcett Ltd., London

Printed and bound in Great Britain for
Coronet Books, Hodder Fawcett Ltd,
St. Paul's House, Warwick Lane,
London, EC4P 4AH
by Hunt Barnard Printing Ltd,
Aylesbury, Bucks.

ISBN 0 340 18991 6

Author's Note

THE ESSENCE of the story you will read is quite true. I've shifted a date, altered a name, even telescoped time where telescoping lent impact. However, in bulk and after thirty-six years, this is the way I remember it.

THE RAJ

1

IN CALCUTTA, INDIA, ON A DECEMBER AFTER-
noon in the early nineteen-thirties, a meeting of the Bengal
Club Board of Governors was called to order. The board
room was high-ceilinged, spare, insulated slightly against the
noises of Chowringhi Road outside. A taxi horn from the
Maidan could be heard now and then but, on the whole, the
only sound was the whirring of the electric ceiling punka,
new in nineteen twenty-six. A framed portrait of His Majesty,
the King-Emperor George the Fifth, presided benevolently
at one end of the room.

Ordinarily a meeting of the board provided only a peace-
able prelude to evening drinks in the lounge. New turbans
for the bearers might be under consideration, or whether or
not the curries at tiffin were being made a shade too hot by
the new kitchen wallah. This meeting, however, was out of
the ordinary.

Old Dermott Bryan was in the chair and was finally forced
to tap his glass with a pencil. "Gentlemen, let us discuss this
a trifle more calmly. No need to be overheated. After all, the
cold weather is nearly with us." He tried a smile at the others
but was met only by a few grunts in response.

He glanced down at a piece of paper. "The question before
us is whether or not for the period December twelve to
February twenty, during the cold-weather season, ladies
should be admitted to the premises of the Bengal Club when
in the company of members."

He peered toward a youngish, rather bland-looking man
in his late thirties. "Young Beauchamp here has proposed the
motion. He has obtained, I see, the signatures of the required
eight members."

"Never." It was Andrew Phillips shouting. Dermott Bryan

9

was never certain whether old Phillips shouted because he was angry or because it was the only way he could hear himself. He was a bit deaf from quinine, as were most of the old "quihais."

"Not never, Andrew. After all, ladies are due to be admitted again in nineteen ninety-four."

"That's sixty-odd years from now. Let them wait. I shan't be here." Old Phillips sat back grudgingly. The men about him nodded.

Sir John Thornton sighed. He was probably the only man there, except for old Phillips, who could remember the last time ladies had been admitted to the premises. That was nearly forty years ago. Once every hundred years, that was the rule on admitting members of the female sex to the club premises. Since the club was not yet two centuries old, there had been only one such visit. Nevertheless, of such stuff could customs be made. Dermott Bryan knew Beauchamp would never be able to alter matters. Still, let the fellow have his say.

Bryan nodded to Beauchamp. "Go on, man. Let's have it."

Beauchamp rose to his feet. No deafness about him, thought Sir John. He probably stays away from gin and tonic, drinks American cocktails.

"Gentlemen," began Beauchamp. "Fellow members of the Bengal Club." He smiled. "I realize that's a bit redundant."

Cheeky fellow, thought Sir John. Means to say the right thing. Just doesn't know these fellows.

"Gentlemen," said Beauchamp more seriously. "I know our proposal is disturbing but, believe me, it is anything but frivolous. After all, I waited several years to become a member of the club and I share your respect for it."

You also share in the advantages, thought Sir John. It's good business to belong to this club. Have all the top business chaps in Calcutta as fellow members.

"It's because I am thinking of the club that this proposal has been made. It's also a question of self-preservation. The club needs this gesture. To show it is still functioning. Not withering away."

That did it. A regular uproar broke out. Sir John wasn't certain who bellowed first. It might have been old Phillips. It might have been Angus Harrison, manager of Imperial Tea. Dermott Bryan banged patiently on his glass.

"Gentlemen, gentlemen," he said. "Beauchamp has the floor."

The uproar subsided. Beauchamp went blandly ahead. Give him credit, thought Sir John. He doesn't lose his head.

"We must face it, gentlemen," he said. "The club is losing old members more quickly than it is gaining new ones. One cannot prevent our respected elders from passing on. No one can live forever. And the younger chaps in town . . ." He hesitated. "We must recognize it. They're not applying for the Bengal Club anymore."

"Nonsense!" shouted Colonel Fenn. He was over from the Fort. "Poppycock. It's still the best club in the city. In all of India I might add."

"Hear . . . hear," muttered Angus Harrison. Andrew Phillips pounded the table.

Beauchamp nodded agreeably. "Of course. If one wants to meet the burra sahibs in Calcutta it cannot be equaled. But this doesn't seem to be enough for the young people today. They are newcomers for the most part. Have been in Calcutta only a year or two and they want sports and a little social life with their clubs."

"We've got snooker tables. And bridge. Jolly good bridge too," said Harrison. Sir John knew he was probably the best bridge player in the club.

"Not that sort of sport. Look at the Slap. They've put in a swimming pool, and they have dances once a week. They have more members than they can accommodate."

"You can't get a decent bridge game at the Slap," said Harrison.

"Look at the Jodhpur Club," said Beauchamp. "They've improved the golf course and put in a tennis court. Those clubs are coining money on new memberships. We're having extra assessments. Two this year. I suggest something has to be done and by opening our doors to the ladies this season we'll be serving notice we're coming to life."

Sir John looked around at his fellow board members. They looked gloomy. He knew what Beauchamp said was true. They knew it too. They were losing members faster than new ones applied.

Beauchamp was continuing. "I suggest this cold weather is an opportunity. We can set aside a day for the ladies, perhaps two days a week. They can be invited to tiffin or perhaps even dinner. That will bring in the young men and they can see what a really fine place we have here."

Or had here, thought Sir John, glancing at the occasional

mold stain on the walls. Have to paint those up a bit if we hope to attract new members.

"This is not a sports club nor is it a dance club," said Andrew Phillips firmly. "The Bengal Club was put together as a meeting place for males, a place to get away from the ladies once in a while. That, by heaven, is what it should remain."

"Hear, hear," said the others.

"Let the women go to the Slap if they want to dance," shouted Harrison. "Or that other club."

"Or Firpo's," snorted Colonel Fenn. "That's a public restaurant. They'll take in anybody."

The others laughed. Phillips patted the colonel on the back.

Dermott Bryan saw the drift of the issue but he was in an awkward position. He didn't want to come down too hard on young Beauchamp and his friends. They represented a fairly up and coming set in Calcutta, particularly in the jute trade. On the other hand he certainly wasn't going to offend the senior members. Something had to be decided and quickly. He knew Angus Harrison had a bridge game to get to.

"Sit down, Beauchamp, please. You have put your case very favorably."

"Thank you." Tom Beauchamp sat down. His expression was noncommittal. It was difficult to know whether he was disappointed.

"Gentlemen," continued Bryan. "I shan't ask for a decision at this moment. I'll simply make a ruling from the chair that the motion be tabled for the immediate future."

"Until nineteen ninety-four," said Angus Harrison. The men laughed.

"That's up to you. I doubt I'll be in the chair then. Meanwhile I propose that we table this proposal. Any objection?"

"Not from me," said Angus Harrison.

The others shook their heads vehemently.

"Beauchamp? Do you insist on a vote?"

"No, sir." Beauchamp knew what the result of a vote would be. This way he could at least preserve his good relations with the other members. No point in antagonizing burra sahibs.

He mustered up a bland smile. "I think you've given me a very fair hearing. Thank you." He bowed.

Dermott Bryan tapped the glass. "This meeting is closed then. I suggest we meet in the lounge. Thank you."

One or two of the senior members patted Beauchamp as they passed. "Good show, lad," said Colonel Fenn. "Bring your women to the Fort." He followed the others out. There was nobody left but Beauchamp and Sir John.

The elderly man nodded. "Good try, Beauchamp. Well said."

"I trust I wasn't impertinent, sir."

"Not at all. Denise would have been proud of you."

"Thank you, sir. I had particularly hoped we could admit ladies this season. We're having a houseguest."

"Lady Thornton told me. This Miss what's-her-name."

"DeGive, sir. Mary deGive."

"We're having a Miss Cranston. Bunty Cranston. Niece of a stamp collector I've been corresponding with." Sir John looked gloomy.

"Very nice of you to have her, sir."

"Yes. Well, we'll see." The old gentleman looked doubtful. "On that notion of yours, better luck next time. In nineteen ninety-four perhaps." Sir John nodded vaguely and moved off toward the stairway leading down to the entrance hall.

Beauchamp looked after Sir John. So they were going to have a houseguest too. Lady Thornton, of course. Everyone knew it was she who insisted on inviting these girls. She had been a "fishing fleeter" herself. Sir John hated the whole thing but put up with it for his wife's sake. Beauchamp shrugged, turned away. He had his own problems this cold weather.

At the entrance to the club Sir John waited for his syce to bring around his car. The kithmaghar at the entrance helped him in and Sir John sank back. He was getting too old to attend these board meetings. Those old chairs were nearly as bad as the ones he had sat on as chief justice. When a man retired he was at least entitled to a more comfortable chair.

"Sahib?" It was the syce turned around to face him.

"Regent's Park. And ahista jao." He didn't want to drive fast. He liked to catch a little nap on the way home.

"Bahut achcha." The syce turned around. He knew better than to hurry. He had been driving Sir John ever since his retirement. The old Daimler moved slowly up Chowringhi and turned left onto Park Road.

Sir John didn't slip into his nap straightaway. He was in

a reminiscent mood. It was, he reflected, probably the reference at the club to the last time ladies had been admitted, in eighteen ninety-four. It had reminded him how much Calcutta had changed.

The horse had been the center of life then. They pulled the gharries, those boxlike, enclosed carriages used for taxis, and they drew the private carriages for an evening's airing in the Maidan or on the Strand. One rode them on paper chases or to picnics, and one bet on them at the races on the Maidan or up at Darjeeling. The horse still had its place but everything now in the way of conveyance seemed to be the motorcar.

Sports had changed too. Tennis, croquet, archery had been the accepted sports when he had first come out. Tennis was still played, particularly the tea tennis parties on private courts. And the Slap had good courts as did the Ballygunge Club, though the latter now accepted Indian members.

Now organized sports were the thing—rugby teams, football, and cricket. And the latter two had been largely taken over by the Indians. It was amazing to see how the Indian football sides played in bare feet. In the rainy season they played rings around the booted British sides. As for cricket, there was hardly a British eleven in India that could stand up to the side fielded by the Indian princes.

It was this swaraj agitation that was most disturbing. In the nineteenth century and before the war it had been confined to legal agitation. Lawyers like this Nehru's father, educated in England, had restricted themselves to legal arguments for representation. Now India had Gandhi or the terrorists stirring things up.

It was all the Great War, Sir John mused. Nothing had been the same since. The Indians had been promised a reward if they would provide troops and they had responded nobly. Now they wanted their pound of flesh and were impatient.

He, for one, was not sorry to be out of things. He had done his stint, forty-six years in the Bengal Courts. He could afford to relax. It was the younger chaps like this Beauchamp he wondered about. He couldn't blame them for wanting to change things about. Damn it, he'd do the same in their place.

Sir John sighed. Now there was another cold weather season about to begin and there'd be the young lady visitors out from England. That at least hadn't changed. He supposed they had to have the Cranston girl. He wondered what this deGive woman would be like. "DeGive." Odd name. He muttered it once or twice. Must be Norman. At least it sounded an old family. He wondered whether she'd be like some of the other visitors the Beauchamps had entertained. He hoped not. A very racy lot, most of them.

The old Daimler went slower now. It had wedged itself behind a bullock cart swaying heavily in the crowded street, the driver asleep on the frontboard. Sir John's syce honked once or twice, then resigned himself to waiting. Sir John opened a sleepy eye on the cart.

"No lantern, of course. Blasted farmers never carry them. Should be hauled up."

His eyes closed, his pale face sank lower against his shirt-front. The white hair and mustache tucked themselves into place. The syce relaxed in his seat. The Daimler followed the bullock cart, the retired chief justice and the bullock driver both peacefully asleep.

While Sir John was being driven slowly out toward Regent's Park, Tom Beauchamp was driving his Ford roadster toward the flat he and Denise occupied in Tollygunge.

Tom and Denise were rather unlike the average youngish married couple in Calcutta. Most were out from the Midlands or Scotland and held only chota sahib jobs in the wholesale trades or insurance or jute.

Tom and Denise were not only Londoners but obviously Mayfair and Cambridge. Tom was said to be the twin brother of a peer but having been born ten minutes later than his brother, the elder had gotten the title and the lands and Tom had migrated to India—to earn a living and to make it less awkward in London for his brother, the earl.

Tom was still young-looking with the rather smooth good looks the Prince of Wales was then making fashionable. He belied his English background by an addiction to American cars, slang, and drinks and associated in Calcutta less with his fellow English than with the small international group, particularly the young Greek bachelors in Ralli Brothers. It was the only hint that he might resent the unlucky hand British law had dealt him.

Denise Beauchamp had her own special aura. It was rumored that she had once been the mistress of a certain Near-Eastern industrialist, that he had set her up comfortably when they parted and Tom had been part of the arrangement. She sunbathed daily on the roof of the Saturday Club, the "Slap," an unheard-of practice for British wives. She also played squash like a man, frequently playing at the Slap with the barefooted, fez-wearing Indian professional. Surprisingly, she was not very pretty for the ex-mistress of an industrialist, being rather plump and sloppy, but she had fine eyes, a quick smile, and a warm good nature. She and Tom were faithful, so far as it was known, so they were accepted, perhaps envied, and even, on occasion, pointed out. The truth, of course, was that they were somewhat sophisticated for Calcutta.

They lived on the top floor of a cumbersome, rambling two-flat house. The top floor in Tollygunge houses was always the more expensive since it had its own verandah, was generally cooler, and was further from street nuisances. The Beauchamps had three bedrooms, two of them large, a broad dining room, the usual bath with hot water geeser, a kitchen and serving pantry, and a small verandah outside their bedroom. Here they sat every evening after dinner for coffee and a little brandy. Sometimes they played two-handed American gin rummy but usually they simply sat and read the magazines—Denise read the *Sporting and Dramatic* and *Sphere* and Tom *The New Yorker*—or watched lizards chase bugs up and down the wall.

They fought occasionally, of course. Denise could never quite forgive Tom for not having hurried up and been born ahead of his brother. To her, ten minutes seemed a trifling matter if one really tried. But they concealed their irritabilities, even in the hot weather and, having no children, had few vexations. It seemed in every way a placid and normal marriage.

Tom drove his car while the syce sat beside him. Tom was depressed and irritated. He had feared the Board of Governors would turn down his group's request but he had at least expected a vote to be taken.

The depressing point of it was that the club actually was on the rocks. He hadn't been merely argumentative when he had pointed out the assessments, the loss of members; it was a damned fact. The club had seen its best days and wouldn't face it.

For that matter, so had Calcutta. An enterprising chap would see the handwriting on the wall and get out of it. The jute trade had slackened off; the demand for tea was steady but not improving. The railway rolling stock was aging with minimal replacements. The country was standing still, partly due to the worldwide slump but also due to all this home-rule agitation. Swaraj.

As though Gandhi weren't bad enough, now had come this Gupta fellow. His terrorists were something new. They added a violence to the swaraj drive that was a little unsettling. Old Saunders, head of the European Association, had been shot and badly wounded while simply driving in the Maidan in his motorcar. And the raid on the Chittagong armory just a few months back. They had killed four constables and picked up a fair amount of guns and ammunition in the bargain.

A smart fellow might get out of India. He had best reconsider that Brazilian paper deal. He hadn't looked at it seriously at first because he didn't think anything could replace jute in the world markets, certainly not a paper product. He would discuss it again with Denise.

As for the Bengal Club meeting, that had been a damned shame. He had wanted very much that his proposal should be passed. It was this Mary deGive. He and Denise would need all the help they could get.

Tom cursed. It had been a joke to permit Denise to have Mary. He thought it might be a lark to spring Mary deGive on Calcutta. She was so damned mid-Victorian. It would be an added bit of fun for the cold weather. Now she promised to be a nuisance. He had hoped he could at least dispose of her at the club once in a while.

Tom drove fretfully, his mouth drooping with self-pity. This promised to be damned bad cold weather. He shivered a little. Then he understood. It had been cool that morning when he had gone to the office. The cold weather was already on them.

2

DR. TOMPKINS, SHIP'S DOCTOR OF THE S.S. *STRATH-naver,* Peninsular & Orient Line, stood at the railing. He had been going back and forth between Southampton and Bombay every voyage of the *Strathnaver* for nearly eight years. One of his few pleasures, if he might name it so, was watching the new passengers embark at Southampton. Sometimes, he told old "Sparks" in the wireless cabin, he felt like Charon.

It was on the late November sailing that he noticed Mary deGive. He noticed her first because she was carrying her own luggage, a rather elderly suitcase bound with a gay bit of yellow cordage. It was most unusual for passengers to fetch their own luggage board. He assumed she must have battled fiercely with some unlucky navvy.

He watched her carefully as she clutched the gangway railing. She peered up at the waiting vessel, her face upturned in undoubted anticipation. She wasn't pretty, that was apparent to him. Nor was she young. He estimated her to be in the middle or late thirties.

But there was something in that face, an excitement perhaps, an eagerness, that set her apart. The doctor had seen many lone women climb aboard the *Strathnaver,* India bound, most of them younger than this one, but he could remember no one climbing the gangway with quite such an air of excitement. She even paused once halfway to close her eyes in sheer happiness. She then rushed ahead to disappear beneath him into the ship's entry.

It was several days before he saw the woman once more. The ship rolled slowly down to Gibraltar, bucking into the heavy seas, pitching doggedly bow to stern. Few passengers appeared in the dining salon.

At Gibraltar he saw her again. The seas were calm beneath

18

the Rock and passengers gratefully flocked into the open air
to gaze at the majestic fortress.

He saw her near the stern, wan and holding to the railing.
It was obvious that it had not been an easy passage so far.

She stood determinedly, almost, the doctor thought, as
though at attention. There was an expression of pride on her
face and something else. He had seen it in new doctors on
receiving their diplomas: dedication.

The ship's horn blasted, deep and prolonged. The woman
turned and went unsteadily from the railing toward the pas-
sageway below. She had completed her ritual of obeisance.

The *Strathnaver* moved eastward now. The November skies
were still gray but the Mediterranean behaved less inhos-
pitably than the Atlantic.

More passengers appeared on deck. Dr. Tompkins saw the
woman again. She wore the same clothing in which he had
first noticed her. It was obvious that the single piece of luggage was not overburdened.

She had a curious way of dressing, almost old-fashioned.
Most of the English lady passengers wore hats, either the little
cloche hat still in style in India or the new Empress Eugenie
hats bought freshly for the voyage. Miss deGive—the doctor
had learned her name—wore no hat and carried her hair
neck-length in a knot as her mother might have done. Her
full skirt was long and she wore a high-necked blouse. Once
he saw her in a turtleneck sweater.

The vessel paused briefly at Alexandria and then moved on
to Port Said. The next morning they entered the Suez Canal.

The *Strathnaver* now came to life. The doctor and other
ship's officers changed into whites: white shorts, high socks,
blouses, caps. A children's play area was constructed on deck,
a large wooden frame strung with heavy ropes. Indian ayahs
appeared with their children-charges and settled comfortably
inside.

A canvas swimming bath was constructed on the forward
deck and, when they moved from the canal into the Red Sea,
warm, brownish water was pumped in and the pool was soon
filled.

The doctor saw Miss deGive again, swimming placidly
about. Her bathing costume was full skirted, knee length, and
hardly modern. The other female swimmers, mostly young
ladies, wore the new French bathing dress: blue flannel shorts
and the sleeveless, striped jumper called a "maillot." The

woman seemed unaware or undaunted, swimming breast stroke, capless head held high, absorbed, happy.

It was inevitable that he speak to her. Her deck chair had been placed on the upper or sports deck and here he had seen her, occasionally with other, younger girls sitting around her, chatting, laughing. She seemed to have taken over the matron duties on the ship. Her chair had become something of a rallying point.

One day after tea, a day short of Aden, he found her quite alone in the chair. There was something unaccustomedly pensive, even fatigued in the way she leaned back.

"May I sit down? I'm Dr. Tompkins, ship's doctor." He smiled his usual shipboard smile.

"Oh, do." She bounced up, quickly alive.

She's really quite nice looking, he thought. Not pretty, her face a trifle too broad perhaps. But a good English complexion, peaches and cream, and the eyes were intelligent, a lovely blue.

He settled back comfortably. "First voyage out?"

"Oh yes." She beamed at him.

"Enjoying it?"

"Marvelous."

"Are you from London?"

"Oh, dear no. Roecroft. I'm a schoolteacher. I was," she added.

"Roecroft." He knew there was no need to identify it further. Roecroft was probably one of the most renowned of England's boarding schools for young ladies.

"Will you teach school in India?"

She shook her head emphatically. "I'm through with that."

"ICS?" He knew the India Civil Service was still hiring British staff.

"No." She hesitated a moment, then laughed quite openly, the blue eyes delighted. "I'm going out to look for a husband."

"Well, you are candid."

"Why not? Most of the girls on this ship are."

"You know what they call you in India?"

"Fishing fleeters. We're in the fishing fleet." She laughed again, delighted with the name.

"Where did you hear of the fishing fleet?"

"I grew up in Cheltenham. I've always known of it."

"Ah." He nodded. Cheltenham, like Bath, was a watering

spa for retired Indian Army officers and retired Indian Civil Service wallahs. It was a pleasant, tranquil spot in the south of England.

She went on. "My father was a doctor like you. I heard lots about India."

"In his waiting room no doubt."

She almost giggled. "They used to take me on their knees, all the old colonels and planters. They used to call me 'miss sahib.' "

"All the old quihais." There was just a touch of bitterness in his tone.

"Yes. They told me all about India. They said there were eight bachelors to every woman out there, every white woman. That's how the fishing fleet came along. Anyway, when I decided . . ." She looked almost hesitant, then shrugged. "When I decided it was time I married, I decided on India."

"Very commendable. But you waited rather long, don't you think? You may be coming in at the end of the line."

"Swaraj?"

"Yes. Home rule. The old Empire may be on its way out."

"I don't believe it." Her broad mouth firmed itself. "That's another reason I'm going out. Marrying in India is the least an Englishwoman can do now. It shows our confidence."

"Hear, hear." Again there was that note of bitterness.

"I'm a member of the Empire Club, Doctor. On Curzon Street. It made us so angry when Gandhi came to London and the government hailed him so. They didn't seem to know what to do."

"They don't."

She turned to him earnestly. "We'll lose India, Dr. Tompkins, if we don't do something. We need the Raj and India needs us."

"Quite true."

"But all that was being done in London was talk. Nobody did anything. Not even in the Empire Club. I wanted to do something but what could I do, just a woman."

"You could marry out there."

"Exactly. My father went out to the Boer War because medical help was needed desperately. He gave up his practice and went. Women are needed in India. Wives. I know this sounds silly."

"Not at all."

"But if we lost the Raj and I hadn't tried at all, hadn't done anything . . ."

"That would be worse."

She said nothing but from her look at him, there was no need. The blue eyes were determined, the broad mouth resolut. He thought the early queen Boadicea might have looked so.

"Do the other girls on the ship feel this way? The fishing fleeters." He smiled.

"Oh, I don't know." She was quickly cheerful again. "They have their reasons, I suppose. They just want to get married. It's easier in India. I want to get married too. It's high time, don't you think? I'm thirty-eight. For me it has to be India."

"It may not be easy."

"I know. They're much younger than I. And some of them are very pretty." She looked at him almost worriedly.

"Some of them."

"They have such nice clothes too. I never seemed to have time to buy clothes."

"You are different."

"There isn't much time either. I'm going to Calcutta. The cold weather doesn't last very long, does it?"

"Eight or ten weeks."

"There must be someone out there for me. If there's someone looking for a wife of thirty-eight, not very pretty or well dressed . . . why, I'll have no competition." She was cheerful again.

"I wasn't thinking of the competition when I said it might not be easy. These are not easy times in India."

"I know. The terrorists. We've read about that." Her broad jaw jutted angrily. "They've killed some of our magistrates."

"India itself is not easy. Heat, disease. You have a nice skin. It might age quickly in India. Crinkle. In ten years an Englishwoman can look twenty-five years older."

"Heavens. That would put me over sixty."

"Not all the English will welcome you. There are some who resent the fishing fleet."

"But why on earth?"

"Oh, it used to be an Englishman settled in India. He took an Indian mistress, learned the language, made it his home. Now what happens?"

He looked at Mary as though awaiting an answer. She could only smile expectantly.

"He marries an English girl, gives up his mistress, and has to run a proper home. If he has children, they're sent back to England to school. This means he has to take the wife home every three or four years to see them. He's just a visitor in India now. Many think the fishing fleet has come between the Englishman and India."

"I hope everyone doesn't feel like that. Not the bachelors."

"They won't." He hesitated. "Please go back, Miss deGive."

"Go back? But I've only just come."

"Believe me, there's nothing you can do in India."

"I can marry."

"Marry in England where we belong."

"I'm not needed in England. Not even in Roecroft." She turned away and he could see a loneliness there. He saw suddenly the need to go to India. Call it loyalty, patriotism . . . whatever name she put on it. This was a lonely woman.

She quickly recovered, chuckled. "I'm already of some use. Some of the girls here are really quite frightened. I cheer them a little."

"I've noticed."

"It's almost like Roecroft. Listening to their problems. It wouldn't do for me to give up."

"I wish you luck. Perhaps the Raj does need you. Well, I should be going. Must preside at the ship's doctor's table."

He spoke with a surprising bitterness. She could see deep lines appear in his round face, almost as though a glacier were to reveal hidden fissures.

He stood up. "I suppose I've become a bit of a crank, going back and forth on this ship for eight years. I watch the girls come out each cold weather and I want to warn them. I had a daughter married in India. She wouldn't be discouraged either. She died out there of the amoebic. She and her boy both."

He stood above her chair, deep in his thoughts. Then he shrugged, the fissures disappeared to leave his face smooth and calm again. "I wish you good luck. Good-bye."

She watched his stout figure as he went down the deck, unhurried, with a curious dignity. Charon himself, as "Sparks" would have told her had he been there.

Mary left her chair, walked slowly to the railing. The sea below hissed quickly past but Mary was barely aware.

She had been warned. Heat, disease, a country that aged

women. Go back while there was still time he had said. She
might be coming in at the end of the Raj.

What, really, did she know about India? Not much actually
beyond the tales told by elderly men. She had never really
studied India. She had busied herself with the Empire Club
and made a fuss over the Raj and its cause but was it out of
interest in the Empire or simply because she was single? She
didn't really know.

For that matter, she didn't really know herself. She had
always assumed she was a lady. She certainly didn't look the
accepted type: broad features instead of slender, large hands
instead of delicate, a husky, even hoarse voice instead of
well pitched. She hardly dressed the part. Her clothing was
nondescript, passé, as though frozen in a style of twenty years
before. As, perhaps, she had been.

Yet she had been educated to be a lady and the name,
deGive, had supposedly come to England with the Normans.
And, Heaven knew, she had certainly interested herself in
ladylike causes, Armenian Relief, Belgian Relief, that sort of
thing. She attended the proper concerts, subscribed to fort-
nightly opera seats, had even spent two summers in France.

Yet was she sufficiently bloodless, remote, high-principled?
She had never really enjoyed the concerts or opera. She had
rather wander into Chelsea or the less fashionable but
rowdier pubs of Soho or Shepherd's Market. She had felt a
fraud. Then, inevitably, there had come the explosion: a
very minor one, more of a popgun than an explosion.

Mary stared down into the water. She could see again that
last meeting with poor Mr. Janeway. He couldn't go on with
their little weekends, he had said. Harmless weekends, God
knew: merely two companionable schoolteachers paying occasional visits to shrines of England's past. Stonehenge, the
Roman ruins at Bath, things like that.

But Mr. Janeway had been brought to heel. The head of
his school, St. Mordred—or St. Morbid as the Roecroft girls
dubbed it—had made it plain. There was no room for him
at St. Mordred's unless he discontinued this relationship with
Miss deGive.

Poor, dear Mr. Janeway . . . he hadn't wanted to break
off with her but, at his age, he needed the school much more
than the school needed him.

She had soon turned in her own resignation. Perhaps she
had been leading up to it, even her taking up with Mr. Jane-

way in the first place. She had wanted a change in her life and knew she might not have the courage of her own will.

A time had come, that was it. Roecroft had been a sanctuary after the Great War, after Tim's death. She had retreated to the old school as a place to hide. But she had mourned long enough. She was on the shady side of thirty-eight. She could remain forever at Roecroft, unused, never knowing what might have been.

Then, as she had told the ship's doctor, it had all come to a head over this swaraj business. Home rule, the Indians called it. Anyone with half an eye knew that it merely meant exchanging one set of rulers for another, less benevolent rule than the British Raj. It had made her blood boil the way in which the Mahatma was welcomed in London. Government seemed to care more for his skinny welfare than it did our fellow British in India.

It all fell into place. The British in India needed reinforcing; she needed a husband. The Raj needed every bit of loyalty available, even a woman's, offering a woman's mite so to speak.

She turned to look forward toward the bow. India lay there, another day and a half across the Indian Ocean to Bombay. Then there'd be a two- or three-day train ride across India to Calcutta.

She would certainly not turn back now.

3

THE MARSH WHERE THE CITY WOULD REST HAD been built by two rivers. One rose in Tibet, north of the Himalayas, then flowed, cold and clear, seven hundred miles to the east to plunge down through a gap in the mountains. It turned southwest then and rolled on between the hills of Burma to the east and the Shansi hills of Western Bengal until it descended a thousand feet to the Bay of Bengal. In Tibet the river was called the Tsangpo but in India, when it had burst south through the mountains, it was called the Brahmaputra, the "Son of Brahma."

The other river was born on the under side of the Himalayan watershed. As the Tsangpo was flowing across the northern side, the Jumna flowed south from the mountains, then east until it met the Upper Ganges at Allahabad. The two rivers greeted, journeyed east together, and were joined by two other rivers hurrying down from the mountains, the Gogra and the Gandak. Then, as a mother who has collected her brood, the majestic Ganges drifted placidly across the broad plains of northern India until it turned south around the Garo Hills and stretched its broad fingers toward the Bay of Bengal.

Now the two rivers worked as one. The Brahmaputra brought silt from the mountains to the north. The Ganges, two hundred miles to the west, came to the end of its broad channel and nosed its silt ahead as a groundhog might burrow through the earth. Islands of mud formed and reformed or disappeared entirely during the rainy seasons under a vast sheet of turgid waters. And always, under the onslaught of the two rivers, the Bay was being pushed stubbornly backward. The great delta of northern Bengal was being born.

In time seeds blew from the mainland and marsh grass and birds appeared. Fish swam up from the Bay and crocodiles preyed on them from the muddy banks. For five months in the year, from March until July, the marshes baked under a sky without clouds. In July rain was swept north from the Bay by the summer monsoon until, trapped by the Garo Hills, it fell on the slopes, washed down to the Ganges, and added to the silt. It rained for four months and the marshes steamed.

In late November the monsoon winds quietly shifted to the north and the rains stopped. A cool dry air from the Himalayas spread over the delta. Birds dipped and soared excitedly. The marshes, limp grass until now, were pennants flung to the breeze. Even the ancient rivers, sluggish and brown, tried to sparkle. It was a respite of three months.

As the marshes grew they were given a purpose. Conquerors were appearing on the mainland from the northwest and pushing down into the plains of India. The inhabitants, the conquered, fled east along the path of the great Ganges. A last few, more adventurous or more desperate, escaped to the delta marshes. Villages grew on the muddy banks and clung tenaciously. The villagers fished, trapped birds, and planted rice. New conquests overran the plains behind them but the villages remained remote and safe in the marshes.

Then a new kind of conqueror appeared, and from a different direction. For thousands of years India had been invaded from the northwest, across the mountains. The newcomers came from the other direction, sailing up from the Bay. And these people, the British, seemed at first only to be traders.

There were three small villages at the western end of the delta on a branch of the Ganges called the Hooghly. The British rented one of the villages from its chief and established a trading area, then a fort to protect the trading area. The fort was named Fort William in honor of the king then ruling England. The village had been named for its patron, the ruling god of the marsh. It was called Kali Ghat.

The British prospered. Other trading areas were established and British control was extended to the mainland. The East India Company, the original private venture that had taken over the delta village, was in time replaced by the British government.

The city grew. Docks and warehouses were built on both sides of the Hooghly. A British residential area grew near Fort William and the commercial district was surrounded by a growing native town.

In the nineteenth century railway lines were laid to the mainland and a great station was built on the west bank of the Hooghly. Jute and engineering factories were raised nearby and a solid bridge was flung across the river.

A palace was erected for the governor as the town was now the capital of Bengal and then, for a while, the capital of all India. The viceroy built a palace and the Indian princes, wishing to be near the seat of power, occupied palaces nearby.

A boulevard appeared, then a park. Squares were laid out, centers for the growing banking and insurance companies. Shipping lines opened offices, not only British lines from nearby Burma or the Straits Settlements but British firms based as far away as China, Japan, or Australia. Foreign lines sent in their ships and opened trade. Foreign governments established official representation.

A great and imperial city was being built. The village of

Kali Ghat, now known to the world as Calcutta, had grown in a hundred and seventy years to a city of more than two million people. By the early nineteen-thirties it was second in size in the Empire only to London. A strange thing had happened. The marshes had reconquered the mainland.

4

ALASTAIR ST. GEORGE FLEMYNG, CAPTAIN IN the Poona Horse, aide-de-camp and bodyguard to His Excellency, the Governor of Bengal, eyed the top of his servant's head. He was seated on his bed, the bearer kneeling before him pulling up his socks. Captain Flemyng stood up, stepped into the underdrawers his bearer held for him, and allowed his servant to pull them up and button the front. He then held up his arms: the servant dropped his undervest over his head, pulled it down.

His blue military trousers were next pulled up and Captain Flemyng, "Tiger" to his occasional friend, sat again on the bed while Fazid knelt to put on his shoes.

It was with a certain grim satisfaction these days that Flemyng permitted his servant these daily ministrations. It was customary, of course, for sahibs to be dressed by their bearers. To do otherwise would disturb the long-established master-servant relationship. But Flemyng wondered now as he looked down at his servant's straight black hair how long this Muslim, the descendant of generations of fighting Pathans, would continue to kneel at the sahib's feet pulling on his socks. Captain Flemyng half hoped that one day his bearer would pull out a kukri and try to slice off a few of the captain-sahib's toes.

Captain Flemyng was grimly irritable that morning. If he needed a reason, he knew he had a whole host from which to select.

In the first place, the cold weather season was about to begin. This was his second cold weather in Calcutta and he knew what to expect. There were the girls, for example. He was a bachelor and wished to remain one. He resented being the object of pursuit. He could barely bring himself to be civil to them.

There was another thing. He was a soldier, yet, with the cold weather season, his social duties as aide-de-camp increased. He was expected to dance with the right ladies, chat with the proper smile. Under ordinary circumstances he knew that some pink young lieutenant would have been chosen for the post.

But these were not ordinary times. The Raj was in trouble. The terrorists were amuck in Bengal. The governor needed a proper soldier by his side. So he had been chosen, plucked from his regiment largely on his war record—two wounds and a DSM at Gallipoli and third wound and a second ribbon in the Mespot. He had accepted because he was ambitious and Calcutta was the center of power. But he was still a soldier and, for the girls and the social nonsense that lay just ahead, he felt a sharp distaste.

He moved away from Fazid and pulled on his dress blouse, scarlet with blue piping, the colors of his regiment. He went to the bureau mirror, gave his black hair, a gift from his Irish mother, a last brushing.

Smile, you bastard, he muttered. You'll never get a battalion with that busted face. He must practice looking gracious.

He went into the living room, finished his tea and rum. He was going to Sunday church and needed all the stimulant permissible.

Ordinarily he looked on church as he did everything else in the line of duty. It was a discipline good for a soldier. He had learned to sit rigidly in his seat, at attention, eyes on the pulpit, neither hearing nor participating. It always reminded him of Indian holy men, sitting on a bed of nails and staring fixedly at the sun.

But today would be different. This would be the first Sunday of the season and there would be women there. Fishing fleeters. He knew he would be left in peace during the service. It was afterward, outside, that he dreaded. He would have to run a damned gauntlet. All because he was an aide to the governor of Bengal and single.

He nodded to Fazid as he went out the door held open for

him. The syce had brought around the Morris. Flemyng briefly returned the syce's salute, climbed into the driver's seat. He would not be like the other sahibs in Calcutta, letting their syces drive them. To him the daily battle in Calcutta traffic was a satisfying outlet.

He drove out into the busy street. A bicyclist cut across his path but he drove straight on, forcing the cyclist to fall off his bike, cursing.

Tiger cursed him back. "Ooloo k foofoo," he yelled, then settled back comfortably. Thank God for these little diversions.

Denise Beauchamp was not in the best of moods that morning. The new gown she had entrusted to the durzi Phyllis Anson had recommended had turned out badly. It had been an economy on her part to have her cold weather gown made by a durzi. Everyone in Calcutta was trying to save money this year. Now it was only money down the drain. She sat over the frock, thread in mouth, eyeglasses on top of her head, picking at the durzi's work.

Tom Beauchamp stood in the bedroom window, still in his pajamas, and scratched his stomach irritably. It was Sunday. He usually felt a little amorous on Sunday mornings from the gins on Saturday night. With Mary deGive in the house, one had to be discreet.

He glanced at his wife, went restlessly to sit on the bed. "How's the dress?" He always called frocks "dresses" in the American way.

"Bloody. Makes me look forty." Since Denise was thirty-nine, she knew that left her little margin. "Too long and too full. I can't think why Phyllis Anson recommended him."

"Phyllis always wears things too long and too full." He took off his pajama top, threw himself full length on the bed.

"Don't bounce. You'll scatter the pins." She knew what Tom might have on his mind. He could be demanding on Sundays. This morning she had something else to think of besides her frock. Mary.

It had been an impulse agreeing to her visit. Mary had shown her about at Roecroft when Tom's brother, the peer in the family, had asked them to accompany him to a governors' meeting. She had quite liked Mary and, when Mary had suddenly cabled and asked if she might visit them in

Calcutta, she had agreed. She hadn't fully realized at Roecroft just how out of place she might seem elsewhere.

The trouble was she rather liked Mary. She had found her surprisingly easy to have around the house. Mary listened to her chatter, gossiped with her in a wry sort of way. She had been good company during her daily visits to the bazaars and shops. She hadn't realized just how much she had wanted a woman friend in Calcutta.

There was another thing. Mary seemed to be enjoying herself so much. She didn't gush but Denise could see that there was an honest satisfaction with Calcutta, as though the bazaars, Chowringhi Road, the Fort, and the Maidan were exactly as she had expected them to be. It was different from their previous visitors who had found the bazaars dirty, Chowringhi a little ridiculous, and the Fort an antique curiosity. There was a reassurance in Mary, and Denise knew she herself needed it sometimes.

"Did the invitations come to the Garden Party?"

"Yes."

"Mary too?"

"Yes. I told Tiger Flemyng she would be visiting."

"Damn. I suppose we have to take her." Tom was aggrieved.

"Of course. It's the first big do. The governor's Garden Party is practically an official welcome. If she's not there, it'll make it that much more difficult for us to take her about."

"She looks such a freak. You never know what she's going to wear. Turtlenecks. I doubt there's been a turtleneck worn in Calcutta since before the war."

"I think she has some very nice clothes. And they suit her."

"I wish to God we'd never invited her." He stretched languidly. "I'm damned if I'm going to do much for her."

"Tom, she's our guest."

"She's your guest. You take care of her." He rose indolently to his feet, went out to the verandah.

"But you're the only one who knows men. You could always produce someone from the office."

"What men? We haven't hired anyone new in a year."

"There's the Bengal Club. There are men her age."

"I tried. The club doesn't want women. Besides, why this bother about men? She can't be coming to get married. Not at her age." His voice carried fretfully from the verandah.

"She was nice to us at Roecroft, Tom. We must give her a good time."

"We must give her a good time." Tom mimicked his wife. His fingers were lifting the top from a green oblong box attached to the railing. He picked up a pronged stick and reached gently inside. He stirred and the flat head of a small snake appeared, a krait, about fourteen inches long. Its velvety mouth was open and holes showed where the fangs had been drawn. The head moved sleepily. "Hello, sleepy," Tom murmured. He moved the stick, stroking the krait's body.

Denise's voice rose unhappily. "It's going to be very difficult for her at the Garden Party. We must help."

"You help." Tom stroked the krait softly, his eyes smiling. "You're the only one who loves me," he murmured. The snake yawned.

At the other end of the house Mary sat in the bath. She had put her tea by the side of the tub and, from time to time, sipped thoughtfully.

It was obvious to Mary after nearly a week that, so far as Tom was concerned, she was not very welcome. He spoke to her as little as possible. He answered her in grunts. He had certainly left all the hospitality, the showing her about Calcutta, to Denise.

Mary dropped her head back against the edge of the tub. It was not the first time she had felt de trop; it had happened too often. She could still remember the first time, with her mother when she was about fifteen. Her mother was beautiful then, one of the famous Taylor sisters, and Mary at fifteen, though far from pretty, had youth and exuberance. There was something in that round little figure, in her friendliness, that made men look at her with equal friendliness.

When, one day, she presented herself for tea, she remembered the silence as she entered the room, the quiet stares and then the smiling attentions from her mother's young men. She could remember the fright she had felt at the growing coolness of her mother and the awful feeling in her stomach that her mother wished her someplace else.

She had been sent off to Roecroft soon after and she soon learned that she was meant to spend her holidays in school. During Christmas week, while he was alive, her father and she always managed a few days in London together but then she returned to Roecroft.

Mary picked up her soap and made a slow, careful rub across her body. Her stomach, now flat and hard, caught her eye. It had no navel. She had never known whether it could have happened naturally, at birth, or whether her mother, like the Wicked Witch, might not have ordered this absurdity for her body to render her more ridiculous to men.

It had pleased Mary as an adolescent to fancy that someday she might meet a prince charming so particular in his choice of wife that he had taken an oath to marry no girl possessed of navel. She had envisioned his awe and rapture as she revealed her secret to all assembled.

In later years she grew unconcerned. With Tim it had caused no more than an amused and gentle pause. There were matters that interested him more than the nonappearance of a navel. They were seldom in the mood to tarry for an anatomy lesson.

Mary drank her tea quickly. Enough of such thoughts. She had been living with the memory of Tim long enough. Dear, dead Tim . . . her one fling, come at age twenty-two, more than half a generation ago. She had given her rather rackety youth to his memory, buried most of her adult life in Roecroft. Now she had come to India to marry.

And what, so far, did she think of India? Was it as wonderful as the tales in her father's waiting room had led her to believe? Or was it as the ship's doctor had warned?

Mary screwed her eyes up in concentration. It was certainly not the cleanest of countries. She had seen enough of the bazaars, the cow droppings, and red betel-nut spit on the sidewalks to know it must be an unsanitary city. There were also unpleasant odors and scrawny beggars; she had not anticipated their abundance.

But it was a colorful city beyond belief. She had the constant sensation that she was attending some sort of masquerade. It was a masque, a carnival in which each person had been commanded to establish an individual personality.

Babel must have resembled the Calcutta streets. Native Hindus and Muslims, Tamils from south India, Pathans from the north, Chinese, brown Malays, Burmese, bearded Sikhs—each group was divided and subdivided into the most minute variations of tongue, skin color, and costume, the latter ranging from the nearly naked to the figure muffled from top to toe except for the eyes.

Through it all moved the occasional "European," the word

that she had learned was applicable to the British and all other white men alike. But the Europeans were so few, an occasional white face in a bazaar, the solitary police sergeant on Chowringhi or Tommie from the Fort. Alone, a speck of white in a sea of brown, yet somehow in command, enduring.

"We are sheep dogs," her father had said. "Have you ever seen a good dog chivvying a group of sheep, rounding them off, controlling them? He's protecting them from the wolves. There are many sheep but few sheep dogs. He must rise to the odds."

Her father would have approved of what she had done. He would have sent her off to India with his cheerful blessing. For her to marry in India was to take her place in the ranks.

One thing was apparent and, at the thought, Mary set her wide mouth firmly. She would get no help in her plans from Tom Beauchamp. The very thought of her marrying would cause a guffaw. She would have to take matters into her own hands.

She lifted herself determinedly from the tub. She was beginning that very morning by attending church service. Alone. She would somehow shift for herself.

St. Paul's Church in Calcutta, the "English Cathedral" as it was locally named, bore no relationship to the crowded city around it. Except for the native syces tending the sahibs' motorcars outside or the ayahs waiting for the few children attending, one might almost be at home in England on a fine April Sunday. The worshipers, the peaceful faces, the Anglican ceremony, even the hymns reflected the England so far away.

There was a city, an alien city, somewhere outside those lofty walls but here there was only England. It was not the Lord who was praised here, Mary reflected, but the Raj. And perhaps it was the way it should be. For a Briton in India, they might well be synonymous.

The voice from the pulpit ceased and the congregation rose dutifully for the next hymn. Mary glanced about. Sunday service was obviously an occasion during the season. She saw Calcutta in all its finery . . . uniforms, long dresses, picture hats. There were many more young ladies than she would have seen at home. And she was apparently the only visitor without an accompanying host or hostess. But then, she reflected, the Beauchamps were probably the only hosts with quite such a guest.

A face caught Mary's attention. It was a soldier in his mid-thirties sitting several rows in front and to the right. She found herself returning from time to time to watch him.

It was a striking face, even handsome in a hard, craggy way. The man was taller than the people around him. She could see there were scars on the face, one on the bony jaw and the other running for an inch beside the very deep-set eyes. The nose seemed to be twisted a trifle as though from a blow. It was certainly not a restful face.

The hymn finished and Mary sank down. She noticed that the man glanced over his shoulder once or twice toward the row behind him. Once his eyes met hers and she smiled calmly.

She turned away. Really, Mary . . . and in church too. If you must be forward, don't waste it on a man perhaps younger.

But she continued to watch him. He didn't look like a churchgoer. He was much too worldly. He looked English, yet the dark skin, the black hair, and the eyes—a hard blue when he had glanced toward her—might have been Irish. Tim was partly Irish. And at the thought, Mary felt a little chill. She made herself turn toward the pulpit.

Tiger Flemyng sat quietly in his pew. He had seen Sir John and Lady Henrietta Thornton behind him and knew their visitor, Bunty Cranston, would be after him. He felt hemmed in. Bunty was cute, even desirable, but he knew no one less likely to be in church of her own accord. If Bunty was there, there must be a man involved, and he was afraid the man was himself.

Bunty Cranston sat between Sir John and Lady Thornton, her eyes fixed dutifully on the pulpit. But her thoughts were directed only toward Tiger Flemyng. She adored Tiger. To Bunty he was all the Bengal Lancers rolled into one.

Bunty might seem like a silly girl but she wasn't. She was twenty-one, adorable, and nearly ruthless. She was an orphan. Her Dad had been killed at Gallipoli when attached too briefly to an Indian regiment. Her Mum hadn't lived long afterward. At sixteen Bunty had moved from her aunt's home, found a job with Withrow & Jenks, Ltd., assurance agents, and had been on her own ever since. It had been years of coping, scrounging, including this visit to the Thorntons, her uncle being a philatelist correspondent of Sir John's, and testing and proving her power over the lads. Beneath that appealing, turned-up face was a tough little nature.

Unfortunately, Bunty had chosen Tiger to adore. She had come out early to Calcutta, had met him through the Thorntons, and felt she had a claim over the other girls. She now sat impatiently, waiting for the service to end.

In his pew Tiger had another thought—the woman who was visiting the Beauchamps. He had accommodated Denise with an invitation to the governor's Garden Party but he was wondering whether he had done the right thing. The last two guests of theirs had been a bit sophisticated for Calcutta. One of them had appeared rather an ex-tart and the other had turned up at the governor's party quite intoxicated. The Beauchamps could hardly be refused. He was the brother of a peer. But His Excellency would want no more awkward guests.

He was regretting his acquiescence. He liked Denise, though not that fake-American husband of hers, and so had sent her the invitation she wished. He had a picture of what this new woman would be: another Beauchamp special, racy, fast, loud-talking, the worst sort of Mayfair.

And now there was Bunty Cranston behind him. He knew she would be after him as soon as the service was finished. He was trapped.

The last hymn was sung and the benediction pronounced. Mary saw the man glance quickly behind him, then look away. She noticed that a young girl seated two rows back had smiled invitingly at him.

Mary rose with the others in her pew and turned up the aisle toward the church door. She was aware that the man had also risen and must now be close behind. The young girl smiled and rose confidently to enter the aisle. The next moment Mary felt her arm gripped firmly from behind and knew that the tall man was escorting her up the church aisle.

Well, Mary thought. Calcutta is full of surprises. She made no effort to release her arm. On the contrary, she smiled companionably up at her escort and accompanied him out of the cathedral vestibule and down the front steps.

There he released her arm and bowed solemnly. "Thank you. It was simply that I wanted to get away from someone."

"Quite all right. I'm afraid that next week you'll have to make other arrangements. I may not be here."

"I think I should introduce myself. Captain Flemyng, aide to Sir Gerald Andrews. Alastair Flemyng."

"My name is Mary deGive. I'm visiting the Tom Beauchamps."

He bowed. "How do you do." Then his eyes widened. "You're the one visiting the Beauchamps?"

"Yes. Is that wrong?"

"No. I mean . . ." He stopped, obviously at a loss.

Mary laughed. "You're embarrassed about something. I shouldn't have thought it of you. Good-bye, Captain. Glad to have been of service."

She walked cheerfully away. Behind her Tiger Flemyng was still staring. It couldn't be. She looked too respectable for the Beauchamps to have as a guest. She must be a relative. Perhaps that was it.

Mary marched smartly toward Chowringhi. She felt giddy. There was a sparkle in her eye, a lift to her step. If she had been carrying a parasol, she would have twirled it.

She had met a man. Not any man but an aide to the governor of Bengal. He might be younger than she but that didn't matter. It was a beginning. She had managed to let him know her name and with whom she was staying.

Of course, it wasn't a ladylike thing to have done but, after all, she was a fishing fleeter. It was a first effort, one might say, to serve the Empire. The cause demanded such indiscretions.

Yes, she had done the right thing. And, best of all, she had done it all herself. With no help from anyone.

The students at Roecroft would have been quite surprised at the awkward Miss deGive. There was no doubt. She seemed to be skipping.

5

GOVERNMENT HOUSE GARDEN PARTY WAS ESPE-
cially prized that year. There was the slump, the swaraj
agitation, and a really bang-up season was needed. The
Garden Party would get it off to a good start.

The hostesses of Calcutta were unusually busy. The durzis
were kept occupied altering dresses. Parasols were mended
and cleaned. Medals were polished. Gossip and rumors were
exchanged over tea at the Slap or tiffin at Firpo's. Mrs.
Bracebridge and Lady Thornton preferred the telephone.
Mary deGive had been mentioned.

"Have you seen her?"

"She was at the Vardens'. I wouldn't say she was very
young."

"I wonder why she's visiting the Beauchamps. She looks
as though she might be a relative."

"I heard her invitation to Garden Party came nearly a
week late."

Lady Thornton made a solicitous sound. "I hope she can
last it. She doesn't look used to garden parties. We think of
this as cold weather but visitors find it jolly hot. I'd say she
might find it tiring standing about."

"I remember my first, Henrietta. I nearly fainted. Well,
I can't worry about her. I have enough problems."

"I'm sure you do, Lydia," murmured Lady Thornton. She
had seen her guest, Margot Danvers.

"You do too, Henrietta. I find your Bunty a bit eager.
Rather a tease, I suspect."

"Weren't we all at one time?"

"Henrietta!" Lydia Bracebridge was shocked.

Lady Thornton laughed. "Good-bye, Lydia. I'll look for
you tomorrow."

"We'll be under the refreshment awning. You know how Rufus hates the sun."

"So does Sir John. These old quihais."

"Good-bye, Henrietta." The ladies hung up.

The afternoon of the party was warm and cloudless. Mary took her place in the auto with Tom and Denise in a mood of anticipation. She was surprisingly excited . . . with just a touch of apprehension. She prayed that everything would go well, not only for her sake but also for that of Tom and Denise.

Mary had done her best to dress up for the occasion. Denise had insisted she wear one of her party frocks—rather short, stylish, quickly adjusted for Mary by a local durzi. Mary's arms were bare and she already felt drops of perspiration. She had bought shoes especially for the occasion, heels higher than she liked but fashionable. She carried a garden party hat and a parasol. Mary had even attempted a touch of makeup, putting a splotch of powder on her face and neck and adding a touch of lipstick to her wide mouth. She did hope she looked presentable.

On Garden Party day all streets leading to Government House had been closed to traffic except for the Esplanade. As the syce drove their auto into position Mary could see that the street ahead was lined with troops. Dense ranks of Indians were pressed back against the high walls of Government House and the buildings opposite.

The line of cars moved slowly and it was twenty minutes in the sun before the Beauchamp motor stopped before the high iron gates of Government House. Tom stepped out and handed down Denise and Mary. The syce moved the car toward the ranking area.

Mary stopped before the lofty gates and gazed inside. It was magnificent, even more impressive than she had expected. This was majesty itself, the panoply of Empire.

Denise whispered. "It's said to be modeled on Versailles."

Mary could only nod. Government House rose inside the gates in white, solid height. It didn't face the gates but stood to the left of the entrance walk, facing a broad green lawn on the walk's right.

"Come on," said Tom impatiently. He moved through the gates and onto the walk.

Mary followed, walking slowly in a line of arriving guests.

The bulk of Government House rose on her left, wide steps leading upward to a broad verandah with white Doric columns. Two cannon flanked the base of the steps. Turbaned and bearded Sikh soldiers stood beside the cannon.

It's like a procession, Mary thought. It was also like something else, a film she had once seen of the Nuremberg clock. There was the same slow, timeless circling of figures, appearing and disappearing.

They followed in position until the path turned left and there Mary stopped, eyes widening. A dense crowd stood on an open lawn . . . colorful, stately . . . but the figures were silent, nearly motionless. The quiet was deepened by the sight of a military band, seated rigidly under an open tent, their instruments held stiffly in their hands.

Mary watched, her breath caught. It was a still life, a colorful and imperial tableau.

"We're on time," said Tom. He sounded relieved. "H.E. isn't down yet."

So that was it. They were waiting for the governor to arrive. A signal was needed, the waving of a wand.

"Isn't the viceroy here?" asked Mary.

"He doesn't come until after Christmas. This is the governor's party."

"Hush," said Denise. "He's coming."

Mary saw the scarlet-coated band briskly pick up its instruments. A moment later she heard the first note of "God Save the King." The crowd stood immediately to attention and eyes turned toward the side verandah of Government House.

Then Mary saw him, the small and slight but erect figure of a man wearing a white Shantung business suit. Behind him and to one side stood a lady. She wore a plain blue frock, a picture hat also in blue.

"Lady Andrews," whispered Denise.

The couple waited silently until the last notes of "The King" had died away, then started slowly down the steps.

"There's Tiger Flemyng," said Denise. Mary saw him behind the governor, tall and erect in his scarlet and black uniform, a plumed helmet on his head as he followed down the steps.

"He's very impressive," Mary murmured.

The governor and his wife moved easily into the crowd, pausing here and there for greetings. Mary saw Captain Flemyng follow impassively. With the arrival of His Excellency and Lady Andrews the crowd began to shift.

"Come on," said Denise. "Let us show you about." She took Mary's arm, smiled encouragingly.

Mary hesitated. It was uncustomarily warm and her shoes did pinch a bit. She set her chin. She certainly wasn't going to let down now. Not after going to all this trouble.

"Come on," she said.

They began a slow parade through the crowd. Gradually Mary forgot her tight dress, the sore feet. This was the Empire in all its color and stateliness.

The variety of guests seemed enormous. There were soldiers in scarlet jackets, blue jackets . . . Sikhs in silk turbans, great height, and majestic beards. There were British churchmen in black coats and gaiters, Indian princes in turbans of silk, their women in saris of orange, green, silver, colorful as butterflies.

There was one group that seemed out of place. The men wore startlingly white topis, long black cutaway coats, and striped trousers.

"What are they, Tom?"

"Americans," he muttered. He seemed somewhat embarrassed. "That's their consul general and his staff."

"Do they have to dress like that in this heat?"

"I guess so. It's sort of a formal uniform." It was evidently one American practice he couldn't approve of.

Mary felt a quick sympathy. They too must find this difficult. But she didn't say it out loud.

They moved slowly on. Groups were breaking up now, dissolving and reforming in coagulating blobs of color. The murmurs were less hushed. The band had shifted into a melange of Strauss, spirited, graceful.

Mary saw Tiger. He was speaking to a white-haired churchman and, in a moment, led him toward the governor. His Excellency greeted him and they chatted.

"Who's that with the governor, Denise?"

"Bishop Anson. He's our top churchman in Bengal."

Mary saw Tiger move away to another group, speaking this time to a short, quiet Indian prince. It was obvious he was the retriever, bringing up to His Excellency those considered suitable for a chat. It was undoubtedly a mark of distinction. She was glad that she would not be chosen. She would never get through it with that crowd watching.

Mary and the Beauchamps moved on. Mary saw quite a

few young ladies, many of whom she recognized as fellow fishing fleeters from the *Strathnaver*. Some strolled with escorts or stood obediently with host and hostess. They all looked so young and healthy to Mary. She was certain their feet did not hurt, nor did they long to sit down.

They pushed slowly ahead. Tom spent as much time as possible moving away to mix with other groups, speaking to acquaintances.

Mary was somewhat irritated. She didn't think she looked quite that badly or out of place. Denise stayed loyally with her but she finally told Denise that she would really like to stroll by herself for a bit. Denise went quickly off to join her husband and Mary went determinedly on by herself.

It was shortly afterward that Mary became aware of a young woman who appeared before her. She seemed to be in her late twenties, thin with angular features. Her high, penciled eyebrows provided an exclamation point to her bony features. Mary felt that the slender figure was shockingly overdressed with lace dripping from her picture hat and even from her parasol. She also sensed strongly that the face was not unfamiliar to her.

"Miss deGive?"

Mary nodded and waited. There seemed to be a certain malice in the face before her.

"You don't remember me, do you? I went to Roecroft. My name is Margot Danvers."

"Of course, Sir Charles is your father." She remembered the young woman now, though not very favorably. Miss Danvers had believed that her occasional residence in Paris had entitled her to a better grade in French.

"You're visiting in Calcutta?" The eyebrows lifted.

"Yes."

"I'm staying with the Rufus Bracebridges. They are friends of father's."

Mary didn't reply. She didn't know "the Rufus Bracebridges" and saw no reason to comment. She waited.

Margot eyed her and the thin mouth sliced the face into a smile. "I saw you on the *Strathnaver* though I doubt you noticed me. You still seemed to be playing the schoolteacher, serving tea to the girls in the Common Room, listening to their tales of woe."

There was now no mistaking the malice. Mary assumed

that this young woman must have watched the gatherings at her deck chair.

Miss Danvers smiled again. "I assume you may have shared a few pointers on being a fishing fleeter. The blind leading the blind."

Mary was stunned. It was breathtaking. She forced herself to be calm. "I'm visiting friends in Calcutta."

"We are all visiting friends. It is *why* we are visiting that matters."

"Miss Danvers, if you will excuse me, please." She tried to sound haughty but glanced around to look for the Beauchamps.

The young woman's voice was now rasping in its intensity. "I happen to know about you and Mr. Janeway, Miss deGive. My father was at a meeting where your behavior with Mr. Janeway was discussed. I don't know which might amuse Calcutta more, the story of you and Mr. Janeway weekending in London together or the thought that you might be hoping to marry out here. Good-bye, Miss deGive. I will say as you once said to me, 'Roecroft girls do not make themselves ridiculous, Miss Danvers!' It is a pity you do not practice what you preach."

Miss Danvers dipped the frilly parasol, moved away in a flouncing of laces and frills.

Mary felt her anger rise. She clenched her fists and nearly moved after Miss Danvers. Damn it, she thought, we failed at Roecroft with that one all right.

Then she got hold of herself. She would meet all sorts out here. Not all of them would be friendly. The season was short, competitive. She must control herself. After all, she should be used to coping with difficult young women.

"Are you all right, Mary? You look flushed." It was Denise.

"It is a bit hot. And my feet hurt."

"Do you want to go?"

"Oh no. We can't do that anyway, can we? Until the governor withdraws."

"That may not be until after five. He has a good many people to chat with."

"What's the matter?" Mary saw that Tom had just come up.

"Mary's hot and her feet hurt. I asked her if she wished to leave."

He smiled openly. "Fine. Plenty of taxis outside. They'll know where we live."

Mary set her firm jaw. "I'm staying to the end." She was pleased to see a slight frown cross Tom's soft face. "Come, Denise. Let's walk."

She limped determinedly off. Denise and Tom glanced at each other but fell in behind.

It was not the most pleasant of strolls. In fact, it was hardly a stroll at all. Mary marched grimly, pausing from time to time to stand immobile. Tom continued to dart off to speak to men he knew, never returning with anyone to present to Mary.

Denise brought up one or two couples, either middle-aged or elderly. Mary would draw herself up firmly and respond obediently to the customary questions.

Yes, Calcutta was very interesting . . . Yes, the Garden Party was charming . . . Yes, it was rather hot.

She persevered. She knew Denise was doing her best, trying to make up for Tom's lack of attention.

Mary and Denise finally sank onto chairs before a tea table. Tom soon joined them but his expression was bleak.

Denise seemed to feel an explanation was owed Mary. "Tom has been talking to friends. He has a scheme for raising money for a Brazilian venture."

"Brazil?" Mary was startled. Brazil seemed so remote at that point.

"Something in jute. He's offering his friends an opportunity to invest. Any luck, dear?"

"No." It was such a savage, grunting reply that the party fell silent. There was no need for Denise to say more.

Mary sat erect, refusing to slump, a fixed smile on her broad mouth. The chair beneath her seemed like iron.

"Miss deGive?" It was a man's voice and she looked up to see Captain Flemyng had presented himself. He bowed formally.

"His Excellency has sent his compliments and requests that you be presented."

"Me?" She stared him. "There must be a mistake."

"I assure you there has been no mistake. His Excellency wishes that you be presented to him."

Denise clapped her hands. "Mary. Go. It's wonderful."

"But I shan't know what to do."

"Simply answer him. He'll do the talking."

"But the governor . . ." Mary felt her face grow red. "I'm not even wearing my own clothes."

Tom grunted. "So much the better."

"Miss deGive?" Tiger held out his hand.

"Just a moment." Mary felt beneath her chair for her shoes.

"Allow me." Tiger knelt and quickly pulled them out for her. She put them on awkwardly, stood up.

"Do I look all right?"

"Marvelous," said Denise. Tom grunted.

Mary turned to Tiger. "Where is he?"

"By the band tent."

"Come on." She gripped his arm determinedly and they started across the lawn, passing through the crowd. She was aware that there were stares as they passed and hung on grimly. She was certainly not going to collapse in front of the elite of Calcutta.

There was only one moment when she faltered. She gripped Tiger's arm. "Do I curtsy?" She didn't add that she might not get up again.

"Do whatever you wish."

Mary closed her eyes. It had been many years since she had made a curtsy, not since a young girl at Roecroft. But the governor was the King's representative in Bengal. There were generations of deGives looking down at her.

She brushed her hair from her forehead. She wished now she hadn't worn Denise's dress, those silly shoes, and that face powder. It was probably gathered in lumps on her damp neck.

"Courage." Tiger grinned down at her and they passed through the watchers to stand before the slight governor. "Allow me to present Miss Mary deGive. Sir Gerald Andrews, Governor of Bengal."

"Miss deGive."

"Sir Gerald," murmured Mary and sank hesitatingly to one knee. She took a deep breath and was up again.

"And Lady Andrews," finished Tiger.

"Lady Andrews," muttered Mary. She swooped down again.

"Hello," said Her Ladyship and gave Mary's hand a slight squeeze. Mary gripped it firmly, hoisted herself upward. She was aware that Her Ladyship had hardly glanced at her but was staring out over her head with a vague smile. Mary relinquished her grip.

She felt a sudden panic. Tiger had withdrawn completely, probably to fetch another guest. She prayed he would come quickly.

Lady Andrews spoke, still not looking at her. "Is this your first trip to Calcutta?" she asked dutifully.

"Yes, Your Ladyship."

"I hope you will like it. It's such a nice season of the year, though it really can be quite hot." Lady Andrews waved her hand vaguely.

Mary said nothing. She was in no condition to discuss the weather.

Sir Gerald spoke. "It was Captain Flemyng suggested I meet you. He said you had helped him out of some predicament at church."

Mary was silent. She felt that if anyone was in a predicament, it was she. The band music nearby had increased its volume with a spirited march and the sound beat against her. The sweet aroma that Lady Andrews was wafting vaguely toward her with each wave of her hand added to her discomfort. She was certain that the drops of perspiration now trickling down the inside of her knee must have formed a slight pool before Sir Gerald.

His Excellency looked up at her appraisingly. "And what are you doing in Calcutta, Miss deGive?"

Mary was silent a moment. Now, Mary, rise above all this . . . the heat, the discomfort, Miss Margot Danvers.

"I'm in the fishing fleet," she said. It was the simplest thing she could think of.

Sir Gerald let out a sudden whoop of a laugh. "Did you hear that, Maude?"

"Yes, Sir Gerald," his wife said placidly.

"She said she was in the fishing fleet." He laughed wheezily. "I'll be damned. An honest woman come to judgment. Bless me, that music's loud. Bandsman! Bandsman!" The governor raised his voice to attract the bandleader but the bandsman's back was turned.

Sir Gerald grabbed Mary's arm. "Come. It's too noisy here." He led her pre-emptorily toward the crowd, Lady Andrews following.

Mary limped gallantly along. The slight governor paused genially from time to time to introduce her. "Miss deGive. She's visiting, says she's a fishing fleeter."

It was obvious that Sir Gerald was enjoying himself. It

was a respite from the usual pomp of the Garden Party. Mary saw that their party had attracted followers and that her passage with His Excellency had become something of a procession. Well, she thought, if one must declare one's intentions oneself, I couldn't have had a more conspicuous occasion.

She began to enjoy herself. Her weariness was being overcome by an excitement, a sense of fun. A half hour before it had been a question of whether or not she became nauseated or fainted.

Yet she was weary. The governor had stopped to introduce her for the seventh or eighth time when she felt a strong hand on her arm and heard Tiger Flemyng's voice.

"Your Excellency, permit me. May I present His Highness, the Maharajah of Puripore."

Mary saw that Tiger was presenting to Sir Gerald a roly-poly little Indian prince and his maharani.

"Good-bye, Miss deGive," said His Excellency. "It has been very entertaining. I wish you good luck in Calcutta."

"Thank you, Your Excellency." Mary started to attempt a curtsy but Sir Gerald put out his hand. "Save your energy. It's too hot."

Mary turned to Lady Andrews, standing patiently nearby. "Your Ladyship." She made a slight dip.

"Good-bye, good-bye. I am so glad you could come. If it weren't for this awful weather." She brushed a handkerchief mechanically across her face. For a moment there was a glimpse of someone a long way from her beloved Scotland.

She and Tiger walked slowly back toward the Beauchamps, Mary walking with more assurance now, completely indifferent to the stares.

When they reached the Beauchamp table, she put out her hand. "Thank you. That was very nice of you."

He held her hand a moment. "What was it you said to His Excellency? It must have amused him."

"I said I was a fishing fleeter." She said it calmly. "He asked me and there seemed no reason not to tell the truth."

"It isn't true, is it?"

"Why not? I am single."

"You certainly aren't the ordinary sort."

"Perhaps there'll be a man who is looking for an extraordinary woman."

"It may not be easy. You'll need help. Someone to show you off. Make you appear special."

"You?"

"I?"

"You are the governor's aide." She laughed. "Don't worry. I'd have no designs on you. You are a bit young for me."

"But what could I do?"

"Lunch perhaps. Excuse me . . . tiffin. What is the name of that restaurant? Firpo's. I understand that Friday tiffin at Firpo's is very special."

"You really are remarkable."

"Shall we say this Friday? At one?"

"When you begin, you really go all out."

"There isn't very much time. One must grasp one's opportunities."

They watched each other, she waiting for some sign of acceptance.

Why not? he thought. Gupta has been quiet for six weeks. There hasn't been a killing since Heyward was murdered up in Midnapore. Besides, being seen out with this woman might keep the other fleeters away, including Bunty Cranston. Besides, though she certainly wasn't a pretty woman, there was something . . . what was it the French called them? Jolielaide. Beautifully ugly or some such description. French was not his cup of tea. But that was it: there was something attractive in her lack of beauty.

She spoke quickly, almost belligerently, as though guessing his thoughts. "This will be on my behalf only, Captain. I'll be using you for my own purposes."

"I had somewhat the same idea."

"I am here to marry. Shall I pay for the tiffin? I don't want you to waste your money."

"I'll pay. And I shan't be wasting money."

"Friday at one?"

"Right. Firpo's."

She extended her hand, shook his vigorously. She turned and walked back toward the Beauchamps.

She felt quite giddy again. Really, she wasn't doing too badly for herself. A man, a luncheon date at a good restaurant. Frankly, Mary, she thought, I never would have suspected it of you.

6

IN THE TOWN OF MIDNAPORE, SOME MILES NORTH of Calcutta, a school passing-out exercise was being held. The students to be graduated were seated in expectant rows, behind them their proud parents. Although the students were Bengali, the boys wore a British school uniform of blue shorts, white shirt, and blue tie. The girls wore the blue skirt and white middy blouse of British schoolgirls.

Mr. Stephens was the speaker. He was the new district magistrate in Midnapore, sent to replace Fenley Heyward who had been murdered by the terrorists. Stephens had been asked to make a few remarks to the students and had welcomed the opportunity. He had children of his own back in Calcutta and felt that the ceremony with these young students might be just what he needed.

He finished his remarks and the school principal rose to direct the students toward the platform. Mr. Stephens received the first certificate from the assistant principal, a thin lady in glasses and a blue sari, and the boys and girls began to move forward.

The magistrate adjusted his glasses and smiled. He was enjoying himself. There was an occasional fumble as he extended a certificate but the ceremony was going well. For the first time in this unfortunate town he was feeling a respite, a touch of relaxation.

He was aware of a particularly pretty girl stepping toward him. She was smiling and he paused in appreciation. She might have been his own daughter. The audience applauded as he walked forward for Suchila Ramdas was the brightest and best liked of all the students. She reached the platform, smiled, and he held out her certificate. She reached her hand from beneath her loose middy blouse.

There was a sharp report and the magistrate fell backward, his glasses slipping loosely across his nose. He tried to get up, stared up confusedly at her, then, still holding her school certificate, slowly collapsed sideways and died.

The girl, frowning now, pointed her revolver at him and fired twice more. The glasses flew off his face in a scattering of glass, metal, and blood.

Sir Gerald Andrews, Governor of Bengal, was awakened by a peremptory hand reaching under his mosquito net.

"Sir Gerald," said an urgent voice. "Sir."

"Yes?" Sir Gerald opened his eyes sleepily and could make out the khaki-covered sleeve of Sergeant Prout, the NCO on duty.

"Telephone, sir. It's Mr. Franklin. Says it's urgent. I'll put the phone under the net."

Sir Gerald accepted the phone. He knew his commissioner of police wouldn't ring him so early unless it was essential. He waited a moment to clear his mind.

"Sir Gerald here." He could hear the voice of his police head. It sounded very far away.

"Sir Gerald. Franklin. I'm sorry to bother you, sir, but I've just been called up to Midnapore. That's where I am now."

"What is it?" Sir Gerald wished his chief would get to the point.

"Can you hear me?"

"I can hear you very well. Get on with it, man."

"It's Stephens, sir. The chap we sent up to Midnapore to replace Heyward. He's been shot."

"Shot." Sir Gerald sat up straight in bed, his forehead touching the side of the net.

"Yes, sir. At the Midnapore school, the passing-out exercise. One of the students did it. A girl."

"Good God. He's dead?"

"Yes, sir. Instantly. The girl's dead too. Took poison."

There was silence from Sir Gerald's end. He knew what this meant. It was the terrorists again. The girl taking poison, the public killing, at a moment when the victim would feel most secure: it was just the Gupta touch. Still, one must be certain.

"Could she have known Stephens, Franklin?"

"Not that we know of, sir. He's only been here five weeks."

"Check on it. It might well be Gupta's crowd but we must make absolutely certain. Check her background, her political interests. Your men can do it but I want it done thoroughly. And I want you here by five o'clock. We'll have work to do."

"Yes, sir."

"Good-bye."

"Good-bye, sir."

Sir Gerald hung up and handed the phone under the net to Sergeant Prout. He leaned back, closed his eyes. Another killing. Just when it looked as though they might have a breathing spell. And just when the season had begun in Calcutta and the viceroy would be coming down from Delhi.

The viceroy. Lord. That would be a catch for the terrorists. The viceroy would have to be informed immediately of the killing. Though he would soon learn from the morning newspaper. That was one reason Gupta picked public occasions, to obtain maximum publicity.

Sir Gerald closed his eyes. Imagine involving a girl in their struggle. None of Bapu's methods for them. None of this fasting, this nonviolent civil disobedience. Gandhi's methods were too patient, too slow. The terrorists wanted quick results.

Sir Gerald stared at the roof of his net. There was a tiny hole at the top and his eyes were drawn to it. That was the second night the hole had been there. Somebody needed a bit of prompting. For a moment his mind focused irritably on the tiny hole, then he went back to his problem.

His ruddy Scottish face set itself. He knew he could be ruthless too if necessary. He hadn't fought his way up in the Scottish textile world by being a soft man. He had dealt with some pretty crafty business rivals in his time and a few very rough labor leaders.

And Ireland, that had been a hard business too. He had held authority there just after the Great War. There had been the same sort of terrorism, the ambushing of police, the assassinations. He had been ruthless but successful. A sort of peace had been established.

But in Ireland there had still been plenty of troops to back him up. Now the Great War had been finished a good many years. Most of the available troops in India were up on the Northwest Frontier Province. In Ireland you were close to your base, dealing with people who were also white and who spoke the same language. Here you were half a world away and only ninety thousand whites among four hundred million Indians. They weren't even decent odds.

There was one other difference between India and Ireland. In Ireland there had been a solid British government to support him. Lloyd George was still Prime Minister and his Irish policy was firm, unequivocal.

Now there was a coalition Conservative—Labour Party government in London, a government that hadn't yet determined what its policy in India would finally be. It might be firmness; that was certainly what the Conservatives and Stanley Baldwin, their leader, would want. But the Prime Minister, Ramsay MacDonald, and his Labour supporters might simply turn their back on India and concentrate their efforts on ending the business slump.

To make matters worse, he suspected that Lord Willingdon, the new viceroy, could not be too sure of his governor of Bengal. The viceroy was undoubtedly a skillful man and experienced in Indian affairs, but now this was the most turbulent province in India.

The governor of Bengal pulled back his mosquito net and sprang actively from his bed. He was not a big man and his feet barely rested on the floor as he sat on the edge of his bed. He took a cigarette from the pack by the bed and lighted it thoughtfully.

He would have a lot to do that day. He would begin by sending a cable to London, reporting the killing, and another to the new viceroy.

He didn't want the viceroy to come to Calcutta. This would now be no place for a social holiday. It had been bad enough at the Garden Party. Despite all the quiet precautions, police in mufti, extra troops, he had never been certain the party might not suddenly be blown sky-high. He certainly hoped the viceroy would keep his distance.

In Delhi the viceroy received Sir Gerald's cable, read the news silently, and stuffed the paper in his pocket. He knew a cable would have gone to London and he was not expected to take action until instructions were received from the secretary of state for India. He would maintain the fiction that he was less fit to decide matters than the new secretary seven thousand miles away.

Meanwhile he puttered in his wife's vegetable garden. It was one of the first things Lady Willingdon had requested of her husband, that a small corner of the vast gardens of Vice-regal Palace should be allotted to her for vegetables. The viceroy had made only one condition, that he should be allowed to putter in it. So this game they played, a stratagem of affection, was put into operation.

It was among the eggplant that his aide, Captain Graham, found His Excellency. The viceroy, his thin, aristocratic, even priestly face very much the representative of the Crown, was bent industriously over his weeding. Little drops of perspiration slipped off his nose but it was plain he was enjoying himself. He wore old flannel trousers, a sweater, and a broad-brimmed Chinese coolie hat acquired during a recent ambassadorial assignment. Despite the worn clothes, so perplexing to the Indian gardeners of the palace, the slender features, white hair, and waxed mustache permitted no mistaking him for other than the representative of a king.

The aide coughed and Lord Willingdon glanced up. "Hello, Graham. Very dry earth you have here. Not a worm to be seen." He glanced at his aide's hand. "For me?"

"A cable, sir. From London."

"India House?"

"Yes, sir."

"Come into the study. Mind the eggplant. Won't take much tramping on."

The aide walked carefully around the small plot and followed the viceroy up the steps of the narrow verandah and into the Viceregal study. It was not a large room but it was neat, white, with a Sudanese mahogany desk, a wicker chair, and two basket chairs placed close at hand. A small photograph of Their Majesties, King George and Queen Mary, he in the naval uniform of an admiral, was hung behind and above the viceroy's chair.

Willingdon closed the French window, casting a last glance toward "Her Ladyship's garden," and extended his thin hand to his aide.

"You've read it, of course."

"Yes, sir."

The viceroy read it quickly. "Hmm, martial law." He looked up, his eyes twinkling. "The secretary's very peremptory about it."

Captain Graham exploded. "It's impossible, sir. The secretary's merely putting you in the middle."

"Now, now. Mustn't jump to conclusions. The secretary

is a very experienced man." He glanced at the telegram. "Very."

He moved to look out on the garden. "Martial law means occupying Calcutta to all intents and purposes. Establishing a curfew, closing places of business, shipping offices, jute factories, tea offices."

"It would be a very strong step, sir."

"Business in Calcutta is having enough troubles these days, isn't that so?"

"Yes, sir. As everywhere else."

"Martial law would not smoke out the terrorists. They would simply lie low. The only people damaged would be the law-abiding."

"I'd protest it, sir. Ask for a confirmation."

"You would? Tell me, Graham, what do you consider our objective in this case?"

"Why, to defeat the terrorists, sir."

"To defeat the terrorists."

"They mustn't be allowed to murder our magistrates."

"I consider our objective—in fact the only reason for my being here—is to keep India within the Empire."

"Of course, sir. I merely meant . . ."

"The terrorists are only one of our enemies. There is also the Mahatma. The little man in Yevrada Gaol. We cannot ignore him, Captain."

"No, sir."

"So our real objective is not to lose India to either of these men. Have you ever been in Calcutta during the cold weather, Graham?"

"No, sir."

"Very gay. I passed a few weeks there when I was governor of Madras."

"May I ask what it is like, sir?"

"You may. Calcutta is very hot normally, you know. Steamy. Then comes that delicious cold weather. For about eight weeks one can breathe again. It's like a holiday."

"Festive?"

"Very. Galas, garden parties, gymkhanas. The girls too."

"Girls, sir?"

"The fishing fleeters." He glanced rather impishly at his aide. "They are all unmarried, Captain. Been coming out for years. Boatloads. They concentrate on Calcutta, most of them. That's where the fun is. And the men."

"I see, sir." The young captain looked uncomfortable.

"We're expected to put in a month there. I should think, this year there'd be more girls than usual, things being rather bad at home. If one were to put on martial law it would rather spoil things."

"Sir, the girls can't be that important."

"Are you against marriage, Graham? Or British womanhood? Dear me, Her Ladyship would be distressed indeed to hear this." The viceroy was obviously enjoying himself.

"No, sir."

"I'm glad to hear it. Perhaps we can put one of these girls on to you. Meanwhile I think we should carry on as usual. Send a cable to Sir Gerald asking if he has any objections to my coming. After all, my safety will be his responsibility. It isn't every day a Scot is asked to be responsible for the life of an Englishman."

"What shall we tell London, sir? The cable did say we should establish martial law."

"London is a long way away. We mustn't bother them with details. They're interested in one thing, that the British Raj be maintained in India. We'll just enlist these girls in the struggle, so to speak. You draft something to Sir Gerald. I'm going back to Her Ladyship's garden." He nodded solemnly to his aide and marched out.

In Calcutta Sir Gerald fingered the cable he had received from Delhi. He knew the viceroy liked his fun but, damn it, this was too much. He read it again.

"WILL VISIT CALCUTTA FOR CUSTOMARY COLD WEATHER SEASON PROVIDED ACCEPTABLE TO YOU. AFTER ALL WE MUST NOT LET DOWN THE FISHING FLEET. WILLINGDON."

Sir Gerald swore briefly to himself. What this meant in plain English was that the viceroy felt the best way to deal with the present situation was not to deal with it at all. To keep the boat steady. The Calcutta "season" would be thrown in the faces of Gupta and his terrorists, also of Gandhi and his National Congress Party, to show them that Britain would not be rushed into concessions. And he, the governor of Bengal, was expected to provide the security for this demonstration.

He swore again in his best Scottish manner. Just like a damned Englishman to make the decision, then toss the ball to a Scot to carry. Right into the thick of the scrum too.

Sir Gerald walked out onto his private verandah. It was on the second floor and he could look down onto the lawn and tennis court. Two malis were cutting and edging the smooth lawn. They squatted on their heels, bony knees thrust before them, snipping and edging as they waddled along.

He could see over the compound wall to the vast park of the Maidan beyond. The grass-covered ramparts of old Fort William stood to the right toward the river, protected on its Maidan side by the moat and an open field of fire. To the left he saw the late afternoon traffic branching through the Maidan roads toward the residential districts of Tollygunge, Ballygunge, or Regent's Park.

He could see cricket games scattered about the Maidan, the white-clad players, mostly Indian, appearing small and silent against the green plain. In the distance the statue of Queen Victoria, seated before her memorial, stared out at the city.

Sir Gerald brooded. Those drivers in the traffic were the burra sahibs, the big bosses of Calcutta business, or their chota sahibs, the junior executives. They were on their way home for a drink and a stretch in the garden with the wife or a pal, or possibly for a game of tennis at the Saturday Club. It was his responsibility to protect them, their families, their businesses too. And protect those Indians on the cricket grounds as well. He was governor of all Bengal, not just the small European part. Now he was expected to protect the viceroy as well.

He turned away from the balustrade. He had a good mind to cable the viceroy in his own manner. "Sorry. Do not have enough troops to protect you nor enough bachelors for the fishing fleet." Except that the latter would be a lie. Young bachelors were the one thing Calcutta had in plenty.

He turned toward his office and caught a glimpse of his aide.

"Captain Flemyng."

"Sir."

"Send a cable to Delhi. Tell His Excellency his cable has been received and we are looking forward to his visit."

"Yes, sir."

"What is the date of today?"

"December tenth, sir. Wednesday."

"That gives us six days to make ready."

The governor went back to the verandah. The malis were

still inching along on their heels. He stared down at them. The noises from the Maidan could hardly be heard.

In Yevrada Gaol, Poona, a thin, bespectacled little man received the news of Stephens' killing as he sat cross-legged at his spinning wheel. The news was brought to him by one of the women allowed to attend him in his quarters. A student, she said; it was a girl who had shot the British magistrate.

Gandhi paused in his spinning; his face became grave. It was clear that this was another terrorist move and that it was aimed not only against the British. It was also at him that the bullet had been fired.

The Mahatma looked toward the little court outside his room. He could see Mirza, his secretary's wife, playing with her little son. He knew his secretary must be nearby, probably in his office gazing out at his wife and child and wishing he could be with them.

The Mahatma sighed. It was so peaceful here, even though it was a jail. He had hoped there might be six months at least before he would have to take action against the new government. He had given the new viceroy six months in which to settle in and establish something of the same trust he and Irwin had reached. That was why he hadn't pressed for release from his jail, hadn't fasted or called for further civil disobedience. He was being patient. But now this killing. Gupta would not wait.

The Mahatma folded his hands, bent his head. Though he loved his fellow man, he understood him. He knew that he and Gupta must always contend for India, and that Gupta might win. He prayed.

7

WHEN THE BENGALI SCHOOLGIRL FIRED THE SHOT in Midnapore and the British magistrate fell back dead on the platform, a man was standing at the back of the hall amid the press of other Indians. He was a young man, about twenty-two, English in his dress though his face, slender, sensitive, even intellectual, was unmistakably Indian.

He saw the girl fire two more shots into the man's head, then put a lozenge between her teeth. He saw her sway, drop the revolver to the floor, and, as the others on the platform rushed toward her, sink to her knees, her long hair touching the upturned feet of the dead man.

The young Indian looked about him. Screams and shouts were rising from the crowd into which he was pressed. Some of the people were running forward, the better to see what was happening. Some were beginning to slip away from the building, to scatter. The man pushed his way out, his eyes lit with satisfaction.

"Rajid." The voice came from one side. The young Indian stopped. He could see a small figure, a boy, standing near a palm tree across the dusty road.

"Go away." He started to move on but the boy came closer. "What has happened? I heard shots."

Rajid glanced about him at the other figures hurrying away, their voices rising excitedly.

The boy pulled again at his arm. "Is Suchila all right?"

"Chup raho!" Rajid pushed the boy roughly away from him and began to walk quickly down the road, the dust scuffing angrily after his feet.

The boy was sobbing now and followed, his arm pressed across his mouth. "I am frightened. My sister . . . there is something wrong."

"Go home. I will kill you if you follow me." The man shoved him. The boy took a few stumbling steps and fell onto the road.

The dust, white in the bright sun, rose querulously, protesting the inert body. The man went down the road.

He looked sharply at a watch he wore on his brown wrist. The train would leave in fifteen minutes. That was one reason this day had been selected. He could get away promptly and make his report to Gupta.

He walked quickly and in a few moments stood in the square before the station. The train already stood on the long platform. There had been no warning whistle. Damn stationmaster, Rajid thought. Anglo-Indian, of course. Mongrel bastards. When we take over this country, they'll be the first people we'll get rid of.

A policeman appeared out of the station and stood by the tidy garden looking toward the square. Rajid stopped. He knew he had just as much to fear from an Indian policeman as from one of the British. Perhaps this one already knew about the killing.

He stood irresolute. He could run full-tilt, knock the constable down, and sprint for the train, or he could retreat, try to get onto the platform from another street.

He made his decision, walked arrogantly toward the watching constable. His hand was on the revolver in his jacket pocket. He knew that if the policeman so much as accosted him he would pull his revolver, shoot him dead, and run for the train. He had been arrested once before, in Calcutta during his university days, and would never be arrested again. Not by an Indian.

He could see the stationmaster raising his red flag of departure. Rajid took a few quick strides and was abreast of the watching constable. He paused, glaring full into the eyes of the helmeted Indian. The policeman's eyes stared mildly, indifferently back, then he turned away. Rajid rushed ahead through the station gate. A door was swung invitingly open on the moving train and Rajid was helpfully pulled in.

He sat on the floor of the crowded compartment, gripping his knees. Two hours and he would be in Calcutta. He hoped Gupta would have more confidence in him now. This was the second killing which he had been sent to watch and to report on. He wanted now to fire the gun himself, to see the face of an Englishman staring up at him, dying, the eyes closing. It

was intolerable that he should not be given as much trust as
a girl. He knew how Gupta felt about him, that he was too
young, too hysterical, that he must first prove he could control himself. Perhaps now he would change his mind.

Rajid dug his fingernails convulsively into his knees. His
eyes lost themselves in his private and cluttered world. The
train rumbled toward the delta and the city.

The position of the crossbred of two races has seldom been
enviable, particularly if one of the two races is white. Which-
ever the country, the offspring of biracial matings has con-
sistently received rejection by both races. In India it was the
Anglo-Indian, a hundred thousand of them.

Some chose to remain Indian, particularly if the father
of the family was Indian. Some, the lighter in skin usually,
tried to claim their British heritage, applying hopefully to
British schools, aping British clothes, British accents. Their
rejection was usually inevitable and total.

So the Anglo-Indians remained suspended in limbo, neither
British nor Indian. Ninety thousand of them lived in Calcutta.
The men filled jobs on the railway as clerks or stationmasters,
taught in the less rewarding schools to the least promising
pupils. The women filled jobs as office clerks or typists, or
worked as sales-girls at small wages in the larger and more
crowded stores. Their incomes were negligible, the past
shadowy, the future as twisty and uncertain as the delta itself.

There was one redeeming birthright to the Anglo-Indian,
the beauty of their women. As with so many mixed races the
union sometimes produced a delicate and special beauty. It
was this that provided for many their only escape from the
community. It was common knowledge among Anglo-Indians
that several of the world's most glamorous motion-picture
stars had been Calcutta-born, had started as the mistress of
a Briton or American and, having been taken to the continent,
had changed their names and eventually emerged into the
bright entertainment world never to return to India.

It was also this beauty that made the girls a marketable
commodity for the bordellos of Calcutta. With few financial
resources, a very limited field in the job market, little chance
of marrying into either of the parents' worlds, the Anglo-
Indian brothel in Calcutta found its supply of girls fully
equal to the steady demand.

Magda, on Acre Lane, was the most successful of the

madams. It was from her house that several had graduated to
mistress-dom and one, at least, had gone on to cinema fame.
The tall, ocher-colored house with portico and columns, once
the stately home of a Victorian sahib and his memsahib, was
a touch of splendor in a section of the city fast disappearing
among a lapping squalor of small shops and narrow alleys.
Here Magda conducted her establishment with discipline and
correctness. No excessive drunkenness or rudeness was permitted. It was the sort of behavior, pseudo-respectable and
efficient, that endeared her to law enforcement authorities
and invited the regular customer. Magda had a very good
thing.

There was only one vexation in her work. The girls, being
part Indian, had occasionally acquired an Indian lover along
the way. Sahibs didn't find a girl attractive if she shared her
bed with an Indian. He would permit an Indian to shave him,
even pull up his trousers for him, but he would not share a
girl with him.

It was up to Magda to keep these dark chaps out of her
house. Let the Indians go to Kuraiya Road if they wanted
a girl. The riffraff of Europe were the "girls" in those houses,
aging tarts from Bucharest, Barcelona, or Naples. They were
good enough for the Indians.

But, since her own girls were not above reproach, vigilance
against their dark lovers was the motto of Magda's day. The
wonder of it was that so few of her girls got caught.

At about the time Rajid's train was entering the outskirts
of Calcutta a girl on the top floor of Magda's, about sixteen,
slender with pale ivory skin, black hair, was slowly dressing
for the evening. She had put on her brown muslin dress and
was hesitantly combing her shoulder-length hair. She paused
once, a rather lost expression on her otherwise blank, even
stupid face. She quickly sat up as there was an impatient
knock on the door.

"Dolly?" It was Magda's voice.

The girl got slowly to her feet and went to the door.
Magda, short, darker than any of her girls, pushed into the
room.

"What nonsense is this? The other girls have been downstairs a half hour."

"I do not feel well." A sullen look darkened her pretty face.

Magda eyed her carefully, crossing her right hand over her
left in front of her stomach. It was said Magda wore a

wedding ring on this hand but always carefully removed it when she opened in the evening for business. She now glanced about the room, went quickly to the bathroom windows, glanced down at the narrow alley three floors below. She turned to the child.

"Come now. This will be a big night. Every Scot in Bengal has come to Calcutta."

"St. Andrew's Night." The girl repeated it mechanically.

"Tomorrow's Sunday. You can sleep late and we'll all go to the cinema in the afternoon."

The girl looked up, a stir of interest in her face. At least that would be something to look forward to. She loved pictures more than almost anything, and the next day there would be a Tom Mix. She especially liked pictures about horses.

"Don't be long now. Five minutes." The woman glanced at the bed, pulled back the green coverlet. There were sheets on the beds in Magda's. It wasn't like those places on Kuraiya Road. She smoothed down the sheets, pulled up the coverlet, patted the pillow neatly.

"Come now." She went out. In the hallway she shook her head. This child was new and she certainly wasn't very bright. She was willing. That was one advantage of having stupid girls, Magda mused. They knew there was little else for them and they tried to please.

Dolly could hear her sturdy shoes clumping down the stairs. She heard a taxi horn at the front of the house and, though her room was at the back, could hear the expectant boisterousness of the first men arriving for the evening.

She cast a last glance at the mirror. Her eyes, dark-shadowed but with the vagueness of a child, looked back at her with uncertainty. "Rajid," she said and put her face in her hands. Then she rose placidly to her feet and turned toward the door.

It was dusk when Rajid's train reached Calcutta. The compartment doors swung open, were banged back against the carriages, and the passengers climbed down onto the platform.

Rajid jumped down, joined the jostling crowd, and pushed his way toward the third-class exit. Outside Howrah station he saw a tram of the Calcutta Street Railway, its green and brown sign reading "Garden Reach Road." A policeman was on duty at the main station exit but he showed little interest in the crowd. Rajid walked calmly across the tram tracks, clutched the handrail of the trolley platform, and, by pushing and cursing, forced his way inside. The passengers settled themselves into grumbling patience and the trolley moved slowly out into the traffic headed for Howrah bridge.

Rajid could see the city across the bridge and the first scattered lights of the evening. On the river the steamers swung at their berths or nosed doggedly to the city docks. It was a crowded and busy scene. Barges clung stubbornly to their tugs. Farm boats, each with its bamboo deck-hut, rowed high and empty as the rivermen worked their way back from the city markets.

Only the jute factories were still, their tall chimneys on the Howrah side of the river silent and smokeless at the end of the day. The trolley gained the Calcutta side of the bridge, turned right onto the Strand Road to begin the long ride behind the Fort and the Maidan, then along the river out toward Garden Reach.

The sight of the river distracted Rajid. He remembered the first time he had seen the Hooghly. He was a student from upcountry beginning his matriculation at Calcutta University. He had wandered to Strand Road one night and saw the river, an arm of the great Ganges. The river's message was clear to his mind, already excited by news of the Mahatma's defiant salt march to the sea. The waters rolling down from the great plains, the heartland of ancient India, had called clearly to him. "Free me . . . free me." Rajid had known then to what he must dedicate himself.

The tram pushed through the center of the native city, passed in sight of the docks and moorings at Kidderpore and, in an hour, reached the half-city, half-country area known as Garden Reach. Here goats grazed between the street cobbles, women carried wash to the water tanks. Rajid left the tram a quarter mile before it would reverse itself for the return ride.

He went quickly up a side street away from the river. He felt safe now and was impatient to see Gupta, to receive his nod of approval. It was a quiet street. On one side, sedately behind an iron railing, stood the rounded dome of a Muslim mosque, its four corners guarded by four minarets. Fifty yards further, on the opposite side of the street, a store front was lettered "Methodist Reading Room." Rajid crossed, paused in front of the store, then went quickly through a side alley to the rear. A stairway led to the second story and he climbed, knocked on the wooden door, waited. He knocked again impatiently and the door was opened.

The Bengali who called himself Gupta lived in a small, bare room and slept on an iron cot. A muslin curtain covered the single window in his room; a kerosene lamp on a low bedside table provided him with light. He was a short, round little Hindu—surprising in so fanatical an ascetic—moon-faced, and, as he sat motionless on the iron cot, the lamp cast the shadow of a brooding Buddha on the wall behind him. This man had arranged the murders of British magistrates, police officials, the leaders of business organizations as well as constables and guards, both British and Indian. He was a true terrorist.

A young man knocked on the room door, entered, and gestured toward the outside door. "Rajid," he said.

The seated man nodded. "Wait."

The guard bowed and returned to his seat in the next room.

Gupta moved back heavily against the wall. He knew what Rajid had to tell him. He knew the English magistrate had been killed before Rajid had left Midnapore. He had his own methods of acquiring information.

There remained only for him to decide whether to see this young follower. To learn what he already knew was to waste his time. To see Rajid merely to compliment him was to extend an unnecessary kindness. Gupta didn't permit himself these gestures.

He knew what Rajid really wanted, to be rewarded with the next killing. He knew the student's nature, the fanatical hysteria he called patriotism. Gupta didn't want to discourage this. He wanted to keep the young man at hand, a cocked pistol, waiting only to be pointed at the proper time and target.

But Gupta distrusted young followers like Rajid. So many of them were pseudo-English. It was curious. They studied in English-modeled universities, were fluent in the English tongue, with English history and literature. They played English games, affected English clothes, even English slang. Yet they were Indian, raised in Bengali homes, of Bengali blood and an Indian religion. It was this dichotomy that confused them. Their resentment of the Raj was a frenzied love-hate.

There was another reason Gupta felt a contempt for his followers. They were terrorists out of patriotism. They believed they loved their country and killed for their country. To Gupta this was nonsense. A true terrorist killed only for the sake of killing. He knew, as Nechayev had written, that the true terrorist entered the world only to destroy it.

Gupta, moving quietly on his cot, called, "Chowdri." The young guard rose from his chair in the front room and entered. Gupta nodded. "Tell him I know his good news. He has done well. Tell him I will send for him soon."

"But he wants to see you, Gupta Guru. He is very impatient."

"Tell him there will be a meeting soon. Tell him to remain in the city." He nodded.

The guard left and Gupta sat back. He knew where Rajid would go now, to that little Anglo-Indian girl in the brothel on Acre Lane. It was just as well. She might cool his impatience. Gupta liked to know these weaknesses of young followers. He would always be able to find a use for them. He sat back against the wall. The shadow settled itself comfortably.

In his flat at Government House, Tiger Flemyng was reading a book called *The Revolutionary Catechism*, written in 1869. Its author was the Russian revolutionary, Sergei Nechayev.

Tiger read the last sentence again. "Our task is terrible, total, universal and merciless destruction."

He thoughtfully put aside the book. What had he learned so far? It was clear that Nechayev had been a very tough man. He had been confined for eight years in a narrow, solitary cell in a Russian prison-fortress. Finally, still chained to the walls of his airless and lightless cell, he was found dead. His only accomplishment, up to his death at the age of thirty-four, had been his own destruction.

Yet Flemyng knew that this book, his *Catechism*, had made him the patron saint to terrorists, beyond even Bakunin, Shelyabov, and the other killers he had studied.

It was clear that if Gupta was a true follower of Nechayev, it would not be a life of indulgence that he led. Nechayev had preached an ascetic dedication, the abandonment of all human relationships, the forswearing of self, of family, of property, of all attachments. The end of this dedication would be destruction. The world was evil, strayed from righteousness. It must be punished, destroyed, so that a cleaner world might arise. He called for a priesthood of terror.

All this merely confirmed for Flemyng what was only too apparent. Finding Gupta might prove impossible. He would never leave his hideaway. He would eat little, shun fresh air and women. He wouldn't even have a friend who might betray him.

They knew he was in Calcutta. That much they had learned from police informers. But Calcutta sprawled on both banks of the Hooghly. It was a rabbit warren of a city—and there were more than two million rabbits. Locating one Indian among so many brown faces made the needle in the haystack seem conspicuous.

Tiger took out a photo. It was the snapshot of an Indian, said to be a former student at the university, suspended some years before for agitation. It was said that he was now a follower of Gupta's and had, in fact, been seen in the area of the Chittagong Armory raid. The photo came from the university files.

Flemyng studied the face. It was not an unusual face in Bengal: delicate, sensitive, large-eyed, almost effeminate to a Briton's eyes. There was intelligence there but also impatience and a certain cruelty. He would now be perhaps twenty-three.

Tiger put the photo suddenly in his pocket. It was only a chance but if he couldn't find Gupta, he might at least find this man and he might lead them to Gupta. Anything was better than waiting.

He would begin with the brothels. This man was young. He might well be unmarried, unattached. There might be little else for him but Kuraiya Road or Acre Lane. At the worst, someone might recognize his photo.

It was a lively night at Acre Lane and Dolly had found herself in demand. She ate her supper about half past nine and went to her room to remake her face. She was already fatigued. She tried not to react to the men's bodies. She knew dimly that it was unprofessional to respond. But once in a while, perhaps every third man, she would find herself clutching the man, whimpering in helpless confusion.

Dolly finished before the mirror, adjusted her dress, went out into the hall and down the stairs toward the parlor.

A voice whispered at her. "Your Rajid is outside."

It was the girl passing her on the way up. Dolly recognized

"Baby," another new girl. A tall, grinning Scot was with her, still wearing his ribboned bonnet.

Dolly paused. "Did you see him?"

"From the window. Ten minutes ago. He's in the lane." The girl slapped at the Scot's hand. "Mind my dress. You are in a hurry."

The Scot laughed uproariously and Baby led him into a bedroom. The door closed.

Dolly stood irresolute. She hadn't seen Rajid in nearly two weeks. He would be angry if she kept him waiting.

Her eyes were perplexed. She wasn't accustomed to decisions. Her pretty face, slightly vacant, tried to arrange itself in thought.

An hour later police inspector Harrison and his sergeant confronted an angry Magda, called from her dinner. The inspector grinned. "Apologies, Magda. We're looking for someone and we thought he might just be here." He produced a snapshot. Behind him, Tiger Flemyng waited patiently.

The inspector shoved the photo at Magda. "Take a look, old girl."

"But this man is an Indian. You know my place. There are no Indians allowed."

"I know. Your girls wouldn't touch one." He grinned again, shoved the picture at her, this time more sharply. "Look again."

"I never see this man."

"Okay. We'll take a look-see. Take me around."

"But the girls have visitors. They will kick up a fuss."

"Too bloody bad. Come on. Every room."

He turned toward the staircase, followed quietly by the unobtrusive Flemyng. Magda knew who he was. She had seen him at parades. He was aide-de-camp to the governor. She wondered only briefly why he might be there. It wasn't her business to pry.

In Dolly's darkened bedroom Rajid, half-clad, stood with his lean, dark face pressed against the half-opened door. Dolly, a cheap Japanese kimono over her pale shoulders, stood behind him, her arms about his waist.

He listened. "They are searching the house."

"Let Magda find you. I don't care."

"It isn't Magda. It's the police." He swung around. "Where can I go?" He shook her roughly. "Quick."

"But why . . ." She stared vacantly.

"Never mind. Tell me." He shook her again.

She pointed. "The bathroom. Outside the window."

"Come." He rushed into the small bathroom, pulled back the oval window, looked out.

She clutched him. "It is dangerous. You would have to reach the balcony."

He shook her off, stepped onto the toilet seat, pulled himself through the window.

Dolly stared after him, her eyes uncomprehending but frightened. She went back into her bedroom, then out into the hall. The voices seemed to be at the foot of her stairs and she waited uncertainly.

"Hello there, you little ducky." Dolly turned to see a large, middle-aged Englishman bearing down on her. He was wobbling a little, wagging his finger. "I saw an Indian in that room. Indians aren't allowed in this place. I'm going in to tell him."

"Go away. You are drunk." Dolly tried to close the door behind her. Rajid, in the window, clung to the bathroom sill, his feet on the vine below.

"I'm going to tell Magda," the man continued. "You're for us, not the wogs."

The voice of the inspector came up the stairs. "Now for the third floor."

"There's only Dolly up there. She's new here."

"Every room, Magda."

Dolly stepped back into her room. The Englishman followed and she swiftly closed the door. Rajid watched from outside, his revolver in his hand. The Englishman wobbled toward her.

"Let's you and I have a go. I'm better'n a wog."

She stepped back, her eyes wide with fright, then she waited submissively.

In the hall outside the inspector paused. "Open up. Last room."

"No, Inspector. She'll be frightened."

"Open up. Quick now." He stepped back. Magda unlocked the door reluctantly, swung it open. The inspector entered, then stopped abruptly. He looked embarrassed.

"Oh. Well, he's certainly not an Indian. Sorry." He closed the door quietly and went toward the stairs.

Rajid clung to the sill, staring in, his eyes wide. There were only a few sounds, the slap of flesh on flesh, an occasional grunt, a faint whimper from Dolly.

Rajid's eyes grew eager, the lips stretching with wild excitement. As he watched, his face slowly became almost mystical, lost in a protective dream.

Then, with a final shout, all noise ceased from the bedroom. Rajid put his head down on his arm, then, sobbing helplessly, he swung down to the verandah below. He slid to a scaffolding and then to the ground. He ran blindly, stumbling.

Tiger Flemyng threw open a window in time to see the lurching figure enter an alley and disappear.

8

FRIDAY WAS CALCUTTA'S GALA DAY FOR TIFFIN. Everyone worked hard four days in the week to get off the home mail on Thursday so that it could cross India and catch the P. & O. boat out of Bombay over the weekend. The incoming mail didn't arrive from Bombay until Sunday morning and wouldn't be coped with until Monday. So Friday meant that a two- or three-hour tiffin could be taken and Firpo's, the most popular restaurant in Calcutta, would have an air of holiday.

Mary had mixed feelings concerning her tiffin with Captain Flemyng. She wasn't certain she had heard of Firpo's from the retired colonels in Cheltenham; the restaurant might well have had a different name when she was young. But the fact that it was a luncheon mecca for the British in Calcutta gave it a special aura.

It was obvious that Tiger was not eligible for her marriage

intentions. He was undoubtedly younger; she judged him to be in his middle thirties. Furthermore, he was an aide-de-camp and she remembered from her childhood that aides in India could not marry. They were required to remain bachelors, due, possibly, to an excess of social responsibilities. She had felt it enormously romantic and even sad, quite appropriate for defenders of the Empire.

She knew it could do no harm to be seen in the company of the governor's aide. There wasn't an unmarried woman in Calcutta who wouldn't give a great deal to be in her position. She must make the most of this opportunity.

She threw caution aside in dressing, wearing for the first time a much-too-expensive print frock she had bought for the trip.

The frock and the one-way ticket she had decided to buy, largely to reinforce her determination to marry, had cost a large share of her savings.

She also wore a brassiere in which she had invested, a total departure from the band she had always worn. Mary even touched up her full mouth and sloshed on a sprinkle of face powder. The effect, if not entirely feminine, was at least spectacular.

She left the flat early and found herself on Chowringhi with a few minutes to spare. She knew that Chowringhi was the principal shopping street for the British in Calcutta and paused at the head of the boulevard. The Maidan lay to the right and to the left an arcade was lined with shops.

The boulevard itself was taken up with trams, taxis, horse-drawn carriages, and bicycles. Coolies hip-swayed through the traffic under heavy burdens carried on their heads. Cows wandered at will under the arcade, the "divine bovine," Tom had called them.

To Mary it was a thrilling sight. This was the center of Empire. On this street Clive had walked and the great Warren Hastings, first governor general of India. Here was the Black Hole of Calcutta, a place of horror yet pride to all English. Here was where the British Raj itself had been born, in Calcutta.

Mary absorbed it all, breathed deeply of the heady air of Empire. She wished only that her father could have been there. He would have understood her feelings. He would have nodded judiciously, approvingly. Everything was in order. Functioning.

Mary crossed to the arcade, started slowly along its length. For the most part the shops appeared to be modest, glass-fronted. She passed a draper's shop, a spirits store, a chemist's. A building appeared with a sign beside the entrance which read "Grand Hotel." The lobby, half-seen behind the wooden doorway, seemed empty.

A cow strayed into her path but Mary walked calmly around it and stopped to peer into another window. Silks were being displayed and Mary considered how she might look in a sari. She had heard that only Indian women could wear saris, that the bright colors made a white woman look pale and insipid. She dismissed the idea. It would be undignified of her.

The calm face of the cow appeared in the window beside her. Mary felt a touch of amusement. The face, above her waist, seemed to be the placid, matronly gaze of a fellow shopper. She started to move on but the cow swung broadside at that instant and its high, bony flanks pressed against her.

Mary felt a slight distaste. She had heard that latrine rights in the streets were sacred to the cows and she had no wish to be splashed.

She pushed against the cow's side but felt only an answering heave. The cow was imperturbable. Mary saw that several Indians had stopped and were watching. She pushed again but its high, sharp hips heaved and Mary found herself pinned against the window.

"This is ridiculous," she thought. "Someone will surely pull the cow away. Meanwhile it is going to push me right through this shop window." She knew a touch of nausea now and, as she glanced at the growing circle of grinning or indifferent faces, a surge of anger.

Mary was about to raise her knee sharply into the cow's belly when it gave a startled cough and moved quickly away. A man stood next to Mary, a heavy walking stick in his hand. It was obvious that he had jammed the handle of the stick into the cow's rear just below the tail. Mary remembered seeing Indian bullock drivers do that in the Maidan. She had thought it cruel but it obviously succeeded.

"Thank you." She couldn't say more. She was feeling shaky.

The man nodded, glanced at her with rather a quick, appraising look, then went on his way. The watching crowd of Indians looked disappointed but melted away.

Mary turned to the window to adjust her dress. This was

truly a startling experience. She tried to imagine a cow on a street in London or even Cheltenham.

She wondered who the man was. He appeared to be English though he had a very peculiar skin . . . yellowish, baked out, even cracked. "The way Spain must look in August," she thought.

There had been nothing hesitant in the way he had jabbed that cow. It had been cruel, shockingly cruel, but very efficient. She would thank him properly if they met again.

There was a crowd at the entrance to Firpo's and Mary stopped to watch. A tall, bearded Sikh with a blue puggree wound around his head, a white cummerbund over his knee-length coat, was opening the doors of a line of private motors and taxis.

Mary watched the newcomers: planters, red-faced from upcountry tea gardens—businessmen, the burra sahibs of Calcutta, with their memsahibs in their party best—and an occasional officer from the Fort. There was obviously no loss of confidence in the Raj on the part of these people. Mary felt a touch of pride. These were her fellow British.

She briefly noted one or two other matters. The name "Firpo" over the door in gilt letters was missing a quarter of the "O" and the magnificent doorman in his knee-length coat had a rip under the armpits. She felt a touch of irritation. The management was really rather lax. Someone should take them in hand.

Now was no time for slackness. She had heard of the killing at Midnapore. Tom had raved and cursed, shouting that "we should shoot them all." Denise had been short with the native bearer.

Mary had been deeply shocked. The magistrate killed might have someday retired to Cheltenham. It was almost as though one of the sweet old ICS gentlemen in her father's office had been murdered. She felt it as an indignity and a horror. There must be no slacking in the face of these people, no "Firpo" sign with half an "O," no doorman with a rip under his armpit.

She had set her chin determinedly when she felt a grip on her arm and turned to see Tiger Flemyng. Immediately her mood changed. She was about to enter Firpo's with an attractive man. The least she could do was seem carefree. After all, he too was a soldier of the Raj. She would not appear glum.

"Shall we go up?" He had bowed. There was fatigue in his face but he was courteous.

She fell in behind and they entered the stairway. She wondered as they climbed why he should look so tired. All the more reason for her to cheer him.

A man waited hospitably at the top of the stairs. He was stout and his black hair was brushed straight back from his high forehead. He looked Italian.

Tiger nodded. "Barrancini. Table for two on the verandah."

"Yes, Captain Flemyng." He smiled and led the way. It was obvious that anyone from Government House stood high on his list. Tiger and Mary followed as he entered the broad verandah.

At the entrance Mary stopped. It was remarkable. The long dining room they had left was nearly empty but the verandah was crowded with people. Tables jostled each other to the railing. An abundance of Indian table bearers filled the narrow aisles. Lowered lattice curtains kept the noise of chatter inside though isolating the verandah from the bustle of Chowringhi below.

Mary followed Tiger as he stalked through the tables to a place at the far end of the verandah. She remembered hearing somewhere that you could tell a man's nationality by the way he entered a dining room with a lady: the Englishman stalked ahead, the American followed behind, the Frenchman went arm in arm. Flemyng was a true Englishman.

She was also aware as she followed that heads turned their way. She tingled. This was marvelous, an entirely new experience for her. She fairly preened as she walked. Floated. They stopped finally at a table Barrancini had chosen and Mary, after parading conspicuously about the table a moment, sank finally into a chair.

"Drink?" Tiger asked. She nodded. "Two gimlets," Tiger said. Barrancini bowed and left, taking the drink order himself.

Mary glanced happily about. There were obviously other fishing fleeters present. She even saw Margot Danvers, her former pupil, watching her. There were no young men at her table, simply the same older couple, the Bracebridges, with whom Margot had been standing at the Garden Party.

Mary smiled toward Margot. It was the impulsive, friendly gesture of a Roecroft teacher toward a former pupil. Besides, she was feeling outgoing that day. Margot glanced away.

The drinks were brought and tiffin ordered. Mary wanted to try a Bengali curry. First a gimlet and then a curry. She could picture a whole row of retired colonels beaming down at her approvingly.

"I wonder if they'll know," she murmured.

"What?"

"That I'm drinking a gimlet and eating a curry at last. I've heard about these things since I was a child." She saw his puzzled expression. "In Cheltenham. As a child from a lot of retired Indian Army officers and ICS men. They were patients of my father's."

"Ah." He nodded wisely.

"I don't know where such people go when they die but, wherever they are, I hope they can look down and see me." She raised a glass and looked upward. "Salaam, sahibs." He raised his. "Salaam."

"Umm, that's good. Could I have another?"

"If you want one."

"Don't worry. I'll wash it down with a little curry. They should get along very well. Fire and ice. Oh, I'm having such a good time. Wherever did you get the name 'Tiger'?"

"My name is Alastair."

"But you're called 'Tiger.' Why?"

"I could give you many explanations. Which would you like?"

"Because you're a devil with the ladies."

"No. That's the least reason."

"Because you're a war hero."

"Probably quite the opposite. I used to sleep a lot up on the Frontier. Possibly the heat and the heavy tiffins. I never seemed to want to begin the day. That was when they started to call me 'Tiger.' Sort of a joke."

"I like the first explanation. The women."

He nodded to the bearer. "Two gimlets. Jeldi." The bearer went quickly toward the bar.

"Why are you called Mary deGive?"

"That's my name." She looked mournful. "I know it doesn't suit me. It belongs to someone glamorous, beautiful, romantic. Ma-ry deGive." She let the words linger, drawing them out softly. Shen she shrugged. "I should be called Phoebe or Agatha. Someone reliable. Phoebe Higginbottham."

"You're not a Phoebe."

"I'm not a Mary deGive. Sometimes I try."

"Like now?"

"Now I'm Phoebe. Here are the curries." She eyed the bearer expectantly. He carefully put down the curry dishes, surrounding their main plates with little tubs of condiments. He then trotted off for the two additional gimlets.

Mary looked helplessly at the five little tubs. "What is in the little dishes?"

"Meat, vegetables, curry pepper. Here are chapatties. That's sort of a bread. You break it up."

"But how do I eat everything?"

"With your right hand."

"You mean I just dip my fingers in. We never had one of these in Cheltenham."

"You can have a knife and fork if you really wish it."

Mary glanced around and saw that she was being watched. "What do others do?"

"They use forks if they eat it at all. It can be very hot."

The bearer returned with two gimlets and put them on the table. Mary took a sip and glanced around defiantly.

"Right hand or left?"

"Right."

"Here goes." She inserted her fingers into the rice pile and then into her mouth. "Now the chicken." She plunged her fingers into the nearest tub and shoved them into her mouth.

"Now the pepper curry," said Tiger. His face was solemn.

"Righto," said Mary. She pushed her fingers into the tub and into her mouth. Her eyes widened, her mouth opened and shut convulsively. She clutched her throat.

Tiger nodded mildly. "Hot, isn't it?"

She made wild, desperate noises, obviously wanted to spit out what her mouth held but, with others watching, she was trapped. She clutched the gimlet glass and swallowed a good half of the drink.

Her expression became nearly beatific. She again sipped the cooling drink and tried another finger of the curry.

"Better. I hardly notice it at all."

"The gimlet or the curry?"

"Either."

"Another gimlet, bearer."

Mary didn't protest. She was enjoying her curry too much, inserting an inquiring finger into the various tubs, putting the contents into her mouth, following placidly with a sip of the gimlet.

Some time later the tiffin was finished. The curry dishes had been taken away and, except for Tiger and Mary, the verandah was empty. The others, evidently the custom, had moved inside for their tiffins.

Mary hiccupped a little. "My first curry since I was a little girl in Cheltenham." She had a little trouble with the word "Cheltenham."

"And your first gimlets ever, I should think."

She nodded. "Curry and gimlets . . . girry and cumlets. Very good. What's next?"

"You mean sweet or dessert?"

"Sweet. I want a mango fool." She spoke the words carefully.

"I doubt mango fool would go well with gimlets and curry."

"Old Colonel Wattrous always liked a mango fool."

"How about a carriage ride?"

"Carriage ride?"

"Through the Maidan. We'll take a gharry. A closed carriage."

"A gharry. Of course. A gharry ride."

Tiger waited. He had to admit it; he hadn't enjoyed himself so much in quite a while. He needed something like this. This Mary deGive was remarkable. Tight as a Lord, drinking more gimlets than most men could consume, yet she had not entirely lost her dignity. She drank as though she owed it to the old colonels in Cheltenham—she was drinking in their stead—yet she also owed it to herself to keep her dignity. She was Queen Victoria with a quiet snoot-full.

Mary stood up, slightly swaying but still regal. "Pay the man."

She waved toward the bearer, began a slow, dignified march through the verandah. Tiger signed the tiffin chit and caught up with Mary at the top of the stairs leading down to the street.

They marched slowly, her generous mouth set determinedly, down the stairs and into the street.

9

AN HOUR LATER MARY AND TIGER WERE DRIFT-
ing down the Hooghly River on the high-waisted cargo boat
of a farmer. Mary reclined on a comfortable pile of sugar-
cane stalks. Tiger sat reflectively at her feet.

Mary wore a damp white cloth on her forehead. She wasn't
entirely certain how they came to be on the boat. Tiger had
stopped the carriage when she had waked and led her down
to the riverbank. It had only been a moment to hail a passing
farm boat, haggle briefly with the good-natured owner, then
she had been led to the high center of the ship and they were
now drifting peacefully with the sluggish river.

Mary had no idea what time it might be. She knew they
had passed under great freight steamers, had drifted past
burning ghats where she had seen a body being attended,
and had once passed a sturdy British naval patrol bustling
up from the Bay. Tiger had said they would not go far,
possibly only to the Sundarbans, the marshes that stretched
down to the Bay, then return.

She wasn't concerned. It seemed the most natural thing
in the world to be drifting on the sugar boat of a Bengali
peasant. It smelled sweet—too sweet—but if the farmer, his
helpers, and Tiger could stand it, so could she. Besides, it
was another page in her book of India.

"So you're a fishing fleeter."

It was Tiger's voice and Mary was startled, not only at
the sudden sound but at what he had said. Then she remembered dimly that it had been she, after all, who had
announced it.

"I am."

"You don't want me, do you?"

Mary glanced down at him. His face was so grim that she was amused. She was beginning to feel herself again.

"Are you available?"

"No. As a matter of fact, aides can't marry. We must remain bachelors."

"I hope you always tell the girls that before it's too late."

"Immediately. The trouble is most don't believe it. What sort of man are you looking for?"

"A single man as a starter."

"A good beginning."

"And someone suitable."

"What does that mean? Rich?"

"When a woman says 'suitable' she means she'll wait and see."

"Wait and see what?"

She shrugged a little. "Who wants her."

He watched her rueful expression. She's an honest woman at least.

"What about love? Do you expect to find someone 'suitable' for that?"

"It would certainly make him more suitable."

"But not essential."

"What is essential is that I marry. I am not young, I have given up my position, and I have little or no money."

"Isn't that called prostitution?" His voice was harsh.

She felt her face flush, then smiled. "Perhaps every woman in her right mind is a bit of a prostitute. It is a giving and taking, that's all. Each comes to terms."

"But not love."

"One must not expect too much."

"By God, you amaze me. You're straight from the prewar days, even Edwardian, yet you talk as though you were more emancipated than the dottiest of flappers."

"A paradox . . . a woman."

"I don't know what you are."

"There is one thing I would like to know. Where are the men in Calcutta?"

"Good God, they are all around the place."

"Young ones, yes. Where are the older ones? I've seen a few playing billiards or snooker at the Saturday Club and there are a few here and there but one never meets them."

Tiger glanced toward the riverbank. They had left the outskirts of the city and were passing fields of rice paddies. He could see women bending over the marshy water, patiently reaching down to sift the ungrained shoots. They moved slowly, their backs bent, several with babies strapped to their backs.

He turned back to Mary, meeting her seriousness with his own. "If you intend to marry in India, you might as well understand something from the beginning. This is a man's world. A woman may be necessary from time to time but for the Englishman out here, she never really fits in."

"But he does marry."

"He marries young. They have a few children, then he reverts to what he is at heart, a man's man. A quihai."

"I've heard that expression but I've forgotten what it means."

"In Hindustani it means literally 'who's there?' It's the way a man calls his servant. It's come to mean what old sahibs are called. It's probably because they're going deaf from all the quinine they've drunk."

"Poor fellows."

"Oh, they're happy enough. All a quihai wants is his daily gin and tonic at the club after work, a game of snooker or a rubber of bridge with his pals, then home to a late dinner and to bed with a book under his mosquito net."

"But where is his wife?"

"Oh, she's in London or the Midlands with the grandchildren. He's fond of the old girl, of course, and he goes back every four years for a reunion. But he hates the climate back home as much as she hates the Indian heat. They'd never divorce. They simply live separately and amicably."

"But it wouldn't have to be like that. I've met several wives here. Lady Henrietta Thornton and Lydia Bracebridge."

"They are exceptions. There are more upcountry. Couples live closer together in the mofussil. They have to. There's no one else."

"Then perhaps I shall marry upcountry." She looked determinedly off at the passing marshland. She wondered if this were upcountry. It wasn't very inviting.

"How far are we going, Tiger?"

"I think this is far enough. We'll be in the Bay in another eighty miles."

"But how are we going to get back?"

"Very simple. The way we've come. We'll just hail another boat."

She leaned back. It really was very simple sometimes. You just let yourself drift.

Two hours later, Mary and Tiger were strolling slowly through Eden Gardens. Tiger hadn't suggested ending their afternoon together. In fact, he had seemed anxious to continue. When Mary felt she might well have worn out her welcome, he had insisted that she see the Gardens, the most truly English bit of garden east of Kensington.

They were seated now near the empty bandstand. It was well after six o'clock and the Gardens were shadowed by the fading winter sun. There were still strollers and Mary could hear quiet English voices and the knock of bat on ball from a nearby cricket club.

Mary was somewhat weary but had no idea of giving up. It was all too seldom that she had spent this much time with an attractive man. It was a test, really. She knew enough about the rules of the game for a woman to know that she should pay a little more personal attention to this man.

"Tell me about yourself. I really know nothing about you."

"This is an anonymous country." Here we go, he thought. He had been exposed before to fishing fleeters.

"You are a soldier, I know that. Wounds too, I see." He looked sharply at her but she smiled. "I was a nurse during the war. One gets used."

"When they're not yours." There was no bitterness in his voice. He had long ago made peace with his face.

"Are you truly English? I would guess you were Irish."

"Half."

"Ah, which half? Your father?" He shook his head and she smiled encouragingly, trying to be helpful. "Your mother then. She was on a tour of England with her parents and she met your father at a concert. They were sitting next each other. They exchanged notes, met, fell in love, and lived happily ever after." She paused, breathless, somewhat pleased at her fancy.

He eyed her somberly. "My father was a lieutenant in the British Army on occupation duty in Ireland. My mother met him when he came to her house to arrest her brother as a rebel. When she married my father her mother spat at her."

"Oh."

"And when I was born the midwife came late, as late as she could. My mother died."

"I'm sorry."

"My father left Ireland for good. He died in the war in a German prisoner-of-war camp, of varicose veins. They'd ruptured." He spoke quietly, his mouth mocking but the eyes were hard.

Mary was silent, a little ashamed. It served her right, trying to be arch, something she wasn't. She should have more respect for the men.

She shrugged a little. "You should marry, Captain."

"I told you. I'm the governor's aide."

"But you might later."

"No. Never."

"Your parents?"

"Perhaps I've been married before. When I was a young subaltern on the Frontier and she couldn't stand the cantonment life. One day when I came back, she was gone. Not even a chit."

"Is this true?"

"Perhaps. Perhaps not." He stood up. "Come. Let's walk."

Mary stood quickly to her feet and fell in submissively beside him. He glanced sideways at her.

"How did you happen to come to India?"

"I've told you. To marry."

"But why India! You could have married in England!"

"I felt I was needed in India. I know that sounds silly but it isn't to me. This is a time of crisis for the Raj. Gandhi and his salt march, his starving himself to win swaraj.

"He's in jail now."

"He's still dangerous. The terrorists too. It just seemed a time to come out. To contribute the little I can. As a wife to someone."

"My God. You really believe in all this. Queen Victoria herself has come."

"You mean in the Empire? Of course I believe in it. I'm English."

"Of course you believe in it." His voice was mocking.

"But don't you?" She looked at him in puzzlement, then shock. "But you must. You're English too. A soldier. An officer."

They stared at each other a moment, then she laughed lightly. "You're joking. Just because I'm new here. Come on. Let's walk."

She took his arm easily and led him through the Gardens.

There were a number of statues on the path. Mary stopped before one to read the inscription.

"General Roberts, the hero of Kandahar, Afghanistan." She smiled up at Tiger, reminding him. He was silent.

She led the way to another statue, a bearded figure seated on a dais. "Hastings," she read. "The great Hastings. First governor of the Raj." She glanced around. "It's almost as though these statues watched over the Gardens. Here is one place that 'shall be forever England.'"

"Rupert Brooke. A poet. You quote the wrong man. You should quote the Indians. Tagore, even Gandhi."

She faced him and for a moment there was anger in her face. Then she controlled herself and spoke softly.

"You really do have doubts. Why? It could be very dangerous for you if someone knew."

"It is dangerous now. I am a soldier. I may have to die for the Raj. Or kill."

"Have you told others?"

"Of course not."

"Are your doubts new?"

"Perhaps a year. Perhaps they have always been there. Inherited from my father in Ireland."

"But we have been good for the Indians! Everybody knows that. They were nothing before the Raj."

"Has it been good for us?" He seemed to be addressing the statues as much as Mary. "We are as much the conquered as the Indians. We force rules on them but we force worse ones on ourselves. We say it takes character to rule. One must be hard. Hard on them and hard on ourselves. Then we are no longer human. We have traded what we are for a sense of power."

"A sense of power?"

"Don't you feel it? It's all around us. We are the masters, the sahibs. We have the power of life or death."

He was looking now at the distant memorial to the Queen-Empress, Victoria. His face was hard, accusing, the scars ugly, unsoftened by the fading light.

Mary watched him. She had known that bitter look only too well. Tim had loved England but hated the war and knew he had to go back to it.

She put a hand to her broad forehead. She knew the fading light could do nothing for her unlovely face. It never had. But there was determination in it and a certain strength.

"If you have doubts, you should give up being an aide. Return to your regiment."

"I took this post because I needed it. I've been passed over twice for promotion. At thirty-five I'm the oldest aide in India."

"Why were you passed over?"

"A British officer doesn't spend his leaves among the Indians, studying in one of their ashrams or living in their villages as I did."

"They picked you as Sir Gerald's aide-de-camp."

"They wanted a bodyguard, a gunman. They wanted a man with two DSMs and a few scars. If we couldn't catch the terrorists, we might at least frighten them."

"You are telling me some shocking things."

"I want you to know what you may be getting into here. It's not all Firpo's and garden parties."

"I never thought it was!" She faced him angrily. He too was angry. There they stood—he, tall, scarred with a broken face; she, for a moment magnificent in her fury.

Then she softened, shrugged a little. "You are a much more complicated soldier than I suspected."

"You are not the usual visitor."

"We each have our problems."

"Shall I see you again?"

"I don't know. I would like to talk to you."

"I could help you, I suppose. You do need someone." Oh, Tim, she thought . . . he's so young. It couldn't be. Not he. "You wouldn't interfere."

"With other men? No."

"We must agree on that. We'll see each other only when it is convenient." She had turned away from him and her own voice was a little harsh.

"I agree."

"Good." She swung around. "It's been a very nice day. Everything. Thank you."

"I'm glad we did it."

They smiled and knew now they would be friends.

10

SO FAR IT HAD NOT BEEN A SUCCESSFUL VISIT for Margot Danvers. Her hostess, Lydia Bracebridge, was out of touch with the younger men in Calcutta and Rufus Bracebridge was proving of little help. Margot had met older married friends of the Bracebridges, and two acquaintances of her father had given a tea. The eligible introductions to date had included a bachelor vicar, likely to remain a bachelor, and a retired botany specialist once connected with the Calcutta Zoological Gardens. Margot had been her usual self, cool, slightly acidulous. She did not suffer fools gladly.

The time was wasting. She had seen several of her ship acquaintances being accompanied by men. She had even seen the deGive woman being squired about, not only by that rather fast-looking Beauchamp couple with whom she was said to be staying but once, at Firpo's, she had seen her with that striking Captain Flemyng, aide to the governor. Men's tastes in women were a source of some bitterness to Margot.

Margot knew very well she was good-looking. Her thin face, lean body, high forehead with shaved eyebrows provided only an exclamation point to her lack of appeal, but she had been taught that good looks in a lady were not quite nice, were somehow vulgar. There could be no mistaking her for other than of good family.

She was particularly vexed with Calcutta because of the special wardrobe she had laid on. Margot prided herself on her taste. She bought her tweeds and shoes in England, her party frocks in Paris. She was that rare thing in county society, a lady who dressed nearly as well as a nobody. One could hardly have told from her appearance that she was the daughter of a title. She might well have been a secretary in the city. But obviously her clothes had cost several times their value—the mark of a lady.

In Calcutta her clothes had brought little recognition. She wore her tweeds, her party frocks, picture hats even, to St. Paul's Church with the Bracebridges. To no avail. Calcutta was simply too provincial, too far from the smart world. If anything, in these days of the slump and the rather defiant dowdiness about her, her clothes were making Margot feel conspicuous.

She began to take long, irritable walks. She would rise early, stride energetically into town to the Maidan, do its entire length, then walk home.

One afternoon she especially felt she needed a walk. She had seen the engagement announcement of another girl from the ship, the younger of two sisters. Margot strode into the Maidan and stopped indifferently to watch a rugby game. She was not a rugby fan. The one game she had seen, with her father at Twickenham, she had found incomprehensible and excessively male.

She paused now, partly to catch her breath, mostly to frown unseeingly over her own bitter thoughts. The next thing she knew the ball was bouncing her way and Margot was being knocked down and overrun by a pack of eager, sweaty males.

She lay breathless a moment, then a brawny arm reached down to help her to her feet.

"Are you all right?" It was a broad face looking down at her, grinning but concerned.

"I'm all right." She pushed angrily at her skirt. It was really too much. These brutes.

"We were chasing the ball. It was a knock-on." He took her arm to steady her.

"Please." She pushed his arm angrily away, trying to achieve some dignity.

"Try the stands, miss. A lot safer there."

"Come on, man," a voice shouted impatiently.

The broad hand dusted vigorously at Margot's skirt. "You're a good sport. We could use you in our scrum line." He winked good-naturedly at her and lumbered back onto the field.

Margot didn't go up into the stands. She walked with slightly unsteady dignity away from the field and toward the street home.

She said nothing to the Bracebridges about her experience. She only hoped that no one she knew might have been there to see her humiliating moment. Imagine being knocked over by a lot of brawny, sweating men. Probably most of them junior clerks, even soldiers from the Fort.

Yet the one who had picked her up had seemed decent. His accent wasn't too bad, possibly Dorset. She wondered who he was. Possibly she should drop him a note of thanks.

She turned to the sports pages of the *Statesman,* the Calcutta newspaper, the next day and determined that the two teams playing rugger on the Maidan the previous day had been the Calcutta Scottish and the Calcutta Rugby Club. Which team was which she had no idea.

"What are the colors of the Rugby Club?" she asked casually at tea that afternoon.

"Colors?" Mrs. Bracebridge looked startled. "Heavens, I don't know. Do they have colors?"

"Of course. How else would one distinguish?" Really, Margot thought. Imagine not knowing something so simple.

"I must ask Mr. Bracebridge. He's quite keen on rugby."

"Colors?" repeated Mr. Bracebridge that evening. They were having dinner, alone as usual, just the three of them. "Let me see. The Rugby Club wears blue. No, that's the Welsh Fusiliers from upcountry. Won the All-Comers last year. Ah, it's red and white. The club side wears a white jersey with red stripes."

Margot was satisfied. He was a member of the Calcutta Rugby Club. She remembered his red and white jersey. And the paper had said that the Rugby Club was playing again the next afternoon.

The next day Margot told Mrs. Bracebridge she was visiting the Zoological Gardens that afternoon and, having paid a perfunctory visit to the Zoo, she took her place in a quiet part of the rugby stands.

Margot saw him, twice as big as life, playing in the very center of the scrum, his forehead and ears bound tight with a black band. Each time the ball was thrown in between the two packs Margot's man, at the apex of his scrum line, would heave and butt against his opponent opposite, simultaneously hooking with his feet to send the ball back through the legs of his teammates to the little scrum half waiting and hopping about behind.

Her man was magnificent. Despite herself Margot caught

her breath. Each time the ball was thrown in, the Rugby Club pack, led by its massive hooker, surged forward like an enraged caterpillar. The hooker opposite would kick vainly for the ball as he and his pack, heaving and digging in with its feet, were slowly, inexorably pushed backward.

Margot felt her flesh grow oddly warm, little red spots appearing on her thin neck and bony shoulders as her man, like some bull-shouldered elephant, led his pack raging up and down before her. When the game was ended she felt quite exhausted.

The next day Margot took the *Statesman* account of the game to her room and locked the door. There seemed to be an interminable list of the players' names but she noticed that they were grouped according to team and, in each case, one name stood alone. It stood at the beginning of the names, solitary, majestic, befitting the apex of a triangle.

"Frank Willis?" said Rufus Bracebridge when asked that evening at dinner. "Hmm, he's the hooker for the Rugby Club. One of the old-timers, I believe. Must be pushing forty."

"Forty." Despite herself Margot felt a shock. This bull elephant, her Atlas bearing the weight of the rugby world, forty? "He seems younger," she murmured. "I saw him play."

"You can't tell with their hooker-bands on. I dare say if he took off that band you'd find he was well scarred. And bald as a coot."

"Scarred." Margot felt a chill. She could hardly be interested in a man with scars. Still, since the Great War there were many such.

"Yes," said Mr. Bracebridge. "He's been twelve years with the club. At least that. Came out after the war. A hooker takes a good deal of butting. You can always tell a veteran by his scarred forehead and torn ears. Very difficult position." He sipped his tea reflectively. "I was a three-quarter myself. Out on the wing. You need speed there."

"I'm sure," murmured Margot. She didn't want to encourage her host's musings. She wanted to digest what she had learned.

Margot spent the next several days in a state of despondent frustration. She wanted very much to know this man, torn ears and all. But there seemed no way to meet. The Brace-bridges would be no good to her even if she were to suggest an introduction, and this she could not do. She thought briefly of waiting again on the touchline at his next game and throwing herself under a scrum once more. She dismissed this as highly impracticable. She might very well be lifted to her feet by a total stranger.

Margot became moody, irritable, forgetting even to smile graciously at the servants each day. She decided to occupy herself with small distractions. She had become expert at that back in England. That day, for example, she would buy a tie for Mr. Bracebridge. Mrs. Bracebridge had said it would be his birthday the next day and Margot felt it suitable to give him that most impersonal of gifts from a lady, a nice tie.

She walked into town and wandered off Chowringhi into an unimpressive street just a short distance off Curzon Way. She realized it was an area she had not seen before, a street of small shops, Anglo-Indian cafés, a petrol station. She was about to retrace her steps when she saw a tidy little store whose neatly lettered sign read "Gentlemen's Furnishings." Encouraged by this and approving the neat window display, Margot went inside. There appeared to be only one person in attendance but, from his clothes, she felt he must be English.

"Could you show me a gentleman's tie?" she asked, then, as she stared at the approaching salesman, she nearly choked. "You," she said, quite humanly.

"Hello," he said cheerfully. "You're the touchline stroller. Hope we didn't hurt you. I've often wondered."

"It was quite all right. I shouldn't have been standing there. It was very clumsy of me." She stood staring up at him. He seemed even more powerful in his business clothes, his jacket barely buttoning across his deep chest. She noted that his forehead did indeed have a few nasty scars and that one ear was slightly puffed but, was grateful to note, he had a full supply of hair. She felt curiously weak in his presence. For a moment she felt that if he had lowered his head to butt her in the familiar fashion she couldn't have denied him.

She recovered herself. "I've come for a tie," she said firmly. "It's for a man."

"For your husband?" He smiled.

"No. It's for the gentleman with whom I'm staying." He smiled more broadly. "I mean . . ." she said. Then she set her chin firmly. She was not going to explain. "Let me see your gentlemen's ties, please."

"Of course."

"I'm visiting Mr. and Mrs. Rufus Bracebridge," she added with dignity.

He led her to a lighted showcase and bent over it. "We have some very fine ties. This one with the stripes, for example."

"Have you anything in solid colors? Dark blue, I think." She knew Mr. Bracebridge had gone to Oxford. She was not a girl to overlook such matters, or not to know the colors.

"Here is a dark blue. It isn't washable. It's silk." He looked at her appraisingly. Most of his customers wanted only washables.

"I doubt Mr. Bracebridge washes his ties," she said primly. "How much, please?"

"Ten rupees. That's fifteen shillings."

"I have the rupees." She counted out the unfamiliar money with stiff, slightly uncertain fingers.

"Thank you. I'll put it in a box." He left her to hand the tie to a young clerk for wrapping. The clerk was of that pale brown color Margot was beginning to recognize as Anglo-Indian.

"Can I show you anything else?" He had come back and was standing beside her, large and friendly. Margot took refuge in staring about the shop.

"No, thank you."

"Is this your first visit to Calcutta?"

"Yes."

"I hope you're enjoying yourself."

"Quite well, thank you." He wasn't overburdened with brains, she thought, judging by his conversation.

"Is that Mr. Rufus Bracebridge you're visiting?"

"Yes."

"I've seen him at rugger matches. He used to play, I think."

"Three-quarter," she said with finality. "I believe my package is ready."

"Oh, a pity." He gave her a shopkeeper's smile yet so openly that she could hardly feel offended. "I hope you will come again."

"Thank you. Good day, Mr. . . ." she hesitated.

"Willis. Frank Willis. Good day."

She turned and walked out. She paused on the outside to glance back at the store sign. In small letters in the right-hand corner she saw the gold lettering. "Frank Willis, Prop." At least he was the owner of the store.

She did her best for the next two days to put this man out of her thoughts but on the third day he telephoned her. At the sound of his deep voice on the phone she felt the spots rising again to her thin neck.

"I rang to see how the tie was liked. A good haberdasher likes to know his goods have given satisfaction."

"It went nicely, thank you." She did wish he would stop referring to himself as a "haberdasher." "Gentlemen's furnishings proprietor" at least.

"I thought if you'd pay the shop a return visit this afternoon I could show you the rest of our tie line. Then we might have a cup of tea afterward."

"Tea?" She felt a little dizzy. A man was actually asking her to have tea with him. And not just any man . . . this particular man.

"Who is it, Margot?" It was Mrs. Bracebridge calling from the top of the stair.

"A gentleman, Mrs. Bracebridge." She knew that, strictly speaking, that wasn't true but she had to say something.

"Oh. That's nice," said Mrs. Bracebridge. At least it was a male who had called Margot.

"Are you still there?" It was Frank Willis, the voice peremptory.

"Yes." Margot hesitated. She knew she shouldn't see him. He was a stranger, a man to whom she hadn't been introduced. And he was a shopkeeper to boot.

But he did play rugby. It was not as though he were a football player. And he had observed the niceties; he had asked her to visit the shop.

"I'd be delighted to come."

"Good. A quarter to four then. I'll shut up shop for an hour or George can take over. We can nip over to the Grand for a spot."

"A quarter to four. Good-bye, Mr. Willis." She hung up.

She dressed carefully that afternoon, wearing a yellow printed frock she had brought back from Paris and carrying a small, neat parasol, white with blue cornflowers around the edge. For a hat she wore a flutter of pale yellow tulle on her thin hair.

She was greeted at the shop with a warming smile of appreciation. It was clear that to Frank at least his visitor was the last word in chic and good taste. He himself was dressed in the best his shop could offer, a tightly fitted blue blazer, complete with the emblem of the Rugby Club, and a pair of gray Oxford flannels. He seemed even more powerful looking than at their previous meeting.

He escorted her briefly about his little shop, eyeing her and her frock with an admiration that brought more spots to her lean shoulders. He then led her out to the crowded street, thence to Chowringhi and the Grand Hotel.

It was the first time Margot had stepped inside the Grand. It was obviously passé, outré, and all the other French words that came to her mind. The bare, faded lobby, decorated only by two forlorn potted palms, struck her immediately as "commercial." It was inhabited at the moment only by a solitary Anglo-Indian whom she took immediately to be a commercial traveler. Nothing spoke more clearly of the slump than the emptiness of this undoubtedly once-bustling lobby.

On Frank it had no effect. He led her genially through the lobby to the "Palm Court" beyond, a square, stone-floored room, dimly lighted through its glass roof. They sat at a wicker table, ordered tea from an elderly Indian bearer, and sat back to look at each other. Margot wondered briefly why he hadn't taken her to Firpo's or to the Slap for tea but put it out of her mind. She was not one to let minor issues divert her from the problem at hand.

"I have enjoyed watching you play rugby." She thought it best to put in the first word.

"It's a grand game. This is my thirteenth season with the club. See my scars?" He bent his head.

"Yes." She closed her eyes.

"Feel them." He took her hand, ran it over his forehead. She explored the skin tentatively, eyes closed. It felt granular.

"How terrible." She tried to sound sympathetic.

"You should see the chaps who played opposite." He grinned, shook his head. She smelled the odor of hair tonic. It gave her pause for a moment but she dismissed the thought.

"It seems such a rough game," she said. "One has to be so strong." She smiled encouragingly with her thin mouth.

"Quick too. We still have some very fast lads in our backfield. Not so fast as we used to be but not too slow either. We'll win the Cup."

"The Cup?"

"The All-Comers. The Fusiliers won it last year. The Scottish won it year before last."

"You have won it?"

"We held it five years running. Nobody could beat us. We'll get it back this year. We're not so old as all that."

"I'm sure you will. I hope you'll invite me." She knew she didn't have a very appealing smile. She did her best, raising the shaved eyebrows. And she knew that by now her expensive French perfume must have reached him.

"Consider yourself invited," he said gallantly. There was no need to say more. The elderly table servant came up quietly on his bare feet and laid down their tea and biscuits with two small saucers of marmalade. "You do the honors," Frank said. "I like plenty of sugar."

"So do I." If he had said he liked it with vinegar she would have said she liked it too. She poured his cup carefully, added the hot milk, stirred in two heaping spoonfuls of sugar. "Enough?"

"Achcha. Perfect."

She handed him his cup, then sat back with her own. He drank in great, hungry gulps, spread marmalade on one of the biscuits.

"Biscuit?"

"Not now."

"Too much of the marm?"

"Oh no, I like marm." Dear heaven, she thought. "Marm." This wasn't going to be easy.

"So do I." He spread his own biscuit lavishly.

"It seems so unusual of a rugby player to be owner of a gentlemen's furnishings store," she said.

"Nothing unusual. I like clothes."

"Oh, I can see that. I meant it seems so small and you're so big."

"Best men's shop in Calcutta," he said. "In all of India for that matter. Things are a bit slow just now but they'll pick up. Bound to."

"Then you'll go on to something larger, of course."

"Larger?"

"Won't you? I mean with your ability."

"I like my shop." He set his jaw belligerently. "I leave the big wholesale business to the burra sahibs. They're just warehouses. I deal with my customers personally."

"It *is* much cozier." She could see she had touched a sore spot.

"Of course I can't go to the Slap."

"You can't?"

"I'm in retail. I can't go to any of the posh clubs. The Slap, the Tollygunge—I'm a shopkeeper." He grinned good-naturedly.

Mary felt her face grow red. "You should really do something about it."

"I don't mind. I have the Rugby Club. They'll probably turn me out when they find a better hooker. They haven't so far." He patted his big chest. "I have my church too."

"Church?"

"The First Congregational. I know it's not posh but we're active. Anglo-Indians mostly. A very decent lot."

"I see. I'm an Episcopalian."

"Then you go to St. Paul's here. Very burra sahib."

"Yes." Suddenly she saw the Palm Court in all its age—the bare, wooden tables, the cold cement floor. It was as though a cloud had passed over the glass roof.

"You feel all right?" He looked anxious.

"Quite."

"Let me give you some more biscuit and marm."

"I've had enough, thank you." She moved. "I think I'd best go. I promised Mrs. Bracebridge I wouldn't be long."

"Too bad. I was enjoying it. Still, just as well. I can go back to the shop and relieve George. Though there's probably not much to do."

He called the kithmaghar, paid the chit, led her from the Grand. He escorted her possessively along Chowringhi, towering even over her yellow and white parasol. Margot, her thin face tired now, said nothing. They found a taxi in front of Firpo's and he helped her inside.

"I'll see you again?" He beamed down at her, one hand on the taxi door.

"I can't say. I'm really the guest of Mr. and Mrs. Bracebridge."

"Oh, that'll be all right. He's keen on rugger."

"I'll speak to them."

He hesitated, then came out with it. "You know it's good to know someone like you. You don't mind my being a haberdasher and you . . . you dress like a queen. You're top hole."

"Thank you. Good-bye."

"Good-bye." He waved to the Sikh driver and the taxi pulled ahead, the driver shouting at two coolies in the way.

Frank Willis moved jauntily under the arcade away from Firpo's.

Margot sat back, her eyes miserable. He was barred from the Slap. That meant if she married him she would be barred from the Slap too. And the Saturday Club was the center of Calcutta social life. Without that one might as well be . . . in the First Congregational Church.

Margot felt her neck crawl with her agitation. Pink blotches appeared on her neck and she scratched them mechanically. She liked Frank. It was a great deal more disturbing than that. He unsettled her. There was something in that great male frame, that vitality, that made her shiver a little when he was near. He was like a great bull in the animal fairs she had attended. She couldn't give him up.

Frank phoned the next day but Margot found an excuse not to see him. He phoned again the second day but she again put him off. She was struggling. On the third day she could resist no longer. She agreed to accompany Frank to the coming Sports Night at the Rugby Club.

Frank was quite serious in his intentions about Margot. He knew she was unmarried, assumed she was a member of the fishing fleet, an institution with which, as a Calcutta male, he was well acquainted. He had no intention of wasting her time, or his own.

The truth was that Frank knew he was coming to the end of his rugby career but, until now, had been uncertain as to what he should put in its place. He had eschewed the girls hitherto because of his dedication to the club and a need to remain in condition. But this year would probably be his last. He had survived longer than any other hooker in Calcutta rugby. It would now be his turn to watch from the stands. He would settle down to one opponent, as he put it to his pal, Gordie Purvis, instead of fifteen.

He liked Margot. She was big, not unlike a rugby hooker. Big hands, big feet. But, curious and awkward as she might be, she had a certain amount of style. He knew he hadn't the most sophisticated taste; in Calcutta he hadn't had much chance to develop one. In Margot he saw the epitome of British good taste. The fact that her afternoon frocks were obviously expensive had not escaped him.

There was another, less admirable quality in his admiration for Margot. Her remarks about the Slap and her obvious distaste for his church had set him to pondering. He wondered if it might not be a good thing to marry Margot. It couldn't hurt a haberdasher to have a posh wife.

Perhaps he had been too conservative with his little shop. It was quite possible that Calcutta might provide bigger things if he had a grander store. He might even build something to rival the biggest in Calcutta. The first step might be to marry someone like Margot.

Sports Night at the Rugby Club would have tested the determination of stronger women than Margot. The clubhouse was old, wooden, bare of furniture, and its walls were decorated largely by photos of past teams. Frank marched Margot proudly from one photo to another, pointing himself out in the teams of the nineteen-twenties. He had more hair then but wore the same good-natured grin.

It was a hearty evening. Margot could see that Frank was popular with his rugger pals. He proudly introduced Margot and boasted with his teammates as to their victory in the coming All-Comers tournament. Eventually she was able to find herself alone with Frank on the verandah.

"Great lads," he said for the fourth or fifth time.

"Very nice," she answered. She would try to be appreciative but there were limits.

"That Gordie Purvis is our fullback. Kicks to touch from any place on the field."

"I'm sure," she said. She remembered Gordie Purvis only as a stringbean of a man. She wondered how he could kick anything.

"He's dead sure on the converts." Then he swung aggressively to the point, as though he were knocking on a loose ball.

"Margot, I'm not much at talking. I have to come to the point. It's my weakness."

"I shouldn't have thought you had a weakness," she murmured.

"What I'm getting at is I've enjoyed your being in Calcutta. I hate to think of your leaving."

"It isn't compulsory to leave."

"Then I think you should stay. Permanently."

"This is a proposal I take it."

"You might put it like that."

"How else could one?"

"It is a proposal. I want you to marry me."

She felt her breath catch. There it was, what she had been longing for. She felt a bit faint and put her hand out to his.

"Are you all right?"

"Yes."

"What do you say, Margot? I can take a week off after the tournament. We could be married and have a little trip. Puri. The Railway Hotel's not half bad."

"I like you, Frank. Very much." She felt almost faint. The tears came to her eyes.

"Well then, it's settled."

"No. I mean I couldn't."

"Couldn't?"

"It's you, Frank. The Slap. Oh, you're a wonderful man but you don't know my father. I couldn't tell my father I was marrying a man who couldn't take me to the Slap." She felt her face was flushed. She wanted so much to be coherent.

"What has the Slap to do with it?"

"Father wants so much for me. If we couldn't go to a club, he wouldn't understand it."

"But I can go to the Slap in the hot weather. If I'm invited."

"But not during the season. And the cold weather is so important." She knew she was wailing but she couldn't control her voice.

Frank looked at her and his face was a mixture of perplexity and affection. "You want me to be admitted to the Slap, is that it? Or no marrying."

"I'm sorry, Frank, because I do want to marry you."

"But they wouldn't take me in the Saturday Club. I'm in retail, a shopkeeper."

"They might. We could make them accept you."

"How?"

"If the right person proposed you and you were seconded properly. Mr. Bracebridge could propose you. He's a former member of their membership committee."

"But he knows I'm in retail."

"He'd do it if I asked him. I'm sure. We'd have a month. We could make you over, Frank. The Slap is a tennis club. I could teach you. I'm not bad. Then you could be seen with us. We could all go to the cinema together and to Firpo's for luncheon."

"I go to the Grand."

"Firpo's, Frank. The Grand's not for us. We would have

a month and then you'd go up before the membership committee." She had taken his big hand fiercely in her own, her fingers holding to it desperately.

Frank snorted. "Bracebridge. He's an old quihai. I'd need a proper second if he proposed me. Someone young, with spit and polish. Bracebridge could never get me in by himself. Who is there? I don't know anybody."

Margot clutched his hand. The nearness of his acquiescence spurred her. "Captain Flemyng," she said. She hardly knew how the name had come out.

"Flemyng! The governor's aide? Don't be daft. He doesn't even know me."

"I know someone who does know him." She could see them now at Firpo's—the tall aide and Miss deGive.

"But he'd never do it."

"Would you try if he would? Would you?" She clutched his fingers.

He stared at her, saw the desperation in her eyes. He also saw the larger building, the vast store he might have.

"Of course. Who wouldn't?"

"Then we'll try." And suddenly she had pulled his hand convulsively to her thin mouth, kissed it passionately, then burst into tears.

11

THE SEASON WAS IN FULL SWING NOW. THE VICE-roy had arrived and taken up residence in "Belvedere." It was the middle of December and the race season had started at the Calcutta Jockey Club. Polo games were being played daily on the Maidan grounds between army teams and teams of the Indian princes. The palaces of the princes were again inhabited, their owners returning from their states of Jodhpur, Cooch Behar, Burdwan, and many others. Despite the terrorists' killing in Midnapore, despite the Mahatma in his jail at Poona, it was said that Calcutta had never seemed gayer.

Mary was in the midst of this. Her acceptance had been assured by her presence at the governor's Garden Party and her subsequent appearance at Firpo's with Sir Gerald's aide, Captain Flemyng. She attended the Jockey Club and polo games with Tom and Denise, was invited with them to tea tennis on private courts and the occasional dinner at Firpo's or the Slap.

She was enjoying herself. She was meeting men though nothing had come of it. She wasn't concerned. There were still several months to go and she knew that she was moving in the correct milieu.

Only Tiger Flemyng marred her enjoyment. She saw him occasionally while with the Beauchamps. He stood near Sir Gerald at the polo matches or attended him in his box at the Jockey Club.

She saw him watching her as she met new men and there was usually a slight smile, somewhat sardonic, on his face. She knew what it meant; he disapproved of what she intended. It made her even more determined to set him straight about his lack of faith.

When Tiger was free of his duties and invited her, Mary continued to go out with him. It was not entirely unselfish, wishing to set him straight, help him with his doubts. She also knew he could tell her things about India she might wish to know. To deny herself his knowledge out of disapproval of his doubts would be foolish.

One night Tiger took her to a swimming match held at the Calcutta Swimming Club. He had said it was an annual affair, a water polo game and swimming match between the Club and the Kokine Club of Rangoon. It seemed odd to Mary that a club side should come all the way from Burma for a match but, if it was that important to both clubs, she looked forward to attending.

It was obvious at first sight that the Swimming Club was considerably less exclusive than the Saturday Club. It was a large and bare rectangular shed, containing an extra-large swimming bath lined with bare wooden benches. A narrow gallery was suspended from the roof on one side of the pool.

It was the crowd that caught her attention. Boisterous, packed happily onto the wooden benches, it filled the suspended gallery as well. She felt the vitality and cheerful, even coarse good nature of the crowd. There were families with children climbing the benches, accents of all sorts with the Scottish or Midland predominating. It was obviously not a burra sahib gathering. She knew she must be among the average of the eight thousand British in Calcutta: the clerks, police sergeants and their families, Tommies from the Fort, the chota sahibs.

She glanced up at Tiger. "This is different. I never would have known Calcutta was like this."

"Do you like it?"

"Of course. It's Elizabethan. The mood, the children running about—there's a family eating from their basket. We might be at the Globe waiting for a performance."

He glanced at her but said nothing. He led the way to two places on the nearest wooden bench. A police sergeant stood near and saluted as they came up. It was obvious that he had been told to save two places.

Mary glanced around at the nearest people. She was struck by the face of a man watching her, the yellowing skin, the hard blue eyes. Then she knew him. It was the man who had so efficiently saved her from the cow on Chowringhi. He seemed to bow slightly and she nodded, then turned away.

There was a sudden shouting and applause from the crowd and she saw that a group of men in bathing trunks had entered at one end.

"The water polo," Tiger said. "We've come in at the second half. Any score, constable?" He turned to the police officer.

"Four each, sir. Nip and tuck."

"A bit rough from the look of them."

Mary saw that two of the players wore bandages on their heads. It reminded her of the war-wounded.

The constable grinned. "It's been a bash, sir. Always is. Good thing it's only once a year. Takes a year to recover."

The two sides, six to each, were lined up at separate ends of the pool. A referee tossed the inflated ball into the center and the teams dove in and swam furiously to be first at it.

The shed was an instant uproar. Mary instinctively put her hands to her ears. The shouting, stamping on the benches, the women shrieking were nearly overwhelming. It was incredible. The sound beat upward against the tin roof and smashed downward again.

The pool was a maelstrom of thrashing, swimming men. One player would grab the ball, pitch it far down to one of his mates, and man and ball would instantly disappear in a swirl of foam, upraised arms, and thrashing legs. It was impossible to tell which side was the Calcutta Swimming Club except for the upswell of noise as friend or foe was encouraged or accused.

"Like it?" It was Tiger shouting down to Mary.

"I don't know. How long does it go on?"

"Till they drop. Or drown."

"There's no fixed time?"

"Supposed to be twenty minutes but nobody cares."

A goal was scored somehow and, from the deep groan that went up, Mary knew it must have been the other side scoring. The players swam heavily back to the ends of the pool, the ball was again tossed in, and the players swam furiously back toward the center.

The noise of the crowd this time had an angrier tone. Its side was a goal behind. The din was continuous. Again there was a thrashing at one end, this time where Mary and Tiger sat.

"Look," Mary pointed. "That water's all red. That's blood."

One player, an enemy player from the triumphant shouts of the crowd, turned slowly on his back, his face pale against the green water. The red was slowly leaking from a deep scratch, a gash, at the side of his forehead.

The nearest players swam furiously toward him, not to render aid, but to revenge themselves on the suspected assailant, now swimming sullenly backward. There was another thrashing, a whistle blew, one or two extra swimmers jumped into the pool to lend a hand, or a foot. The crowd was whistling and, to Mary's eyes, thoroughly enjoying the terrible battle.

She touched Tiger. "I think I've seen enough."

"It quiets down after a bit. Exhaustion."

"It simply doesn't appeal to me. Do you mind?"

"I'm ready."

They walked slowly out of the shed and turned toward the Maidan. The river was behind Mary and it was the first time she had approached the Maidan from the river side.

Neither she nor Tiger said anything for a few moments. The sound behind them slowly faded as they walked. It might never have been heard.

"What did it mean, Tiger?"

"It was worse than usual tonight."

"Why?"

"Could be many things. The Slump. People are worried about their jobs. They see their friends losing their positions, having to leave. Some of them have families, children. Calcutta is their home now and they see everything slipping away. Tonight was sort of a flight from all that."

"It was horrible. Some of them actually sounded as though they wanted to see someone drowned."

He said nothing. They walked a long time silently. It was a moon-brightened night and Tiger stopped once or twice to stare toward the distant Fort, its grass-covered ramparts barely visible in the moonlight.

When he spoke it was almost as though he were musing. "They don't usually behave like that."

"The people at the pool?"

"They're a decent lot on the whole. Considering that they are a long way from home, they maintain their behavior very well. It's the ones who have been out here the longest who are the worst."

"Homesick?"

"No. They don't know the meaning any more. Not consciously. They think of themselves as the sahibs, the masters of India. There's no one so imperial as some of these little clerks. They're nobody back home but give them five or ten years out here and they're all nabobs. Masters."

"That's why you took me there. You wanted me to see them."

"You might as well know."

"But they were just excited. It's only once a year. You said yourself they're worried about things. They were letting go."

"That's only part of it. I told you what the Raj is, what any Empire is. It's having your own way over someone, holding him down. Nobody can be a part of it long without becoming brute. Even the lowest of clerks. It's in the air."

"I don't want to listen to this sort of talk."

"You think I'm trying to discourage you from marrying here."

"You *are* trying."

"Are you angry?"

"I am. You're a British officer."

"Damn it, woman."

"I don't want to hear more."

"You listen. By God, this isn't only for you I'm talking. I need to talk. Here, sit here."

He led her toward a bench. Mary saw with surprise that they had crossed the Maidan and were near the great memorial to Queen Victoria, seated on her solid throne.

Tiger walked nearby. "Never mind the British out here. What about the Indians?"

"We've been good for them. Everybody knows that."

"Good for them." It was almost a snarl. "Let me tell you about this country."

Mary started to rise. Nothing he could say would change her mind about marrying in India.

"Sit down." His voice was angry, commanding. Mary sank back.

His voice was quieter. "India is ninety percent villages. The villages were run by the village councils, the panchayats —a council of five. The members knew the village, knew everything about each other for generations. If there was a problem the panchayat worked it out. We promised they could keep the councils but what happened? We abolished them."

He raised his face to the Memorial. "We put in our British system with one court for every three hundred villages. Now there aren't enough courts and the witnesses don't understand the procedures. Judges, lawyers, rules of testimony—to make the system work it's had to be corrupted."

Mary forced herself upright. It was stupid of her to listen to this talk.

He went on. "In one village I was told a story. A gang of cattle thieves had been caught. Other members of the gang told the owners that if they identified the cattle as theirs, they would be murdered. What did they do? The police rounded up twenty other people who swore the cattle was theirs and the gang was convicted. Then the fake owners sold the cattle to the real owners and split the proceeds with the police. Everybody was happy but the thieves."

He laughed. There was no reply from Mary. "Do you know who really owns India? It isn't the Raj—it's the moneylender. If he's British he's called an investor. He puts his money into jute, tea, or our few telephone lines."

"He risks his money," Mary said.

"Not even that. He's guaranteed his investment by law. He gets his nine percent before even the coolies are paid. As a matter of fact our British investor receives nearer twenty percent."

He turned savagely back toward the stone figure. "The Indian moneylender, the bania! The villagers have to borrow to pay our taxes and still exist. The bania gets from seventy-five to two hundred percent on his loan. The villager can never pay his debt. We don't change the system because we want the taxes. It's our rope around their necks."

"Why do you stay on if you feel this way?"

"I stay because I'm a soldier. If you can marry without loving, I can kill without believing."

Anger came quickly to Mary, then slowly slipped away. She must remember. Tim had been like that. Tim too had known doubts. But she had comforted Tim and lost him. She must not go that way again.

She made herself look away from Tiger. She must not watch him or she would harm them both. She was there to marry.

She stood up. "Let's talk of something else. Do you know a man named Frank Willis?"

"Willis? No."

"He owns a retail shop. Gentlemen's clothing."

"That fellow. A rugby player. You're not interested in him, are you!"

"A former pupil of mine came to see me yesterday. Margot Danvers. She's staying with the Bracebridges. She wants to marry Willis."

She turned away. She could still remember her surprise at Margot's visit and her shock that Margot should ask her for help. It had been but a few weeks since Margot had been so rude at the Garden Party.

Yet she had agreed to help. Even now she wasn't certain just why. It might have been out of a habit of helping her Roecroft students. She was still their schoolmistress. Or it might have been because she caught a glimpse of Margot's desperation. She could understand that very well.

"Let her," said Tiger.

"She wants to marry him but she also says she must be in the Saturday Club. She says her father, Sir Charles Danvers, would never forgive her if she married someone who couldn't be."

"She said that!"

"Is it true people in retail here can't be in the Slap?"

"It's true enough."

"She really cares for him. She says he would have a chance if the right people put him up. Rufus Bracebridge would propose him. She asked me to ask you if you would second him."

Tiger stared at her, then broke into a great laugh. "You mean it!"

"I said I would ask you."

"You mean she actually won't marry Willis unless he's in the Slap!"

"That's what she says."

"Then let her stay single! Or marry some other fellow! Refusing would be the best thing I could do for both of them."

"Tiger, you don't understand."

"I certainly don't."

"Here is a young woman who has been raised in the most exclusive manner imaginable—family, school, presentation at Court. Yet she has allowed herself to fall in love with Frank Willis. Her one reservation—her one effort to hold to some sense of what is familiar—is that he should be admitted to a club. It's as though she were reassuring herself that if a club will take him he must be all right for her. She knows so little of men. How could she? A club is the one familiar reassurance she has here."

"You really want me to help her."

"I think it would be a kindness."

"I would almost like to do it. It would be a joke on the Slap. Marriages aren't made in heaven out here! They're made in the Saturday Club!"

"You're being cruel to this girl. It would cost you so little and it would mean so much to her."

"You simply want to play Lady Bountiful to your former pupil. You talk to me about the Empire. You see how the Raj is. One has to be in the right club even to marry!"

There was anger in his face and Mary flushed with an answering anger. It was her father he was attacking, and all those retired old men in Cheltenham who had given their lives to the Raj.

Then she laughed. "You're right. I'm such a busybody."

"Florence Nightingale."

"I'm still wanting to help people. Just a schoolteacher at heart."

"Not at heart. There you're something else, though God

knows what." He threw up his hands. "All right. I'll help your Miss Danvers."

"You will!"

"Just tell him to give up that hair-stink he uses."

"Oh, I will."

"Marriage, the crimes we commit in thy name here."

"It isn't that. She simply loves him." She said it so simply, almost wistfully, that Tiger could sense the envy in her. Margot had found her love. She might need the reassurance of the Slap's approval of her choice—after all, she was in a strange land—but she dared to humiliate herself for him. There was love in her. Mary had no such love as yet. So she wrapped herself in the flag, in the Raj for reassurance, while she waited.

"You're such a damned Englishwoman. So loyal."

"No, I simply feel that all of us out here are sort of a family. We must help."

"Family. That's blasphemy."

He was outraged but Mary smiled. She knew what his anger meant. There was still a spark of loyalty in him too.

On the verandah of their home Denise Beauchamp went quietly to the little green box attached to the railing. She lifted the lid and the tiny head of the krait lifted itself from the leaves at the bottom.

Denise picked up the prong and prodded gently. The snake bit sluggishly at the prong, its open mouth moist and velvety.

She lifted the box from its cradle and went back into the bedroom. She sat on the bed on which Tom now lay, naked legs outstretched, the aroma of coconut oil rising from his loins. Tom reached out greedily, took the box, and Denise settled herself gently beside him.

She looked away. She knew it would do no good to plead with her husband. She had tried that at the beginning when she had realized this terrible thing she would have to share. Now Denise knew she could only wait, as she had always waited. She did it because he was weak and she loved him.

Denise focused as always on the mosquito net, folded back and tied to the bed's headposts. There was a gauzy mistiness about the white net that let her thoughts sink into the billows, protecting.

She was glad that Mary wasn't there. It was only when Mary left the house that this could happen. She sometimes dreaded Mary's departure, knowing what might come. Tom was unpredictable in his tastes; it might be her he would want, it might be "Mud-Pie." With Mary gone, she could prepare her mind, overcome her shame. She had tried to make peace with this sharing long ago.

Her husband moaned, then again. Denise looked down at him. His breathing had quickened, his eyes were half-closed, only the whites showing, the eyes rolled up.

Denise took his hand. She knew it wouldn't be long now. She held his hand tighter, her worldly, rather puffy face patient. But still her eyes were averted, fastened on some inner sight.

He was breathing jerkily now, his face contorted, the teeth clenched. He moved convulsively on the bed, his head thrashing from side to side.

Then his head lifted, the eyes opened wide. "Oh, Denise." It was a cry of despair, self-hatred.

Denise leaned down, kissed the sweating forehead, comforted.

12

THE NEXT MORNING MARY AND DENISE WERE having their coffee as usual on Denise's verandah. Mary's thoughts were on the night before. It might be wise to see less of Tiger Flemyng. There was a complexity in him that was disturbing.

The bearer appeared. "Telephone, memsahib. Beauchamp sahib."

Denise rose. "Tom doesn't usually telephone in the morning. I wonder." She left and Mary could hear her voice from the bedroom. When she returned there was a look of excitement about her.

"Whom do you think Tom is bringing to tiffin?"

"I have no idea."

"Edward Goad! He's the biggest jute planter in Bengal. He owns York House estate. My God, what an opportunity." She saw that Mary didn't understand and rushed on. "Tom's plan for setting up jute factories in Brazil. He has the Brazilians interested. He just needs more money. Goad could be just the man."

"Does Goad know?"

"I don't know. Tom said Goad spoke to him at the Bengal Club. They had a drink and Tom asked him to tiffin. Oh, what does a jute planter eat. What!"

"Meat and potatoes, just as any man."

"This is important. You don't know!"

"You make it sound as though this Goad might be difficult."

"But he is! Tom says he's the most dynamic and ruthless man in the jute trade. He's self-made."

"Is he English?"

"He's a Yorkshireman, I think. Tom says he's even made over his accent. I must have a good tiffin. I must." She screwed up her plump face, her eyes closed in desperation, and rushed out.

It was shortly before noon when Tom arrived with the guest. Mary could hear her husband making hearty small talk as he led the way up the stairs. Mary was dressed and waiting with Denise on the verandah. She had to confess a certain excitement. She was meeting a jute sahib, one of the pillars of the Empire. She noticed as Tom talked that there was no answering voice from the visitor. It was as though Tom were talking to a stone wall.

"I must greet him," said Denise and she rushed to present herself at the top of the stairs. Mary could hear her voice in its most hospitable tones.

"Do come up, Mr. Goad. Tom and I are quite honored. After all, you don't come into Calcutta very often."

There was a reply Mary could not catch, then Denise could be heard leading the way toward the verandah. Mary stood up expectantly. Denise led out the newcomer and Mary's eyes widened. This was the man from the Swimming Club the night before, the man who had helped her on Chowringhi that day, driving the cow away.

Her second reaction was one of puzzlement. This man didn't seem English at all. His skin was as old as she had remembered it. It should have been ruddy to match his reddish hair and pale blue eyes but it was yellowish ocher, faded as some of the Calcutta houses she had seen.

Tom made the introductions. "Mary, this is Edward Goad. Mr. Goad is in the jute industry. He *is* the jute industry I should say." He laughed rather fulsomely, then nodded toward her. "Mary deGive."

"Hello," she said. "We've met. On Chowringhi—that cow you saved me from."

"I was glad to be of service." His voice was low and his bow rather formal for such an earthy-looking man. Mary remembered the cow. There was nothing formal about that.

Denise broke in. "Miss deGive is from London. Out for the cold weather." It was an obvious enough statement but Mary thought the guest looked at her more speculatively.

"I hope you will have a nice visit," he said. His diction was careful. As though any accent had by now been disciplined.

"Thank you." He's not a gentleman, Mary thought, but he's confident. There was authority there.

It was Tom who broke up the slight tension. "You girls have your drinks here. There are one or two things we want to talk about. Come on, Goad. Let's go into the sitting room."

He turned to lead the way but Goad paused to bow formally, almost ironically, first to Denise, then to Mary, then preceded his host from the room. How easily he moves, Mary thought. Like a big cat.

"Denise, he's the man who helped me that day. I told you. When that awful cow trapped me."

"Goad?"

"I remember that strange color. So yellow."

"Quinine probably. A lot of the quihais get that color. But he seems pleasant. Not at all what one hears."

"Has he a reputation?"

"You can't get where he has without breaking a few heads. He's said to be a monster. I wonder why he's in Calcutta."

"Is that so unusual?"

"They say he hardly ever comes." She eyed Mary speculatively. "He is a bachelor."

"Denise!"

"He's never come before during the season. And it was he who spoke to Tom first at the club. He may have found you were our houseguest."

"He's probably here on business."

"He could do his business from the estate." She looked quite pleased for Mary.

It was a curious luncheon. Tom's business venture had evidently drawn little response. Tom continued his efforts during lunch but his visitor's silence finally led to a sullen withdrawal and increased drinking.

It was Mary who bore the brunt of Goad's attention. She felt his eyes on her even when Tom had been speaking to him. Denise took up the conversation when Tom fell silent but Goad gave her only the briefest of replies while, from his bulk across the table, he watched Mary.

He finally spoke to her. "How do you like Calcutta, Miss deGive?"

"Very nice."

"You know, you look just as young as ever."

"Oh?" It was such a blunt remark that Mary was startled. She groped for an explanation. "Have you seen a photo of me?"

"In the *Illustrated London News*. I used to subscribe."

"But that was nearly eighteen years ago." She remembered that there had been a photo of her taken during the early days of the war. Her name had been printed as well.

He nodded. "I remember. You were a nurse. And the name was unusual. Miss Mary deGive." He pronounced it "deGive" as though "giving" a present.

"DeGive," she murmured. "Norman." Good heavens, she thought. Imagine remembering all this time. Imagine noticing me in the first place.

He continued stubbornly. "You have improved with the years." He then fell silent, concentrating on his eating.

The luncheon had broken up soon after and Goad, speaking in his careful way, had thanked Denise, bowed formally to Mary, and left with Tom. Denise had been very cool with her husband, barely speaking when he left.

She turned to Mary. "Tom. He's such a fool sometimes. Drinking like that. He'll never persuade anyone that way." She shrugged. "What did you think of him?"

"Goad? He's remarkable."

"He liked you. I think you may have a suitor."

Mary said nothing. She was remembering the cow and the stick Goad had jabbed into it.

"Imagine remembering me all this time. I wonder. He is rather fascinating." She felt a curious excitement. No man had ever before remembered her in this way. She wondered whether this man might be the one.

The next day Tom gave a tiffin at Firpo's to which he invited Goad and Mary. The following night he gave a dinner party at the Slap which again included Goad and Mary.

Mary tried to be a cheerful companion but found Goad very silent. He watched her as she'd chat, then would stare at Tom, his gaze swinging back to her, careful, estimating.

"You're not enjoying yourself, Mr. Goad." It was toward the end of the dinner party. Mary had found him heavy going.

"Tell me, do you know about this plan of Tom Beauchamp's for raising money?"

"For his Brazil plans? I know a little."

"Has it occurred to you that you were being used by him?"

"How? To bring you to the table?"

"Aye."

"It has." She spoke calmly. "In fact, it seems obvious."

"Yet you go along with it. Are you being paid?"

"You're very candid. I shan't say rude."

"Are ye?"

"No."

"Then why do ye lend yourself to this? You seem like a good woman."

"I thought you could take care of yourself." She smiled.

He peered at her and gradually the suspicion left his face. He liked what he saw. "Aye. You did right."

"Besides, I had my own reason for coming." She smiled frankly at him this time and he suddenly laughed, hitting the table with his fist.

"Damn, an honest woman."

After that evening Goad began to entertain. He gave dinners, elaborate affairs, usually at the Great Eastern Hotel where he was staying instead of at one of the clubs.

There were always the same five guests: Mary, the Beauchamps, and the Thorntons. Sir John was Goad's legal adviser. Flowers decorated the table and gifts always appeared for the ladies. Mary once found at her place the carved jade figure of an Indian deer.

She hesitated. A lady did not accept such gifts from a gentleman. It was obviously expensive. But she did not wish to offend their host and she did love the little figure, so delicate and graceful. She ended by accepting it.

It was after a dinner at the Great Eastern that Mary saw Tiger again. She was waiting in the lobby for Denise. Tom and Goad still sat at the table.

Tiger approached Mary quietly. "Hello. I see you have met Edward Goad. I was with Sir Gerald in the private dining room and saw you."

"Yes. He's very nice."

He smiled pleasantly. "I think I should warn you. Goad's ruthless, even for a jute wallah. We watch him but there's not much that can be done. He's very powerful in Bengal."

Mary felt her face flush. "I'm his guest, Tiger. You shouldn't say such things."

The smile left his face and it was very quickly hard. "Not Goad. Anybody but him."

"But why!"

"You're too good for him. He's bad, everything that's wrong here."

"Please, that's enough. Here he is with Tom." She turned abruptly to greet them. Denise had entered and was watching.

Tiger and Goad eyed each other. They were a contrast. The soldier was slender and oddly aristocratic despite his busted face. The jute sahib, in his late forties but still powerful looking, was a man of the earth.

"Goad." Tiger nodded briefly and left. Goad had said nothing.

"Come," said Mary to their host. "It's getting late. Time to go home." She and Denise led the way. The men fell in behind and that was that.

The next morning Mary lay thoughtfully in her bed. She liked Goad. He was certainly the most eligible man she had met, or would be likely to meet. There was also something elemental about him to which she responded. It was disquieting. But he was not a gentleman and now there was this warning by Tiger.

"Ruthless," Tiger had said of him. Were not most men? Certainly empire builders were. Mary knew enough of her history to know that. But what sort of ruthlessness? One might say there had been a certain ruthlessness in her approach to marriage in India. She could hardly scorn him for his own.

"Mary?" Denise could be heard at the door. "Can I come in? I've brought my tea."

"Achcha, memsahib. Ao," Mary called. She laughed as Denise entered. "That was Hindustani. What did I say?"

"You said, 'Good, Madame. Come in.' You are learning."

"That's encouraging after only three weeks. Sit down here on the bed." She made room for her friend. "That was a very fine dinner our host provided last night."

"Tom was quiet, thank heaven. I told him if he brought up that Brazil scheme once more I would leave the table."

"Mr. Goad thought I was involved. He thought perhaps Tom was going to give me a commission if we landed him."

"No. How awful of him."

"I didn't deny it. I thought it made me more Machiavellian. I simply told him I felt certain he could take care of himself. Which is true." She leaned back. "Denise, I'm not certain I should go on seeing Mr. Goad."

"Why ever not? He's unmarried and very rich. You are interested in marrying, aren't you? You haven't said but I should hate to think all this was for nothing."

"I'm not certain I am interested in him."

"He's interested in you. He told me last night he would like to give a barge party for you."

"A barge party?"

"On the Hooghly. He'd bring down one of his jute-barges, fix it up with canopies, hire the Firpo orchestra, and invite a hundred guests. It would all be for you."

"I should feel like Cleopatra."

"Perhaps that's the idea. He is sort of a Caesar."

"It would be too much."

"Would you visit his estate?"

"Has he suggested that too?"

"He wants all of us. The Thorntons too."

"His estate. I'd like to see that." Mary rose from the bed and slipped on a dressing gown. She walked to the window jalousies still lowered to the floor. She tugged on a cord and the jalousies rose in a slow rustle above her head. A faint breeze picked at the folds of her nightgown and slipped across her bare feet.

Denise thought, looking at Mary, that she had never fully realized how striking a woman she could be. Mary's long hair, unbound, fell about her shoulders. Even without make-up, which she knew Mary wore little of anyway, there was a richness in the lovely skin, in the broad mouth, the high and broad cheekbones that impressed Denise. She made Denise feel dowdy, sloppy beside her. She wondered again how this decent, intelligent woman had failed to marry.

She blurted it out. "Why haven't you married before?"

"Denise."

"Seriously. I can understand why a mug like me hadn't. I was lucky to find Tom. But you're interesting looking. You've got brains too. Yet you've never married, have you?"

"No."

"Why not? I'm dying to know. You had someone but he was married and couldn't marry you?"

"No." Mary laughed.

"You swore you'd never leave Roecroft. You took a solemn oath."

"Frankly, I came to hate Roecroft."

"Then why haven't you married?"

"There's no simple answer." Mary hadn't turned to look at her friend. How much could she tell Denise? It was embarrassing to talk about Roecroft and Mr. Janeway. It was not the sort of ending to her career there that one wanted to tell.

Yet she did owe Denise something. Denise had been good to her, hospitable, and if anyone would understand why she was still unwed, it would be Denise. Telling might also clear up a few things for herself.

She turned to her friend. "I was brought up in Cheltenham. My father was a doctor, Doctors did very well there. Though the diseases they dealt with were not always the usual."

"Foreign diseases." Denise smiled. She'd said it as though they had no right to be in England.

"There weren't many young men there. At least, there didn't seem to be many. Perhaps when one grows up in a doctor's office and lives among retired people, it conditions one somehow. One doesn't notice young people. If one does, they don't seem right. They're healthy." She laughed briefly.

"Then the war came and there were even less young men." Denise shrugged. "I know."

"That's right. They opened a hospital in Cheltenham. I became a nurse. It was that way I met Tim."

"Tim?"

Mary shrugged. "The usual thing. He was wounded. We

fell in love. When he went back, he was killed. I think he was the first young man I'd ever known very well."

"Mary."

"Oh, there were others who lost their men. Plenty. But after the war I went back to Roecroft. There was something about life in the early twenties . . ."

Denise giggled. "The Jazz Age. That was my downfall."

"I spent the next twelve years at Roecroft, most of my adult life." Mary was silent a moment, remembering. "Finally, there came a day. Most of my life I had occupied myself with things that happened to other people. My father's last illness, even Tim. I had been living second-hand. I wanted life first-hand again."

"But why India?"

"I had grown up with India. Listening to all the retired colonels, the old Kipling wallahs. I'd always heard of the fishing fleet. You know the extra girls who come out each cold weather. When it came my turn, it seemed the only place to come. I felt needed too. You know, the swaraj agitation."

"Florence Nightingale."

"I still think it was right. Why did you come?"

"Oh, I had nowhere else. I'd been living a long time in Beirut. I'd been a very naughty girl. I couldn't go back to England. I really had no other place."

"We fishing fleeters. We really come trailing our past."

"I'm glad you're here."

"So am I. But I'm not going to come cheaply. I've had my life. I want to like the man, of course, and respect him but that other sort of love isn't essential. I have a good many years to make up. Has Goad really invited us to York House?"

"This Friday for the weekend."

"Tiger Flemyng has warned me against Goad. I don't want to make a mistake but neither do I want to miss an opportunity. I haven't seen very many here."

"There are very few single men the right age."

"I'd rather like to see York House."

"Please say yes. I know Tom's a nuisance about his scheme but this would mean so much to him. He might have a better chance up there." Her rather puffy face was earnest, even desperate.

"I won't go just because of Tom."

"I know but it would help. I do hope you'll accept."

Mary turned away and looked out at the nearby house and the compound behind it. A wall intervened but she could look over the wall to the grass tennis court behind, empty at the moment, waiting. She had never yet seen anyone using the court. It was a lovely grass, green, well rolled, but just waiting, unused. Like herself.

"I'll go," she said. "Tell Tom." She ignored Denise's thanks. The plump little woman rushed to the door to tell her husband.

Mary turned to the window again. It might be now or never. This could be her chance.

Tiger learned of Mary's trip in a very simple way. The Thorntons had included their houseguest, Bunty, in their acceptance of Goad's invitation and Bunty had wanted Tiger. He had soon learned from Bunty who the other guests would be. He told Bunty he would let her know.

Tiger wanted to go. He tried to tell himself that it was none of his business what happened to Mary deGive but he knew it was his business.

It was mad. There were so many stories about Goad, mostly rumors it was true, but Tiger was certain Goad was not for Mary.

But he couldn't simply disappear for several days on a weekend visit, not these days. There were killers loose and his job was to protect Sir Gerald.

Then something happened at Government House. Sir Gerald later suggested it be filed in His Majesty's archives under "C" for comical. The governor was given to a bizarre sense of humor.

It began with a simple tennis match. Sir Gerald enjoyed his early morning tennis, usually about seven, and Tiger was his customary opponent. They played on the Government House court, a green and well-watered lawn court inside the compound wall, and were always attended by a British police sergeant. Two young chhokras or ball boys were also present.

It had been a brisk match, nippy-cool in the early air. Sir Gerald had sent the sergeant into the house to fetch a sweater. The sergeant had been gone only a moment and Tiger stood at the baseline preparing for his first serve. His Excellency stood alone at the far side of the court near the compound wall waiting to receive. One chhokra stood behind Tiger and the other at midcourt.

There was a rhododendron bush at the foot of the wall and behind this a small shed was used by the gardeners to store their tools. The padlock on its door was tested each night and morning by the police constable on duty. What now took place happened so quickly that every action thenceforth was purely a reaction. It was as though a camera focused on a tableau—the green court and the two players—were to see its picture explode into sudden and grotesque animation.

There was the sound of wood splintering and a man burst from the shed, crashed through the rhododendron bush, and rushed silently across the law toward His Excellency. Tiger had time only to realize that the man was nearly naked, was covered from pate to legs with a heavy grease, and was holding high over his head an enormous two-handed sword. It was this silent figure who galvanized the tableau into its grotesque action.

The chhokras screamed and ran toward the deepest part of the compound. The governor bolted instantly for the far side of the court, the naked swordsman in pursuit. Tiger, into his serve, had time only to belt the ball toward the pursuer, then rushed at him with his tennis racket.

It was ridiculous but horrible. The governor was circling the net, the assassin was chasing the governor, and Tiger was chasing the assassin. The only thing saving the governor from being chopped to pieces was the heavy sword the Indian carried. Then came the end.

Sir Gerald and his pursuer paused on opposite sides of the net, then the murderer, still silent, bounded to clear the net, his sword held above his head. His foot caught and, as Tiger came up, he sprawled on his chest and one knee. Tiger had just time to bring down his racket hard on the man's neck, heard two cracks as both racket and vertebra were split. He then wrenched the huge sword from the man's hand as Sir Gerald threw himself on the greasy back.

The man struggled, sliding His Excellency off his back, and was reaching blindly for his sword when Tiger brought it down heavily, all the power of his frustrations over Gupta and with himself in the blows. The head rolled loose on the lush grass, the body and legs flapped while Sir Gerald clung, then the body lay still. The head slithered a few feet away, the eyes opening and shutting convulsively like a spinning window blind.

His Excellency pushed himself away from the headless body. There had been no sounds at all in their struggle. The murderer had been silent and the sounds of their scuttling feet had been deadened by the thick green lawn. There was no sign of the chhokras and the British police sergeant was only now returning tranquilly from the house, holding the governor's sweater.

That was the end of it so far as His Excellency was concerned. The dead man was hauled off to the burning ghats and there, head wrapped neatly to the body in a shroud, he was disposed of.

There was a moment immediately after the killing when Sir Gerald had looked rather quizzically at Tiger and remarked on the fury with which he had struck at the assassin.

Tiger said nothing. He was feeling surprisingly shaky. He hadn't known he was capable of such complete savagery.

Sir Gerald wished everything to be kept quiet. He was not certain whether the assassin was a terrorist of Gupta's or merely a homicidal fanatic. If he were Gupta's man, the governor wished Gupta not to know what had happened to him, hence the quiet disposition of the body in the ghats. He also suggested that Tiger take a few days off. It would be an added touch to deceive Gupta.

Two days later Mary and Denise, with Tom driving, left for Edward Goad's estate. They drove over an uneven dirt road. The Hooghly River wound heavily past.

They had driven more than two hours when the river and the road bent slightly to the right. It was plain from the fields and the terraced riverbanks that they were now entering a great estate.

Denise pointed. "There, that must be York House."

Mary could see a deep clump of acacia trees above the river and, half-hidden, the white turrets and gables of a mansion. It resembled the enormous Victorian homes she had seen in Calcutta.

"It looks haunted," said Denise. "All those windows."

Tom giggled. "York House. I wonder if he thinks of himself as the Duke of York."

They drove up a winding road to the grove of acacia trees and halted in an open space. The driveway stretched ahead of them to a portico and the great house.

"Good God," said Tom.

"Buckingham Palace," said Denise. She was awed.

Mary felt her heart catch. This house wasn't the faded ocher of the Calcutta mausoleums. It was a brilliant, defiant white. There was magnificence in the way it reared itself above the river slope. She knew she was seeing one of the great estate houses.

Tom pointed to the broad verandah. "Look. The servants."

"Tom," exclaimed Denise. "They're in livery."

It was true. There were nearly a dozen servants rushing toward them and Mary could see on the crimson chest of each white tunic a white emblem.

"It's a rose," murmured Tom. "He's dressed his servants in the white rose of York."

Then the tension broke for Tom and Denise. Denise put her hand to her mouth and broke into uncontrollable giggles. Tom laughed and swore alternately.

Mary was silent. The costumes were ostentatious and probably vulgar but there was something colorful about them. They stirred something deep in her—a vision of Hampton Court, he was the royal owner, King Henry himself.

The vision passed. This was a King Henry with a yellowing skin, wearing khaki shorts. He was a monarch in his home, bursting with calm assurance, but still a jute wallah.

The servants fell back as Goad approached. Mary and the Beauchamps alighted.

"Welcome to York House," said Goad to Tom, each syllable carefully enunciated.

"Thanks. Glad to be here." Tom was being breezy. He wasn't going to let this fellow know how much this visit meant to him.

Goad waved to his head bearer. "The kithmaghar will show you to your rooms and you can refresh yourselves before tea." He bowed before Mary. "I am glad you could come."

"I am happy to be here. I've never seen a jute estate."

"The best in India," said Tom ebulliently. He beamed at their host.

Goad ignored him. "Now you will come into the house." He led the way up the verandah steps. The servants disappeared with the luggage toward a side entrance. The kithmaghar directed a syce to take away the auto.

Goad led his guests across the verandah and through a double-doored entrance. Mary blinked as she came out of the sunshine but she was aware that their host had paused inside and seemed to be looking at them expectantly.

They stood in a large hall that extended the depth of the house. At the far end a broad stairway led upward to a gallery and what Mary assumed must be the bedrooms.

The hall itself was dark, shadowy. There seemed to be an office in one corner but its walls extended only partway to the ceiling.

Patches of colored sunlight glowed on the dark floor and Mary saw that the room windows were narrow louvered slits, six or seven in all. Each window contained mosaics of different colored glass and these filtered the sunlight into patches of blue, red, and green.

It was like a cavern—deep, remote. She was aware of a faint tinkling sound and realized that in the open spaces above the walls tiny bells and pieces of glass had been hung. They revolved in the delicate breeze from the opened door and provided the distant tinkle.

She closed her eyes. It was strange, eerie, yet it didn't frighten her. It was private, cool after the sun outside—an inner refuge.

"Do you like it?" Goad was looking at Mary.

She turned a candid gaze on him. "I don't know."

He nodded approvingly. "It takes time."

"The walls," exclaimed Denise. "They're covered with jute."

"Burlap," said Goad. "From the estate mill."

"Could we go to our rooms?" asked Mary. She could see that Tom and Denise were enormously amused by the room. She didn't want to offend their host. He was not a fool.

"The ayah will show you." Goad gestured to a shadowy corner and a woman came forward and moved toward the stairway. The guests followed.

"Fantastic," breathed Denise to Mary. "I can't wait to see our bedroom."

But Goad hadn't finished. He called to them from the foot of the stairs. "I forgot to mention. There will be additional guests."

Denise nodded. "Sir John and Lady Thornton."

"Miss Cranston, their houseguest, is coming. And they are bringing Captain Flemyng, the governor's aide. Do you know him?"

"Yes," said Tom. "Nice guy. Sort of."

"Good." Their host smiled. "I wouldn't want anyone at York House who might be a nuisance."

"Come on, Mary." Denise put out her hand.

Mary's mouth was dry. Tiger had dared to follow her. He was intruding himself on her efforts.

She didn't want him there. She would need a clear head. And for what she might decide to do she didn't want a witness. Least of all he. It would be like having Tim see.

Mary took Denise's hand and followed her silently up the stairs.

The Daimler that carried Tiger to York House contained four passengers with mixed moods. Sir John was irritated because he never liked to go into the country. He held himself stiffly, cursed silently at each swerve in the dirt road, and swore that never again would he venture into the mofussil.

Lady Thornton had resigned herself to the visit. If Bunty were interested in Tiger Flemyng, she would at least give her a chance. Personally she thought it a waste of time.

Bunty was a kitten with a bowl of milk. She pressed her soft thighs together in anticipation and moved closer to Tiger, taking advantage of each bump to sway her legs against him. She was a sensuous child and the bumps being rather frequent on the dirt road, Bunty was finding herself soft-eyed. She was dimly aware that Lady Henrietta was beside her. She didn't care. She would have Tiger to herself for two whole days and was not going to waste it by playing the lady. She would make full use of what God gave her. And at the next bump she moved her thighs closer toward Tiger.

Tiger was peering impatiently ahead. He told himself that he was following Mary to keep her from making a fool of herself with Goad. Otherwise, he hardly knew why he had come on this trip. It might have been Bunty. She had made it obvious she was available and he was in the mood for a little romp. There was something about cutting a man's head off that restored the animal in a man.

Meanwhile, he let Bunty slip her hand softly into his pocket, gently scratch her fingernail along his thigh. Damn, he thought, this is going to be a complicated weekend.

13

"THERE IT IS. THE JUTE PLANT." GOAD WAVED HIS
hand expansively toward the fields below the house. The
slender plant, brown with tendrils and small leaves, looked
to Mary like bamboo.

"I didn't realize it would be so tall."

"Those plants are only six feet. Some of it grows to sixteen.
Here, let me show you how they begin."

He strode to the edge of the nearest field and bent to scoop
from the ground what seemed to Mary like a small, green
pebble. So small that she could barely see it between his
fingers.

"That's the baby of the crop, just the seed. In three months
it will have grown to six feet. Like those down there."

He put the green pebble back into the soil, smoothing
down the earth with his fingers.

"Will it grow after pulling it out like that?"

"It will grow. It's strong. Like everything else that survives
out here."

She noticed that as he talked about the jute his accent was
less careful. He had reverted to his natural Yorkshire.

"Come. I'll show ye more."

"Don't you think we'd best be going in? The others will
be down by now."

"The bearer will take care of them. There's still a half hour
to dinner."

She thought it best not to disagree. They were out on the
terrace now, the great house behind them in the fading light.
She walked beside him as he led the way to the far end of
the terrace.

He waved toward the fields sloping down to the river.
"There. All in jute."

"There's a village over there. Is that the estate?"

"Aye. There are two more beyond the ridge. I have near a thousand workers. That means a lot of women and children."

"A thousand workers for the fields?"

"I have mills too. Up the river there. They're over the rise."

"I thought the mills were all in Calcutta. In Howrah across the river."

He laughed. "That's where most of the companies have their mills. I have mine here. They said that wouldn't work."

"It obviously does."

"Aye. I have three mills with twenty looms each. That's more than six hundred spindles. We do it all here, from the first seed to the finished burlap. And we still have enough raw jute left over to press a hundred thousand bales for export."

Mary was impressed. "Jute means a great deal to you."

"It isn't just jute. It's cords and ropes for ships. It's burlap for trade and carpets and curtains for homes. We make it all." He waved his arm toward the fields and villages.

"It sounds so substantial." He had made it seem so self-sufficient, strong.

He looked at her. "There's one thing missing. That's why I went down to Calcutta. This place needs a memsahib. A man in my position needs a wife."

Mary caught her breath. There it was. Suddenly this man had come out with it.

She nodded calmly. "That is why you asked me here."

"Aye."

"It would be ridiculous of me, I assume, to deny I am interested."

He gave a quick laugh. "You're in the fishing fleet, aren't ye? That's why you've come to Calcutta. I want a wife. You're the one who would suit me."

He said it boldly. There was nothing careful or cautious about him now. He was in his own realm.

Mary wondered whether she should deny being a fleeter. It would give her time. But could she deny it? She had admitted it openly before this. Denying it would complicate matters. Facing it would clear the decks.

She shivered a little. Suddenly she felt the evening chill in the air. Funny, back in England now, this would have seemed warm. Perhaps her blood was already thinning.

"I think we had best be going in," she said.

"I don't want to offend ye but neither do I want to waste your time."

"Or yours." She smiled.

He laughed. "Either of us. We both have jobs to do out here." She started to move away but he caught her arm, gripped it. "I'm serious, woman."

"I know you are. I shall give it thought, Mr. Goad." This was ridiculous, she thought, using only his last name. Right out of Trollope or Congreve.

He hesitated. "One thing more. I'm not entirely a clod. I know a man shouldn't speak to a woman like this. There's more to a marriage for a woman than just making her a business proposition."

"There is."

"I'll tell ye this. I like your looks. I'd be proud to have ye for my wife."

He said it straight out, no smirk or sheepish grin. He meant it. He would be proud.

"Are you certain I'm the wife you want? I may be quite different than you expect."

"You're a classy one. You'd be a credit to me. To York House." He took her arms so that she could feel the strength in his hands.

"We must go in," she said.

"Not yet."

"The others will be waiting." She pushed firmly at his hand and he dropped his arms.

"Aye." He extended his arm, again the careful burra sahib, the great estate owner. "Come."

They moved toward the house. At least, she thought, he has proposed. Now she knew exactly where she stood.

Dinner that night was not without its undercurrents. The meal itself was elaborately English with a clear soup, roast beef, treacle pudding, and, before the fruit, a savory of egg on cheese. Mary was puzzled as to whether the sumptuousness of the dinner on this remote estate reflected his own enormous appetites or was a warm gesture of hospitality. He produced beer and whiskey for all with the fruit.

Mary was aware of Tiger watching her, looking from her to Goad, a slightly ironic expression in his deep eyes. There was a moment when Tiger differed with Goad over some triviality—Tiger pointed out that the use of the white rose of York for his servants was probably illegal. Goad said he had assumed it was. That made it more enjoyable.

The Beauchamps laughed dutifully. The Thorntons were silent. Mary knew she should have been disturbed at this slight affrontery to the Crown but she put it aside. Goad was a law unto himself.

After dinner Mary went to stand alone on the verandah. The ladies remained inside, apart from the men. She was aware in a few moments that Tiger had appeared beside her.

"Please. You are supposed to be with the gentlemen."

"I wanted to speak to you."

"Does our host know?"

"Probably. Beauchamp was beginning to tell one of his golf club jokes. That seemed excuse enough." He held her arm. "Don't worry. I shan't be difficult. How did it go this afternoon?"

"He showed me his jute. He's very proud of it."

"Did he say anything personal?"

"He asked me to marry him."

"What did you say?"

"I told him I would consider it."

"Are you? Going to consider it, I mean."

"Yes."

"He's a brute, Mary."

"It's possible."

"He's ruthless. Unprincipled."

There was a quick touch of anger in her eyes. "I don't think you are in a position to discuss principles at this moment."

He laughed. "Go ahead. Marry him. You'll have to live in this crazy house. They say he has one wing done in jute. Everything. Curtains, carpets—probably even his pajamas."

"He raises jute."

"You'd never get away from this place. He never comes to Calcutta."

"There should be enough here. We might build a tennis court."

"Tennis! This isn't Bournemouth or Cheltenham. It can be murderously hot here, worse than Calcutta. It's further from the Bay."

"There are other things. There are neighbors."

"There might be ten British within twenty miles. And they'd never come here. He's not liked, Mary. I've told you.

The district medical officer might turn up or the district engineer. They'd have to drop in occasionally. Otherwise— nobody."

"Why isn't he liked? You say he's important in Bengal."

"I don't know. It had something to do with the war. He stayed here while others got killed."

"Perhaps he was essential."

"A jute overseer? Hardly. All I know is that he and York House have a bad name. That's why he always entertained you at the Great Eastern. He knows he's not welcome at the clubs."

"It's wrong of people to treat him like this. He's a bulwark of the Raj! A pillar of the Empire!"

"Oh, Mary."

"He's doing me an honor in asking me to marry him. This estate means everything to him. It's his whole life and he's offering to share it with me."

"What about his bed?"

"What do you mean?"

"You'll have to share that too. Can you do it?"

"Don't be disgusting."

"Leave here, Mary! Now, while there's still time! I'll take you."

There was a movement in the dining room entrance and they turned to see Edward Goad. In the half light his big frame, dark red hair, and yellowing skin filled the doorway.

"Is everything all right?"

"I was talking to Miss deGive. This is a private conversation."

Goad smiled. "In my house there is very little private from me. That is one of the privileges of being host."

Mary put a calming hand on Tiger's arm. "I'm sorry to have come out but it was hot in there. I think I'll go up to my room."

"But the night is still early," said Goad.

"It's been a long day. I'm more tired than I'd thought. Please make my apologies to Lady Thornton, Edward. Good night, Alastair."

Tiger watched her go, then returned abruptly to the dining room. Goad remained thoughtfully on the verandah.

In her room Mary went to her little verandah. She sat in the wicker chair, hair unbound, hanging loosely on her shoulders. She leaned back, made herself be calm, eyes closed.

It was silent on the estate and gradually Mary's full mouth relaxed, the clear eyes were calm. The only sound one could hear was a faint singing from one of the distant village huts. Mary wondered for a moment what a coolie found to sing about.

It was wrong of Tiger to have followed her that way, or to have come to York House at all. He must know he was making it harder for her. It was callous of him.

And what was it he had said about Goad? Could she share his bed? That was a revolting thing to have mentioned. One did not think about such things. There had been Tim in her life . . . it had been glorious, sweet, and brief. There would never be another Tim.

Mary put Tiger's words from her mind. There were other and more important matters to consider. Edward Goad was wealthy, that was apparent. She would never have to worry about security again. It was also clear that he was not an educated man, certainly not as she thought of education, and one must consider this. They might have little to say to each other.

He was a strong man but this could be a fault. As his wife she might not be allowed any life, any thoughts of her own. She could become a nobody.

On the other hand she would be taking her place in the ranks. Edward Goad was a jute sahib, a backbone of the Raj. As his wife she would be serving as her father had, as every British woman should.

Mary shook her head. It was difficult. Goad was an unknown. So far her womanly instincts told her nothing.

Mary put away her thoughts and went into the room. She closed the jalousies but the faint coolie singing could still be heard. It was ridiculous, she thought, but it had a certain reedy appeal. High, faint plaintive.

Suddenly Mary felt alone, very far from England. She was just a woman, alone in a still-alien land.

She leaned her head against the half-open jalousies. She could hear the singing plainly now, spreading to the silent fields and the quiet river. It was the only sound on the estate.

14

IN YEVRADA GAOL MAHATMA GANDHI SAT quietly turning his spinning wheel. In the courtyard of his quarters his secretary's wife and the few attendants permitted him went about their business.

From his desk the secretary could see Bapu seated cross-legged before his wheel and was troubled. The Mahatma had been deeply preoccupied since the murder in Midnapore. Each terrorist killing, as it had been reported, had left Bapu increasingly sad. He no longer teased the secretary's wife or chattered with their children. He remained quietly at the far end of his room, thoughtful and withdrawn.

The secretary wondered if he should speak to their jailer, Colonel Morgan, and try to initiate steps for Bapu's release. He knew it would be useless. Bapu did not really wish to be released. He knew that so long as he was in Yevrada Gaol, he remained a symbol to India of the constant struggle against the Raj.

Yet the secretary knew the Mahatma well enough to know that this brooding must end in some sort of action. He watched the Mahatma silently.

The next night in Calcutta, Lord Willingdon, Viceroy of India, received a message. He and Lady Willingdon were entertaining Sir Gerald and Lady Andrews, their hosts in Bengal, at a small dinner in Belvedere. Lord Willingdon had lost none of his lean looks since arriving in India. He was still the slender, distinguished-looking aristocrat sent to represent His Majesty.

He read the message his aide brought, excused himself, and, beckoning to Sir Gerald, led the way to his small library.

He handed the message to the governor. "From the prison

at Poona. The Mahatma has announced a hunger strike. To begin next week."

"No!" Sir Gerald stared at the message in his hand. There had been no intimation of this.

Lord Willingdon nodded. "It's the terrorism, of course. He may even know of that attempt on your life the other day. This is the Mahatma's answer."

"But this says it will be on behalf of the Untouchables. Gandhi says he will fast until they get representation in the Congress."

"Do you think that's his real reason?"

"That's what it says." Sir Gerald waved the message. His literal Scottish mind went by the facts.

The Viceroy frowned. "The Mahatma is a very profound man. Don't forget he has strong convictions about the path to independence. He wants it won in the right way or not at all. He has said that if won by the wrong methods it will be lost again. Ahimsa. Nonviolence—that's his way."

"It's not Gupta's."

"Exactly." The viceroy pointed to the cable. "This issue of the Untouchables is not his real objective. Gandhi knows we could concede representation for them without his going on a fast. This is a challenge. He wants to show the people of India that he can do more for them than Gupta can."

"Then we should concede, sir. Give the Untouchables some voice. Help Gandhi."

"I don't know." Lord Willingdon looked thoughtfully at the governor. "This may be an opportunity. What do we have? The Mahatma pushing at us from one side; Gupta pushing from the other. They're both after the same thing. Swaraj. Independence. It's our job—my job, if I may say so— to push them both back." Looking almost quizzical, he turned to Sir Gerald. "Did you notice the color of Her Ladyship's gown this evening?"

"Her Ladyship's gown? I can't say that I did, sir. My wife says I'm not very good at such things."

"It is mauve. My wife always wears mauve. You'll notice it before long, I daresay."

"Yes, sir." He wondered what the color of Lady Willingdon's gown had to do with the Mahatma or the terrorists.

"When Her Ladyship was very young, her father always wanted her to wear blue. It was his favorite color. Her mother, for some inexplicable reason, favored red. Said it brought something out in her daughter."

"Yes, sir." This was really far afield, thought Sir Gerald. He had never enjoyed conundrums. He liked things out in the open.

The viceroy smiled companionably at Sir Gerald. "Her parents rather kept at Her Ladyship, one way or the other, until one day my wife bought her own dress. It was neither red nor blue but mauve, a combination of both. She was never bothered again."

"But how . . . I mean, sir, neither Bapu nor Gupta exactly qualifies as a dress expert."

Lord Willingdon strolled calmly past Sir Gerald, his fingertips together. It was almost as though he were in a royal procession. It was a gesture Sir Gerald had noted before.

"We are in somewhat the same position as Her Ladyship," said the viceroy. "We cannot give in either to violence or nonviolence. We must 'mauve' them both."

"I don't understand, sir."

"If we let Gandhi fast that will take the spotlight off Gupta. Old Bapu will have all of India praying for him. And a large part of the world besides. Then, at the proper point, we'll give in. We'll concede something on these Untouchables. Meanwhile Gupta may have held his hand; it would be pointless to kill while the world watches Gandhi. Then when we concede to Bapu, India will turn to him again."

"But he may die in the meanwhile."

"He may."

"They would say we'd killed the Mahatma."

"How long did he last on his previous hunger strike?"

"Twenty-one days. He might not last that long again. He's older."

"It's a gamble, isn't it?" Lord Willingdon looked at his slender hands.

"It is that, sir."

"It's largely a question of timing. If we yield too soon we shan't have gotten the most from it. Shan't have damped down Gupta sufficiently. If we let him fast too long—well, no need to say what that would mean. The Sepoy Mutiny could look like child's play."

"Yes, sir." Sir Gerald wiped his forehead.

"The hazards of authority, Sir Gerald. Always on the edge

of the knife." He shrugged cheerfully. "It worked in the case
of my wife. Now she'll wear nothing but mauve."

Sir Gerald smiled. "Very becoming, sir." He was beginning
to feel more confident. There was something about this viceroy.

"We'll use this Mahatma, Sir Gerald." The viceroy's face
was grim for a moment, then he smiled. "Come, let us finish
our dinner. One man fasting is enough." He led the way
back to the dining room.

In Kidderpore, in the room over the Methodist Reading
Room, the round little man sat hunched over his bed. He
had sat there all day, ever since he had heard of Gandhi's
fasting. His eyes were half closed as his heavy, slow-grinding
mind considered this information.

To Gupta the issue was clear enough. No man would risk
his life on behalf of the Untouchables. They were an irrele-
vance, a side issue in India. This fast was aimed against the
Raj and also against him. Gandhi was trying to kill two birds
with one stone. It suited his frugal nature.

Gupta considered his choices. He could fight Gandhi, reply
by arranging another killing. The murder of another magistrate would obtain at least temporary attention. That was
certainly what he would like to do, defy this pseudosaint.

Gupta's eyes relaxed; his smooth face softened. Why should
he kill when the greatest murder of all might now be taking
place? If Gandhi died it would certainly be judged as murder
and the British would be condemned as the killers. They
would be held guilty not only by India but by the whole
world. Then there would be chaos in India and in chaos
Gupta knew he walked with a sure foot.

The little man sat back. He would do nothing for a while.
He would see how this new viceroy dealt with this problem.
Lord Irwin, his predecessor, was easy to predict. He would
do the moral, the humane thing. He would probably have
gone to the prison and he and Gandhi would have prayed
together, then reached an understanding.

But this Willingdon—Gupta considered him—he might not
be such a fop as he appeared. One had best wait. Meanwhile,
it was always possible that fool in Yevrada Gaol might die
by not eating.

Gupta helped himself to the litchi nuts beside his bed. It
was the only luxury he permitted himself. It took the place of

regular food. But this Mahatma—Gupta shook his head—he fasted to save the world, not destroy it. Bapu was a fool.

15

AT YORK HOUSE EDWARD GOAD HAD ARRANGED a ride and a picnic. He wished to show Mary over his estate and had invited his guests and a few neighbors to join them.

Mary had considered refusing. She wondered whether accepting his invitation might not indicate a commitment to marry him.

She decided that was nonsense. She *was* considering him. That was why she had come. To come so far and not see the estate would be ridiculous.

She now stood critically in front of her mirror. She knew this day might be some sort of climax in her visit to York House, if not to India. If he would show her his estate, she would match his gesture by looking her best.

She was not afraid of her riding ability. She had become accustomed to horses at Roecroft. Her costume would be the same full skirt and high sweater she had always worn. Her only indulgence was a shiny black bowler. She knew there was a slight incongruity but she had seen it in Southampton before sailing and hadn't been able to resist it. She had brought along her old familiar riding hat, a leghorn straw that she treasured, and was even now putting on first one and then the other, unable to decide.

She eyed herself critically in each. The beautiful bowler did not really go with her skirt and sweater but it was magnificent and showed her high cheekbones and remarkable eyes. Those blue eyes which Tim, an amateur racing driver before the war, had said should be the color for warning flags. He said no driver would pass by. But Tim had also said that her voice reminded him of one of his autos in low throttle. Her voice, which her mother had said was too hoarse to be ladylike, he had called powerful, reassuring.

The thoughts of Tim made Mary pull at her new bowler angrily. She would not make so much of this Edward Goad. She would wear her battered old leghorn. She placed it on top of her head, one side sagging down, the other askew, and then snatched it off and quickly clapped on the bowler. Enough of Tim. This was a new start all around. She went swiftly out of her room and down to the driveway and the assembling riders.

She was startled to see how few had gathered. She knew that the Thorntons would not come. Sir John had muttered something about preferring to eat tiffin on the verandah in comfort. But neither Tiger nor Bunty was in sight. Mary glanced toward the verandah, then went on toward the riders.

The Beauchamps were there, Tom on his heartiest behavior and obviously looking forward to another chance to present his Brazilian scheme. Denise was looking slightly apprehensive.

There were only four newcomers. Goad made a gesture. "This is Dr. and Mrs. MacDonough. Dr. MacDonough is the district medical officer. This is Miss Mary deGive." He waved to the other two. "The Jolliffes, Ian and Kitty. Jolliffe is our district engineer."

They nodded to each other. Mary saw that Kitty Jolliffe was quite young, that she smiled rather tremulously, and that her husband, young and blond, was rather the usual product of a good English public school. They were obviously new to marriage and probably to India.

It was the MacDonoughs who caught her eye. He was in his late forties and surprisingly handsome and worldly looking for a DMO in such a remote area. His flushed face and slightly red-streaked eyes gave Mary some indication why he was in so minor a post. He seemed sober at the moment and sat his horse steadily.

Mrs. MacDonough was formidable looking. She gripped the horse with strong knees and obviously tolerated no nonsense. Mary wondered whether this lady might not at one time have been the doctor's nurse.

"Everyone's here," said Goad. "We'd best be going." He didn't mention the absence of other neighbors. Evidently his only guests would be this seedy DMO and his wife and the young newlyweds.

It was a beautiful afternoon for a ride. The horses were small but looked sure-footed. Denise whispered that they were descended from "tats," Himalayan mountain ponies. She said they were used in races in Darjeeling and small village fairs.

Goad waved away Mary's syce and helped her into the saddle himself. He mounted his own tat and led the way briskly down the slope toward the river. He rode close beside Mary, his reddish hair bare in the winter sun, the only man not wearing a topi. Then came the other guests and the two syces with a hamper.

Mary looked at the bright sunshine, the river drifting heavily at their feet. She touched her hat gaily. She felt alive and nearly young.

In her room on an upper floor Bunty Cranston watched the riding group disappear toward the river. She knew the Thorntons would be taking their "ziz" as Lady Henrietta termed it, that long after-tiffin nap. There were only Tiger and herself left and she meant to make the most of it.

Bunty began slowly to undress. She knew it might be now or never with Tiger and she would not pass up the opportunity.

Bunty was not a stupid girl, far from it, but with Tiger she knew she really had only one asset, her body. She knew nothing about politics. She heard everyone talking about "the Raj" and the terrorists and this Gandhi crank. She tried to interest herself, even poring over the *Statesman* when Sir John had finished and trying to read the editorials.

She was soon bored and found herself reading the cinema reviews. At least there she was on familiar footing. The cinemas were showing much the same films as in London, though six or seven months later.

She had never had the chance to play sports and probably wouldn't have if she had. She couldn't very well talk about Withrow & Jenks, Ltd. That was really the sum total of her experience—that and the lads.

Bunty went to stand before her mirror, combing out her short, curly bob. She barely glanced at her body, quite nude now. She had no concern about that. She knew what it did to the male.

It was a cute face that looked back at her. More than once she'd been told that she looked like that former American film star, Clara Bow. The one they called the "It" girl. She knew that one had to look closely behind that cute face to see the tough little nature.

She wondered what her friend May would say now. May had been her one friend at Withrow & Jenks. She and May understood each other. "It's war, dear," her friend used to say. "It's them or us." And there was no doubt who "them" was—the lads. Bunty knew that May would approve of what she was about to do.

Bunty ran her hands slowly down the sides of her body, then turned toward the window. She could barely see the riders now. They were climbing the slope again toward a distant ridge. In a few moments she could begin.

In his nearby room Tiger also watched the riders move upward. His eyes never left the group until they passed over the ridge and out of sight.

He turned away. He knew he should feel noble. He had done the right thing in not going with Mary. He was giving her a free hand with Goad. Galahad himself.

Tiger dropped on the bed and stared at the ceiling. What in God's name was wrong with him? Here he was, nearly thirty-six, free as the air, yet concerning himself over a woman older than he. Why? He was damned if he knew. He simply had a talent for confusing his life.

That was why killing was sometimes so simple, so releasing for him. It had been the same way on the Frontier. After the war, when he had first come to India, he had known a different set of confusions. He had already seen too many men killed, had killed enough himself, yet was expected to go on.

He had tried indolence, indifference, even fatigue; it was then he had mockingly acquired the name "Tiger."

Finally, under orders, he had gone on a punitive raid through the Khyber and up into Afghan country. They had caught a raiding party unawares and he had slashed and shot until exhausted. It had been the sweet, cleansing simplicity of killing.

And the joke, as he well knew, was that he now looked the killer role. No one with his scars, his busted face, could possibly be uncertain. It was the face of Dorian Gray in reverse. It was the outside that was horrible.

With a sudden raging oath, Tiger moved from his bed

toward the bureau. There was a bottle of whiskey waiting. It was then that he saw Bunty.

She had pushed aside the latticed entrance to his room and stood quietly in the doorway. It was clear from her dressing gown that she wore little or nothing underneath.

When he spoke it was almost a snarl. "You know what you're doing, I suppose."

"I do."

"Sir John and Lady Thornton are still in the house."

"They're asleep. So are the servants."

"There'd be nothing in this. No promises. It'd just be for now."

She smiled up at him, calmly. "Don't worry about it."

As he still hesitated, she let the dressing gown slip slowly from her shoulders and sink past her waist to the floor.

She waited. But there was no need to do more.

Mary moved her body slowly against the walk of her small horse. She had found that whether going down the slopes or up toward the ridge, his pace was the same. Neither hill nor hollow would change that purposeful, methodical gait.

There was peace in it and Mary let her thoughts drift. She knew that in England there might well be fog on a ride like this and sleet could be forming. Here there was only the bright sun and the canopied Indian sky.

It was Tom who intruded. He pulled beside Goad and pointed to a ditch near the river. "You wouldn't have to irrigate in Brazil. They have plenty of water."

Goad glanced at him but said nothing. A few hundred yards further Tom spoke again, pointing to the faraway coolie village. "Supporting those coolies must cost you a lot of dough. Their wives and kids. You wouldn't have to do that in Brazil." Goad didn't even glance at him.

Tom sank back into a gloomy silence. It might have been Denise, riding forward to put a gentle hand on her husband's arm, that kept him quiet or it might have been Goad's indifference.

It was obvious to Mary by now that Goad's resistance to the Brazil plan was well-founded. He had created a mammoth estate. They had ridden away from the river and in a half hour had crossed the ridge to a whole new vista of fields.

Goad paused and the others reined in. It was awesome. As far as one could see there appeared to be fields of the tall, bamboolike plants. The extent of it made the fields Mary had seen by the river only a fraction of the estate. Even Tom looked impressed.

"Are those the mills?" She pointed toward three half-hidden buildings, their chimneys jutting behind clumps of palm. Goad nodded.

"And are those irrigation ditches?" She indicated long, brown lines streaking the fields.

He looked at her. He thinks I'm merely humoring him, thought Mary, but it really is remarkable. "How do you bring the water in?" she asked. "It must come from the river and we've just crossed a ridge."

Young Jolliffe spoke up. "Hydraulic. He did the engineering himself. He uses hydraulic power to press the bales of his extra jute too. How much do you export, Goad?"

"A hundred thousand bales a year," said Goad.

"Those villages are clean too," said MacDonough. "I know. I inspect them twice a year."

Goad looked at Tom. "Do you have all this in Brazil?" Tom looked sullen and Goad suddenly laughed and slapped him on the back.

Goad chose a shaded spot for tea, in a gully just off the ridge. A bamboo hut had been built in the sloping side, with a palm-frond roof. During the hot weather Mary thought it must provide a restful spot for their host.

It was peaceful. During lunch she could hear crickets in the field below and a woodpecker was laboriously picking out his own tiffin from a nearby mahogany tree. She could see over the gully rise to the river and watched a pair of red-legged cranes moving sedately beside the bank.

She found herself watching Goad. He was setting the pace for his other guests, eating with gusto, talking animatedly. It was different from the reserved, silent man she had known. It was more than just being the good host; there was something about being on his own land that revivified him. He was one with his earth.

She wondered what it was that had made him so successful. He was a strong man but so were many others who had accomplished less. Tiger for example. There was something else in that face, a shrewdness. And something more which she could not define. She felt a faint unease. This man was much less simple than he appeared.

After tiffin Mary found herself alone with Goad. It might

have been a discreet courtesy on the part of the other guests, or Goad might have arranged for Jolliffe to lead the others off toward the mills.

"You have a very impressive estate," she said. Mary had walked to the top of the ridge. He had followed her. She spoke calmly, unhurried. "Now I can understand better why you're not interested in going in with Tom on his Brazil scheme."

"He thinks India is finished. He says the Japanese are planting jute, and the Mexicans."

"Are they?"

He nodded. "So have others. It hasn't come to anything."

"Tom says jute is in a slump. He said fifteen percent of the looms in Bengal were closed last year."

"More. It'll be worse this year."

"You might listen to Tom. If you could develop substitutes in Brazil, why do you stay here?"

"Beauchamp doesn't see the possibilities. None of them do, not even in Calcutta."

"You're not going to buy more land."

He laughed grimly. "I have enough land. It's developing what's here that must be done." He waved toward the fields. "What do you see there? Jute fields—isn't that all?"

"Yes."

"I see laboratories—for research, scientists, chemists. I'll develop new fibers here, find new uses for jute. This is a time for expanding, not running out."

Mary felt herself caught up. This was the same hunger, the same passion that her father had found in medicine. The Empire had been built by such men.

"You see it, don't you?" He looked at her suspiciously.

"You're very convincing."

"Beauchamp's a fool. He talks about paper substitutes or cotton. When I bring jute and science together, they'll be as old-fashioned as animal skins."

"You'll be very rich."

He swung sharply toward her, his face ugly for a moment, suspecting a mocking quality in the words but Mary's face was calm. She had stated a truth. But there was suspicion still in him. He eyed her carefully.

"It won't all be roses for the woman who marries here. We shan't go into Calcutta much."

Mary waited. She knew he was testing her now, probing, watching.

"She wouldn't go back to England much either. My life is here in India. India can be hard on a woman. A man has his work but a woman is alone much of the time. She has to be strong."

He seemed to be challenging her, his face closer. "Then there's the heat." He spoke softly now, as though he had saved this for the last, his eyes never leaving her face.

"You can taste it, the sweat running down into your mouth and turning to salt. You can smell it, a mixture of rot and mildew. There's heat rash and the skin itching, the weight of the air on you before the rains begin, then the steam around you and the air more water than air."

He stared down at the river as though even now he could see the steam on it, then the rains falling and turning the river brown with mud from the Garo Hills.

"You go to bed tired and you wake up in a bed of sweat. Even the mosquito net is heavy."

He swung back to her, his eyes testing her. "You love England but even that would change. England's cold when you go home. Even in the summer you'd find it cold and shivery. You'd be fit then only for India."

"You make it sound impossible." She tried to speak defiantly.

He spoke as though he hadn't even listened. "Then, at the end, it may be for nothing. You might endure it all, as we have, then be kicked out anyway."

"Swaraj."

"Aye. Be kicked out of India and be unfit for England as well."

"As a former schoolmistress, I can appreciate your skill in giving tests."

"I have given you a warning."

"It was very convincing."

"Then you'll be leaving."

"I don't know."

"Only a fool would stay. Mad."

"If this is a sample of your salesmanship, Edward, I wonder you've sold any jute at all."

Smiling at him, she took his arm. "Here come the others." She moved with him toward the hollow. Flee, Mary, said an inner voice. While there is still time. But her stride was even and unhurried.

16

THE NEXT MORNING MARY WAS HAVING TEA with the Beauchamps on their verandah when she heard the sound of shouting and running.

"I must see," said Tom. He went to the rail. A young Indian was running past, and Tom shouted, "Hi. Kaheka shorgul?"

The Indian looked up, waving his arm excitedly toward the river. "Bagh, sahib. Shikar." He grinned and ran on.

"Bless me." Tom turned in from the rail. "He said there's a tiger down by the river. There's going to be a hunt."

"Tiger." Denise looked startled. "I didn't know there were any this close to Calcutta."

"I didn't either," Tom said. "I don't believe it."

There was a knock on the bedroom door. "Sahib. Beauchamp sahib."

"That's Goad's bearer. I'd better see." He went to the door and Mary could hear the bearer greet him, then there followed a rapid conversation in Hindustani of which she could make out only a few words.

"Goad sahib . . . bagh shikar . . . das budghey." She knew the latter words meant "ten o'clock."

The door closed and Tom came back. "It's true all right. One of the villagers spotted a tiger down in the marshes. He says it's probably an old tiger but Goad wants to get rid of him. They can be dangerous when they're old. We're all invited."

"Not I. I'll stay here," said Denise.

"There wouldn't be room for everybody. There'll only be two elephants."

"An elephant?" Mary was startled. "I thought one hunted from a platform in a tree."

"A machan? I doubt you could build a machan down there. There aren't any trees. Only marsh. Besides, you wouldn't like machan hunting. You have to sit up all night and the mosquitoes are ferocious." Tom was being expansive. He had listened to a great many hunters' tales at the Bengal Club.

Denise looked puzzled. "I haven't seen any elephants here. Where would he get them?"

"He probably has some for pulling logs when he's building a road. And the coolies could build the howdahs." He turned expansively to Mary. "A howdah is what you sit in on the elephant's back."

Mary smiled. "Elephants that build roads to carry people who've never hunted to shoot an old tiger. It's like something the Mad Hatter might organize."

"Are you going?" asked Denise.

"I haven't been invited yet."

"Tom?"

"Not I. You don't get me on an elephant. I don't want you to go either, Denise."

"I'm not exactly a sportswoman."

Mary made her decision. "If he invites me I think I will go."

"Mary!"

"I know. I'm hardly a sportswoman either. I just think I shall." It was a test, she thought. She must prove to herself that she can accept things like this. Otherwise she might as well stop now with any thought of living in India. This was no country for the cowardly.

Goad invited Mary and the hunt was scheduled for ten o'clock. It was a ragtag group that assembled. The variety of guns would have startled an experienced tiger hunter. Only Goad had a proper gun, a high-powered .577 Nitro-Express rifle which he handled with obvious familiarity. Jolliffe had come along with a 28-gauge shotgun, very useful for shooting marsh snipe, even crocs, but not tiger. Sir John, whom Mary was surprised to see, carried a heavy-bore elephant gun but was persuaded to exchange it for something less awesome. Mary was given no gun at all.

There were only these four. The others had begged off or been told there was no room. Mary saw that Bunty and Tiger were watching the proceedings with some amusement. She saw Goad trying to bring some efficiency into the hunt, marshaling the bearers, bringing up the elephants.

He now came up to her. He looked confident in the cool air. "It's not too late to change your mind."

"No." Mary shook her head.

"It may get a little bloody out there."

"I'll try not to be a nuisance." She swallowed a little nervously. At least they couldn't say she wasn't willing.

"Good." He eyed her with approval. "We'll be ready in a few moments. This is the first time we've had a hunt here but we'll get him."

"Are you sure you have to kill it? I hear it's an old tiger."

"It may kill some of the village children if left alone. It's already torn up some of our best young jute plants." It was clear that the plants were not the least of his reasons for wanting to kill the animal.

"I'm ready."

"We'll leave from below the terrace." He turned to look toward the village. "Here come the coolies. I want to get them into line."

He walked quickly down the slope. He was the sahib and this tiger was on his land. He was showing her how he handled these matters.

Mary walked around to the terrace. It was apparent that the coolies had responded with enthusiasm. It might have been the promise of tiger meat or the possibility of a celebration afterward.

They were assembling below the terrace with every sort of noise-maker. Mary could see drums, iron bars, rusted pans from surplus mill machinery, flutes, and whistles. They had been told to bring anything they could blow or hammer and they had complied with thoroughness.

Tiger appeared beside her. His hard face was angry. "The man's crazy. Look at those beaters—they're just coolies. Field workers or from the mills. The tiger'll laugh himself to death. And look at those howdahs."

He pointed to the approaching elephants. Mary had never seen any sort of howdah but she had to admit these looked makeshift. The villagers must have been working since early morning to make them.

"You shoot from those," he said. "You'd be safer on the

ground. And those elephants are working elephants. They've never seen a tiger."

"Oh, do stop."

"You'd better not go near a tree. Those elephants will try to knock off the howdahs. And if they can't they'll rub against the tree to break the straps. The way a dog rubs his back. And just keep them away from the river. Elephants love to sit in the water. If they get into the river, there you'll sit." It was obvious Tiger was beginning to enjoy himself.

"Edward says the tiger may kill someone if he's left there."

"You tell Edward the tiger will just die of old age if he's left alone. Edward is thinking of his jute fields."

"You simply don't like him."

"I don't. Neither do I want to see you killed. Do stay, Mary."

"No."

"You're trying to prove you're not afraid."

"Oh, I'm afraid all right."

"Then stay."

"No. I've said I'd go. Good-bye. I'll see you later." She went down the slope. She heard him call angrily but didn't answer.

She saw that the elephants had been brought lumbering into place, ropes for the howdahs strapped under their stomachs. She hoped that the ropes were made of Goad's best jute.

She saw that ladders had been placed against the wrinkled hides and that the mahouts were already seated astride their necks. The crowd of beaters had been sent toward the river and were already running exuberantly out of control. Goad stood beside the first elephant, waiting to help Mary up the ladder.

A closer sight of the elephants was not reassuring. They stood heavy-headed and apathetic. The howdah on one seemed to have been put together from a packing case and a pad of gunny sacking. The other howdah was enormous, bearing a canopy of red brocade and having four peeling columns of gilt at each corner.

Mary stared. "What's that?"

"It belonged to one of the old princes for this area," said Goad. "It was used in ceremonial processions. Must be a hundred and fifty years old. One of the coolies found it in a godown."

"But it looks top-heavy."

"There isn't time to make two. You and Sir John will ride in that. Jolliffe and I will go in the other. Time to go."

He led her to the ladder. She looked up. It seemed so far to the top. Sir John was peering down, looking very pleased with the rifle in his arms.

Mary grumbled to herself. "I thought he didn't like the mofussil, yet here he is. Perhaps he's going to shoot everything in sight. Avenge himself."

She grabbed the ladder rungs, closed her eyes, and climbed. The elephant seemed to sigh mournfully from deep inside but didn't move. She reached the top, scrambled hastily in, and sank tentatively onto the dilapidated throne. Sir John was seated on a chair before her. The ladder was taken away and the hunt was ready to begin.

It didn't take Mary long to wonder whether she shouldn't have remained with the other ladies. Her elephant had a side-to-side sway as it walked that soon made her feel queasy. The howdah lurched with each swing and, though Mary kept her eyes fastened on Sir John's back, she knew what a look-out sailor at the top of a swaying mast must feel.

To break up the sway the elephant would stop from time to time and try awkwardly to raise his rear leg to paw at the ropes under his belly. It was just as Tiger had said. She was thankful there were no trees against which the elephant might have knocked off the howdah.

I'll never last, she thought. I'll be ill any moment, all over the inside of the prince's howdah. Yet, as the elephant settled into a steady gait, she found herself becoming used to the sway, learning to sway in turn. She began to relax a bit. She could not really enjoy the experience. There was something grotesque in this hunt: the silly howdahs, the amateur beaters, the apathetic work elephants. It was a sham, a masquerade.

The elephants were moving now in the open space between the jute fields and the edge of the marsh grass. They advanced in a line parallel to the river. The beaters, below them, were working their noisy way, their heads showing above the tall grass. The mahout kept up a cheerful chatter while prodding the elephant with his logging hook.

Then it happened. The beaters at the near end of the line came to a confused halt and Mary heard the growing murmur. "Rajbagh." She saw that some of the beaters were pointing to the long grass before them and, as she watched, the grass began to sway at the top, swelling toward them. The grass at the nearest edge suddenly parted and a tiger bounded into sight.

"Good God," said Sir John. "He's a real one."

Mary stared toward it. This was not an old tiger. Even she could tell that. Its coat was not patchy but rich and glossy and the black and yellow stripes stood out strongly.

They all watched the waiting animal. The only sounds were the faint snarling from the tiger forty yards away and the slowly rising squeal from the elephants.

Suddenly there was a "whomp" from Sir John's rifle and a puff of dust shot up at the tiger's feet. It quickly lurched to one side and bounded back into the grass toward the line of beaters. The nearest coolie broke wildly from the grass and fled screaming past them up the slope toward the jute fields. The tiger broke from the grass after him.

Mary saw Goad stand up in his howdah and bellow, "Nahin." She saw him wave wildly as the coolie ran crazily into his jute field—one with young plantings—with the tiger bounding behind. There was a shot, then another, and Mary saw Goad standing motionless with his rifle in his hands. The tiger lay on the ground, thrashing, then lay still. The coolie lay loosely in a heap.

"My God," said Sir John. "He shot the coolie too." His face was incredulous. "It was the jute field."

Mary was bewildered. It had all happened so quickly. Then, at the sight of the coolie's hand flapping faintly against the dirt, she felt sick. It was like a chicken she had once seen beheaded, its legs tapping and kicking slower and slower in the dust.

She was suddenly aware of the bright sun, the snuffling elephants, and the deep stillness from the beaters; all silent except for one coolie at the far end of the line, still marching dimwittedly ahead, his flute blowing its high, thin tunelessness. She knew then that all the ridiculousness of the day, this bizarre tiger hunt, had been leading them to this.

She touched Sir John on the shoulder. "I want to go back." She wanted to be away from that hand, tapping slowly in the dust.

It was a quiet, even solemn tiffin that day. Only Goad and Mary, Tiger and Bunty were present. Bunty chattered, flirted with Tiger. He was curiously silent, even detached. Goad was calm, giving quiet orders to the servants. It was not a festive meal.

After tiffin Sir John sent word he wished to speak to Goad and when their host returned he told Mary that Sir John and Lady Thornton were leaving. "He said he had a golfing engagement in Calcutta." He laughed shortly. "He doesn't play golf."

"He may have some legal work to do," said Mary.

"Then he should say so."

It was Tom who left no doubts as to his motives. He marched out to the verandah after tiffin and said he and Denise were leaving. He looked surprisingly spunky.

"Yes," said Tom. "That was a damn fool thing to do, Goad, shooting that bearer. Mind you, I don't give a hoot in hell personally if you shoot your coolies. They're yours and I suppose you can do as you like with them. It's just that there's this swaraj talk these days."

He faltered a moment as Goad looked at him, then went on. "I mean, if we stayed on, it'd look as though we shot up our own servants."

That was all. Tom and Denise went up to pack. Sir John and Lady Thornton had already done so. Bunty was still on the verandah. Goad turned to the young girl, surprisingly courteous.

"You will go also I presume, Miss Cranston. With Sir John and Lady Thornton."

"I did come with them."

"Of course."

"I'm sorry, Mr. Goad," Bunty said impulsively. "You have been awfully nice to me."

He smiled at her. "I am sorry we have not had more time to talk. Perhaps you and your hosts can come again sometime."

"Thank you." Bunty glanced at Tiger and went into the house.

Goad turned to Mary. "I must go down to the coolie village. That beater will live, you know. He will not walk again. His hip is shattered."

"Won't that make it difficult for you with the others?" Mary asked.

"No. They laugh at him already. They know he will be taken care of."

"Do you want me to come with you?"

"You will stay here, please." He turned to go.

"Oh, Goad." It was Tiger speaking to him, almost casually.

It was practically the first word he had spoken since the tiger hunt. He sounded almost off-hand.

"Yes?" Their host turned to glance at him.

"I received word this morning that the Mahatma is going on a hunger strike. I'll have to go back to Calcutta. The word came over Dr. MacDonough's phone. He sent over a chit." He paused. "Did you know about the hunger strike?"

"The word came to you, Captain, not me."

"I noticed the coolies chattering a lot yesterday. Coolies are usually the first to learn these things. You know, 'cooliegraph.' I thought perhaps you might have heard all this yesterday from your bearer."

Goad contemplated Tiger but he kept silent. Tiger continued. "You had a hartal here the last time Gandhi went on a hunger strike, isn't that true?" He nodded to Mary. "A hartal is a sympathy demonstration. Practically a strike. You had one here, as I remember, Goad. It's in our records. The hartal cut into your jute production pretty badly."

"If you have it in your records that should be enough."

"A hartal right now could be very bad for you." He laughed. "You'd do anything to divert your coolies from another hartal. Even arrange a tiger shoot."

"Tiger, what are you saying?" Mary was astonished.

"That was a very lucky thing, having that tiger turn up. Such a young tiger too. He wouldn't need to wander down here to hunt."

"You know a great deal about tigers, don't you, Flemyng? That is your nickname, I believe." Goad looked amused.

"I know there's nothing that diverts coolies more than a big celebration with lots of tiger meat."

"Coolies are easily diverted, like children. If I wished to arrange a tiger shoot I would hardly buy one that would trample my jute plants."

"That was an accident."

"Or shoot one of my coolies?"

"That you hadn't counted on."

"I suggest, Captain, that you report all this to your governor. I also recommend that you have proof other than suspicion. Now I must go down to see my coolie. I will hurry because I want to be here when you leave." He smiled at Tiger and left.

"Tiger, what was that about?"

"He arranged that hunt, just to divert his men from a hartal. That could have shut down his estate."

"You don't know this."

"You know what he's like. He'd commit murder to protect York House. He nearly did."

"He didn't kill the coolie. It was a good shot."

"You're protecting him, of course."

"We are his guests."

"He's losing his guests." He laughed. He had recovered his temper.

"I'm ashamed of Tom! It isn't the shooting that's making him leave. It's because Goad won't go in with him on his Brazil plan. Wild horses couldn't drag Tom away if Edward would reconsider Brazil. Edward knows that."

"Sir John and Lady Thornton? They're not involved in any Brazil plan."

"Sir John has hated it ever since he came. He just wanted an excuse."

"What about you? You're going."

"I don't know."

"Good God, you've seen what he is! Even if he didn't arrange the hunt, he did shoot that coolie. For a few jute plants."

"He killed the tiger too. He saved the coolie!" She didn't want to think of that crumpled figure in the dust.

"Mary, come with me. We can be in Calcutta in a few hours. We can have dinner and a walk to the Memorial."

"No."

"But if you stay you'll be alone here."

"I know."

"Does this mean you intend to marry him?"

"I don't know."

"But he's so wrong for you."

"He may be exactly right. He loves his land. That's why he shot that coolie. If he did arrange the hunt, he did it to protect what is his."

"And that's what you want to be?"

"I just know that he has all of you against him—the neighbors too, according to you. I don't feel I should desert him in this way."

"Mary . . . Mary."

"Please, Tiger."

"You don't know what you may be letting yourself into.
You can't take on all of India!"

"He has."

He hesitated. "I like you, Mary. I have considered you my
friend."

"I am."

"Not if you are to be beside him. That is the India I
doubt."

"His India would have to be mine. It is as simple as that.
And that is the problem too." She suddenly smiled and
leaned up to kiss him on the cheek. "Good-bye, Alastair.
For now, at least."

In midafternoon the autos gathered in the driveway. The
word of the Mahatma's hunger strike had reached the guests
by now. Tom Beauchamp was depressed at the thought that
the market value of jute shares would fall as they had during
the Mahatma's last hunger strike. He was all for reopening
the Brazil proposition with Goad then and there but Denise
restrained him and got him into their motorcar.

Sir John was also depressed at the Gandhi news. He said he
always seemed to receive bad news in the mofussil. Lady
Thornton was concerned lest her servants in Calcutta go on
a hartal as they had during his last hunger strike.

Denise cried a little at leaving her friend. Tom impatiently
shushed his wife and started them on their way.

Mary didn't volunteer any explanation as to why she was
staying, simply standing near the host as he said his good-
bye. Lady Thornton was too experienced a hostess to show
any curiosity. She mercly gave Mary a shrewd look as though
to say, "I'm sure you know what you're doing, my dear."
Sir John nodded good-bye and muttered some advice about
staying out of howdahs in the future.

Goad was very correct and formal. He waited until Tiger
and Bunty came down. Goad bid them a brief good-bye, then
stood carefully back while his servants placed the luggage
in the autos.

Tiger spoke quietly. "Good luck, Mary. No more tiger
shoots."

"No." She turned quickly to the waiting Bunty. "Good-bye.
Take care." She found herself kissing the young girl's cheek,
either from an impulsive fondness or a flight to her Roecroft
habit.

"Good-bye." Bunty was a little abrupt. She had just learned

from Tiger that he would not dine with her. He had meant what he had said.

There was a bit more handshaking between Mary and Tiger, then he and Bunty climbed in with Sir John and Lady Thornton, and the auto, the syce driving, descended to the river road and turned toward Calcutta.

Mary watched it out of sight. She knew Goad waited on the verandah and hesitated to turn around.

"Mary." His voice was impatient.

"I'm coming." She strode quickly up to the verandah. "Edward, I'm going up to pack. I'd like to leave as well. Couldn't you have someone drive me?"

"Why didn't you leave with the others?"

"I didn't want to walk out when they did. It seemed like desertion."

"Very commendable. My proposal of marriage . . . are you walking out on that too?"

"For the moment." He saw the indecision and took a step toward her, his whole body eager for her.

"Edward, no." Mary pulled herself away. She was trembling. "I'm sorry. It's been too much. The tiger shoot, the coolie. This Gandhi news; it is true, isn't it?"

"It's true enough."

"And you did arrange that tiger kill, just as Tiger said. To prevent a hartal."

"That is no one's business but mine." His face was set but there was no denial in it.

"Edward, listen. I am considering your proposal. Believe me." Her voice was near breaking. "I want to stay in India. I came out because I thought I might be of some use. But I don't know. I may not be as strong as I thought. There could be trouble now."

"There could be."

"I want to be certain of myself, and my husband too. After that tiger hunt today, I'm not so certain." Her eyes were troubled, then she pulled herself together. "I want to go back to Calcutta. Not to Tom and Denise's. I simply want to be by myself for a while."

"Mary." He took a hungry step toward her but she moved away.

"No. You must know someplace I can stay. Not the Great Eastern or the Grand Hotel. I don't want to be noticed."

"It might not be safe in Calcutta now."

"Riots."

"Probably. If anything happens to Gandhi."

"Then I might as well find out. I'm afraid but I'm more afraid of making a mistake in marrying. That could be worse."

Goad watched her. He could not have imagined that this woman could be distressed by anything. She had seemed so strong, superior. He found himself surprisingly moved. He wanted her more than ever but he knew he must wait.

"I know a guesthouse. It's small but quiet. I'll have Ahmed take you."

"You do understand?"

"No. Nevertheless, I will wait." He bowed, again in control. "Good-bye."

17

IF HE WISHED TO DRINK FROM THE PUBLIC WELL of a village not his own, he would be driven away. If he wished to worship in a church of his own religion but not his own separate church, he would be excluded. If his shadow crossed the path of the orthodox Hindu, the Hindu would walk around the shadow.

These "untouchable" people were the casteless, the seventy million outcasts among more than two hundred million fellow Hindus, half the population of India. Confined to their own villages, denied the right to vote, even of education, they were restricted to the most menial and degrading work. They had been the original inhabitants of India but had been conquered and scattered. It was for these outcasts the Mahatma proposed to risk his life.

The leaders must first be induced to sit down together, to confer. The Mahatma knew there was only one thing, their affection for him, that could bring this about. Now the mere threat of his fasting had brought the leaders quickly to Poona, then to a conference in nearby Bombay.

They were stubborn men. The Untouchable leaders had been hardened by centuries of oppression and would accept nothing but full representation in the National Congress. The caste leaders were proud and deeply orthodox. To extend the vote to the casteless was contrary to a thousand years of history. Worse, it was profane, a denial of what to them had been ordained by holy scripture.

The word was soon brought to Yevrada Gaol that the conference had been unable to agree and had disbanded. The Mahatma now had little choice. He had said that no people deserved swaraj that could not first rule themselves.

He announced that he would now begin his fast, unto death if necessary. He would test his fellow Hindus' love for him and he would test his own for them. "My fast," he said, "is based on faith in my cause, faith in the Hindu community, faith in human nature itself. My cry must rise to the throne of the Almighty God."

The frail man, now sixty-three, rose early as usual on the appointed day and had sung to him his favorite verse. "He alone is the true Vaishnava Who Knows and Feels for Another's Woe."

He ate his customary breakfast of milk and fruit and from half past six until eight o'clock, he had one of his companions read to him from the Bhagavad Gita. At half past eleven the Mahatma had his last meal, lemon juice and honey with hot water. He and his little group sang a song written especially for the occasion, "O Traveller, arise. It is dawn. Where is the Night that Thou Still Sleepest." The jail bell struck noon and the Mahatma's fast began.

The world outside responded. All over India cookfires were left unlighted. Millions began a fasting of their own. In some places public wells were opened to the Untouchables. In some even the temples, the citadels of orthodoxy, were declared open. In Bombay seven temples asked their worshipers to decide by ballot. Pebbles were to be dropped into a white box if they wished their temples thrown open to the Harijans, the "children of God" as the Mahatma called them, and into a black box if exclusion were to be continued. On the second day the boxes were opened. The white box contained more than twenty-four thousand pebbles; the black box only four hundred.

The world outside India, even the sophisticated cities of the Occident, paused to watch, first with skepticism, then wonder. "Let us imagine," said the London *Economist,* "that in the United States the Democratic President-elect, Franklin D. Roosevelt, were to announce his intention of fasting to death unless the Southern Democrats abolished Jim Crow cars and allowed their colored fellow-citizens a genuine exercise of the vote. In that event Mr. Roosevelt would be a doomed man. He would just starve."

In India delegations were calling at the prison at Poona. Children, even Untouchables, asked that Bapu give up his fasting. It was the fourth day and he was known to be weaker. Bapu sent them word that he would continue until he could truly believe in their love for each other and for him.

In Calcutta the viceroy played croquet and received reports. He was maintaining a close observation of the Mahatma's health. He had advised the jail superintendent that all necessary medical assistance was to be extended. It was a dangerous knife-edged patience he had forced on himself but he knew as well as Gandhi what the stakes were and he too could be resolute.

He was playing croquet when he recognized Captain Flemyng, the governor's aide, approaching with Lieutenant Vickson, his own junior aide. "Is that the report?"

"Yes, sir." Tiger halted to salute, then handed the cable to the viceroy.

"Come here while I rest. I'm afraid I'm not yet accustomed to your so-called 'cold weather.' I find it jolly hot." Lord Willingdon led the way to an arbor and a bench, then seated himself. He squinted at the report.

"I have your glasses, sir." Lieutenant Vickson handed them over.

"Thank you." The viceroy placed them on his nose. They gave his thin face something of the look of a careful bank examiner as he bent over the paper.

"Nausea, aches, too weak to bathe," he read. "Has this just come in, Captain?"

"Yes, sir," said Tiger. "It was sent at nine Bombay time."

"It says this is the seven o'clock examination. Those doctors are getting up early."

"Dr. Mehta is living at the jail, sir. He and Dr. Gilder are seeing the Mahatma twice a day."

"Too weak to bathe. I don't like that. He has always been

a very clean man." He paused, then continued from the paper. "Voice growing weaker, blood pressure high, to conserve energy is now carried from place to place on a stretcher." He looked up. "Why must he be carried from place to place? Where are they keeping him?"

"In a courtyard, I believe, sir," said Tiger. "It's what he wanted. A cot has been set up and he lies there most of the day."

"In this sun?"

"There's a mango tree, sir, and the cot's been placed there. He's moved only for natural functions so to speak."

"And this is only the fourth day." The viceroy shook his head.

Lieutenant Vickson spoke up. "He survived before, sir. Twenty-one days."

"He's eight years older now. Sixty-three. Besides, he wasn't in jail then. He was in the home of friends, surrounded by people who loved him, who nursed him." The viceroy's voice rose. It was plain that, despite himself, he cared about this feeble man.

He sat back. "Is he still giving interviews?"

"No, sir." Tiger shook his head. "He's not seeing any delegations either. He says they know what has to be done."

"He's right, of course." He bent over the report. "An enema. It says 'enemas of soda bicarbonate dissolved in water." That must be for the high blood pressure. On top of everything he has to take enemas. He's a stalwart man."

"Yes, sir."

"Completely purposeful, even at the cost of his own life. It's like Jesus. He died for others. But Jesus still had his position to establish. It was his dying that gave him the great impetus. This man has already won his people. It's really unique in history."

"There was Daniel the Stylite, sir." It was Lieutenant Vickson speaking.

"Who?"

"Daniel the Stylite, sir. The Stylites were holy men more than a thousand years ago. They sat up on tall pillars, for penance or something. Daniel said he'd sit on his pillar until he died unless the Emperor—he was a Merovingian Emperor, sir . . ."

"Thank you, Vickson."

"Unless the Emperor would renounce his heresy from the

church. The Emperor wouldn't and Daniel finally came down. But, when he was led in to see the Emperor, feeble and shaky, the Emperor yielded. You see, he couldn't give in before because he was the Emperor, but now he could."

"Very interesting, Vickson. But that was a thousand years ago. These are modern times." The viceroy sounded a bit testy. Tiger wondered whether Vickson had been trying to compare Lord Willingdon with the Emperor. After all, the viceroy too had the power to end this demonstration against his authority. By forced feeding if necessary. He glanced at young Vickson but the aide's face was innocent.

The viceroy shook his head, almost as though he were answering the lieutenant's accusation. "It is the Hindus who will have to stop this fast, by agreeing among themselves. I wouldn't interfere if I could. Nor would the Mahatma want me to. It must be played out to an end. That's all, Captain. I hope the next report will be better. I hope there will be a next report."

He nodded to Tiger and he and Lieutenant Vickson withdrew. They had walked out of earshot when the young man looked up.

"What do you think?"

"About what?"

"About Gandhi. There was a time he'd have been stood up in front of a cannon."

"That was eighty years ago."

"That still might be the best way. This is dangerous. The Mahatma is getting all of India excited."

"All the more reason for us not to be."

The lieutenant looked at him curiously. "You sound so detached. You do care, don't you? I mean about what's happening. I'm surprised His Lordship doesn't shoot old Bapu. That's what they'd have done in the old days."

Tiger glanced at him. "Old Bapu, as you call him, is using an even older weapon. Jesus used it. It's called love. He's appealing to man's conscience."

"Are you comparing old Bapu to Jesus?"

"I'm comparing his methods. They worked the last time they were used. The Mahatma might be just as dangerous to us as Jesus was to the Romans. As a weapon love is nearly unique. Has hardly ever been used."

"You sound so cynical. Gandhi's our enemy as far as I'm

concerned. We've got this damned Gupta on one side and Gandhi on the other. I'd shoot both of them."

"I'm glad you feel so strongly about it."

"Don't you? I mean, sir, as Sir Gerald's aide you have a responsible position."

Tiger closed his eyes. He was in no mood these days to listen to such simplicities. He would have liked to kick this young and overheated lad in the pants. He forbore. The lieutenant's heart was in the right place, dedicated to the viceroy.

Vickson went on. "We can't let them kick us out of here."

"We have a duty to civilize them," Tiger murmured.

"Exactly. I mean we are civilized."

"Perhaps that's what the Mahatma wants us to be. Civilized and Christian. That's what defeated Rome. Perhaps we should simply shoot old Bapu in a civilized way."

"Now you've got it." The lieutenant nodded happily.

"I think Lord Willingdon is waving for you. You're wanted."

"Good Lord. Thanks." Vickson started to go, then stopped to eye Tiger. "You said shoot him in a civilized way?" He stared at Tiger, baffled, shook his head, and hurried away.

Tiger turned toward the lodge gates and the road beyond. He really shouldn't twit the lieutenant that way. It was becoming a habit with him. It could be dangerous. Anyone might think he were not a hundred percent Kipling wallah.

But was he? There was no point in denying it any longer, not to himself. Something was happening to him. He had told Mary the causes of some of his doubts—the poverty and hopelessness of the Indian peasants. They were ground between British taxes and the Indian moneylender. He'd also mentioned the inequities he had seen develop in attempting to clamp British justice onto the Indian masses.

But there was more, much more. There was the destruction of India's once-strong village industries—the weaving trade, the small cotton mills. The Lancashire mills had seen to it that India should become a market instead of a producer and the village industries couldn't compete. A tariff on Lancashire goods would have protected the local skills but this the faraway mills and their government wouldn't permit.

Tiger was familiar with all these charges. He had been reading the "enemy" literature, so to speak. He had had the usual disbelief, even contempt, for the nationalist arguments, but he had dug deeper and found considerable truth. He had pored over old histories during his holidays and come on disturbing confirmations. It seemed there were actually cultures and entire civilizations prior to the British Raj. This was difficult for an Englishman to appreciate but it was apparently true and unsettling.

Tiger knew that the British had brought a unity of sorts to the Indian peninsula but so had a great emperor named Asoka, three hundred years before Christ. As for religious strife, so sporadic and savage under British rule, under the Mogul emperors, notably the renowned Akbar in the seventeenth century, there had been little or no strife.

But the British had brought peace to India, no one could deny that. There had not been a major bloodletting since the terrible Mutiny of nearly eighty years before. Yet there hadn't really been peace. No one knew that better than Tiger. He had seen too many Indian soldiers dead. Not in India, to be sure, but in Gallipoli, with Allenby in the Messpot or beyond the Khyber. Indians died now outside the motherland and in the wars of India's conquerors. And the irony of it, as Tiger knew, was that the cost of these Indian expeditionary forces was borne by the Indians themselves.

Tiger had fought and bled for Britain. He was an Englishman with the Englishman's training and convictions. He had been nourished at Harrow, shaped at Sandhurst, and tempered at the Dardanelles. He had early shown signs of willfulness, to be sure. Suspended briefly from Harrow for irreverence, disciplined twice at Sandhurst, even passed over twice for promotion, once at Gallipoli and once in Mesopotamia, for "arrogant disregard of personal safety amounting to insubordination." Yet he was still an Englishman, so admired by the world, and he was a gentleman and an officer.

Tiger stopped in the roadway and fingered his scars. The one beside his jaw itched occasionally in the cold weather. They both itched during the rest of the year. He looked ahead. He could see the Maidan beyond his auto and, in the distance, the towering memorial to Queen Victoria.

He wondered sometimes these days why he kept on in India. If he had growing doubts as to the rightness of the Raj, he should clear out. He should resign his commission in good conscience. It would certainly be the sensible thing to do. If Britain's day was indeed done he was being quixotic to stay on. Aides-de-camp, particularly those passed over twice for promotion, would have little future. They would be an anachronism. Why then did he stay?

He was used to the damn country for one thing. It was the only place now that he felt at home. He liked the size of it, its misty, snow-topped mountains, its broad, eye-stretching plains, its great rivers, even the barren, baked northwest frontier. And, perhaps above all, he liked the rich mixture of its people, Muslims, Hindus, Sikhs, Parsees, Tamils—the variety was infinite.

There was another reason he stayed. He would have grinned cynically if anyone had mentioned it to his face but it was true. He felt a sneaking affinity with his fellow British out there. It wasn't the pomp and circumstance, the power and the glory of the Raj that held him. It was the people: the soldiers, the hard-working sahibs, the old "quihais," the children and their ayahs in the parks, the wives—the generations of British, India-born, reaching back to "John Company," as the East India Company became known.

Tiger slowly continued toward his auto. He could see the autos in the Maidan as sahibs went home for their tiffins. He stopped.

There was another reason he stayed in India, of course—the most compelling. He had nowhere else to go. He was a damned remittance man in a way, supported by the government. He could stay on in India, live like a sahib on condition that he seldom went to England.

He really had a very good thing, come to think of it, as did most remittance men. The only trouble was that he had an inconvenient conscience. If he had any sense he'd forget all about the rights or wrongs of the Raj and make the most of things.

Tiger saw the Memorial in the Maidan and glanced toward the statue of the Empress. She was alone up there too. For her, perhaps, it was not so difficult. All it took was a heart of iron.

For four days Mary had remained by herself in the Calcutta hotel to which Goad had directed her. It was a small hotel near the river, really a guesthouse. The others besides Mary at the large dining room table included a young German and his family, newly assigned to the German Trade Commission office, two Anglo-Indian couples of varying degrees of color, and an Indian professor from Calcutta University. Mary seemed to be the only pukka Englishwoman.

Yet Mary enjoyed the little hotel and felt almost at home with her fellow guests. It seemed just the sort of place Goad himself might have used and, from the respect with which his name was mentioned by the Anglo-Indian proprietor, she gathered that this was his customary home when he visited Calcutta.

Mary had not let Denise know where she was. She had phoned her on arrival and told her she was staying in Calcutta for a few days but had not mentioned the reason. She had no doubt that Denise had assumed Goad was with her. Nor had she rung Tiger. He was the last person she wished to see.

For she had to come to a decision. She had neither the time nor the money to go on much longer. But a wrong decision could be worse than no decision at all. She wanted to sort things out.

It would not be easy. If ever there were a time not suitable for sorting things out, it was then. It was the fifth day of the Mahatma's fasting. There was tension in the air. It was not a time for tranquillity.

Goad kept himself in her mind in a very simple way. Each morning there were fresh flowers in her room. Each evening there was a special bottle of wine at her place. On the third day, Christmas Eve, Mary had been greeted before dinner by the announcement that a present from Goad sahib had arrived. Ahmed had appeared with a strong, grinning young house servant she had seen at York House.

"Salaam," said Ahmed. He had gestured to the young servant. "His name Gopal. Goad sahib send him to be your bearer."

That was all. Ahmed had bowed again and left. Gopal had remained to attend Mary at table, to sleep in the hallway outside her door. And to remind her that someone waited for her at York House.

On Christmas Day Mary left the hotel for a long walk through the city. She wasn't depressed. It had been a gay little party the night before. The dining room had been hung with ribbons, a small tree had been placed on a table, and the evening had ended with an effort at carols. The German family had added its own version of "Silent Night" and it had been easy to forget that in Mary's mind they were still the enemy nation.

Mary walked quickly along the embankment, then turned along the Strand in the general direction of Fort William and the center of the city. It was hard to remember that this was Christmas. To her Christmas meant rain or fog, an occasional snow, always a Christmas party at the school for all remaining students. It meant a spiced wine, friends or family, green trees and ornaments.

Here there was warmth instead of snow, a warmth to her nearly tropical. There were palm trees instead of pines. Instead of a Yule Log, there were bougainvilleas and a banyan tree in the Zoo. There were bullock carts and a brown world of strangers to whom Christmas meant nothing.

Mary moved steadily along the embankment until she had reached the Howrah bridge. She paused at the near end to eye the jostling crowd, the crossing trains, the bathers on the steps below dipping themselves into this arm of the sacred Ganges.

There was a little shrine on the bridge and, in the midst of the pushing traffic—the bicyclists, the hurrying coolies with freight on their heads, the gharries and trolleys—she saw a native kneeling before a Hindu priest. The holy man was intoning soundlessly in the noisy air, waving his prayer flag methodically above the bowed head.

A different sound caught Mary's ear, the familiar drumbeat and strident horns of a Salvation Army band. Then she saw the players, grouped on the bridge directly across from the Hindu shrine, standing calmly at the edge of the traffic.

She watched them. She had recognized the discordant tune. "O Come, All Ye Faithful." She heard the words being raised loudly above the bridge noises.

She listened, a frown of puzzlement in her eyes. The words should have been familiar. She had sung them often enough at Roecroft. Her lips formed the hymn soundlessly. Then she realized what was wrong. The words were being sung in Bengali.

Mary turned away and tears came to her eyes. It was silly to be disturbed by such a curious event. This was India, a country of contrasts. Instead of Christmas trees, there would be palms, heat instead of snow, Salvation Army bands who sang the old hymns and carols in Bengali. She would have many such Christmases if she married Edward Goad.

Mary strode back toward the embankment. The cacophony from the bridge—trolley wheels, shouts, taxi horns, the tuneless "O Come, All Ye Faithful"—reached after her.

18

IN BOMBAY A NEW MEETING OF THE CASTE AND Untouchable leaders was arranged and an agreement in principle was reached. Representation of the Untouchables was conceded. It was the sixth day.

But in Poona the Mahatma was adamant. He told the jubilant delegation that a specific agreement must be reached as to the number of Untouchable delegates.

"But they are only entitled to seventy seats. That is numerically obvious," said the caste spokesman.

"Then they must have a hundred and seventy," said Bapu. "There are things besides numbers."

The delegates went back to Bombay and struggled with their problem. The sixth day became the seventh and the seventh the eighth. Then the delegates went back to Poona. Gandhi, on his cot in the courtyard, seemed even more frail.

"One hundred and forty-one seats," said the Untouchable leader gratefully. "A hundred and forty-one, Bapu."

"Have you agreed?" said the Mahatma to the caste leader and the latter nodded gravely. He had been stubborn but no one could hold out longer. All of India was behind this frail man.

The Mahatma's eyes flickered. "Now the British must approve."

The leaders were astonished. "But we have agreed."

The head moved feebly. "There can be no real agreement until the British approve."

The doctors cut short any further pleas and the leaders were shown from the prison. Their faces showed a common conviction, a common sense of grief. The British would never accept the agreed representation. They had already put forward their own communal plan providing for Untouchable representation to be elected separately from the other Congress members. The cynics said the British plan would divide the Hindus even further, thereby making the rule of the Raj that much easier. They would never withdraw this plan, even if there were time to do so. The British Cabinet had announced it could not again discuss the Hindu problem unless the Prime Minister were present and the Prime Minister had suddenly been called out of London to Sussex to attend the funeral of an aunt. Meanwhile the Mahatma starved.

In Calcutta the races were held as usual at the Royal Calcutta Turf Club. The eighth running of the Cooch Behar Cup was attended by His Excellency the Viceroy and Lady Willingdon, as well as Calcutta society. The Cup race, one mile three furlongs, was won by the outsider, *Golden Carp*, by two lengths over the favorite, *Shipshape*. It paid its supporters the whopping price of three hundred eighteen rupees for an eight rupee bet.

The Calcutta Amateur Theatrical Society presented its Christmas pantomime as usual at the Old Empire Cinema. "Cinderella" was well received by adults and children alike, though there were a few who said it was high time old Major Fenton was replaced as the female comic by someone less given to forgetting when to enter.

The Love Parade, starring Maurice Chevalier, Jeanette MacDonald, and Jack Buchanan was playing at the New Empire. A visitor, seeing the fishing fleeters and their escorts in the bar during the interval, must have considered the film's title very suitable.

There were daily bulletins in the *Statesman* on developments in Poona. Even if one wished to ignore the Mahatma's fasting it would have been difficult. There had been riots at the university and there had been a sympathy strike by trainmen of the Bengal-Nagpur Railway. One realized that if the Mahatma died the British would be held accountable and that they were only eight thousand in a city of two million.

But to ignore the "cold weather" or the young lady guests would not only be bad manners but an indication of panic. So one went to Firpo's as usual, attended the races and the cricket matches, and turned an encouraging smile toward the courtships that were developing. Each day the *Statesman* carried the notice of another engagement or marriage. The same issue carried the latest bulletin from Yevrada Gaol.

On the tenth day of the fast, the day before the New Year, a message from London was delivered to the viceroy at Belvedere. The Prime Minister had made an emergency return from Sussex, the Cabinet had met, and Lord Willingdon was advised of the seriousness with which it viewed the Mahatma's fasting. It was shortly afterward that Tiger Flemyng came from Government House with the latest medical report from Poona.

"We have examined today Mr. M. K. Gandhi," the viceroy read. "Blood presure 1.3; systolic, 185 m.m.; diastolic, 110 m.m. Both the acetone and urea content in his urine have increased, the latter to 1.5 percent.

"We are definitely of the opinion that this portends entry into the danger zone. Mahatmaji has no reserve fat and he is living on muscle. This is the stage when an attack of paralysis may intervene any time. We are of opinion that he has entered into that stage that is bringing him nearer his end. There is danger even if the fast is broken."

The viceroy put down the message. He was no longer the witty, slightly mocking strategist. He was grave.

"I also have a message from Sir Gerald, sir." Tiger spoke up. "Sir Gerald urges that you give every consideration to accepting the Untouchable agreement. It is the opinion of Sir Gerald and his council that the fast has gone long enough."

"They've had a meeting, have they?"

"Yes, sir. The city is in rather an ugly mood. There have been parades, riots. If anything were to happen to the Mahatma . . ." Tiger stopped. There was no need to say more.

The viceroy was thoughtful. "We have kept Gupta quiet for ten days. Not much but it may have been enough. By giving in we may lose a battle but one can lose a battle and still win the war, eh, Captain? As Fabius did."

Tiger said nothing. He didn't trust these little analogies. History never repeated itself exactly. It was as varied as man.

"But Fabius had only one enemy," continued the viceroy. "The Carthaginians. We have two, Gandhi and Gupta."

"Yes, sir." And ourselves, Tiger thought. Never fail to look within for the enemy.

"We must improve on Fabius. We might wring one more day from the Mahatma. When we give in it must obtain the maximum in publicity. That might squash Gupta once and for all."

"But one more day will be New Year's Day, sir. There will be the Proclamation Parade. Sir Gerald believes the crowd might be dangerous."

"It will be. Very. But we don't want to disappoint the troops, do we? They have come all the way from their cantonments."

He smiled now, quite cheerful. "And the militia—those business chaps give up a great deal of time in preparation. And we certainly don't want to disappoint all the pretty girls out from England, do we? Or the Indians."

"No, sir." I wish he would stop playing, Tiger thought. He knows damn well why he's not canceling the parade.

The viceroy went on. "I was rather looking forward to it myself. You tell Sir Gerald we'll have it as usual."

He smiled, remaining seated on his desk, quite perky. If Tiger could have looked behind him as he left he would have seen His Excellency's expression change when the door had closed. It was very grim indeed.

Tiger went out early that evening. He wanted to get the feel of the city, its mood. He wandered from bazaar to back alley, from the Chowringhi of the sahibs to the Kidderpore dock area, from the Chinese quarter to the alley behind Magda's in Acre Lane. He walked or rode the crowded trams, pushing himself inside, testing the reactions of the people.

No one pushed back. When he shoved someone aside, on a tram or in an alley, he was met only with sullen withdrawal. He lost his temper once, cursing the people in their own language and in Pushto, the alien and feared dialect of the tribesmen of the Frontier. He was reminding the Bengali of what everyone said, that they were not a warrior people, that they had always been among the defeated. They were suited only to be babus. Even now, with their Bapu fasting his life away for them, they allowed this scarred white sahib to push among them, ridiculing them.

Finally, Tiger went back to his flat, poured himself a burra peg, and went out to sit on his verandah. He wanted to settle himself. He knew enough of the Indian to know how little the night had told him. If ever there were two sides to a coin, the Indian showed them. One side of him was docile, the holy, gentle side to which Gandhi appealed. The other showed the bloody, cruel face of killers, murdering in a sudden and unpredictable frenzy, as in their terrible religious riots.

Yet the viceroy wished to test this people. He would have his parade, make one last use of the Mahatma's fast before yielding. It was dangerous and cruel. It also took nerves of iron.

But, Tiger wondered, why was he himself so unsettled? It wasn't the possibilities of danger. He was too experienced a soldier for that. He wondered whether it was Mary, last seen at York House. One really had to hand it to that woman. She had never lost sight of why she had come to India. There was no confusion, no uncertainty there. Perhaps that was why he missed her so much.

He shrugged. So be it. You're born alone and you die alone. And, except for the occasional passer-by, you're alone most of the time in between.

He raised his glass. Bungho, Alastair old boy. Tomorrow will be a new year.

The New Year proclamation parade in Calcutta always began at eight in the morning. Some said the English had chosen this hour to demonstrate to the Indians their hardiness and self-discipline. Others said that the English, comparatively sober on New Year's Eve, had chosen this hour to punish the Scots. The Scots didn't complain since they didn't go to bed anyway on Hogmanay. The Scottish regiments marched on New Year's morning with a certain bleary doggedness.

Tiger took up his position behind Sir Gerald on the reviewing stand promptly at ten minutes to eight. He wore full regimentals and was wide awake and watchful, though a trifle bloodshot.

He peered at the scene. The Maidan parade ground was surrounded by a vast crowd of silent Indians. He estimated it at a quarter of a million at least.

There was more constabulary than usual and ropes had been slung to keep the throng from the line of march. There also seemed to be more British than usual. It was possible, Tiger thought, that they were making a public demonstration of their own. Children, exuberant with a good night's sleep, ran happily about. Parents stood watchfully to one side. Strollers, mostly young men and fishing fleet visitors, wandered within the European enclosure. Seeing Margot Danvers with Frank Willis, he remembered that he had promised Mary to help them. He even saw Bunty and several new young men. She glanced once at him, then turned her back. Well, he had warned her. It was "just for now." She hadn't believed.

Tiger glanced at his watch. Nearly eight o'clock. Time for the viceroy to arrive. To the right, beyond Queen's Way, he could see the assembled troops, the rising sun picking out a misty panorama of horse, foot, and artillery. It was a moving and ordinarily a thrilling sight, even to the Indians. This year Tiger heard no murmurs of excitement from the crowd, no standing on tiptoes to watch the marching troops. There was only that sullen silence.

Mary deGive stood deep among the mass of Indians. She was a tall woman and her gaze stretched over the crowd to the distant reviewing platform and its tiny uniformed figures. She knew that Tiger must be there but she felt safe. He would never know that she moved in that vast mass before him.

She walked slowly, calmly, among the Indians. She had made no attempt to disguise her Englishness, wearing her customary garb and going hatless. She was testing herself and testing them. But she met no hostility, only indifference. Perhaps they thought she was a missionary lady, accustomed to moving among them. Perhaps, in their aching anxiety for their beloved Bapu, there was no room for hostility. Not yet.

To Mary it was a colorful crowd. It might almost have been a carnival or one of the great religious gatherings in Benares. There were entertainers of all sorts, dancing bears with rings through their noses, snake charmers with their wicker baskets, jugglers, and groups of acrobats. She saw drink hawkers and peddlers pushing through the crowd and holy men smeared with white ashes, squatting on mats of nails or reciting the traditional tales to circles of listeners.

There were merchants of all sorts, strolling or in impromptu booths, selling brass pots, pans, ornaments, bangles, sweetmeats. She saw that a small enclosure had been set aside for barbers, and some men were having their heads shaved to the pate, while others were having every hair on their bodies removed. Other booths sheltered dentists. There were no chairs, dentist and patient sat together on the ground, dentist seated behind, one hand around the patient's waist while the other grappled for the tooth.

Mary watched it all. She felt calm, even joyous. She wasn't certain why she had come. She just knew she had a decision to make and couldn't delay much longer. She knew also that Edward Goad wouldn't wait. Each day there had been winter flowers delivered, asters, chrysanthemums. Flowers were not the most sophisticated of gifts but Ahmed had brought them with such dignity, such relentless regularity that they bore a meaning too deep to be ignored. Edward was hungry for her and impatient.

A gun boomed and Mary shaded her eyes to peer toward the distant platform. She saw the small figures, all in uniform, turn their heads expectantly in the same direction.

The crowd about her stirred. A sullen murmur rose. Then Mary knew. The parade was about to begin.

As the gun from the Fort boomed the hour, Tiger and Sir Gerald turned their heads toward the early morning mists lying over Eden Gardens. Precisely at the hour Tiger could see appear the lance heads and pennons of His Excellency's scarlet-coated mounted bodyguard. The horses and men emerged from the mist and then came the low-slung state carriage in which Lord and Lady Willingdon rode. Sir Gerald motioned to his aide and they descended from the reviewing stand.

The state carriage proceeded slowly the length of the parade ground to come to rest in front of the governor and Captain Flemyng. The viceroy and vicereine were helped from the carriage by Captain Graham and Lieutenant Vickson, their aides. As they stepped to the ground, the massed regimental bands began the national anthem. All froze respectfully to attention. Tiger, hand at salute, saw that the Indians, restless and indifferent, had continued to move.

The anthem drew to its majestic close and Lord and Lady Willingdon were led to inspection of their bodyguard. Conducted by its commanding officer they marched slowly past the double ranks. Sir Gerald then stepped forward to conduct them back to the reviewing stand, and, as they took their places, a "feu-de-joie," a cannon salute of six resounding "booms," was heard. Lord Willingdon then called for "Three Cheers for His Majesty, King-Emperor, George the Fifth," and was followed heartily by the surrounding British. The bands then struck up a familiar march and there appeared the first ranks of the march-past.

Tiger moved his hand slowly to touch his Webley and felt its squat power beneath his tunic. His left hand rested firmly on the sword at his side. He knew that this could be the moment. The long files of British troops were a challenge to the Indian watchers. It was a gauntlet annually flung in their faces, a demonstration that the power and the glory belonged to the Raj. If ever they would rebel it should be now.

Three regiments of cavalry came first, the Calcutta Light Horse, the Bengal Bodyguard, and the 15th Lancers. Horse-drawn artillery brigades came next, then the quickstepping rifle regiments, the Durhams and the King's Royal Rifle Corps. Short men for the most part, their rifles held at arm's length, parallel to the ground, they marched past the Indians in the short, quick steps of the infantry.

Tiger looked over the heads of the riflemen to the sullen crowd beyond. He began to notice something. He could see a few heads jumping up and down. An occasional bright-colored handkerchief was being waved. He watched more closely. The next group of marchers might tell the story. They would be Scots and the Indians had always responded to the bagpipes.

The first faint wailings of the pipes sounded as the pipe-band came out of the mists. Tiger waited. There was something about the pipes that reminded these people of their own music. It was said that the bagpipe had originated in India. It was an insult in a way. They were being cajoled by their own music.

He saw the first kilted troops, the Calcutta and Presidency Battalion. Then came the swinging kilts of the Calcutta Scottish. The English in the crowd smiled and applauded politely. The Scots jumped up and down, yelling wild Highland yells, and some waved empty bottles. Only the Indians were silent, pressing forward.

Then Tiger heard it, a rising murmur and chatter from the Indians, a few loud hurrahs. He could see more heads jumping, a growing frenzy of colorful waving. It swelled until the applause was a roar to match the skirling pipes.

The bagpipes had won. It was now time to make a decision.

The viceroy turned to his aide. "Cable Poona, Graham. His Majesty's government accepts without reservation the communal plan agreed upon and withdraws its own plan."

The viceroy hesitated, then smiled. "Add my own personal wishes for the Mahatma's speedy recovery and return to good health. I would like to wish him bon appetit but shall restrain myself. Now, it is time to return to Belvedere."

Tiger closed his eyes. They had won. Mercurial people, the Indians, even childlike at times, but the anger and sullenness were gone. He watched the viceroy and Lady Willingdon descend from the platform and walk toward their carriage. Remarkable man, he thought. Walking a tightrope, right to the end.

Mary, a quarter mile away, felt the change in the crowd. She heard the bagpipes approach and saw the sudden exuberance, the quick replacement of anger by open pleasure.

They pressed forward about her, running, standing on tiptoe to watch the approaching pipe-band. The fierce, high skirl of the pipes sent shivers through Mary as well. This was a victory tune. There was no doubt of it. The Raj and these people were one.

For the first time, Mary knew the meaning of patriotism. She had always taken England and the Empire for granted. It was not something one discussed, much less questioned. But now she felt a pride in her people. No one had panicked. They had been worthy of their ancestors, as she must be. She looked about her and, for the first time, felt at home in India.

The viceroy's cable was quick to reach Poona, and the Mahatma, after some hesitation, pondering whether or not acceptance of the British concession might not now be up to the leaders of the Untouchables rather than himself, agreed to break his fast. He was persuaded that he had already wrung from his body the full measure of sacrifice.

At five o'clock on the twelfth day of his fast nearly two hundred people gathered in the familiar courtyard. The yard had been freshly sprinkled with water and Bapu lay on his cot under the mango tree. About him were gathered friends, inmates of his ashram, Hindu leaders, both caste and Untouchables, his wife and son.

At five o'clock his wife, only recently released from prison herself, handed the Mahatma a glass of orange juice. He drank it and his struggle—against Hindu narrowness, against the British—was finished. Men applauded and smiled. They said that the hand of love had been clasped in love. The cry that was "to reach to the throne of God" had been heard.

Gandhi was silent. He knew there was one adversary still unheard. He looked beyond the courtyard toward Calcutta.

At York House Edward Goad was sitting down to his midday tiffin. He had just heard the news of Gandhi's fast-breaking and paused for an unaccustomed moment of silent thanks. He had weathered another threat of hartal. York House was still safe.

Ahmed entered and stood in the doorway. "Sahib." He gestured silently to the doorway.

Goad jumped instantly to his feet and went quickly to the verandah. He stopped as Mary ascended the steps. Goad's servants were unloading her luggage from an auto.

Goad waited, his curious skin reddening beneath the yellow.

"Hello, Edward." She stopped before him. "Do you still want me?" She smiled up at him.

"Are ye certain?"

"Yes. That's why I'm here."

It was a small wedding. The Jolliffes came and the district medical officer and Mrs. MacDonough. The wedding was held on the verandah with a vicar Goad had brought out especially from Calcutta. He was the only Calcutta resident Goad had invited. Mary had asked the Beauchamps but Denise said she wouldn't let Tom come and spoil the wedding by trying to talk business with Goad.

There was a small reception and afterward the village coolies massed about the great house and Goad presented their new memsahib. The villagers salaamed and, led by Dr. MacDonough, already flushed and a little tipsy, gave three grinning "hip-hip-hoorays" in English fashion.

Mary laughed and tried to say a few words in Hindustani, then Goad waved the villagers away to their celebration, and shortly afterward he and Mary said good-bye to the few guests.

That night Mary lay waiting in her bed. She knew that she and her husband were now alone in the great house. The servants had been given the night off and were joining in the celebrations in the coolie village. She had heard her husband roaming restlessly through York House, even in the corridors on the top floor. She knew that he was now outside on the terrace.

Mary gazed up into the shadowy room. There were faint sounds of drums and flutes from the coolie village but the house itself lay in a circle of silence. Only the thumping of her heart betrayed her, seeming to Mary to sound through the room.

Get up, Mary, it seemed to say. Flee this man. You're not prepared for what's ahead. It's been sixteen years since Tim, and you loved him.

Mary got restlessly from her bed and went to the verandah. She looked down at the ground. She could jump down somehow and run across the fields. There might be someone on the river road or she could get somehow to the Jolliffe house. Anywhere.

Mary gripped the railing, unable to move. She'd wait five minutes more. Then if he didn't come she would flee.

Edward, on the terrace below, was looking out over his jute fields. Below him lay the heavy river, dark against its marshy banks. A bat from the godown swooped past him, soaring hungrily.

Goad neither saw the river nor heard the rush of the bat. He knew Mary waited for him and he knew that he wanted her. He had known that since their first meeting on Chowringhi. Now she was his wife, waiting in her bedroom, yet he hesitated.

It was as though he were waiting for a call. He almost seemed to be listening—waiting for permission. His big shoulders were hunched forward, his head tilted to one side. "Julie," he said. It sounded almost like a plea . . . a plea for understanding.

There was no answer. The jute fields stretched silently down to the river. Only the faint sound of flutes came to the terrace.

On the verandah Mary heard her husband come up the stairs, and approach her door. There was hesitation, then a firm, commanding knock.

Mary moved back against the railing. There was another knock, stronger, and Mary's face was set. She walked calmly into the room to the door and opened it. Her husband could see the tall woman before him, her body full and inviting.

Later, when he went back to his own room, Mary lay on the bed, eyes wide. It was over, her first test. But at no time had there been a kiss. She had taken her place in the ranks.

19

THE TIME HAD COME FOR MARGOT DANVERS TO broach to the Bracebridges the matter of Frank and the Saturday Club. She had spent three weeks in quiet preparation for Frank's tennis, rising each morning early to chivvy him about one of the public courts. Now the moment had arrived for approaching Rufus Bracebridge. The difficulty was that neither he nor Mrs. Bracebridge was even aware that she knew Frank Willis.

One Friday, having persuaded Frank to lunch with her at Firpo's, Margot was gratified to see that several of the Bracebridge friends were present. She was quite prepared for the questioning that evening.

"I understand you took tiffin at Firpo's today, Margot," said Mrs. Bracebridge. They were having coffee in the sitting room. Mr. Bracebridge preferred that to the verandah during the cold weather. A fire could be made up in the sitting-room grate and he always sat close to it, a sweater under his tweed jacket, a blanket across his knees. His blood had thinned to such a point that in anything less than bright sunlight he felt a chill.

Margot nodded casually and Mrs. Bracebridge continued, her voice carefully placid. "The Dunhams were there. They said you were with this rugby fellow. What's his name?"

"Frank Willis," said Margot.

"He was evidently quite attentive to you." Lydia Bracebridge beamed at Margot benignly. She was a short woman, as small as her husband was tall, and her feet barely touched the floor. Margot always had an impulse to jerk down on her feet just to see if she would topple forward.

"He's quite nice," said Margot firmly. She wasn't going

171

to defy Mr. and Mrs. Bracebridge but neither was she going to show uncertainty.

Mrs. Bracebridge glanced at her husband, holding his blanket about his waist. "Mr. Bracebridge is somewhat concerned. Your father has entrusted you to us."

Margot decided that the time had come. "He has asked me to marry him."

"Marry him!" Mrs. Bracebridge leaned forward in her surprise, coffee cup suspended in midair. Now, thought Margot, it would be easy. Just rush over and pull her forward.

"Marry him?" echoed Rufus Bracebridge. He sounded puzzled.

"I know what you think. He is a shopkeeper. In retail. But he likes me and I like him."

"Of course, said Mrs. Bracebridge. Her voice rose to a squeak when she was deeply moved. "But you must think what it would mean if you married him. Calcutta isn't London; it's really quite small. Tell her, Rufus."

"Retail," said Rufus Bracebridge, shaking his head. "Unfortunate but there it is."

"I know," said Margot. "We'd have a very thin time of it. That's why I thought you might help."

"We?" said Lydia Bracebridge.

"Us?" said Mr. Bracebridge.

"I know you've done your best," said Margot. "Introducing me to your friends, taking me about."

"I'm afraid there aren't many bachelors among our friends, Margot."

"I know. So I found one for myself. We could make Frank acceptable, all of us. And we must begin by getting him into the Slap."

"The Slap!" said Rufus Bracebridge.

"It would just need the right person to back him. You could do it, sir. You were a member of the membership committee once."

"Fifteen years ago."

"They still look up to you. If you proposed Frank it would put him over. I'm certain."

"But he's in retail. It's not the custom."

"We can overcome that. He's promised to learn tennis. We have a court here and I can teach him."

"You are a good player," said Mr. Bracebridge grudgingly.

"If he learns to play tennis and gets into the Slap he'll go beyond retail. He's ambitious."

"You do like this man, don't you?" said Lydia Bracebridge. She had settled back in the chair again and was peering at Margot.

"Yes. He likes me too." She didn't add what seemed obvious. There was nobody else.

Mrs. Bracebridge turned tartly to her husband. "We haven't been much help to her, Rufus. We did promise her father."

Mr. Bracebridge was contemplating the wall. It was just like that other time. He had a shikar trophy he wanted to hang on that wall. Every man out there had a trophy of some sort, a tiger skin, a boar's head, a pair of elephant tusks, something to show he had been on shikar. His trophy was a python. He had wanted to mount it on the wall but, being nearly twenty feet long, it would have meant winding it around two sides. Lydia had objected.

Rufus Bracebridge sighed. He could still remember the awful breath of that python. He had sat on a rock to rest, having found no deer to shoot, and the snake had reared itself up to wind around him, staring right into his face. Luckily, his gun bearer had been nearby and had blown its head off. It had been a near thing and he had wanted to mount that snake, head and all. He had been compelled to yield.

Now he was faced with female pressure again. His wife wanted to help Margot with this chap, no doubt of that. She would do anything not to fail her guest, if only not to let Henrietta Thornton pull ahead of her.

"I hope your father will approve of this fellow."

"He will if he's a member of the Saturday Club."

"Humph," said the older man. He wasn't so sure. "The next meeting of the membership committee is in three weeks. Anson Potter is chairman. He can be very difficult. And he doesn't play rugger."

"You'll beat him. I know you will." Margot took her host's cold hand and squeezed it gratefully. He raised his eyes toward the top of the wall. The great length of a python seemed to wiggle derisively. He pulled his blanket closer.

Bunty Cranston could have been depressed. She hadn't seen Tiger Flemyng since York House and she now believed his "Just for now."

She had put so much into her adoration of Tiger but she now saw it was hopeless. He was the only man who had known her body and denied himself more. She should have been frightened, much as a duelist might feel who has used his best thrust and seen it go for naught.

But Bunty was young and healthy and now she was restless. Tiger had let her down and the other young men she had met had seemed much like the too eager or earnest young men she had known in London.

Even Calcutta had disappointed her. There were palaces, to be sure, and the enormous homes of some of the princes. But most of the city seemed to have passed its peak. The business district was crowded and the great homes in Tollygunge, Ballygunge, or around the Maidan may have been impressive in the last century but now looked run-down, even seedy. If this was the Empire, her father might well have died in a lost cause. She felt bitter.

One empty afternoon, walking near Government House, Bunty saw an American flag hanging out over the sidewalk. Something in her responded. She had seen enough films to know that America was exciting. She made her way toward the building. At least there should be Americans in that office, perhaps a cowboy. She might even emigrate.

James Fentress Wilson, United States Vice Consul, was young and Calcutta was his first post. He was not happy. He had not yet found a place to live. He had also found that his work in his first post would include visa issuance. He knew that under his country's immigration laws, the Indian quota was nearly nonexistent. To be visa officer in an office which issued few or no visas seemed to provide little opportunity for advancement. When the office bearer announced a visitor, young Wilson readied himself efficiently.

He cleared his desk of frivolous-seeming papers, a half-finished letter home, his college alumni magazine, a solicitation from his church in Ohio. He checked his appearance, finding a clean, decent-looking young man in black horn-rimmed glasses and the open, earnest look apparently required in representatives of his country.

He went to the door, cleared his throat, and called out the only words he had learned in Hindustani. "Tik hai." They sounded much like his American "okay" and apparently meant the same thing. He retreated to his desk as the office bearer entered, soon followed by the most luscious young lady he had ever seen. He sprang to his feet, nearly upsetting his chair, a typewriter stand, and the desk itself. He recovered, motioned Bunty to a seat, and sank back toward his chair.

Their meeting proceeded according to plan. Not their plan —nature's. Bunty made her inquiry regarding a visa for America, James gave her appropriate forms to complete. It was quickly determined that she also was new to Calcutta. They soon found they had other matters in common, they liked travel, going to the New Empire cinema, Greta Garbo. They disliked the dirty streets in Calcutta, noisy traffic, and pi-dogs. They were obviously highly special people and well-matched.

The result of their meeting was that Wilson pulled himself together rather formally at the end and said that he would be happy to bring to Miss Cranston's house such literature on the United States as might appear suitable. Bunty gave him her address and, when she left, she knew she had put in a well-spent hour.

A week afterward Tiger Flemyng waited in the driveway of the Thornton house for Bunty to come down. Tiger was reluctant to go into the house and wait. Seeing the Thorntons might turn the conversation toward their last meeting at York House and Mary's marriage, which had been announced in the newspaper.

Tiger wondered why Sir John had asked him to accompany Bunty to this party. It had been Sir John and not Lady Thornton who had telephoned him and that in itself seemed odd. Bunty's social life in Calcutta was largely of Her Ladyship's choosing.

Sir John had been a bit vague on the telephone, even somewhat evasive. Tiger had agreed to accompany Bunty. He had that afternoon free of his duties. He also felt he owed it to Bunty for having neglected her since York House. He only wondered what it could be about this party that made the Thorntons ask him to accompany her.

He saw her at that moment trotting down the steps, eager, cute, and with just a trace of that sly look, a kitten that has found the cream.

"Oh, Tiger, it's so nice to see you again." She climbed in, hugged him affectionately, sat back, spread wide her long skirt.

"I made an oath I'd never see you again after York House but then today I relented. As a favor to Sir John and Lady Thornton, that's all. I can't imagine why I need anyone to take me to this party. I could just as easily go by myself."

"I'm pleased to be invited." It was obvious to Tiger she had not missed him in the last few weeks. He had the impression she wasn't even interested in him anymore. There was a too friendly ease about her forgiveness. He wondered again why Sir John had phoned him. It certainly wasn't of her maneuvering.

He drove out of the lane into the side street and then into the Maidan. The afternoon traffic had cleared away and there were only the usual homeward-bound bullock carts.

"It's Regent's Park, isn't it?"

"That's right. I don't know the number but I can find it when we get there."

"You've been there before." He smiled down at her.

She looked a little shy, yet pleased. "Once or twice." Then she blurted it out impulsively. "He's really quite nice, Tiger. His name is Jim. James Fentress Wilson. He's an American."

An American? Tiger wondered for a moment whether this could be the reason he had been asked to go with Bunty. Then he dismissed the idea. Sir John was very friendly with the Americans. One of his poker cronies was the American consul general. There must be another reason.

"Where did you meet him?"

"At his office." She giggled. "I went there to find out something about America. Then I met him formally at the Slap. He was with his burra sahib, the consul general."

"Ammon Walker." Tiger had met him at official affairs, a man nearing the end of his career. Tiger understood that Walker and his wife were childless, were much attached to an aging dog they had carted about the world to various posts, and had made themselves something of an authority on Indian rugs. He was also allegedly a shrewd poker player.

"It was proper as anything with the Walkers. We had to laugh. He's terribly nice. This is his first post."

She rushed on while Tiger half listened. "He's twenty-five and he collects stamps and his father was a missionary."

"Sounds very worthy," said Tiger. He felt relieved that she had found someone else. These days he had enough to concern him without taking on Bunty's eagerness.

He drove carefully. They were out of the Maidan now and

were heading out on crowded Prince Street. The stores of the European shopping district had been left behind and the smaller native stalls appeared.

He was aware that Bunty was speaking to him.

"What is a 'chummery,' Tiger?"

"A 'chummery'?" He wondered why on earth she would be asking a question like that.

"This is a chummery party we're going to. Jim's new chummery. Sir John and Lady Thornton said I could go provided you came. It sounds so dangerous." She smiled up at him, her mouth wide with anticipation.

So this was the reason Sir John had asked him to go. It was a chummery party and he wanted Bunty to be chaperoned. But if just a chummery party, why should she need a chaperon? They were harmless enough affairs.

"Chummeries are the houses bachelors share out here, that's all. Three or four bachelors get together and share expenses. It's the basic system."

"What happens when one marries?" She looked almost mischievous.

"They find someone else. A chummery might lose every one of its original members but by taking new ones in it still goes along. It becomes sort of an institution, even acquires a character of its own."

He wondered in which one Jim had been accepted. It wasn't easy for a newcomer to be taken in so quickly.

"Jim says he was lucky. The other Americans at his office are either married or their chummery is already full. He's in with Ian Palmer-Martin."

"Palmer-Martin?" Tiger tried to recall the name. There was someone on the Calcutta Rowing Club by that name. A big, sturdy fellow, very handsome as he recalled. He had been pointed out to him at Firpo's.

"Jim says he's the only American they've taken in. He says he doesn't understand why but I said he was just modest. Anyone would be happy living with him. Even permanently." She giggled.

"Are there going to be others there?" he asked.

"Oh yes. Jim says there are going to be lots of girls. You know, fishing fleeters like me. I don't care. The more the merrier."

She sat back defiantly. She looked so young, Tiger thought, with her wide mouth and cute nose. It made her whole face look turned up, expectant. And there was something else there he had not really noticed before . . . a glisten in the eye, a moistness on the lips. He sighed. She was ripe, that was it. For the picking.

The house in Regent's Park sat behind a high wall and Tiger parked the auto on the street outside. They were obviously not the first to arrive. They went in through the driveway gate in the wall, crossed a path to the house, and entered. Tiger had seen enough of the compound inside the wall—the tennis court, the garden—to know that this was a well-established and comparatively prosperous chummery. He wondered again what he knew of Ian Palmer-Martin.

They were barely inside the house and his topi taken by a bearer—a surprisingly sloppy and rotund servant for so orderly an establishment—when a young man came flying down the stairs calling Bunty's name. By the blissful expression on Bunty's face Tiger knew this must be "Jim."

He and Bunty clutched each other's hand, then the young man turned abruptly to Tiger.

"You must be Captain Flemyng. I'm Jim Wilson. Welcome to our chummery."

Tiger took the outstretched hand. It was a firm grip, quite strong for such an intellectual-looking young man. Tiger took another look at him. He was what he had heard Americans describe as "wholesome." Below average height but muscular, with blond hair. There was a fresh, open quality about his young face that made it clear why Bunty liked him. In fact, looking at them, both shorter than average, both eager-faced, one might suspect they were brother and sister.

"Come on upstairs," Jim said. "That's where the party is. There aren't too many girls as yet but there'll probably be more later."

He led the way up the stairs. It was obvious to Tiger that if many of the girls hadn't yet arrived, there were plenty of men. He could hear male voices and he could see men's topis and felt hats on the second-floor rack.

"This is our host," said Jim at the top of the stairs. He gestured toward a tall man who was approaching. "Ian Palmer-Martin. This is Bunty Cranston and this is Captain Flemyng. He's the governor's aide as you probably know."

"How do you do, Miss Cranston." The voice was very quiet but deep.

"Hullo." She smiled at the young man, appraisingly.

He turned and again Tiger heard the deep voice, very calm and quiet. "I know Captain Flemyng. Only by sight, however . . . and by reputation."

Tiger was a little amused. It wasn't the most discreet remark to make. There was nothing mocking in the young man's expression, however. This strong-looking man was very sure of himself.

"Please come in," their host said and turned toward the living room.

"I'll take care of Bunty," said Jim and he tucked his arm possessively in hers and led her toward the verandah.

Tiger saw Palmer-Martin glance after them, a rather speculative look, then he turned to Tiger. "Come in." He led the way.

Tiger followed the host. He felt Bunty was entitled to be left alone with her young man.

He could see as he stood in the living room doorway that Jim had been right. There weren't as many young women as one might expect at a cold-weather party, perhaps eight or ten. He did recognize two rather horsy young women who were permanent residents of Calcutta and not fishing fleeters. They had gone back to England for their education, as did nearly all India-born British, but then had returned to Calcutta to take a flat and open a small riding academy. They sat off to one side by themselves but seemed to be quite at home.

Tiger noticed one rather odd note to the party. None of the girls seemed to be very much in demand, not even the strangers. One rather embarrassed young man was sitting with the two sisters, fetching them drinks and chatting dutifully. Another slightly older, corpulent man was also busying himself with drinks for the visitors. They were otherwise quite unattended.

Of men there were plenty. There were at least twenty in the living room and he saw another ten or fifteen in the cardroom and on the verandah at the end of the upstairs hall. They were young, under thirty for the most part. He saw several sturdy-looking young men he surmised might be fellow oarsmen from Palmer-Martin's Rowing Club. The rest were a mixed lot, several of them very good-looking though slightly feminine in feature. He wondered where all these young men had been keeping themselves during his time in Calcutta. Except for the host he recognized none of them.

Palmer-Martin came to him. "Let me order something to drink for you."

"A peg, please. Chotha."

The tall man turned to a nearby bearer. "Chotha peg. Captain sahib."

Tiger noticed that he spoke Hindustani without an accent, not the usual simplified master-servant type Hindustani. He also noticed that the bearer, though young and good-looking, was quite slovenly in his appearance and didn't even bother to acknowledge his sahib's order with the usual "achcha" but strolled indifferently away.

"I'd kick your backside if you worked for me, my lad," thought Tiger. He wondered again how such an obviously superior young man as their host could employ such indifferent, almost insolent servants.

Palmer-Martin turned calmly to Tiger. "He will bring you the drink. If you will excuse me, I will speak with our guests." He stopped to glance toward the verandah.

"Our young James has apparently been diverted. American unpredictability."

He spoke calmly, even gravely, but Tiger felt there was just the trace of an edge to the quiet voice and that the handsome, full mouth tightened a little.

He watched as the host walked among his guests. He stopped briefly at each group of young men to speak and smile, much as a lord of the manor might have circulated among the tenants. Or a Father Superior, Tiger mused, among the faithful.

There was a good bit of drinking as the party went on. No new girls appeared and the eight or dozen already there were left largely to themselves. Some of the young men seemed to take turns chatting briefly. The ones who were replaced returned to grinning with their groups of friends. The girls became increasingly quiet.

It was three quarters of an hour before Tiger saw Bunty again and when she reappeared from the verandah, she seemed distressed.

"Jim's hat is missing," she said. "We can't find it anywhere. It's a white hat. It's called a Panama." Jim came up from downstairs then and she turned to him. "Find it?"

"No." He looked puzzled. "Doesn't seem to be anywhere."

"But I saw it," said Bunty. "It was on the hall rack here when we came upstairs."

"Oh well, it'll turn up. It's just that I've had it several years. Dad gave it to me."

Shortly afterward Tiger, strolling out to a side verandah, noticed a snickering going on among a group of the young men and saw that one of them, an enormously fat and sweating fellow called "Tiny," was wearing a Panama hat.

The hat disappeared as he came out and the snickering stopped abruptly. "Looking for something, Captain?" said Tiny. His face was innocent but his hands were holding something behind him over the railing.

"There's a hat missing. Wilson's Panama."

"A Panama? That's the name of a canal." He stared impudently at Tiger and the others broke into a nervous laugh. "Nobody should wear hats named after canals."

Tiger returned to the living room. He certainly wasn't going to make a scene.

He saw young Wilson and Palmer-Martin facing each other in the living room. Jim looked perplexed and irritated. The tall Rowing Club oarsman was facing him impassively.

"But Tiny took the hat," said Wilson. "I know he did."

"Tiny wouldn't take a Panama. He has better taste."

"Ask him, please. He's your friend. That hat was a present."

"You've mislaid it, that's all."

"But why won't you ask him? I don't understand."

"Because I don't choose to. Simple as that." Palmer-Martin smiled quite calmly.

Bunty now took Jim by the arm. "I think it's time to take me home. Please."

"But it's my good hat. I know someone here has taken it."

"Please, I'd like to go." She glanced from Palmer-Martin to Tiger. The others in the room had stopped their whispering and were watching. "Do you mind?" She glanced at the host.

He ignored her to address Jim. "I think your Bunty wants to go, James. And the other young ladies probably wish to go also."

There were a few embarrassed laughs from the young men as the girls rose silently to their feet. Palmer-Martin turned back to Jim. "I suggest your friends might wish you to go too." He said it as though he were dismissing Jim. Tiger saw that even the servants were listening now, outside in the hall. They were grinning.

"I see," said Wilson. He drew himself up. Quite a change, Tiger thought. He can actually have dignity. The young vice consul turned to him. "You'll take Bunty home, won't you, Captain? There are a few things I'd like to go over with Ian."

"James," said Bunty, putting her hand on his arm.

"It's all right. After all, I do live here."

"Shall I see you tonight?"

"I'll call you."

Palmer-Martin smiled. "That means 'ring you' in American."

Bunty glanced at him, again that appraising look. She looked quite cool, even regal in a diminutive sort of way, it struck Tiger.

"Thank you for . . . for a very nice party," she said, then turned and walked out the door.

Tiger nodded to the host, said, "Good-bye, Wilson," and followed her. The other girls, he noticed when he reached the foot of the stairs, had already gone. He wondered who had found them taxis.

In the car Tiger drove slowly while Bunty sat silently in her corner. So that was why Sir John had asked him to go. He knew something about the Palmer-Martin chummery that even he hadn't known. Sir John probably wouldn't have let Bunty go if Wilson hadn't worked for Ammon Walker.

Bunty finally moved in her seat, her pretty face quiet, calculating. "Those fellows were sissies, weren't they?"

"Probably."

She eyed him. "Do you think Jim is one?"

"Palmer-Martin thought so."

"A girl would really be wasting her time, wouldn't she? And there isn't very much time." Tiger kept silent. "What do you think I should do?"

"That's up to you."

"Do you think I should continue to see him?"

"Do you like him?"

"Very much."

"Then why not?"

"But what if he is . . . one of them?"

"I doubt that he is."

"But he might be. Damn it, Tiger!"

"There's always one way to find out." He smiled down at her, driving the car carefully around a bullock cart.

She shrugged. "That's not infallible I'm told."

"It's a beginning."

"You are immoral, Tiger."

"Fight fire with fire."

She shook her head. "No need for that yet. First we have to find him another chummery."

"I'd let him deal with this."

"He's a stranger here. I'll inquire around. We'll show that Palmer-Martin." Tiger looked at her. He saw that beneath that cute little face was a very tough competitor. He wondered if he hadn't underestimated the little Bunty.

"Those poor girls. Nobody even spoke to them."

Tiger said nothing but he couldn't help thinking. Fishing fleeters really ran into the damndest things. Chummeries like Palmer-Martin's, men like himself. To say nothing of the terrorists or Mr. Gandhi. A girl really had to keep her wits about her.

Then it occurred to him . . . the way Mary did.

The horse and rider galloped wildly across the screen. The film flickered quickly to the rider ahead, twisting backward in his saddle to fire at the pursuer. The theater rang with shots and the music pounded excitedly.

Dolly clutched Rajid's arm, twisting in her seat toward him. The other people in the cinema sat in silence, eyes fastened on the screen.

Rajid sat immobile. It had been a week since New Year's Day and they had spent every evening at a cinema, six o'clock showing. They had attended the Elphinstone the first two days, seeing "Gold Diggers of Broadway." He hated it because the girls wore too little clothing and the hero and heroine kissed each other on the mouth. And he loathed a Tom Mix film because so much was made of the hero's affection for his horse.

Most of all he hated the Indians around him, enjoying themselves, forgetting they were not free. He wanted to stand up and shout, "These films are your narcotics, sent to keep you slaves." He knew he would be laughed at so he sat quietly, hating everything around him, even Dolly.

It had been a week since the British had given in to the Mahatma and still no word from Gupta. It was inexplicable. There had been a few days of excitement in Calcutta when the Mahatma's triumph became known, then the city became normal again. The Indians had resumed their daily lives; the

English were still masters. And Gupta remained quiet. To Rajid it was maddening.

He glanced toward Dolly in the darkness. She sat, one soft leg tucked under her, eyes fastened on the screen, hands clinging to his arm.

It had been a week's holiday for Dolly. Magda had worked her too hard over New Year's. The tea planters, jute wallahs, the Scots on holiday—all had descended on Magda's in even more numbers than usual. They had a lot of time to make up, a certain hunger. There was a savagery about the men this cold weather. Times were uncertain and jobs were shaky. There was more hard drinking than usual.

Dolly was new and luscious. But she was too tender for the use to which Magda had put her. According to the doctor she had been a bit torn inside. She had to take a week off. No male intimacy of any kind, and that included Rajid.

It had been a terrible week. He had spent six interminable evenings in cinemas, being clutched by this delicious girl, being pressed against, fondled, clung to, then sent home to his room with only a kiss. It might have been funny to some people but for Rajid it was only one more reason to hate the cinemas.

The film ended in a last burst of gunfire. Tom Mix and his faithful horse rode away into the desert and "The End" appeared. A recording of "God Save the King" began its customary closing and the few Europeans in the balcony struggled to attention. The Indians in the pit filed indifferently toward the exits.

Rajid walked up the aisle and Dolly fell obediently in behind, still bemused by the film. They pushed out of the cinema and turned off toward a narrow street. Rajid lit a cigarette and they left the small square and the chattering crowd.

"It was such a lovely film," she said blissfully. She took his arm shyly. "That's the last time we'll see it."

He grunted. They walked in the narrow street.

"It's such a pretty night." She drew a contented breath.

"It smells in this alley. It always smells."

"I like the way it smells. It's comfy."

He turned savagely on her. "You never see anything wrong. That's urine you smell, and sewer rot. We have no proper sewers."

"Rajid, you're hurting me." He dropped his hands from

her arm. She took his arm affectionately, leaning her head against his shoulder.

"I know it hasn't been easy for you this week. Perhaps I can stay with you in your room all night tonight."

"Not in my room," he said harshly. He lived behind a brass-worker's shop. It was noisy because the old Tamil, a skilled metal-worker, heated and hammered his pans, trays, and pots for the next day's market. It had been safe there for Rajid. The police would never think of a man hiding behind such a conspicuous noise.

"I don't mind. I like the noise." She knew Rajid was ashamed of his room. He cursed the noise when they made love but she always drew him closer to her, soothed him.

He searched her face, suddenly hungry for her. "Are you all right? Could you stay?"

"If you want." She went on. "It would be nice if I didn't have to go back to Magda's at all now."

"Why not?"

"I'm sixteen. It's time I was living a bit different."

He knew what she was getting at. She was beginning to feel he should find a job and help support her. She would be wanting to marry him next. And she an Anglo-Indian—an Anglo-Indian whore.

"It's the films you've been seeing," he said harshly.

"I'd just like to be someplace where I could see you whenever we wanted to." She moved closer to him. She knew he cared about her. It was just like the movies. Tom Mix couldn't tell a girl he loved her either. He had to tell his horse about it. Rajid was proud, that was the trouble. It was because he had been to the university while she hadn't even finished grammar school.

Rajid looked down at her childish face smiling up. She reminded him for an instant of a rubber toy he had found as a child. It had a rubbery face that he liked to twist.

He gripped her. "We'll go to my place."

She slipped her hand gratefully through his arm.

She couldn't see his face, the angry eyes. For Rajid knew what he would do now. He would rip up in one night what it had taken the British a whole weekend to do. He would make this Anglo-Indian whore scream.

He walked with his arm around her waist. The sweet-acrid stench of burnt ghee filled the alley. The houses leaned toward each other overhead as though to protect heaven from the sight of them. The winter stars winked jocularly.

A few days later Rajid had a summons from Gupta and again took the tram out to Garden Reach. He was not surprised to find six or seven other young men already present. Several were in dhotis and blouses, ordinary Bengali dress, but most wore English-style clothing and were student types like himself. One even sported a large, pointed mustache, English Army style. They were all volubly excited at the victory of the Mahatma over the British.

Rajid was tired and sullen. It might have been fatigue from the two days he had spent with Dolly. Or it might have been resentment at Gupta's failure to get in touch sooner with his followers. In the surrounding gabble he said nothing.

Gupta's aide came to lead them into the small bedroom and Rajid followed. He didn't like this being herded about, even by Gupta. He watched as some of the young men waved newspapers reporting the Mahatma's victory. They said jubilantly it was another blow for swaraj.

Gupta, seated on his cot, listened quietly. His soft, round face was impassive and ageless in the dim light. He played quietly with something that twitched across his lap and Rajid could see that it was the tail of a small monkey. Finally, at their leader's silence, the young men became quiet.

"You are wrong," Gupta said finally. "This is a defeat, not a victory."

The young men looked at each other uncomprehendingly. "But they gave in," one said.

"They gave in on the wrong cause. They let the light fall on Untouchability as an issue. What do they care about Untouchability? What do we care! That is a minor issue."

"Not to the Mahatma," said one.

"To us. We are revolutionaries. A revolution cannot be brought about by a man not eating. A revolution must be violent. There must be destruction, chaos. As in Russia. There was a war and everything was destroyed. Then there was a revolution. Not by a man saying, 'I will not eat.' "

For a moment there was anger in his round, placid face, then he controlled himself, looked down at the monkey in his lap, and slowly stroked its ratlike tail. "We have been quiet while this man fasted because if the English had let him die he would have done our work for us. The streets would have run with blood. But the English let him die just enough. This viceroy is very wise. Now they have drawn Gandhi away from independence into Untouchability. We must bring the people back. There must be another killing."

The men breathed heavily. This they understood. "Another magistrate?" asked one.

"He has not yet been selected. This is very important. Whoever it is he must be the spark. Meanwhile you will keep yourselves in readiness."

"You have brought us here only to tell us to wait more?" It was Rajid. He was pushing himself through the others. "It is more than a month since the last killing. I am tired of hiding in this city."

He stared down at the man on the cot. The others shifted uneasily. There were murmurs. "Rajid wishes to kill everyone himself—he is a great shikar." There was laughing.

"Why are you so impatient?" said Gupta. "You are hiding in a very pleasant place."

The others laughed. Rajid's arrangement with Dolly was not unknown to them. Gupta nodded judiciously. "You could perhaps dress as a girl and persuade Magda to hire you."

The young men broke into wild laughter. Rajid, delicate and slender, was not the most male-looking of men.

Gupta looked up at the angry face. "I will select the proper person and then I will let you know. Especially you, Rajid." Then he turned to the others, put his hands together. "That is all. Salaam."

"Salaam." The others bowed obediently and turned toward the door.

"Rajid," Gupta called. Rajid came back to the little man. Gupta looked up at him thoughtfully. "This Dolly is very pretty I am told."

Rajid said nothing. The soft little man below him spread his hands in explanation. "A revolutionary cannot play too long with a woman. It ceases to be play."

The face above him was angry, Rajid's chest heaving with fury. Gupta nodded placidly. "That is all." Rajid hesitated, then rushed out the door.

Gupta sat silently on the cot. His bodyguard entered and opened the window, pulling aside the thin muslin hanging to admit the evening light. A soft breeze pushed at the curtain and found its way into the shadowy room. The guard returned to the anteroom, came back with a plate of ghee mixed with pani which he set beside the bed, then withdrew.

Gupta set the monkey beside the bed. It hopped toward the plate, sniffed at its evening meal, then glanced cautiously toward the shadowy corners of the room. Satisfied, it bobbed its head quickly toward the plate.

Gupta, on the cot above, pondered the visit of his young followers. They had a cause, the freedom of India. This was a weakness. Terrorism must be an end in itself. It should be directed not only against the British but against all humanity.

Gupta could remember his own first violence. It was perfect because it was so purposeless. He had simply walked up to an old man and bitten off his ear. He was sixteen but he knew then the first holy joy of senseless violence. His mother had called him a crazy boy, a vain and egotistical fanatic. She didn't know. It was his father who had understood but he had died in an asylum when Gupta was not quite twenty.

Now someone must be killed. It was his holy duty to kill someone. People must be reminded that nature was cruel, that one could not ignore nature or the species would disappear. There remained only to select the person and the executioner.

Gupta pondered. The Englishman to be killed did not matter. In fact he preferred an unimportant victim. It was more senseless, therefore more suitable. The manner of the killing was important—the victim to be at some commonplace activity. It added to the horror of it.

It was the executioner who must be carefully selected this time. Gupta considered his followers as a surgeon might examine his instruments. Then he nodded. He knew whom he would select. Rajid. Rajid didn't know it himself but he was afflicted with the torments of a love peculiarly his own. He hated this Dolly; she was an Anglo-Indian and she was a whore. Yet Gupta knew Rajid was with her every night, even sat with her through those films the stupid girl liked. Rajid was in turmoil. He was a man of hate and he was in love.

Gupta was pleased. This would be a very satisfying killing. Both the victim and the executioner would be destroyed. It would be worthy of Nechayev himself.

20

THE RICKSHAW SLID DOWN THE INCLINE ON ITS
snowy runners. The two hillmen behind and the two in front
leaned back against their shaft harnesses and brought the
rickshaw slowly to the bottom of the street. With a grunt
from the leader they shifted forward against the harness and
Mary felt the pull as the rickshaw tilted for the climb to
the next rise.

One of the men at the rear coughed and spat in the snow.
An answering cough came from one of the heaving men at
the front. He spat to one side and, as the rickshaw climbed
heavily past the spittle in the white snow, Mary could see
that it was red.

She closed her eyes. "This is far enough, Edward."

"There's just another rise. Then it's downhill most of the
way." He sounded hearty, full of gusto.

"We can walk it."

"All right." He put his foot firmly on the shoulder of the
front man to the right of the shaft and the Sikkimese turned
up his Asiatic face, still pushing at the shaft.

"Achcha," said Goad. He gestured to the ground and the
men stopped, holding the snow runners steady. They had
reached the top of the slope and Mary could see the street
slanted away before them to rise a hundred feet beyond. It
looks, she thought, like a roller coaster at Brighton. She loved
roller coasters. She always felt sick on them but she loved
that first plunge.

Her husband stepped down and gripped her hand hard
as she climbed out. The four men maneuvered the rickshaw
to face the other way and then went sliding back down the
narrow street toward the hotel. Now, she thought, they'll

take their stand under our window and I'll hear them coughing all night.

"Let's sit a moment," she said. "Here's a bench."

"Won't it be cold for you?"

"It's all right." She sat, pulling her heavy coat tighter. It
belonged to the wife of the hotel proprietor, a considerably
smaller and stouter woman than Mary. It kept most of her
warm, however.

Edward sat beside her. He was wearing his heavy sweater
beneath his jacket, better prepared than Mary since he had
been in Darjeeling before in wintertime.

"What is that mountain? There across the valley."

"That's Kanchenjunga." He flapped his arms heavily across
his chest.

"Kanchenjunga. It's as beautiful as its name. Does it always
have snow on it?"

"Always. It's twenty-eight thousand feet," he recited.

"It seems so close, almost as though you could reach out
and touch it."

"You'd need a long arm. That's over forty miles."

"It looks three or four. The air is very clear up here." She
shivered.

"Cold?"

"A little. It's so high. It must be terrible for those rickshaw
men. Did you hear them? One of them was spitting blood. It
sounded like TB."

"It probably was."

"Why do they do this kind of work? It must be killing for
them."

"They don't do it long. Four or five years."

"Then they retire?"

"Some. Some die." He sounded cheerful.

"How terrible." Suddenly the mountains didn't seem so
majestic, but rather like great oppressive monsters peering
down at them. And the village, clinging to the hillside, its
two streets winding up and down like spidery threads, was the
center of a web. Their conversation, always so carefully impersonal, had suddenly the note of a terrible reality.

He shrugged. "There isn't much work up here during the
winter. These men are lucky to have any work at all. If they
live, they'll be well off in Sikkim or Nepal or wherever they
come from."

"And if they don't?"

"There are hazards in every work."

"Let's walk from now on."

"Are you ready to go on?"

"Yes."

She took his arm and they started down the street toward the village center and the marketplace. She knew from previous trips that there'd be no one there but at least it was a place to go. They walked and slid down the street, up the other side. After a half mile Mary felt herself puffing in the high mountain air but she wasn't going to slow down. Goad walked purposefully ahead, holding out his hand to her going up the slopes, steadying her going down. They reached the market square in a half hour.

It was deserted as usual. It did no good for Goad to tell her that market days in the hot weather were gala and colorful, that the market square was always crowded and the products of these hills—pottery, woven goods, teas from nearby gardens, bright shawls—were plentiful and cheap. The market square that day was forlorn and unused.

"Would you like to go further?" asked Goad. "There's a tea shop at the far end of the village. It might be open today."

"I think I'd rather go back. We can save the tea shop for tomorrow's walk."

"Do you want me to fetch a rickshaw? There might be one near the Residence. There's bound to be someone there who might use one, even a caretaker."

"I'll walk. You ride if you wish."

"As a matter of fact, I think I'll just go on. It's another two hours before dinner. It's quite safe for you up here alone." His expression was solicitous.

"Of course, Edward. You have a good time."

"I shan't be long. I might discover some place for us to walk tomorrow. Some place new."

"Good. Take your time."

"Cheerio, Mary."

"Cheerio."

He nodded to his wife, then walked away.

Mary started out of the square toward the upper street. The cold air bit into her cheeks and brought a faint touch of pink. The sharp wind picked at the blue scarf she wore over her hair and a few loose strands rustled against her neck. She turned to look back and saw her husband climbing out of the square on the same street. He turned when she did and waved. She waved dutifully, then they went on.

She wondered momentarily whether she should go with him. This was her honeymoon. She was expected to be wifely and companionable, to go where he goes, like what he likes. Even rickshaws with tubercular, undersized hillmen, two to each end, all coughing. She looked toward her husband but he was already out of sight.

It was only a mile to the hotel but the path went up, then down, and she was constantly climbing and sliding. She was glad to see the elderly, wooden hotel and the few lights in the wing still kept open. A Christmas tree, wan and peaked in its scanty decorations, beckoned from the lobby with thin, naked branches. Mary hurried past the lone rickshaw, the men motionless in their yellow blankets, opened the leaded, colored glass door, and entered the hotel.

It was late afternoon and the lounge had its customary predinner complement of two bachelor tea planters, apparently spending their holidays over a game of draughts. The little Portuguese schoolteacher from Goa and his wife were nowhere to be seen and she assumed that they and their three solemn children might be taking their afternoon hike. From their seeming bewilderment at their surroundings and the great distance from Goa, Mary had wondered whether the parents had really known where and what Darjeeling was.

She shook the few flakes of snow from her scarf and coat, paused to get her breath, then climbed the wooden stairs to their corner bedroom. She stirred the grate fire, then threw herself on the creaky bed. She lay there a long time, trying to sum up. What so far could she say of her marriage?

The bad things made her close her eyes. It was strange, even frightening at times. She had never known anyone like Edward. Sometimes he was hearty, even gay, striding briskly through the snow with her. But sometimes he didn't speak at all, an hour at a time, but simply sat staring out at Kanchenjunga or went for walks by himself as just now. And always, beneath the heartiness and solicitousness, there was a certain mocking quality, as though there were a joke on someone, perhaps both of them.

There was one place where he seemed his true self and that was in bed with her. The evening would begin well. He would buy a bottle of wine at dinner, acting very jaunty, then would walk with her afterward on the snowy terrace, being attentive. Once he had even hired a native band, flutes and cymbals, a cacophony of hill music. Then he would lead her politely to their room.

Then there would be a change. He would hover impatiently while she undressed, would finally pull at her clothing himself, tearing at her much as he might have unwrapped a bale of jute, then, with no preliminaries, he would savage her on the bed to a mutually frustrating exhaustion. He would then leap from the bed—no tenderness, no peace afterward—to disappear into the bathroom for noisy soaping and sloshing of towels. It was all hygienic and horrible.

She wanted to leave, return to York House. She wanted to lose herself in her job. Things would be different then. She would run the house, learn to ride, study Hindustani. She would be everything a proper memsahib was supposed to be.

But he didn't seem to want to leave. He couldn't be enjoying this cold honeymoon—the deserted streets, the cold drizzle—any more than she was. Yet he stayed on. It was almost as though he were afraid to return. Why?

Edward Goad was walking on the hill above the village. He had visited the tea shop and found it closed, as he knew it would be. He now put off returning to the hotel.

He looked down at the village. It was all so damned out of season. The hotel had seemed lively on his previous visits, a place in which to forget things. Now he saw that it was just a drafty, ramshackle old barn.

Nor had he realized how cold it would be. He had to drink wine each night at dinner just to keep warm. He always arrived early for meals because the dining room was at least warmer than their bedrooms. As for those turns on the terrace before turning in at night, it was all he could do to keep his teeth from chattering.

The trouble, of course, was that he wasn't certain just how much he was expected to put into this marriage. Was it a marriage or just a business arrangement? A man couldn't go about showing tenderness and affection where it wasn't expected. He'd make a fool of himself. For the moment it was certainly best to keep it impersonal, including the bed business. At least he tried to get that over with as quickly as he could.

Then why, he wondered, didn't he return to York House if it was so bad? It was clear enough that Mary wanted to get away. She was probably just as confused as he was about the whole thing. Why the blazes didn't he take her home?

A groan broke from the big man. He knew why he stayed on. He was afraid to go back. He had betrayed . . . there would be punishment.

He stayed on and made Mary pay. He walked her up and down the slippery streets, exposed her to TB, the coughing and bloody spittle. By punishing her he was easing his sense of betrayal.

But he couldn't stay on forever in Darjeeling. Sooner or later he would have to go back to York House.

The next afternoon Mary and her husband strode briskly from one end of the village to the other, not once but several times. Mary finally sank onto a bench.

"I must get my breath." She glanced up at her husband. He looked so big and bulky in his sweater and coat. His reddish hair was covered with an old felt hat but his nose, cherry red in the cold, made his curious skin seem almost pale.

"Edward, how long are we staying in Darjeeling?"

"You don't like it. You are not happy on your honeymoon."

"Not at all. I simply think it is time we went back to York House. It's our home."

"You are bored. On our wedding trip." Again that terrible mocking quality.

"Edward, listen. I want to speak frankly with you. I know this is a fishing fleet marriage. You might very well look on it as purely a marriage of convenience for us. But that doesn't mean we cannot have a good marriage. I want to be a good wife, Edward. I intend to be. I want to go back so I can begin."

"I feel we have already begun. Very handsomely." He patted her quite vulgarly.

Mary felt herself flush but she spoke calmly. "I am glad you are pleased. That is part of it, of course. But there are other things. Running your home, making friends with the neighbors . . ."

"You are determined. Come, no more of it now. Tomorrow we'll climb Tiger Hill. You can see Everest from there. Over a hundred miles."

That night the temperature warmed and Mary could hear rain pelting on the wooden roof and tin gutters. She lay awake and listened. There would be no climbing Tiger Hill that morning.

Her husband said little at breakfast and disappeared soon afterward. He returned in a few moments.

"The proporietor says Tiger Hill should be perfect tomorrow. He suggests we get an early start even if it is raining."

"Very well. I'll be ready."

"I've told him we were returning to York House now." He said it so abruptly that Mary thought she had misunderstood. Then a curious smile twisted his mouth. "We will leave in an hour."

An hour later they began the long drive out of Darjeeling down the crooked mountain road to the railway junction at the foot of the mountains. It was a silent drive. Mary watched the fir trees change into pine and finally she saw the first palm trees. It was at the final turn in the road.

"Stop," Edward said to the driver. "Chup." He tapped him on the shoulder. The auto stopped at the shoulder of the turn and Edward pointed. "There's India."

It was breathtaking. Below them Mary could see the flat plains stretching south to the horizon. Behind her the rain and fog were withdrawing into the mountains and the fields and villages below were bright with sunshine.

"Oh, Edward, it's beautiful."

"All the way to Ceylon. More than twelve hundred miles."

"I want to get home." She moved closer to her husband. He looked down at her, a searching, brooding look.

He tapped the driver's shoulder. "Jao." The syce released the brake and the car rolled ahead toward the plains.

Back at York House Mary set about becoming a mem. Her husband resumed his personal management of the estate, even eating his tiffin in the fields with his overseers. Mary had plenty of free time to devote to her plans.

She wished to begin by learning Hindustani. She knew it would be difficult—her memory was no longer young—but she was determined. She had a grammar sent out from Thacker, Spink & Company, booksellers in Calcutta, and had a native munshi sent up from the coolie village, a wizened little man who taught the coolie children. Each morning, reading glasses set determinedly on her nose, Mary spent two hours with the munshi.

"Ek . . . dho . . . teen," he would say. "One . . . two . . . tree."

"Ek, dho, teen."

"Chau . . . punch . . . chhe. Four . . . fibe . . . six."

"Cau, panch, chhe," repeated Mary.

"Not panch," he corrected. "Punch. Like dee drink. Dee drink hab fibe juices."

"That is why it is called punch."

"Ah," he said, shaking his head sideways in that maddening affirmative that to Mary looked so negative. "Sat . . . ath . . . nau . . . das," he continued. "Seven . . . eight . . . nine . . . ten."

"Sat . . . ath . . . nau . . . das. It is very like French," she exclaimed. "Sept . . . huit . . . neuf . . . dix."

"French and Hindustani . . . dey bot come from Sanskrit, dee mudder of tongues."

She wondered why, since he seemed to know some French, he spoke English so badly. "Seben" for "seven" and "bot" for "both." She hoped she would grow accustomed.

Mary also thought it high time she knew how many servants she would have to manage. At first she tried to find out for herself. If she saw a strange Indian face in the house she would follow it, hoping to catch it at work. She felt rather silly and, since she couldn't have spoken to the Indian anyway to inquire as to his duties, she finally went to Goad's office babu.

"Bannerjee babu, you keep the accounts. Please tell me how many servants we have in York House."

"Oh, memsahib. Bhery many . . . bhery many."

"How many? Four? Eight?"

"Four? Eight?" The elderly man laughed wheezily.

"Tell me." She knew she had to be patient with these old employees of her husband's.

"Let me tink." He slowly opened his ponderous account book. He then glanced sharply up at her. "Dis tik hai by Goad sahib?"

"Hah." She waggled her head in the negative-affirmative. "Tik hai by Goad sahib." She actually hadn't asked her husband for permission to query his babu but she didn't see why she shouldn't know how many servants they had. She would mention it to Edward later.

"Tik hai," Bannerjee repeated. He glanced into his ledger. "Ahmed. He is head bearer."

"Ahmed. Ek," she said, counting on her fingers.

"Sooshi. He Ahmed helper. Assistant to head bearer."

"Dho," she said.

"Indra. She your ayah."

"Teen."

"Hamid and Ghopal. Two table bearer."

"Chau . . . punch."

"Samid . . . Feelah . . . Bumtoo. Cook and two cook helper."

"Chhe . . . sat . . . ath."

"Chumaree . . . Sinthal. Sweeper and sweeper helper. Sinthal dee son. Chumaree dee fadder. Bot harijans, mem. Untouchables. Dey good sweeper."

"Nau . . . das."

"Duleep . . . Muntra. Dey work in garden."

"Eleven . . . twelve." Mary had run out of numbers. "Never mind the names, Bannerjee babu. I will never remember so many."

"Der is one auto syce. He take care of sahib auto."

"Thirteen."

"Horse syce for sahib horse, anoder syce for memsahib horse."

"Fourteen and fifteen." She had counted all the fingers on both hands, one hand twice.

"Subhidar. He night watchman for York House. Once Gurkha soldier."

"Sixteen."

"Dhobee. Dat is laundryman."

"Seventeen."

The babu closed his ledger. "Dat is all regular serbant. Dey is few more do little tings. Repairs. Tings like dat."

"Seventeen servants." The prospect was wearying. "Ahmed runs them all?"

"Ah, mem." He nodded sideways. "He hire serbants, he pay serbants, he feed serbants. He also sack serbants." His old eyes twinkled.

"What else does Ahmed do?"

"Ebbheryting. He buy all food for York House, all spirits. He tell cook what sahib hab for hazri, tiffin, and khana. Ebbhery meal. Ahmed wit Goad sahib fourteen year. Ahmed bhery important."

"I see he is. Thank you, Bannerjee babu."

"I not sure sahib want you know all dis. Sahib leab ebbhery-ting to Ahmed."

"I won't mention it, not yet at least. How much do we pay all these servants?"

"I tink it come mebee to six hundred fifty rupee ebbhery mont. Dat is twentee-fibe pound."

"Twenty-five pounds. Each?"

He laughed. "All, mem."

"Good heavens. Thank you." She walked away. She was stunned. She had never run a home of any sort. Here she would not only have the responsibility of managing seventeen servants but they were paid only twenty-five pounds in all, about what one might pay two servants in England. They couldn't be the most efficient of servants.

One thing was clear. Ahmed was the uncrowned ruler of York House. He had complete control over Goad sahib's daily living. She could either accept his dominance over her home or try running the house herself. She decided that for the moment at least, she would let sleeping dogs lie. She would turn her attention to other things.

One night after dinner with her husband Mary spoke up. They had retired to the verandah and he had buried himself behind his *Statesman*. Mary went to sit in front of him.

"Edward, I want to ask you something. Please." She took away his newspaper. "It's surprising, I know, but I would like to learn something about jute."

"Jute?" He peered at her. "There are books."

"I want to take part in it, the way you do."

"Jute is man's work. It's not for ladies."

"I should know. This is the greatest jute estate in Bengal. Where better could I learn?"

"What do you want to learn?"

"What is the estate doing now?"

"Harvesting. We'll be stripping the stalks soon."

"What are you doing?"

"I?" He laughed grimly. "All of it. Checking the retting mostly. That's just before the stripping."

"That's what I want to do."

"Retting!" He broke into a roar of laughter. "You're daft. You have to stand in water right up to your waist."

"Have you done it?"

"I've done everything connected with jute."

"If you can so can I."

"But you have to work right with the coolies."

"You do?"

"I'm the sahib."

"I'm the memsahib. Let's do it tomorrow."

He searched her face. "You fishing fleeters take your jobs seriously." He sounded angry, brutal.

"I want to try."

His expression became almost cruel. "All right. Tomorrow."

He waked her early the next morning, carrying what seemed to be an armful of rubber. He pulled up her mosquito net and tossed the load on her bed. "Put this on. It's a rubber suit. Belongs to one of the overseers. The motor'll be ready in a half hour."

Mary dressed hesitantly but was finally clothed in the awkward rubber. She clumped primly down the stairs, aware that in the enormous boots, the long rubber legs, she looked anything but a dignified ex-instructress in a girls' school. She had decided not to wear a bathing costume underneath but had modestly put on riding jodhpurs, blouse, and sweater. Her hair was tucked under a scarf.

"Ready?" said Goad. She nodded. She noticed he was also dressed in a rubber suit and that it looked patched and well used. "I'll explain what we do as we go. Did you have tea?"

"Yes. Chota hazri." At least she had learned that much Hindustani.

"I've left orders for tea and biscuits to be brought down later. It's best not to work on a full stomach. The water can be cold this time of year."

She climbed heavily into the motorcar and the syce started down the drive.

"Retting is soaking the jute stalks," her husband said. "The stalk is soaked so the fiber is soft enough to be separated from the tissue. It usually takes about ten days. You have to check it every day. Too little and you can't separate the fiber. Too much and the fiber's rotted."

"Is that what we'll be doing?"

"The stalks we'll be stripping have already been retted. They're exactly right."

"Then we'll be doing the separating."

"The stripping. It's not easy."

"I know." She looked down at her rubber suit. "Obviously."

"In the first place we use running water here. Stagnant water would let the fibers soften quicker—they could be loosened in a few days less—but the fibers would be dirtier. Poorer grade. We use clear, hard running water. That means irrigation and that means the stripping ditches are by the river."

"Crocs," she smiled. "Crocodiles."

"Occasionally. And snakes. Water boas mostly." He looked grim. She felt a little less eager. "We keep a guard handy."

"There are hazards in every profession," she reminded him softly. "As you said in Darjeeling." He looked straight ahead. It wasn't funny.

The motor turned a bend in the road, climbed a small rise away from the river, and there it was, the "working area" of the estate. Mary gasped. It was busy and colorful beyond anything she had expected.

On the left she saw lines of irrigation ditches, a half dozen miniature Suez Canals running straight away from the river for a few yards, then parallel to it for a quarter mile. Then, aided by the irrigation pumps, the clear flowing water was lifted back into the river. It was a triumph of engineering, harnessing the flow of the river to the slope of the land.

In each canal she saw long lines of coolies waist deep in the running water. "What are they doing?" she asked. "They seem to be waving snakes in the air."

"That's the jute fiber. They're flailing it in the running water to wash away the dirt and the parasites."

"You said it had to be retted first. Soaked."

"That's already been retted. It was drawn up yesterday. Over there they're drawing up more."

He pointed to the far end of the ditches. She could see coolies, naked except for dhotis, bending down into the flowing water, pulling up long stalks, then tossing them to another line of coolies squatting behind them on the bank. These men were hitting the root ends of the long stalks with heavy paddles, their arms rising and falling rhythmically as they pounded. The softened stalks were then passed along the ditch to another squatting line of coolies—Mary could see women among them—who seemed to be slicing off the broken roots, perhaps a foot from the stem. The shortened stalks were tossed back into the ditch to drift toward the coolies at the nearer end.

It was these coolies who jerked out the fibers from the

loosened tissues and were waving them and swirling them through the running water. They would drop the finished fibers behind them into the stream and at the end of the ditch a line of coolie women was reaching in with long hooked poles to pull the floating fibers to the banks where more women were waiting to carry the cleaned fibers to hang on nearby wooden racks.

"They dry on those racks," said Goad. "Takes a week in this cool weather. Then they're sorted, graded, and baled." He waved toward the high ground over which Mary had seen the mills on her first visit to the estate weeks before. "We raise the best quality jute in Bengal. Uttariya. It's clean, it's soft, and it's strong."

"I had no idea. It's like—what do they call it—an assembly line."

"They said it couldn't be done in jute. There it is."

Mary watched it absorbedly, the lines of coolies bending in the flowing water to pull up the ripened stalks or standing waist deep, their arms waving and flailing the sinuous fibers. She could hear the hollow "thonk" of the coolies on the bank as they pounded the stem roots and the "swish" of the sharp kukris as the squatting coolies slashed off the stems. The water flowed with an even, limpid sigh. Guards with rifles stood watchfully near the raised river sluices and overseers dotted the banks of the parallel canals.

"What are those?" she asked. "Those flowers." She pointed to distant fields of the tall jute stalks and what appeared to be bright yellow flowers on the leaves.

"Those fields will be harvested next. The flowers mean they're ripe. We harvest when they start to fade. Then those stalks are put into retting. That way we always have a supply."

"It's so efficient—the canals, the fields, and the flowers. It's beautiful too." She hesitated, rapt at what she was seeing, then she turned abruptly to him.

"Take me back."

"But you wanted to do something."

She shook her head. "I had no idea. It would be presumptuous of me to butt in."

He was eyeing her again in that appraising way. She felt herself becoming angry. "It was an impulse last night. Call it backing down if you wish."

He slowly began to smile, a bit grimly but a smile. He

leaned forward toward the driver. "Jao. York House." The syce turned the car around.

"I could have stuck it, Edward."

"It's a wiser woman who isn't afraid to beg off. We'll go now and have a good breakfast."

"A burra hazri." She slipped her hand companionably through his arm. He slowly drew away.

For the next few days Mary kept thoughtfully to herself. She had been greatly impressed by the working of the jute estate. It was clear that her husband was a hardworking organizer and a credit to the jute industry. She really must measure up to this man.

One evening they were sitting on the verandah after dinner over coffee. Mary decided it was time he knew her views on a certain matter. She had already broached the question of their neighbors and here, at least, she could be of use.

"Edward, I want to speak to you a moment. Could I interrupt?"

He looked up from his newspaper, waiting.

"I told you in Darjeeling that I should like to know our neighbors better. I feel that is something I can perhaps manage. We might make a few friends among them."

"Very commendable."

"How many neighbors do we have?"

"Near York House? I should say that within ten or fifteen miles, we have perhaps eight."

"English?"

"All English."

"I thought I should begin by paying a call on each."

He put down his newspaper and spoke softly. "Isn't it up to our neighbors to call on you? You are the newcomer."

"But they haven't. We have been home nearly two weeks. There hasn't even been a note."

"Then I think we should let them alone."

"But it's ridiculous. We should have friends in the neighborhood. You are a great man, Edward, a jute sahib. It is high time they ceased resenting you. Jealousy." She paused, flushed and indignant.

"I appreciate your defense of me."

"You don't wish me to go, do you?"

"I think it would be wiser not to."

"But I cannot do nothing here. I will not meddle in your jute work. Ahmed runs our home. That leaves me very little.

And I would like to have some friends. The Jolliffe girl or Mrs. MacDonough, the doctor's wife."

"Mrs. MacDonough." His expression did not change.

"There must be someone I can make friends with. I am not too difficult if I try. Please, Edward. Let me."

He was silent a moment, withdrawn, then he slowly nodded. "Go on. Pay your calls."

"Oh, thank you. I shall start tomorrow."

He went quietly back to his newspaper.

21

"IT'S SUCH A PRETTY BABY." MARY LOOKED DOWN at the sleeping child. "It's a boy, isn't it?" She said it softly. The baby, inside its mosquito net, slept quietly on the cot. The room was shadowy from the lowered blinds.

Kitty Jolliffe nodded. "Ian. After his father."

"I'm afraid we'll waken him in here. Let's go outside."

"If you like. He's a very heavy sleeper." Kitty's pretty face was flushed in the warm room. She cast a last look toward the baby, then followed Mary out to the verandah. It was brighter there and quiet except for the faint sound of a typewriter.

"That's Ian," Kitty said. "He works out in the godown. Then he doesn't disturb the baby. Will you have more tea?"

"No, thank you. Did you have the baby in England?"

"No. I had Ian at the hospital in Calcutta."

"Was it difficult?"

"I suppose so." Kitty puckered up her nose. Kitty seemed so terribly young to have been a mother. "Dr. Allenson is a very good doctor they say. I wanted some sort of—you know —anesthesia. I was a bit frightened."

"Didn't he give it?"

The girl shook her head. "He didn't believe in it. Said

it was a bad example to the Indians." The pretty girl giggled. "We are the sahibs."

"Kipling had it only half right. There is a white woman's burden too."

"Yes. Are you thinking of having a baby?"

"No. I'm a bit old."

"It would be rather nice if someone else here had a baby. There are really no other young women here."

"Thank you."

"I mean . . . well, you seem nearer my age than Mrs. MacDonough." The pretty face frowned.

"What about other problems with a baby? Feeding him and things like that."

"I still nurse Ian myself." She blushed. "I know he's a bit old but I don't mind. Ian wants me to."

"What will you do when that stops?"

"I don't know. Buy things in Calcutta probably. Or have something sent out from England." The girl looked troubled.

"What about local food? What the other babies eat?"

"Ian doesn't want me to. He says it isn't healthy. Dr. Mac-Donough says it's all right but Ian says the baby would get amoebic."

"I see." It was obvious that Ian's wishes were the law in the home. Mary had no desire to cast any reflections on the young father. She hesitated. "I want to ask you something."

"Yes, Mrs. Goad?" The girl blushed. "I hesitate to call you Mary. Your husband is so important."

"Please call me Mary. We are both newly married."

"Thank you."

"I wanted to ask you something . . . it's rather odd. My husband doesn't seem to have many friends in the area. There has never been anyone to call since our return. There have been no chits or anything."

"I haven't come because of the baby. He has had such a heat rash. Ian said he would give you our greetings."

"I wasn't really thinking of you. I have spent the last two days dropping in on other people up here. On the Andersons over at the vicarage, on Mr. Thomas, the schoolmaster, and his wife. I dropped by the Brittingham and Robertshaw estates yesterday. I told them who I was and said I had simply called to make their acquaintance. I wasn't exactly turned out but no one was cordial."

"They're so old, Mrs. Goad. I mean Mary."

"The Thomases perhaps but not the others. After all, we are the only British up here."

"They're just stuffy. They're very settled." The girl seemed embarrassed, even evasive.

"It's something else. I said I hoped they could call on me some day, perhaps drop by for a cup of tea. I even tried to let them name a day. You never heard so many excuses. Is it I? Please be frank."

"You?"

"They may think me a little ridiculous. I am not the youngest of brides."

"Oh no, Mrs. Goad. No one would think that."

"Then what?"

"I don't know. Perhaps you should ask Ian."

"What would Ian know?"

"I can't say. Something that happened at York House once."

The girl stopped. It was plain she was terrified but whether of her husband or what she might know Mary couldn't tell.

Mary stood up. "Thank you for the tea, Kitty. I do hope you will come to York House."

"Oh, I'd like to . . . I would. If only it weren't for the baby."

"Of course."

"Mrs. Goad, please don't tell Ian I said anything."

"You haven't really."

"I know he's rather angry at your husband right now. There's been some trouble. I don't know what it is."

"I shan't bother him. I'm on my way over now to Mrs. MacDonough's."

"Mrs. MacDonough's? Oh, I shouldn't." A frightened look widened the girl's eyes.

"She's the only neighbor I haven't yet called on."

"I don't think I should." Then she blurted it out. "She hates your husband, Mrs. Goad. More than anybody."

Mary felt her face tighten. "She sounds as though she were just the person I should see. Good-bye, Kitty." She moved toward the door.

"Good-bye." Kitty's voice was doubtful. As Mary left she saw the young girl still standing in the verandah door, watching her.

Mary walked slowly down the slight slope toward her motorcar. She passed the godown where Ian Jolliffe worked and she could see him through the open door at his type-writer. His blond, young head was bent in concentration.

She paused, deciding whether to approach him. He looked up and, as he saw who it was, his face took on a sullen expression.

"Good morning," she said.

He muttered something that may have been "hello," then bent again to his typewriter. Mary passed on. This was no time to mention her husband.

She drove her car slowly down the slope toward the river and turned right along the dusty road toward her home. She knew the MacDonough house lay between the Jolliffes and York House and, if she wished, she could stop. It was at least seven or eight miles and on the narrow, twisting river road she would have plenty of time to consider. She wanted to be certain that she wanted to see Mrs. MacDonough.

Mary tried to sum up her impressions of the last few days. What was it about these people that made them dislike her husband?

The homes she had visited seemed typical of British houses in the country. They were bungalows, one story high with a flat roof, part tin, part thatch. There were no cellars and the bungalows were raised on stilts two or three feet off the ground, largely, Mary assumed, as a protection against rain or snakes.

A broad verandah ran across the front of the house, with a railing and lattice curtains of rattan that could be lowered to the floor. The verandahs seemed to be the living rooms of the houses and were covered with cane-bottom chairs, couches, grass rugs. The vicar had an iron-framed piano on his verandah and the retired schoolmaster had a well-used pump organ.

The bungalows stood in clearings, apart from the cooking quarters, and there was always a kitchen garden. They were not large but contained potatoes, pumpkins, eggplants, and green beans. A grove of coconut palms usually stood near the cooking area and the fields behind were dotted with a variety of fruit trees including custard apple, mango, and banana.

Except for Kitty Jolliffe's house Mary had never been invited inside but she had stood long enough on the verandah waiting for her knock to be answered—there were no door-bells—to gain an impression.

There seemed to be no halls. Each bedroom opened onto

the verandah. The walls inside were whitewashed and the floors seemed to be cement. The interiors were shadowy since the only sunlight had first to be filtered past the verandah and through very small windows. It was dark but at least, Mary reflected, it was cooler.

There was one factor that was common to all the homes, the profusion of photos. There was always at least one table on the verandah that contained pictures, some of them slightly yellowing or the frames stained from mildew. There were photos of bridal parties, christenings, regimental groups in the uniforms of the Great War, sports sides—usually a long-ago school cricket team—and photos of parents, uncles, aunts. Most conspicuous were pictures, some only enlarged snapshots of the young and very young, even babies. Mary had no doubt that these were photos of long-absent sons or daughters.

The people themselves she recognized as average, decent. Except for the Jolliffes they were middle-aged for the most part. They were Anglo-Indian families in the old sense of the word, English families who had spent most of their lives in India, as children and adults, as had in most cases their parents and grandparents before them. They were bilingual, speaking Hindustani to their servants as well as they spoke English, and they probably knew Bengali as well. Their servants were as old as the sahibs and served them as their parents had served the sahib's parents. It was feudalism on a very small scale, modest, makeshift, as unpretentious as their bungalows. And, like feudalism, stubborn and long-lived.

But why this aversion for her husband? It was true that their homes suffered considerably in comparison with York House; it was comparing a bungalow with a great, turreted estate house. It was also true that her husband was a new-comer to India, had worked as an overseer, and certainly had no public school or university education. Mary could recognize these handicaps easily enough.

But these people were first and last Raj wallahs. They were imperialists through and through. Edward was a leader in the jute industry and jute was the backbone of the economy. Then why did they avoid York House? What was there about her husband?

She knew the house of Dr. and Mrs. MacDonough lay just

beyond the next turn of the river. She would soon be there. She wondered inconsequentially whether she were correctly dressed for Mrs. MacDonough. She had felt a little conspicuous at her other calls. The wives' clothes had been swadeshi-made by a local durzi, some Indian tailor who had served the countryside for years. For today's calls she had worn a hat and a printed cotton. No one could say she was too casual.

Mary remembered Mrs. MacDonough at the wedding reception. Kitty Jolliffe had been her usual pretty and silly young self, bubbly and preening, befitting a happy young wife. Mrs. MacDonough had stood silently peering at Mary through her steel-rimmed glasses. The rims seemed to Mary less cold than the eyes.

Kitty had said that Mrs. MacDonough hated Edward Goad and Mary suspected her capacity for hatred was nearly limitless. She remembered at the wedding reception that Mrs. MacDonough had used up their brief conversation in scathing remarks about the Indians, calling them "ungrateful" and "feckless" for wishing swaraj. She had managed in the same conversation to make bitter remarks about the absence of her school-age children, in England. Mary knew that most parents in India sent their children home for educating. They managed to be restrained about it through years of separation. Mrs. MacDonough had apparently seized on the separation as one more excuse to berate India and, inferentially, her marriage.

It was also evident at the reception that the doctor drank too much. Mary recognized a trapped quality about him. He was a bon vivant married to this difficult woman. It was a strange marriage.

The car made the turn around the river bend and Mary chugged up the little road toward the house. The Austin, trailing its plume of dust, nosed defiantly about a clump of guava trees and pulled up before the MacDonough bungalow.

There was little difference between this and the other homes. The stilts were a trifle higher than the others perhaps, and an apron of tin had been embedded between the earth and the verandah. It looked shiny and hard, a barrier.

Mary went up on the verandah, knocked on the wall beside the central door, and waited. There was no answer so she moved to glance over the verandah. It was nearly noon, the verandah blinds had been dropped halfway to the railing, and the room was in shadow.

There was a bit more iron than on the other verandahs. The basket chairs had iron casters on the legs and iron sheathing protected the sides of a large, round, and very ugly table. Even the hanging pots of fern had metal bottoms.

There were photographs on the table. One of them seemed to be that of a young handsome man in the uniform of a naval medical officer. Mary was startled to recognize the puffed features of Dr. MacDonough.

There was another photo of two children, a boy of seven or eight and a girl a few years younger. The boy was holding the girl's hand and both peered solemnly out from beneath topis far too big for them. The background was the bungalow and the verandah steps. It was obvious that these were the two absent children.

"Yes?" It was a voice behind her and Mary turned to see that Mrs. MacDonough had come from one of the bedroom doors.

"Oh, good morning. I was afraid there was no one home." She moved pleasantly forward but Mrs. MacDonough made no move to greet her. "I am simply paying a call. I thought it high time I became more acquainted in the neighborhood."

There was no welcome in the woman's face and Mary hesitated. She felt suddenly overdressed. Mrs. MacDonough was wearing some sort of seersucker dress, shapeless and wrinkled.

"Dr. MacDonough is asleep. We have tiffin early." The woman jerked her head back toward the shadowy room.

"Oh. Then I shouldn't disturb you."

To her surprise the woman moved forward. "You can stay. I've wanted to talk to you." There was a certain grim smile behind the hard face and Mary had the feeling that the woman's words were true, that the spider had finally captured the fly.

"I shan't stay long. I know how important it is that your husband have his sleep. He works hard." Mrs. MacDonough grunted noncommittally and Mary changed the subject. "Are these your children? I was just looking at their photos. I can well understand how much you miss them."

"Yes." She didn't even glance at the photos.

"What are their names?"

"Jeremy and Anne." She bit off the names sharply.

14

"Very pretty names. I see Jeremy is the elder." She glanced at Mrs. MacDonough but there was no comment.

Mary felt a touch of amusement. This was really too ridiculous. It was like something out of Madame Tussaud's, speaking to a wax figure in the Chamber of Horrors. Perhaps I should ask her if she's met Jack the Ripper. "I think I should be getting on. I don't wish to disturb the doctor."

"Don't go. I want to speak to you." The woman moved slightly toward her, waited, confident. She was now the spider sure of the fly.

"I understand you've been taking an interest in your husband's jute, Mrs. Goad."

"Oh?" Mary was startled. She hadn't fully appreciated the extent of servant talk.

"You should know that the neighborhood doesn't approve of his methods. They are very unusual." Mrs. MacDonough fairly spat out the last word, in it all the venom of a righteous woman. Mary waited.

"There should be only one crop of jute each year, Mrs. Goad. One October crop. York House has two crops. January and April. He's murdering that land." Her voice rose, then she paused, gathering herself. Her voice was controlled now, soft.

"It's the water too. Water is life in India. In the dry season each drop is valuable. He steals the water with those irrigation ditches he's built. Even in the dry season those fields are irrigated. He wants crops so he bleeds the rivers."

"Ian Jolliffe must approve this. He is the district engineer."

"Jolliffe." The voice broke to a sort of laugh. "He's a boy. He tried to fight Goad. He did only this week. But your husband is Edward Goad, the biggest jute producer in Bengal. They think they need Goad a lot more than a young engineer."

She glared at Mary, then her voice softened. She paused and Mary knew there would be more.

"It isn't only the two crops' ruining the land and stealing the little water . . . it's the way he works his coolies."

Mary knew she should leave. It was wrong to listen to these terrible accusations. "I think I should go."

"You listen." Mrs. MacDonough gripped her sleeve. "He gives his coolies ganja. Bhang."

"Ganja," repeated Mary. She tried to sound knowledgeable.

"Those patches you may have noticed by the coolie village. He's probably told you they were another kind of jute. That's ganja, Mrs. Goad. A drug. Your husband gives it to his coolies so they'll produce more. He forces them as he has forced the land." She came close to Mary, glaring full in her face. Mary thought that Savonarola must have looked like this as he condemned the unrighteous.

Mary spoke evenly. "I am sure my husband would not harm his land or his coolies. The estate speaks for itself."

"It is a disgrace."

"Then speak to your husband. If the coolies are harmed, they are his responsibility as district medical officer. As for stealing the water, as you put it, I am sure there are other estates on the river. Let Jolliffe look into the Brittingham estate for example. Their land is above my husband's."

"It is not they!"

"As for the coolies, I suggest this is entirely up to the DMO, your husband."

"My husband has nothing to do with it." But there was a touch of fear in the woman's eyes.

"Then neither have you," said Mary calmly. "I am sorry we have had this disagreement. Please pay my respects to Dr. MacDonough."

She nodded, her tall figure dominating the verandah, then she moved easily down the verandah steps. She was shaky as she climbed into her motorcar but Mary wouldn't allow the watching woman to see it.

She drove slowly down the road. It wasn't true. It was malice on that woman's part. But she drove faster, barely seeing the road.

When Mary reached York House she went quickly to the small library.

There she found what she was looking for. *Sissal and Hemp*, written by a Scot from Dundee named MacCauley.

She looked through the index until she found under "hemp" the section termed "use as drug." She leafed to the page given, took a deep breath to calm herself, then read.

"The leaves and other tissues of the hemp (cannabis) plant produce a resin from which the cannabis drug is obtainable. As a narcotic it is either smoked or eaten and is known as bhang, charas, or ganja in India, as hashish in Egypt and Asia Minor, as kif in northern Africa, and as marijuana in the western hemisphere."

Mary repeated the last words to herself, then read on. "Potency varies in different regions and the most potent preparations come from plants grown in hot, relatively dry climes and in parts of India." Mary shivered a little. York House fitted both those requirements.

She leafed quickly through the pages for a photo and found one. Her eyes widened. It was undoubtedly a picture of plants she had seen near the coolie village.

The rest of the afternoon Mary fought to control herself. She watched for her husband but he was remaining a long time in the fields. She waited on the verandah, then went to her room, and watched from the verandah. Her strong face was somber now, waiting.

Finally she saw him ride in from the fields and heard him go to his office below. Mary made an effort to calm herself, even pausing to apply a pat of powder to her face and touch up her generous mouth.

She finally descended to the big hall. She could see her husband alone at his office desk and knocked. He looked up as she entered.

"Am I disturbing you?"

"Of course not. Never." He rose politely, gesturing elaborately to a chair. "Please."

"Edward, I would like to speak with you." Mary seated herself. The fields outside the office lattice seemed so tranquil, so lawful in the late afternoon light. Such tranquillity could never be obtained with the methods of which her husband was accused.

"Edward, I have, as you know, been paying visits to our neighbors. During my visits certain things were said concerning your methods of raising jute."

"Oh?" He settled himself comfortably behind his desk.

"It was said that you obtain two crops from our land instead of the proper one, that you use water for irrigation when water is so scarce. It was also said that you work the coolies harder by means of a drug."

"I see you have been calling on Mrs. MacDonough." He nodded genially.

"I shan't say where these accusations were made. I am only concerned with the truth of the statements." Mary was aware that she was speaking like a teacher at Roecroft.

He shrugged. "It doesn't matter. You could have heard this from anyone."

"Is it true?"

"Oh, it's true enough."

"But it's monstrous! It's immoral!" The words had burst from her.

Her husband looked at her and his eyes were contemplative. "I think, Mary, it's time you learned a few things." He walked to the door and closed it. "There's nothing the servants like more than a row between the sahib and his mem." He sat opposite her. "Mind if I finish my tea?"

"It's cold."

"I like cold tea. Very un-British of me but tea is tea." He poured himself a cup and sipped it reflectively. "Let us review this. You have just discovered that the little garden patch by the coolie villages is not a special jute, is not jute at all, but is hemp. And you suspect that the coolies are raising this hemp with my consent in order to make ganja."

"You've just said so."

"Oh, it's quite true. It's not only with my consent but at my orders."

"Edward."

"Let us examine the reasons for this."

"I don't want to know the reasons! It's wrong! You know it else you wouldn't have kept it from me!"

"That had nothing to do with right or wrong. Merely a question of rendering unto Caesar what belongs to Caesar."

"Meaning yourself."

"There is no other Caesar in York Estate. Nor will there be. The only thing you are entitled to know about my business is that it supports us. Very handsomely." He held up his hand as Mary started to interrupt.

"Let me tell you about the jute business. In the first place it is highly competitive. It is so competitive that, as you may have noticed, ours is the only estate of any size in Bengal that is not owned by a company."

"There's Andrew Yule, Tom Beauchamp's firm."

"A company. Andrew Yule died years ago. It has a chairman and fourteen directors. Birla Brothers. A family company for over a hundred years. Jardine Mathison. That goes back to the John Company days."

"The East India Company!" Mary was getting fed up with these localisms.

"It's big. All of them are big. They've grown big by

swallowing up smaller companies, weaker men. York House has fought and survived and will survive."

"By forcing the land, the coolies."

"And myself, don't forget that."

"Not with ganja," she said bitterly.

"There are other ganjas. Pride, ambition. My father was a watchmaker, Mary. A damn good one. He couldn't compete with the new factories, the assembly-line watchmakers. He became an itinerant watchman. We traveled together when I was a boy, all over the Midlands; he repairing and fixing, driving himself until he couldn't anymore and just died."

"I'm sorry."

"No need to be. He never felt sorry for himself, nor did I. But I wasn't going to be a craftsman like him. I was going to be like the big companies, beat them at their own game."

"That's why the working area is the way it is."

"An assembly line. I came out here twenty-eight years ago. Well before the war. I was seventeen. I worked as an apprentice in Calcutta first, then in the jute fields as an overseer when I was twenty-two. That's when I got this yellow skin. Too much sun and quinine. I worked hard and I worked others hard. Now there isn't a jute company in Bengal that could take this away from me."

"Does Sir John know about this? The ganja?"

"Thornton? Of course. So does young Jolliffe and Doctor MacDonough. They can't do anything. Jolliffe tried but they laughed at him in Calcutta. Because I raise the best jute in the Empire."

"Can't you work the coolies without ganja?"

"It works. Why change it?"

"It's wrong!"

"You're sentimental. Empires cost money, Mary. Those parties you went to in Calcutta—the big balls and garden parties you love. They're paid for by scoundrels like me. Those fine neighbors of ours out here, the good vicar and his wife, the nice schoolteacher so happily retired. Who do you think supports their blessed mission schools or pays Mr. Thomas's pension? They know it comes from me, and men like me. That's why they snub me. They may have to take my money but they don't have to drink with me." He was walking restlessly, angrily. It was the first time Mary had seen his face so hard, full of contempt.

"Then all this—the pension for the Thomases, the vicar's school, even York House—is built on ganja for our coolies."

He shrugged. "They'd take it anyway. At least this way they accomplish something."

"I don't know that I'll be able to accept this, Edward. You should give your coolies a chance. Forget the profits. If your father failed you're failing too. As a human being!"

"I'm succeeding as a businessman."

"But you're my husband! I want to respect you. We have to have a marriage!"

"It's a fishing fleet marriage, isn't it? By God, you want too much, Mary!"

He looked so angry that Mary was afraid he would hit her. He recovered himself. "Excuse me. One shouldn't shout at his wife."

There was silence. When Mary spoke it was quietly. "It isn't just the marriage, Edward. I know one mustn't expect too much of that yet. Nor is it the morality of what you're doing. In view of our 'marriage de convenance' I may not be in a position to point to that."

He said nothing. He certainly didn't disagree.

She went on. "We have no position in this country. I found that out this week. I know it doesn't mean anything to you but it does to me. It does to any woman. I would like to be accepted, Edward."

"Marriage isn't enough for you."

"Not the way it is. You have your work but I have nothing to do really. I can't even run this house with Ahmed in charge. We don't have any social position. We don't even go to Calcutta."

"Calcutta doesn't want me there. I embarrass them."

"I would like to give a little party here but, if we did, I doubt anyone would come. They may have to put up with your methods but they don't have to accept us."

"It isn't just morality that makes you want to change me, it's your social position. At least you are honest."

"It's also something else." She hesitated, almost as though unwilling to disclose her views. "I have a very high opinion of the Empire. I know that may not be fashionable today but I happen to believe in it. To me the Empire is a trust. It is a responsibility on us to do our best. Not only for ourselves but for these people too."

"You are old-fashioned."

"Please, Edward, we have to consider our coolies. Give up their ganja."

He saw the plea in her face and, for a moment, he wanted to conciliate her. Then he remembered why he drove his estate.

He shrugged. "You'll just have to take the marriage as it is. I'm not a man to concede to others. I know what they think of me in this area. It's not only my methods. It's because I won't concede to them. I wouldn't join their army during the war. I won't bow at their garden parties. This is my world at York House. I made it and I've invited you to share it. But you'll share it on my terms."

"You'll continue to force the land."

"I will."

"And the coolies."

"Yes."

"At least now I know."

"Now you know."

Mary stayed away from her husband as much as possible for the next few days. She slept in her old room and ate her lunch alone. She and Goad ate their dinners together in silence and, afterward on the verandah, Mary drank her coffee while her husband buried himself in the *Statesman*.

Mary was bitter, shocked. The Empire was better than this. Edward's methods offended her loyalty and every sense of decency. He was wrong, bitterly wrong.

Yet, as she watched him each night reading his newspaper, isolating himself behind the business pages, he seemed terribly alone. He seemed to Mary somehow forlorn, trying to reassure himself with these commercial reports that he was indeed a sahib.

She found herself touched by his nightly isolation. How long he must have sat this way, taking refuge in this ritual! In asking her to marry him, this might well have been what he wished to escape.

It wasn't up to her now to criticize him. He was her husband. Perhaps this was part of a wife's burden in the Raj. She might not always agree with his methods or his morality but no one could deny their success. To criticize him would be to criticize the Raj itself in all its splendor. This she could not do.

One evening Mary left her chair and sank impulsively on her knees before him. "Edward, let's not be this way. I'm sorry for what has happened. Come and have tiffin with me tomorrow."

His eyes were hard. "You are forgetting who I am. I'm the brute who forces the land into two crops a year . . . the lout who feeds his coolies ganja."

"You are also my husband. Have tiffin with me. We can rest upstairs afterwards."

He looked down at her—at the dark hair now cut shorter to be less bother in the coming heat, at the good decent face without lipstick or powder. This was a good woman but he couldn't let anyone tell him how to run York House. Yet he wanted her and she was his, just as York House was.

"Do I have to wait until tomorrow?"

"You're welcome now." She waited until he had lifted her from her knees, then they walked together toward the stairs.

She tried to be an affectionate and yielding woman that night, as obedient as he was hungry for her. There was the same savagery that always caused her wonder. It was a desperation, as though he were trying to put something from his mind.

In the end he won a victory. They sank finally into a mutual exhaustion and sleep. But the bed had been a battle-ground.

The next day her husband told Mary that she could have her party. She could arrange it all. He would tell Ahmed to stay out of it.

22

NOW THAT MARY HAD BEEN GIVEN PERMISSION to have a party she really didn't know what to do with it. She was not very experienced at entertaining. She had presided at teas at Roecroft and had given several small dinners for colleagues. Even her own coming-of-age party, a tea given by her parents at their home for suitable relatives and close parental friends, had required only her presence.

The thought of giving a great ball crossed her mind, a gala with lanterns on the terrace of York House, a string orchestra, the ladies in long, graceful ball gowns. It would be a splendid affair, a Victorian ball in a great estate or something from the American antebellum deep south.

The thought was reluctantly dismissed. Even if it were possible, a ball at York House was no way for her to begin. It might well be considered ostentatious of her, vulgar. It would further alienate York House in the neighborhood.

The invitations also presented a difficulty. Mary didn't want refusals for her first party. There must be acceptances, otherwise a disaster. But who would accept?

There would be the MacDonoughs and the Jolliffes. She thought she could count on them. She would invite the Beauchamps, of course. She and Denise hadn't seen each other since her marriage. The Thorntons . . . she would have to count on Sir John's business relationship with her husband to bring them. But she would not invite Tiger. That must be definite. She wouldn't have him eyeing her marriage in that sardonic way.

As for the other neighbors, she could only invite them and hope for the best. The presence of Sir John and Lady Thornton might induce them. Mary would see that their acceptance, if it came, was soon known.

The only question that presented no difficulties was where the party should be held. At York House, their home.

"How is the party coming?" her husband asked Mary. They were seated on the verandah as usual after dinner. Mary was trying to make up an invitation.

"Slowly."

"When are we having it?"

"I thought in about ten days."

"Have you picked a place?"

"Why, I thought we'd have it here." She looked at him in some surprise.

"York House? I doubt anybody would come. Not the Robertshaws or the Brittinghams. They resent York House. It's a larger estate. Besides, I'm not certain I want them here."

"Not . . . but this is our home." She was astonished. "Do you feel embarrassed that York House is in harvest?"

"Embarrassed!" He roared with laughter. "I don't want

them prying about, counting the stalk flowers, testing the earth. I don't think the vicar would come here anyway. He'd feel he had to go over to the coolie village and set fire to our ganja patch."

"Edward, we have to have a place. It never occurred to me it shouldn't be our home."

"What about the dak bungalow? That's where there used to be parties."

"The dak bungalow? Dak means post, doesn't it?"

He nodded. "They used to run the post and about every forty miles they had a place for the dak wallah to sleep. Now they carry the mail by bicycle or lorry. They've closed most of the bungalows."

"Is there one here?"

"On the river near Duleep-chauraha."

"I don't know. What sort of party could one have?"

"They used to have very good parties. It was used as sort of a club. When the rains stopped each year and the rivers went down there was always a sort of get-together. People from opposite sides of the river who hadn't seen each other in four or five months would come together for about a three-day bash. It hasn't been done, I understand, in a long time. May be all the swaraj talk."

"But what did they do at the parties?" It was all totally new to Mary, almost incomprehensible. She didn't want to make any errors.

"Talk mostly. Gossip. There'd be a lot to say after four months. There'd be card playing, a little dancing to the gramophone. The men might have a shoot and there'd be a paper chase. And there were always children." He was thoughtful a moment. "There seemed to be more children then. They always had a better time than anybody."

"Do you think the neighbors would come there? The Thomases and the rest."

"They used to."

"It might be just the thing." Despite herself Mary felt a thrill. There was something about this; it was the way India should be. She certainly had no other plans for a party.

"There'd been a bar put in and there was a gramophone last time I looked."

"Did you go?"

"Before the war. No much afterward."

"It would be good having everyone together again. I'll go

down tomorrow and look at it." She was pleased, even excited. Goad said nothing.

The next morning Mary and the auto syce drove down to the dak bungalow. It stood in a small clearing over the river and from its verandah Mary could see the hand ferry at Duleep-chauraha and the ferryman hauling on the rope stretched between the river banks.

The bungalow was smaller than any other Mary had seen, having only one room and a verandah, but the room was large, fully twenty feet across. The bungalow rested on the customary stilts and had a sheet iron roof. It might be hot during most of the year but it would be comfortable now. There was no godown or separate kitchen quarters, no vegetable garden or fruit trees.

Mary was encouraged. The floors were still solid. She and the syce tramped heavily on the verandah and the inner floor. There was one solid table inside, a bar at one end, and a gramophone in the corner.

She wound the handle and it squeaked but the turntable still worked. A few records rested to one side; she blew the dust off one and read the label. It was "Dardanella."

She inserted the record, switched the release on, and listened. It was appalling, faint, scratchy, tinny. Yet there was something about it that appealed to her; it seemed just the right touch.

She looked at the other records, blowing off dust to read the labels. "Pack Up Your Troubles in Your Old Kit Bag," "Tipperary," "Just a Japanese Sandman."

Mary was delighted. She would have to send to Calcutta for more records, newer ones, but she would certainly keep these. They would supply the right mood. If the guests were made to feel a trifle nostalgic they might not be in a mood to dislike her husband or her. She had to admit she liked the records too. They brought back her younger days, during the war.

She took a last look about, then went back to York House. She found Edward in his office.

"I like that bungalow. There's quite a bit of work to be done, of course."

"Did you find any snakes?"

"Would there be any?"

"There might well be. In any place that hasn't been occupied for some years."

"I hadn't thought of that."

"There might also be fleas, cockroaches, and scorpions."

"Oh dear."

"Do you still want to try it?"

"I would. Yes, I would."

"Very well. I'll have it put in shape." He turned away.

"Thank you." She wanted to go to him, kiss his yellow cheek, but she restrained herself. She had his consent, that was the main thing.

That day Mary wrote up the invitations. She said there would be a party at the dak bungalow on Friday, January twenty-fifth, and she hoped they would come. She said it would be an "after-the-rains-stop-and-the-river-goes-down" party, the way it used to be.

She sent the invitations and hoped for the best. She counted on servant talk and a general excitement over the fixing up of the dak house to stir up sufficient curiosity to lead to acceptances.

The next week was exciting for Mary. The coolies sent down by her husband were already at work on the bungalow and Mary spent most of her time there. She couldn't talk with them except by hand signals but she could watch.

The estate carpenter found a hole in the floor of the only room, lowered a smoke pot, and three snakes slithered out to be chopped up by the waiting coolies. Mary felt a little sick but the coolies laughed and chattered. The carpenter then boarded up the hole.

The sweepers, father and son, sloshed water inside the bungalow and on the verandah. They then scoured and rubbed on their hands and knees for two days.

Ahmed returned from Calcutta with the list Mary had given him. He had brought as many of the records as were available, "Alice Blue Gown," "Three O'Clock in the Morning," solid, safe tunes, and a few more modern, "Night and Day," "All the Things You Are," and a dozen others.

He also brought back cotton goods for table covers, paper streamers, fancy hats, tiny balloons, and a few nonsense favors. Mary felt such things should be suitable. She and the ayah then set about hanging decorations.

Replies began to come in by bearer. They were all acceptances. Denise added a note saying she was dying to see Mary, "had so much to talk about." Mary felt touched. She hadn't realized how much she had missed Denise.

She redoubled her efforts. She had ordered a croquet set sent up from Bourne, Sheppherd Company, a department store in Calcutta, and would have that set up on the newly cut grass at the bungalow. She would try to arrange for a few boats to be present in case anyone wanted a row on the river. She also considered a paper chase but doubted there would be enough horses. There would be decks of cards for bridge or poker for the men. There would be an outdoor picnic for tiffin and a dinner brought down from York House for khana. They would sit at three or four tables instead of the one large one. It would be less formal.

As for the dinner itself Mary decided to give a proper memsahib's dinner. She ordered a khana that she knew the York House cook could cope with, chicken fricassee, boiled potatoes, sprouts, treacle pudding. For the savoury before the fruit she knew the cook could provide a fried egg on cheese or cauliflower.

The days went by full of activity. The dak bungalow took on the desired appearance. Mary could almost imagine it as it must have once been, with the countryside gathering on horseback or in carriages, full of enthusiasm and talk after four months of being separated by the river. She wondered why the occasion had been allowed to lapse. She doubted it was the swaraj agitation, as Edward had suggested. She felt that the custom was still carried on elsewhere in India, in the tea garden area of Assam for example, where the rains were even more dreadful. She wondered whether the neighborhood might not have lacked a leader. She hoped York House might now remedy that.

Mary was feeling pleased and dedicated. She was even more affectionate with her husband. Goad was coming home at noon each day for tiffin, would take a brief rest with her in their room, then would go down to his office for a few hours of work before returning to the fields. Even he seemed interested in her party preparations.

On the day before the party Mary was awake early, checking in her mind the few last-moment details. Her husband lay sleeping heavily beside her. There was a sudden, quick knocking on their door and Mary could hear Ahmed's voice.

"Sahib . . . sahib!"

Her husband waked immediately. "Quihai?" he called.

"Ahmed, sahib. Jeldi ao. Burra hooroosh."

Goad was instantly awake. "Hum aiga," he called. He

pulled up the mosquito net, jumped from the bed, and went quickly to the door. Mary could hear Ahmed's voice, urgent, low.

"Auto syce bulao," her husband said. "Jeldi." He closed the door, came back toward her, his face tense.

"What is it?"

"You stay in bed." He stepped into his work clothes, khaki shorts, khaki shirt and pulled on his heavy socks and boots.

"But what is it? What is that noise out there?" Mary stepped from the bed and hurried to the verandah. "It's the servants. They're all in the driveway looking toward the village."

Her husband roared at her. "Get away from that verandah!"

"What is it?"

"This isn't for you! Get back into bed. I'll come back as soon as I can." He practically flung her toward the bed, then left.

Mary lay uneasily in her bed. The ayah appeared a few moments later with morning tea but, when Mary asked her what was the trouble, she shook her head fearfully. "Hum ne junta, mem."

"But you must know. Something has happened!"

"Hum nahin junta," she repeated, and went out.

Mary finished her morning tea and went to stand just inside the verandah window, trying to see the village. She could see nothing.

Edward didn't reappear, nor did she see any of the servants going about their usual duties. About ten o'clock she saw the old auto of Dr. MacDonough bouncing crazily toward the coolie village, its tail of dust following apprehensively. Shortly afterward she saw Ian Jolliffe's car also rushing toward the village. She waited an hour but saw neither motorcar return.

Her husband came home after tiffin and, from her room, Mary saw that he was accompanied by Dr. MacDonough and young Jolliffe. She heard angry words from Edward's office and, as she hurried down the stairs, she saw the doctor and the young engineer leave and get into their autos.

She knocked on the office door and Edward rose as she entered. She stopped. She had never seen her husband look so tired. He hesitated, then shrugged.

"One of the coolies went amuck. He killed two women and a child."

"No."

"He sliced up a few others too. They'll recover, thanks to MacDonough." He sat down. "Those kukris are terrible knives. It wasn't very pretty."

"It was ganja, wasn't it?" Somehow she had known it was something like this.

"He was saturated with it. We had to kill him."

"This wasn't the first time, was it?"

He shook his head. "It was the worst."

Mary was silent. The full horror of it tightened her throat, made her feel nauseous. "I must get down there. I can help somehow."

"Dr. MacDonough's there. You have your party to think of."

She stared. "You're not going to have the party!"

"Why not?"

"But . . . there are people dead there! Our coolies!"

He watched her, his face hardening. "Get hold of yourself, Mary. People die every day in India. Thousands. It's a land of death."

"No, Edward."

He gripped her arms, hard, his face savage. "Grow up, woman. That is the way it is here."

Mary wrenched her arm away, tried to speak. Then she kept silent. She knew there was nothing she could say.

The first regret came from Sir John. A bearer brought the chit early the next morning. The note said that "unexpected business in town would prevent Lady Thornton and myself from attending."

An hour later a note came from the Beauchamps. Denise's chit was less formal. "Dear Mary, I'm so sorry we can't come but Tom feels that under the circumstances it would be best if we not turn up."

Mary showed the note to her husband. He laughed grimly. "Bad news travels fast here."

"But how would they know?"

"Probably Dr. MacDonough. He had to telephone it into Calcutta yesterday." He eyed her a moment. "Do you want to quit?"

"I don't know." Mary felt her face flush. It was monstrous that she should even consider going ahead with the party. It should be halted out of respect for the dead.

"As you said yesterday there are people dead out there." His expression was mocking now.

"I know."

"You certainly have a good excuse to quit. Probably no one will come."

"You think I can't do it, don't you. You want me to quit so that you may laugh at me."

"It is a terrible thing that has happened. You are a decent, humane woman. True blue."

"Last week you wanted me not to give a party. Now you are urging it. Why?"

"It is our first party. It is a special occasion."

Mary put her hand shakily to her head. The room seemed suddenly enormous. She felt like Alice in Wonderland, shrunken, lost in a strange room. Somewhere she must find a solution to this curious world. Meanwhile she must not lose her head.

She nodded. "Very well. I'll go through with it."

Shortly before noon the next day Mary and her husband drove down to the dak bungalow. Ahmed and the bearers followed in an estate lorry with the picnic food, the drink, and the croquet set. Mary supervised the distribution, then sat beside her husband on the verandah.

They waited silently. There was no one in sight, neither on the river nor on the dirt road beside it.

Mary sat back. Calmness is what you need now, Mary. Let your eyes rule your mouth. You really want to shout, to run down to the river or up that road . . . searching, calling. "Come in, come in wherever you are." It was like that game you played as a child. You are supposed to count to a hundred, then go and look for them.

Mary sat silently. It was her first party as a married woman and she wasn't going to panic. A hawk drifted down toward the river and slanted upward again, a black rip in the blue sky.

A half hour passed, then fifteen minutes more. Ahmed and the bearers were watching the sahib and the mem. Mary was now sitting straight in her chair, erect, uncompromising. Goad lounged silently beside her, a cigar held casually in his fist. From time to time his blue eyes shifted toward the river road, then returned to examine his cigar or the river before them.

After an hour Mary spoke abruptly. "I suppose we can use some of the picnic at the house."

"Perhaps."

15

"We might let Ahmed take it to the coolie village."

"Coolies eat rice. They wouldn't touch it."

"I wonder if it's I that's wrong. Perhaps they just don't like me, Edward."

"Perhaps." He eyed her, expressionless.

Mary stood up. "I think we had best start back."

"Wait!" He pointed with his cigar toward the river road. Mary shaded her eyes. "I see dust. It's a bicycle!"

"Two bicycles. It's the vicar and his wife. If they come, the others will."

"Ahmed! They're coming!" She sat down again beside her husband. She should have known better than to doubt their coming. These were English people. They would never have had such bad manners.

Then Mary glanced at her husband. His face was grim. She understood. For him the ordeal was not over. It may have just begun.

Each of the arrivals came in his own method of transportation. The vicar and his wife, the Andersons, arrived first. He was an athletic man in his early forties and, since his vicarage and the parish school were only four miles upriver, they had come by bicycle.

The Robertshaws and the Brittinghams came chugging down-river in a launch. A half bale of jute still rested in the bow.

Old Gorton Thomas, the retired schoolteacher, came with his wife, a trumpet firmly held to her deaf ear—alternating the instrument in the direction of the speaker. They arrived by closed gharry, the old-fashioned horse-drawn carriage Mary had seen so often on Calcutta streets.

The MacDonoughs and Jolliffes came last, arriving together, and were the only guests to arrive by motorcar. It was obvious that Dr. MacDonough had already consumed considerable drink. Young Jolliffe looked blond and sullen as usual.

As the last guest arrived, Goad grunted toward his wife. "Do ye notice they've all come at once? They probably all talked it over and decided on a time. They'll probably all leave at once too."

"No matter. They're here." She pressed his arm fiercely.

The party got under way with croquet for some, for others badminton. The vicar undoubtedly entered fully into the sports at his school. He took off his jacket, hit the croquet ball with zest, chaffed Edward good-naturedly for his awkwardness.

Thomas, the retired schoolmaster, was very democratic with Goad, drinking with him after badminton and barely referring to his own days at Cambridge. He was not going to have his wife accuse him later of not putting Goad at his ease.

Mary watched the Brittingham and Robertshaw men with some apprehension. They were much less successful jute planters than her husband. She recognized from the scars on Robertshaw's face and Brittingham's artificial hand that they were wounded veterans of the war. They had every reason to be resentful of Goad and they certainly now had the opportunity to be malicious, even rude.

But as the afternoon went on, Mary was able to feel easier about the two men. No one could have taken offense at their quiet courtesy to her husband. They referred to the war and their dreadful lives in the trenches only once. It was a demonstration, she realized proudly, of simple British decency.

The hours passed but the guests stayed to tea. Mary had half expected they would leave after tea. Certainly that was what Edward had expected. But after tea there was a general relaxation. The gentlemen took a slow walk down to the river; the ladies retired for brief rests in the shade. Old Mrs. Thomas stretched out on a bedroll her bearer had brought and went to sleep, her trumpet still cupped to her cheek.

There was no sign of leaving after tea. The men returned from their stroll with renewed energy. There was a bit more drinking now. Mary was happy to see there was a certain joviality in the air. Even the ladies drank a few pegs. She was pleased. The party was going over.

Edward felt no such reassurance. He knew—or thought he knew—what was in the wind. Now the baiting would begin in earnest. The pleasant walk down to the river had given the men a chance to chuckle to themselves, to exchange amused remarks on their host, then they had returned reinvigorated.

He watched as they circled him, drinks in hand, elaborately courteous, oversolicitous as to his opinions. What did Goad think of the jute situation? Were prices going to rise? Give us your opinion, Goad. You are the burra sahib among us, old boy.

Goad hunched his shoulders, muttering little answers. He knew they wouldn't be shaken off; they merely changed places from time to time. He glanced at Mary once or twice but saw only her pleasure at the courtesy of their neighbors. He knew she would never see the cruelty, the deep hatred beneath the elaborate attentions paid him. He wanted to break free, to lumber out to the verandah. He was a bull being stuck with barbs but so gently, so solicitously, that only the ribbons showed. He stayed, head lowered to his drink, monosyllabic.

It was not until after dinner that the trouble came. There had been a solid amount of drinking before khana. Mrs. MacDonough had grown more bitter during the meal over her separation from her children. Dr. MacDonough was quite drunk by now and finally told his wife to shut her mouth about the children. If he could put up with the separation, so could she.

"You're drunk." It was a sound full of hatred.

"I am. That I am. Around here a man has to drink to keep his reason."

There was a silence. The Thomases glanced at each other. There was no doubt that Mrs. Thomas had picked this up on her ear trumpet. She jerked it up and down with anticipation. The Andersons looked demure though a certain smile of pleasure tightened the lips of the vicar's wife, as though to say "at last."

But Kitty Jolliffe broke into a sudden sobbing.

"Hush, Kitty." It was her husband hissing at her.

She shook her head desperately. "You made me come to this party. You knew what would happen."

"Hush." He squeezed her arm between his fingernails. She screamed sharply once, then subsided into a whimpering.

The meal came to an abrupt end not long afterward. The Andersons said there was a football match the next morning and they really had to be going back early to the vicarage.

Old Gorton Thomas and his wife made few bones about leaving. They thanked Mary carefully for the evening, bowed briefly toward Edward, and shambled out toward their closed gharry, old Thomas reciting Kitty Jolliffe's remark loudly into the greedy ear trumpet.

Only the Brittenhams and Robertshaws bade a hearty good night, befitting men more earthy than their neighbors. They clapped Goad cheerfully on the back and swept out with their wives, the men laughing uproariously as they scrambled down the path toward the river, the wives giggling and chaffing their men as they piled toward their motorboat.

Mary had asked each to stay a little longer. She said there would be dancing; she had put the gramophone in order and had all the latest records. She had even tried putting on a record during their good-byes. She had seen to it that Ahmed had hurried in with a fresh tray of drinks.

Nothing had quite succeeded, however. She accompanied each couple to the door, thanking them for coming, refusing to note that nothing was said about her returning their visit.

The Jolliffes left. Kitty trying to apologize for her tears. Her husband, tight-lipped, led his wife away. Their ride home would not be an affectionate one.

Finally, Mrs. MacDonough led her by now quite drunken doctor to the door. There she turned to Mary with a look of grim satisfaction, wasting no time on preliminaries. "You're one of us now, Mrs. Goad. With Mrs. Jolliffe and all the rest of us. Now you'll know what it is to live here." Dr. MacDonough muttered at his wife and she turned on him, "Yes, she'll learn. I have you and Kitty has that weak husband of hers but Mrs. Goad may have the worst ahead of us all." She turned to glare at Edward Goad, standing silently to one side.

Mary felt a chill. This was it. At last it was coming out. "If you are referring to what happened yesterday at York House, my husband regrets it just as much as you."

"Yesterday." Mrs. MacDonough hooted derisively. "That was nothing."

The doctor pushed drunkenly at his wife. "Get on. You've said enough."

Goad put a restraining hand on the doctor. "Let her speak. Go on, Mrs. MacDonough. Tell my wife."

"You know well enough what I'm talking about." She swung around to Mary. "Get out of here, woman. While there's still time."

"That's enough!" her husband shouted. He pushed heavily against her. "Get out."

Mrs. MacDonough looked at him bitterly. "I wish to God I had left long ago." She turned and walked out.

Dr. MacDonough waited uncertainly. He tried to say his thanks to Goad for his dinner, then he went slowly, wearily, out.

Goad looked after the departing guests and his face was angry. "Bloody bastards."

"Edward."

"You never did see through them. You thought they were being decent." There was a bitterness in his fury.

"They were decent. It was good of them to come."

"Patronizing bastards."

Mary put her hand wearily to her head. "Edward, I think I would like to have a little holiday. I am tired. I'd like to go up to Calcutta. Perhaps shop."

"You belong here."

"We could both go. Give ourselves a holiday."

"I don't go to Calcutta and neither should my wife."

"I'm tired, Edward." She knew her voice was getting out of control.

"You will stay here where you belong."

Mary watched him go. She wanted to rush after him, shake him, hit him—anything to let him know the weary anger that was in her.

She turned away to collect the things that must go back to York House. One of the records waited on the gramophone and Mary put down the needle.

The words—wheezy, cracked—blared from the horn. "Pack Up Your Troubles in Your Old Kit Bag."

How many times she and Tim had bellowed those words at some rally. It was really a little ridiculous, those inane words.

But there was nothing ridiculous about this. She wanted to get away, to flee to Calcutta even for a week, but it was forbidden. She was trapped in this house, in the marriage.

The tears began to come, then the giggles. The tinny words answered. "What's the Use of Worrying? It Never Was Worthwhile!"

Mary began to laugh. It was quite true. Life wasn't really as terrible as it seemed sometimes. It just took getting used to.

23

THE FILM FINISHED AND TIGER GOT TO HIS FEET. He saw that Magda sat a few rows behind him with two young girls. He had heard it was customary for Magda on Sunday afternoon to take several of her girls to the matinee. It was a reward and after the cinema they all went dutifully back to Acre Lane.

He strolled out of the theater and into the small square. He was undecided whether to go back to his flat or drop in at the Slap for a game of billiards. He rejected both ideas and had turned toward the Maidan when he felt a touch on his sleeve. It was Magda and she was now alone.

"Excuse me, sir. I am most embarrassed that we speak this way but it is important to me." She looked very respectable in her Sunday dress and Tiger noticed that the hand holding the parasol wore a wedding ring.

He glanced about the quiet street. He knew that as the governor's aide he was known to all sorts of people in Calcutta but he was in no mood these days to be harangued.

She continued determinedly. "I am Magda. You know who I am, I think. Acre Lane. I wish, please, that you speak to this young American, James Wilson."

Despite himself, Tiger was startled.

"I know you must know him, sir. He is at their American office. I wish that you speak to him, sir, that he does not come to my place."

"Wilson goes to your place?" He was astonished.

"Oh, not as a customer, sir. That is the trouble. He always comes with Mr. Windendorp."

"Mr. Max Windendorp?"

"Yes, sir. They share a chummery."

"No!" Max Windendorp. It was astonishing.

"The trouble is, sir, James Wilson just sits in the parlor waiting for his friend. It is very disturbing for the other customers. It is bad for business."

"I can imagine." Tiger suppressed a desire to laugh. He put on his most grave manner. "Perhaps you should speak to Mr. Windendorp."

"I have. I asked Mr. Windendorp not to bring him but he said he is his chummery mate. So the young American waits. Mr. Windendorp is very slow, sir."

"You have a problem there, Magda. You might ask Mr. Windendorp not to come."

"He is one of our best customers."

"I am sorry, Magda. There is really nothing I can do."

"I have my rights. Magda's is important in Calcutta. Especially now when there are so many visitors here."

"Most of the visitors are girls."

"That's just it. If anything happens to Magda's, those girls are not safe."

"I see your point. You are in competition in a way."

"You will not do something? Have this American sent somewhere else?"

"I am afraid the ground for declaring a vice consul non grata does not include . . . how shall we put it . . . a lack of interest in Magda's girls. I am sorry, Magda. You have an interesting problem." He nodded solemnly and turned to go. "Please excuse me."

She watched him as he left. "There will be trouble with that young man!" She shouted it. He didn't look back. "Damn," he heard her say. He turned to watch as she stumped angrily down the street, her parasol tapping the pavement furiously.

Tiger turned toward the Maidan. In a way he would have liked to have fun with Magda's problem. Perhaps a formal note from Government House to Wilson suggesting that he either take up with one of Magda's girls when he visited or stay home. He was making himself conspicuous.

This was a curious chummery in the first place. He wondered whether Bunty knew of it. He tried to remember what he knew about Max Windendorp. He was a South African, a Boer who was managing a small office in Calcutta for a large Belgian engineering firm. He was a small man, about fifty, dark with a long, slightly hooked nose and curly, almost wiry hair.

The point was that Windendorp was excessively male. There was an intense, electric quality about him and Tiger had heard it said that every night, after dining at Firpo's—always alone in black dinner jacket and tie—he would light his long, black cigar and disappear in a taxi toward Acre Lane. It was said that Windendorp was a regular customer at Magda's, his nightly visits as systematic as a ritual.

Because of these habits, his alien appearance, and his Boer background, he was something of an outsider in Calcutta. A more unlikely chummery mate for a young American vice consul would be hard to find.

Tiger wondered why Wilson accompanied Windendorp to Magda's if he didn't participate. It must have been out of a sense of loyalty to Max.

He also wondered why Max allowed Wilson to accompany him. It was probably either let the boy go or not go himself and that would have been intolerable. In a way it was a tribute to the chummery system.

Tiger entered the Maidan and walked until he found a bench. He realized it was in the same area in which he and Mary had sat. He stretched his long legs, peering up at the great Queen's memorial.

He wanted to ponder. Matters in Calcutta were coming to some sort of climax. The warmer weather had already reached Madras, five hundred miles to the south. The season had only a few more weeks to go.

The fishing fleeters sensed it. Those not yet engaged could still be seen at the Slap or Firpo's, a little too gay, even strident. They knew there wasn't very much time.

Meanwhile the parties were going full blast—balls, garden parties, tennis teas. The Saturday Club masquerade, always the high point of the season, was not far away. The theme this year would be "Durbar, 1877." That was the year Queen Victoria had been proclaimed Empress of India. It was pretty defiant of the old Slap to choose that.

The sound of band music roused Tiger and he looked toward Eden Gardens. It was time for the regular Sunday afternoon concert in the Maidan and it was just beginning.

He could see the circular bandstand in the distance, roofed, girdled by an iron railing already festooned with climbing children. He could see the white coats and the red caps of the police band, their leader, a solitary, erect figure.

Tiger stood up restlessly and went to sit on the root of a

banyan tree. He could see and hear the music better. It wasn't that he was a music lover. He could barely recognize the tune of his own regimental march. He simply had to think.

Tiger knew he wasn't doing his job, that was the trouble. He had been a social aide long enough. He was impatient to deal with Gupta.

But finding Gupta seemed an impossibility. The city of Calcutta contained more than two million Indians. The central part of the city and the few green residential areas contained the eight thousand-odd Europeans. The rest of the city, sprawling on both banks of the Hooghly, knowing no simple boundaries, was a giant rabbit warren. To locate one man in the hodgepodge of villages was to search a beach for a special grain of sand. And to control that vast area, to aid in the search, the Raj maintained a police force of a few hundred, only twenty-two of them British.

Tiger knew there might not be much time. Neither Gandhi nor Gupta had made a move since the end of the hunger strike. Something had to happen. If nature abhorred a vacuum, so did revolutionaries.

Meanwhile he wasted his time dancing awkwardly at parties, prowling empty alleys. He hadn't even heard from Margot Danvers about seconding her rugby player for the Slap. The only person who had paid him any attention was Magda, a madam concerned about her brothel.

Tiger suddenly sat up. The music, the strolling people were forgotten. Magda's. Of course. That was where that follower of Gupta's might be found. Rajid.

Tiger lifted himself from the banyan root, then, walking, put his thoughts together. It had been Rajid they were looking for the night he and the police sergeant had searched Magda's. He had learned since then that there was a girl at Magda's named Dolly who was involved with Rajid. They had followed her but it had led to nothing.

It was Rajid they must follow. The way to Gupta might lie through Rajid. And the way to Rajid must begin at Magda's.

Tiger suddenly laughed. It was the first time he had felt right in a long time. How sprightly that music was. How green and lovely the grass. And the strollers—Tommies from the Fort and their girls, Anglo-Indians most of them—how right it all was. God was in his heaven. He, Captain Flemyng, would have something to do at last.

Margot Danvers was devoting herself to the transformation of Frank Willis. She was determined that he should become a member of the Saturday Club by the time of the Slap's masquerade. She understood that it was the climax of the season and if a girl weren't engaged by then she was in difficulties. Mr. Bracebridge had already entered Frank's name for membership and it was now up to her.

She worked Frank hard at tennis, taking him each evening to the Bracebridge's grass court to drive him grimly about. He was stumbling and awkward but he made progress. She had also made him give up his aromatic hair tonic.

Frank was not the brightest of men but he began to realize what he had gotten into. He hated tennis. The ball was too small. He tripped over his racket. He felt a little like the proverbial bull being led to the slaughter. He also found Margot's social acquaintances extremely stuffy. They obviously were not interested when he talked rugby.

Yet he persisted. He still wanted to marry Margot. He was flattered and a little awed that a woman of her class should have selected him. He had also begun plans to enlarge his men's shop. The Saturday Club had become a sort of Grail.

Margot could almost smell the orange blossoms and hear the wedding bells of the English Cathedral in Calcutta, St. Paul's. (She was not going to be married in any First Congregational Church. It would be like no wedding at all.) She was using the remaining days before he appeared before the membership committee to tie Frank tighter into her life. She lunched with him daily at Firpo's. She accompanied him nightly to the cinema, parading him during the interval.

Margot saw the appealing yet quite mature young Bunty Cranston with a young man she took from his accent to be an American. He was rather nice-looking for an American, hardly a match for the demure yet sophisticated Bunty. And Margot would slip her arm possessively through Frank's.

She and Frank made an odd couple. Calcutta was not unused to watching odd combinations during the cold weather but this one, coupling the bony, rather overdressed Margot with the big, brawny rugby player, was especially noticeable. It was said, however, that Rufus Bracebridge had proposed Willis for membership in the Slap and that no less than Captain Flemyng, aide to Sir Gerald, would second the proposal. Margot could sense the approval about them and knew that,

thanks to Mary deGive, her man was as good as accepted.
The wedding bells were ringing more clearly each day.

There was one slight vexation for Margot, the coming
rugby matches for the Governor's Cup. For five days Frank
would be entirely out of her hands. She urged that he allow
a substitute to play but he was stubborn. He would not let
his side down. When Margot argued, Frank lowered his head
doggedly.

They compromised. Margot withdrew her objection and
he agreed that it would be his last match. Margot even
promised to attend. She would watch over her property even
on the rugby field.

Each day Margot took her place in the stands and, as the
matches proceeded, she began to sense again the power in
this man of hers, began to react to Frank in a very primitive
way. When he lowered his head and butted forward against
the opposite side, she felt a fierce warmth take hold. She
wanted to be there beside him, pushing with him, kicking
fiercely at the legs opposite. And when, tired and exhausted,
he still found the strength to knock on the loose ball and fall
on it, she wanted to fall there with him, stretched over him
protectively.

Margot approached the last game in a very wrought-up
condition. She had found herself dreaming the past few nights
in a very unladylike way. She seemed to be at the bottom of
the scrum, being used as the ball more or less, and each time
Frank kicked down at her, she would moan deliciously in
her sleep. She always awoke early, then would fall asleep
again for a long rest.

She sat with Mr. and Mrs. Bracebridge in the center of
the stands. The other Cup finalists, the Welsh Fusiliers, a
military side from upcountry, were younger, faster, and fit
from regimental training. At half time the Fusiliers were fresh
as ever, jogging about the fields, while the club players
sprawled on the hard turf.

In the second half the club played with dogged anger. Its
backs, overrun by the young backs opposite, would turn and
stumble after them. Frank, his headband now jammed over
his eyes, was still heaving and pushing against the squat young
hooker opposite and, when the ball rolled loose, would lead
his pack in weary, stumbling pursuit.

Margot watched Frank and felt herself shiver. He would
be knocked down but get to his feet roaring. He was like

that Greek mythological giant who was knocked down time and time again but each time rose refreshed by Mother Earth. Margot found herself panting, trembling, trying to shout encouragement but her mouth shut tight with tenseness. Frank, now bleeding from a dozen reopened scars about the head, was like a bull she had once seen in a Spanish bullring, still pawing defiantly at the ground, blood leaking from a dozen banderillas.

The match ended in a draw; cheers were given, the Welsh cheering the club players with something like wonder in their eyes. The governor attended by his aide, Captain Flemyng, came out to present the Governor's Cup.

Margot sat immobile. She knew she should have been furious at what she had seen; it was stupid, male, and purposeless. Frank was jeopardizing his health at the least.

Yet her eyes were shining and, as the Bracebridges glanced at her, she turned away. She felt shivery. She wanted Frank. She didn't care about the proprieties. She wanted to lie down with him, anywhere, right there under the stands if he wished. She loved this man and she felt like a woman.

There was a dinner that evening at the Rugby Club for the two teams. No women were invited so Margot went back to the Bracebridges for a restless dinner, a hot tub, and a long evening with a book.

It was a hearty party at the club, full of windy speeches, heavy drinking, and noisy fellowship. The party broke up finally, not from a lack of liquor or energy but an excess of both. Those Rugby Club players with wives went home. Others went to Firpo's or the Slap. Some of the Fusiliers, being new to Calcutta, wanted to visit Magda's. Frank and Gordie Purvis, refusing to admit they were less fit than the military, went along to show the way.

It was a noisy arrival, six or eight in an open taxi. Frank led them exuberantly up the stairs to Magda's living room and hardly noticed the gradual disappearance of his pals with one or another of Magda's friendly girls.

He himself was more in the mood for drinking than girls. He felt tired but proud. They had been overwhelmed in everything but the score but they had done their damndest. He was in no mood to be diminished.

He noticed that there was only one other man in the living room, a Yank by his accent. He suggested he buy the Yank a drink but was rather shyly turned down. He insisted—he was feeling very expansive—but was again turned down, this time less shyly.

That was how the trouble began. Frank couldn't understand why the other fellow wouldn't drink with him. He didn't particularly like chaps who wore horn-rimmed glasses. He didn't particularly like Yanks; they had too much money, dressed badly, and didn't play rugger.

He couldn't have said how the trouble actually developed. The Yank finally left the living room and started wandering around the house calling for someone named "Max." He had wandered argumentatively after him. He had come on the Yank opening and closing doors and, finally, the Yank had actually walked in on one of the Fusiliers and a girl.

That had done it. The Welshman had hit the Yank, the Yank had hit him back. Frank had tried to stop the fight and been cuffed on the chin. Then everyone had run after the Yank while the girl stood screaming, the Yank yelling, "Max," opening and closing doors and, in short order, it seemed the entire house was chasing him.

Magda had come along about then. Police whistles had blown and very soon Frank and his rugby pals, most of the Fusiliers in partial uniform, were hauled off to jail. The Yank and his Max had disappeared. Frank was upset because he had caught a glimpse of a man standing quietly in the shadows, a man he recognized as Captain Flemyng, his seconder for the Slap.

They weren't detained long at the police station. After all, it was the night of the Cup Final and men will be boys. They were reprimanded and released. The Welsh Fusiliers were turned over to their provost and were soon on their way out of Calcutta. It had been a short but sweet visit—two Cup wins, five fights, and a police raid. "That night at Magda's" would become a brief but hilarious episode in the regimental history.

Frank's night was not yet over. When he returned to the rather shabby ground-floor flat where he lived, he found Margot waiting. She was restless, solicitous and, finally, reckless.

It was Frank who had reservations. He was surprisingly restrained for so bullish a male. But Frank too let go eventually. He still had a sum of energy.

So Margot gave herself to him. It was a desperate gift on

her part, loving, comforting. It was sweet and painful and total.

At the police station Magda put on quite a scene. She knew that the fate of her establishment was being decided in that nearby office behind closed doors. She was not even being allowed in there but that didn't deter Magda from trying her case in absentia, so to speak.

She marched up and down furiously, full of protestations, loud and directed toward the closed office door. "They can't do this to me," she shouted. "I'm a decent, law-abiding woman! I run a brothel for decent people, not one of these hookshops on Karaiya Road."

The bored sergeant before her seemed to infuriate her further. "I have my rights! I'm a loyal subject of the King. You have no right bursting into my house that way. It'll cost me a thousand rupees to repair those carpets, all the tramping about you police did. You'd think I was running a pub for lascars instead of a gentleman's tart-house."

"Hush, Magda," murmured the sergeant.

"I will not hush. Let them hush." And she went closer to the closed office door. She hesitated carefully a moment, then raised her voice in a fury.

"British justice, that's what I want. British justice!" she bellowed at the door, twisting her wedding ring nervously. There was a trace of fear in her eyes.

Three men sat quietly inside the room. Two were police, the sergeant, his captain, and the third man was Tiger Flemyng. Magda's voice could be heard but they ignored her.

The police inspector spoke deferentially to Tiger. "What do you say, sir? Shall we close her?"

"Do you have the evidence?"

The inspector laughed, large teeth showing beneath his mustache. "Plenty. She also serves liquor. Unlicensed."

Tiger's scarred face was grim. "It's that Rajid we want. Dolly's man."

"He won't come when she's open. Not if Magda can help it."

"If she were closed, he might come. Magda might even invite him."

"Magda."

"How much does Magda take in on a night?"

"She has about ten girls. At twenty rupees a man that's about twelve hundred rupees a night. With drinks perhaps fifteen hundred."

"An Indian might look awfully light to her after a week or so."

"I see what you mean, sir. It's a chance."

"We have no choice. Close her, inspector. Two weeks. That may be just enough."

Magda could still be heard shouting. "Yell, woman. You'll be some use to us at last." His hard face was suddenly relaxed, almost gay.

He put his face close to the door, mimicking Magda. "Ow. British justice."

The inspector stared. Captain Flemyng seemed almost cheerful.

24

MARGOT CLOSED HER EYES. SHE COULD FEEL THE little Indian doctor poking around. Finally he stood back and smiled down at her.

"Dat is all. Put on dee clothing." He turned away to rub his hands on a torn towel. "You hab a bhery unfortunate condition. Der will be more information later. I hab taken de smear. But der is no doubt."

Margot went unsteadily to the corner of the little office to pull up her clothing. She wanted only to get away from this shabby room. It was hardly even an office. It seemed to be part office, part living room–bedroom. She had found it by walking desperately in the narrow lanes behind the bazaar until she saw a doctor's sign. Now she wanted to get away from this oily little doctor.

"When shall I know?" she asked.

He spread his hands. "Two . . . tree day."

"I'll come back in three days. Is there another exit?"

"Exit?"

"Another door from this house. In the rear perhaps."

"I fear no. Dis is not so fine here as Chowringhi." He barely troubled to hide his malice.

"If . . . if I do have something wrong can you treat me?"

"You come and we see. Dat will be fortee rupee please."

Forty rupees! Nearly two pounds, probably four times what he would charge one of his regular patients, if he had any patients.

Margot pushed the money at him. "Here. I'll come back in three days." She went toward the front door, hesitated before opening it, then stepped quickly out into the narrow street.

She pulled nervously at her dress as she walked, smoothing down the skirt. She felt dirty, sickened. That this should have happened to her, Margot Danvers, was unthinkable. She barely knew such matters existed.

She cursed Frank. He must have known what he had, yet he had taken her. He was a lout, a swine, a careless, heedless male.

For the next few days Margot kept very much to herself. She saw the Bracebridges only when it was absolutely necessary, at tiffin or at dinner. She would then sit silently at the table, feeling soiled, afraid that her condition must be known to her host and hostess, even to the servants.

Most of the time she sat alone in her room. She would walk slowly from wall to wall, then sit and stare unseeingly out at the garden behind the house. There were two thin and fruitless mango trees standing side by side and she found herself watching their aging branches. Once they seemed to bow, take hands, perform a skittish minuet before her.

Margot clung to that room, refusing to answer Frank's telephone calls or his note. She wanted only to crawl under the bed . . . to hide from the world. The world was a cruel place where you finally found a man to love, gave yourself to him, and then found this done to you.

Once she left the house on the pretext of visiting the Zoological Gardens. She later found herself by the river, staring down at its brown waters. It seemed to whisper comfortingly, assuring her it understood, promising it would solve all her problems if only she would accept its welcome.

She took a step toward the river, went slowly nearer, then

fled, rushing back to the Bracebridge house to hide the rest
of the day in her room.

It was the next day that the telephone rang. The Bracebridges were out for the morning and the bearer was evidently asleep somewhere because the phone rang until Margot
slipped from her room, compelled by its ring through the
empty house.

"Hello, Miss Danvers?"

"Yes." Margot answered mechanically. It seemed strange
to her dulled mind that there should be a voice at the other
end, that there should be people out there.

"This is Captain Flemyng. Alastair Flemyng?" There was
a pause as though the voice were requiring confirmation.
Margot wasn't certain what she was supposed to confirm.
That he was Captain Flemyng? It seemed simpler to say
nothing.

The voice continued. "Hallo? Are you there?"

"Yes."

"I haven't heard from you or Mr. Bracebridge as to when
I would be required to appear with your friend Willis, so I
thought I'd best ring the committee on my account." There
was no sound from Margot and the voice spoke impatiently.
"Hallo?"

"Yes."

"The committee is meeting next week. Since I have seconded your friend, I thought you had best let him know.
It is Tuesday, February eighteenth. He must be on the Slap
verandah at six o'clock. There will be three of the committee
members there as well as Willis, Bracebridge, and myself.
Tik hai?"

"Yes." Again that dull, barely heard voice.

"I'm sorry to seem pushy on this but I shan't be available
much from now on. We'd best get at this. Well, cheerio,
Miss Danvers."

"Good-bye." Margot slowly put down the receiver, the
last word nearly inaudible at the other end. She turned toward the stairs. It seemed so far from the phone table, so
steep to the second floor and so many steps to climb. But she
had to get there because at the top there would be the safety
of her room. Except that now, even there, there would be
no safety.

Tiger put down the phone in his office. There was no

doubt something was wrong. Margot was not the sort, from what he had observed, to be monosyllabic. There had nearly been no voice at all at the other end of the phone. No person.

Well, it didn't matter to him whether or not Willis appeared for the meeting. He had promised Mary to help, had written his name on the application blank. Now he wanted only to eliminate these social responsibilities. He would have no time for anything but Gupta. That name should henceforth be written in fire on his calendar.

He was in this mood of impatience when the phone rang and it was another feminine voice. This time he knew it to be Bunty. There was no mistaking that low yet breathless voice.

"Tiger, I need your help." At least, he thought, she can be heard. But were those tears in her voice? Bunty!

"I'm afraid I was just leaving."

"Please, I'm desperate, Tiger. I haven't seen Jamie in a week. Do you know what has happened to him?"

"No."

"I don't like to ring him. I rang once at his office but what can I say! Can you do something?"

Oh Lord, Tiger thought. "I'm sorry, Bunty. I'm afraid this is between you and Jamie."

"But what can I do! You must help. Ring him or send a chit to him. I like him, Tiger. I do!" There was no doubt now of the bewilderment, the despair in the girl's voice. Her sobs could be plainly heard. It was surprising. Bunty, that man-eater.

Tiger hardened his voice. "Go see him. Right to his house. Have it out with him."

"I couldn't."

"You can if you have to. I'm sorry, Bunty. I was just leaving."

"Tiger. Please!"

"Good-bye. I must ring off." He hung up, the scars on his jaw seeming to throb with his anger. Damned women, don't they know there's a battle on! The Raj itself may be shaken and they are concerned only with their damned problems. Then it occurred to him—for them it was a battle too.

Bunty's taxi reached the house in Tollygunge and she climbed the stairs to the Wilson-Windendorp chummery. She

was wearing her most feminine of frocks and knew that it
favored her. She took courage.

As she entered she saw by the white Panama hat on the
chummery rack that James must be at home. Matthew,
Jamie's Christian bearer, appeared.

Bunty nodded. "Wilson sahib hai?"

The bearer gestured toward the living room and stood
back. Bunty could see James and Max at the far end. They
were sitting over a game of checkers.

"Salaam," she said brightly. "I haven't heard from you
so I thought I'd best see whether you were still alive." She
bent cheerfully over the startled Jamie and kissed him on
the cheek.

Max stood up. "If you'll excuse me."

"Don't go." He seemed almost pleading. "Bunty's just
visiting."

Max nodded toward her, not unkindly. "I think you should
talk to Bunty. Excuse me." He bowed to Bunty and left.

Bunty glanced after him. She was surprised to see how pale
Max had looked. He had dark rings under his sharp eyes.

"Jamie, what's the matter with him? He looks awful."

"Let me get you a lime squash, Bunty."

"No. I came to see you." She sat herself very near him.
"You do like me, don't you?"

"Yes." It was a fervent, even desperate answer.

"Then what is it? You haven't even rung me. A whole
week."

"It's so hard to tell you. I can't."

"Have I done anything wrong?"

"No!" Again that ringing tone.

"Have you?"

"No! Of course not."

"Then what is it?"

He swallowed. "All right. I'll tell you." He pulled himself
together. "You know how it is with men. Some men," he
added hastily.

Bunty stared at him. She had a feeling this was entering
on familiar ground, familiar yet dangerous. "No. What do
you mean?"

"It's hard to explain. Max is very . . . very robust. Some
men are more robust than others and . . . and if they're not
married, they sometimes go to . . . to houses." He swallowed,

then rushed ahead. "The house Max went to has been closed."

"But why was it closed?"

"There was a fight. That was a week ago. And that is why I haven't seen you."

"But what has that to do with you and me?" Bunty knew that her voice was rising angrily but she didn't care.

"I can't leave him while he's in this condition."

"But whyever not! He's a grown man."

"Because . . . because I caused the fight. It was on account of me that they closed Max's place."

"You!"

He nodded his head miserably, the glasses nearly falling sideways. "I always went with him. Just because we are friends. Now on account of me he can't see Vera."

"Vera."

"That was his special girl."

Bunty drew a deep breath. She could see the whole problem very clearly, as well as the solution.

"Then let him bring Vera here."

"Here!"

"If he can't go there and you won't leave him, then let her come here. And I'll come too. Then people won't be able to talk." And I can keep an eye on things, she might have added.

"But this is a chummery. It isn't a . . . a . . . we can't have Vera here."

"You want to help Max."

"Oh yes."

"You want to see me."

"Yes." It was a cry of despair.

"Then there's no other way."

"You'd come here?" She nodded firmly. "As a matter of fact, Max did sort of suggest it, bringing Vera here." He eyed Bunty hopefully. "You're sure you wouldn't mind?"

"Let's just say it's my bit to help Max."

He stared at her, his face rosy with admiration at her sacrifice. "Gee, Bunty . . ." He kissed her impulsively. "I'll go tell Max."

Bunty's face was placid as he left. She knew she had made a beginning.

That very night Vera paid her first visit. Bunty was informed by James and, while Max entertained Vera in the bedroom, Bunty and James remained in the living room. They played loud music and James danced with Bunty rather feverishly.

The next night Vera paid her second visit and again Bunty was summoned. They again danced busily in the living room. There was a moment when Jamie caught sight of Vera, a rather porcine figure, nude except for a towel, trotting dutifully to the bathroom.

When Bunty left that night James pulled her close and kissed her. Bunty agreed to come again the next night. But when she arrived she was met by a pale James.

"What's the trouble?" she asked.

"Vera isn't coming. She wants to bring two of her friends from Magda's. She said the girls have no place to take their gentlemen and, with all this space here, she just can't enjoy herself."

Bunty frowned. She could quite see the porcine Vera, stout but obviously with a stubborn will.

"How many gentlemen would they bring?" she asked.

"Just one. Their favorite customers."

"Can't they take them to a hotel?"

"Vera says hotels are too public."

"How long is Magda's going to be closed? Max might be able to wait."

He groaned. "Another week. Max won't wait."

"Then let them come here too."

"You wouldn't mind?"

"There would be only one man to a girl?"

"Oh yes. After all, this a chummery."

"Very well. Just so long as I come too," she said firmly.

So the arrangement continued. Bunty and James seldom saw the new girls or their customers. They came and left by the servants' stairs, each couple one hour apart. And each night Jamie gripped Bunty more tightly as they danced.

One night they found themselves alone. Max had taken Vera home. The other girls and their gentlemen had also gone. It had been a particularly sensuous sort of evening with the comings and goings of the kimono-clad girls to the bathroom. It might almost have been Magda's.

When Jamie and Bunty danced he gripped her in a trembling frenzy. She responded and he responded to her response. Jamie soon led Bunty into his bedroom.

She made it as easy for him as possible, undoing her blouse

and bra, stepping willingly from her skirt and climbing into bed.

James approached her hesitantly, no longer the frenzied young man. Bunty was aware that he was nude but also that something was wrong. She certainly knew enough of young men to know that what was now limp should have been eager.

Smiling, she held out her arms. Jamie groaned but got quickly in beside her. Bunty kissed him gently, kissed him again, and gradually became aware of a success. She pulled him possessively toward her.

It had not been a carefree time for Frank Willis. He knew very well he was the first man Margot had given herself to. He also knew that in his condition to have done what he did was not the mark of a gentleman.

But Frank had never claimed to be a gentleman. He was a reckless, virile male who took his rugby and his women where he found them. He regretted his infection but, as he tried to tell himself in the popular idiom, it was "no worse than a bad cold." He would have it treated sooner or later.

Frank had not seen Margot in nearly a week. She had given herself to him each night since that first time after the Cup final. Then she had suddenly stopped seeing him. She answered neither his messages nor his rings. It was obvious that something was wrong and Frank, rather sheepishly, felt certain he knew what the trouble was. To add to his uncertainties he knew the day for his appearance before the Slap membership committee must be approaching and he didn't know whether he was still to appear.

Frank told himself he didn't care. He had better things to think about than joining a club like the Slap, full of snobby people. His bad conscience was making him truculent.

One evening, in his ground-floor flat, he had just about decided to tell Mr. Rufus Bracebridge to withdraw his name when there was a knock on the door. He opened it.

"Margot."

"May I come in?"

"Of course." He stood aside uncertainly as she entered. She seemed to him to be unusually calm. "I tried to ring you, Margot. Several times. You were always out. You didn't answer my chits either."

"I know."

The paleness in her face told him the answer, the dark

shadows under her eyes confirmed her pain. He spread his hands helplessly. "I expect I know why you haven't seen me."

"Yes, Frank."

"I . . . I'm sorry. You know how those things are."

"I don't how they are!" Her calm was broken now. Her voice was nearly breaking. "It was a despicable thing to do."

"I know. I said I'm sorry."

They waited. Frank shifted his bulky frame uneasily. Somewhere in that simple mind, he knew he had betrayed something . . . his manhood, Margot, even his rugger pals. Life had always been so simple for him. It was a matter of butting heads with the hooker opposite, of drinking with his pals, taking the easy woman. Now here was a new one. He was out of his depth.

Yet he did want to do the right thing. He didn't fancy wearing the best clothes for nothing. Clothes make the gentleman he'd always said. He had something to live up to. If only he knew what was the right thing.

"I guess you won't have to worry about the Slap now," he mumbled.

"What do you mean?"

"Mr. Bracebridge can hardly propose me now."

"Mr. Bracebridge doesn't know."

"You haven't told him?"

"Of course not." She faced him now. "Captain Flemyng phoned this week. He wants to get on with the Slap application."

"My application!" She nodded. "But surely you don't want me to go through with it now. That was tied in with our engagement."

"I've said nothing about our engagement. That will stand."

"But . . . I've done a terrible thing to you. I've given you a disease." Even he, in his simple mind, could see there was something grotesque in this.

Her face was white, tense. "You'll be cured, just as I shall be. We'll take our cure together. When we've finished with our . . . our treatment . . . we will then announce our engagement."

"The Slap too?"

"Yes." She knew that now she would need the Slap more than ever. It would be a sort of protection.

He shook his head stubbornly. He had some pride left. "No. I don't belong in the Slap. You must see that now. I'll marry you but there's the Grand Hotel if we need fun or the Rugby Club. I don't belong in the Slap."

"We've started this and we'll finish it."

"Margot."

"You don't wish me to have you dropped from the Rugby Club, do you? If I told Mr. Bracebridge of your disease, he would have you out in no time. I doubt that little church of which you are a vestryman . . . Congregationalist, isn't it . . . I doubt they would welcome you either."

He knew he was beaten. "When is the meeting?"

"You will be at the Slap Tuesday. That's three days from now. Sharp at six."

They watched each other. Frank knew there was something different now about Margot, a certainty that made him uneasy. She was like someone who had peered over the brink and had overcome whatever had taken her there.

Margot waited for him to fight back at her, to tell her it wasn't right, letting her run the show. She waited for his rebellion and was afraid. Then she saw there would be none.

Frank arrived promptly at the Slap on Tuesday, accompanied by Mr. Rufus Bracebridge and an efficient but somewhat impatient Captain Flemyng. Mr. Bracebridge quickly presented Frank to the three committee members, "Clipper" Sloan, Tony Wilkington, and old Colonel Taggart. Frank nodded, adjusting his big frame to one of the small wicker chairs.

For the next half hour Frank spoke when spoken to, smiled when smiled at—jumped through all the proper hoops. Captain Flemyng conducted Willis through the ceremony with efficient dispatch, never giving Frank a chance to say the wrong thing.

When it was over and it was clear that Willis would be approved, the committee members stood to withdraw. Tiger Flemyng bade them all his good-byes, murmured something about being needed at Government House, and turned to go. He paused once on his way out to face the woman he had glimpsed alone behind a pillar.

He bowed briefly to Margot, nodding back toward the group as though to say, "There you are. He's in." He then walked on. For him that was the end of it.

Margot, unseen by all but Flemyng, sat back. It was over. Her great hulk of a man would be accepted.

Tears came to her eyes. Not tears of joy or pride. She wept for Frank Willis and for herself.

25

A WEEK LATER AT YORK HOUSE AHMED AP-peared at Mary's bedroom door shortly before tiffin. "Beau-champ memsahib hai, mem."

"Denise," Mary exclaimed. It hardly seemed believable.

She rushed downstairs to find her friend standing in the verandah. They embraced.

"Denise, I am glad to see you."

"Hello, Mary."

"Did Tom come?"

"No. He's at the office. I just thought I'd drive out to see what had happened to you. You never come to Calcutta."

Mary embraced her again. "I'm glad you came." She was surprised how much she had missed her dumpy little friend. "Edward is in the fields. He'll be having his tiffin out there. We can have tiffin alone. You will stay, of course. That's a two-hour drive back to Calcutta."

"Three hours the way I drive. I can't even follow the river properly. Nearly ran in once or twice. Now give me a drink. I think I deserve one."

Denise stayed. They chatted a good deal, about the season in Calcutta and who had become engaged or married. Denise described the principal social events so far—the Governor's Ball at Government House, the Viceregal Ball at Belvedere Lodge. A good bit had happened in the past month and a half.

But mostly Denise drank. Mary had never seen her drink quite so much or so nervously. And as she drank she fell into long, morose silences. There was clearly something on her mind other than the Calcutta social season.

They retired to the verandah after tiffin and Denise helped herself to another whiskey, then sank into a chair.

"You want water?" Mary had noticed Denise was using very little with her drink.

"It's unhealthy." She sipped her peg and leaned back. "It's been a long day."

Mary looked at her friend. Denise really did look as though she needed a rest. Her eyes were heavy, dull. And she seemed even more sloppy than usual. Her stocking seams were crooked and her lipstick smeared as though put on in a frenzy.

Yet this was nothing new. Denise had always been a disorderly warm-hearted, even impulsive person. That had probably been her undoing from time to time.

"Anything wrong, Denise? It's not like you to drink this early."

"I'm just enjoying myself. I don't often drive for three hours. But if you don't come to see me, I have to come to you."

"Edward doesn't want to come into town. I didn't want to come alone."

"I know. I disgrace you now that you're a married lady."

There was no mistaking the bitterness now. Mary put down her glass. "Something's wrong. What is it?"

"You know that I'm a former kept woman. A tart."

"No, I didn't."

"Everybody else in Calcutta knows it. It's too good not to get around. The thing is, he's coming to Calcutta. 'Big Boy,' as Tom calls him. That damned American expression." She was silent a moment, then shook her head. "Tom wants me to raise the Brazilian money from him."

"No."

Denise laughed. "I know. Bizarre, isn't it. My own husband." Suddenly Mary could see that her face was contorted with the effort to keep from tears.

Mary shivered a little. It was bewildering, too much to absorb at once. She couldn't sort it out. She hadn't the experience. She knew only that her friend was in trouble.

"Denise." She put her arm around her friend.

"Oh, Mary. It's so awful. Tom wants me to ask Alec for ten thousand pounds."

"Perhaps Tom doesn't know that you and Alec were . . . whatever you were."

"Not know? That's how we were married. I was a fishing fleeter too, you know." She laughed a little sheepishly. "Alec said it was time I got married. He said that was what I was made for, a sloppy woman like me. He said I'd need all the help I could get. So he gave me a lot of money, practically carte blanche through his agents, and shipped me off to Calcutta."

"No." Mary knew she should not be amused. Denise had been a kept woman, immoral, yet there was something so incongruous in this round little woman's being a rich man's mistress and then playing the rich catch.

Denise giggled. "I really cut a swath here."

"Tom didn't know?"

"No, but I didn't know he wasn't an earl. He looked like an earl. Then, when I found out, it didn't matter. I told him about Alec."

"That was right."

"It was awful. Tom wouldn't see me. It was nearly three weeks before he came back. Then he asked me to marry him."

"He must love you."

"I thought so too then. Now I think he just hated himself."

"But why?"

Denise eyed the taller woman. There was still an innocence about Mary. What could she know of a man who preferred a snake to his wife, or who could take his wife only if she went nude with black stockings, and carried a parasol . . . who must titillate him with the grotesque?

Denise shrugged. "It's too complicated. Anyway, I know now why Tom married me. Any woman who'd been discarded by another man and who was using his money to find a husband was what he deserved. The point is, what do I do now?"

"Tom's your husband."

"You mean I should ask Alec for the money? But he may want to . . . you know. He was my lover."

"But he's your friend too. You said he gave you that money. He must have liked you."

"He's a man."

"It doesn't matter. Go to him as a friend. He can only say no. And he may even lend it to you. Then you'll have the money and a friend too. And your husband."

"I don't even want to see him. I wanted all that to be past."

"It is past. You must remember that. And remember Tom is your husband. You may have married him for your own reasons. We all do that. But we do owe them something."

"You make it all sound so simple."

"Isn't it really?"

"I suppose so. If only Alec were all."

"There's more?" Denise was silent, contemplating her. "Tell me. I'm not very experienced but I'm not stupid."

"No. What's the use? You're just lucky you don't have any problems." Mary said nothing. Denise hesitated, then stood up. "I've said enough. I feel better now."

"Don't go. Edward will return for tea in an hour."

"I must go back. My lord and master may wonder where I am when he returns. If he ever notices."

She leaned up to kiss Mary on the cheek. "Don't worry about me. I'm a pretty tough old trollop. I'll think of something."

Mary followed the shorter woman to the verandah steps. Denise hesitated. "You have a beautiful place here. Sometimes I wish Tom and I lived out of Calcutta. In the country, like this."

"In the mofussil." Mary smiled.

"Yeah, the mofussil." Denise was aware that she had lapsed into American slang. Just like Tom.

She looked up at the taller woman. Mary was so lovely with her clear skin and deep blue eyes. She felt a pang of envy. Perhaps if she looked like that there'd be no snake as a rival.

She shrugged. "The mofussil certainly suits you." She brushed her hand across her face, weary, suddenly dreading the drive ahead.

"Thank you." Mary kissed her cheek. "So long," she said, imitating her friend, and smiled.

"Cheerio . . . damn it."

The little woman clumped down the verandah stairs to her auto. Ahmed held open the roadster door and Denise hoisted herself in. She fitted herself behind the wheel, turned on the ignition, and stepped on the starter. The motor hiccupped into life. Denise waved jauntily to Mary and the roadster lurched forward.

Mary heard the horn bleat at the river road, then saw the little car burst onto the road and scuttle along the river. She and Ahmed watched it out of sight around the bend, then Mary turned back to the house.

She stood at the entrance to the shadowy hall. The colored patches on the floor winked up at her, a ribald message from the sun. The tiny bells above the partitions tinkled fretfully, protesting the opened door.

Mary shivered. It was a shadowy world in which she lived . . . a world in which one's friend lived some sort of personal horror, in which one's husband used his wife's past for his own advancement. Life now was a far cry from her childhood in Cheltenham or her adult years at Roecroft. There was nothing familiar here, no certainty with which she could reassure herself.

Yet there was a normal life in India. There were normal people . . . marrying, having children, raising families. Mary remembered the personal columns in the *Statesman* . . . the notices of births and deaths, of engagements and weddings. All the dear, familiar happenings of British India. India was not all shadows and whisperings; there was normalcy. There had to be.

That night on the verandah Mary put down her coffee cup and addressed her husband. "Edward, I have been thinking. I would like us to have a baby."

He looked up sharply but Mary went calmly on. "If we are ever to have a baby now would be the time."

"I am forty-six years old."

"You're in marvelous health. For that matter, I'm not very young but I'm willing."

"It would be something to do, I suppose." He eyed her carefully, the same calculation with which he might size up a business opponent.

"It's more than something to do. I want a baby. That's natural for a woman. Please, Edward. I do."

She went to kneel before him, her eyes beseeching, even desperate.

He smiled. "I tell you what. I know it must be boring for you here at times. Let me have some dresses sent in for you to look at. From Perry's in Bombay. We can have a proper style show."

"I don't want a style show."

"We can have some jewelry sent in. Old Schweitzer up in Delhi has some fabulous emeralds. He would be glad to send a man."

"I don't want emeralds, Edward."

"No need to buy, just look. Besides, I'd like to see the models." He tried to look roguish.

"I want the baby, Edward."

"I'm sure you do. Very commendable. You want to live up to your contract."

"It isn't a contract! Please." She gripped his knees.

"I'll consider it."

"When?"

"When it is the right time. Now please go back to your chair. Ahmed may come in."

He watched her as she moved away. His eyes were careful, on guard.

The thought of babies had never before interested Mary. She wasn't even certain that she could have a child at her age.

She knew it wouldn't be easy to raise a baby in India. There would be the heat, disease, insects, even the special difficulties of having a baby in a Calcutta hospital, several hours away over a bumpy road. Kitty Jolliffe had done it but Kitty was young and had led a healthy, outdoor life. Mary knew she could claim neither virtue.

She would talk to Dr. MacDonough. She didn't want to go against her husband's wishes but, before approaching Edward again, she felt she might at least begin by learning what would be involved.

She took the estate auto—the only motor car she had yet learned to drive—and crossed the river on the Duleep-chauraha hand ferry. She then drove the few miles to the Mac-Donough bungalow.

She was fortunate on several counts—Dr. MacDonough was at home, he was sober, and Mrs. MacDonough was absent visiting a sister in Madras. Mary wondered briefly whether the doctor drank only when his wife was present.

The doctor welcomed Mary and led her to the small go-down he used as an office. It was crowded with a desk, a rickety wicker chair, and the bric-a-brac of medicine—books, instruments, bottles, charts. Despite the confusion the doctor's manner was brisk, pure Harley Street.

Mary told him why she had come. He beamed professionally.

"A baby? Splendid. We can't have too many Britons here."

"I'm really just inquiring. Is there any reason I shouldn't?"

"Have a baby? None at all. Done all the time."

"I mean at my age. I'm thirty-eight."

"You haven't completed the life change?"

"I haven't begun." Mary felt herself grow red.

"You're still equipped then."

"What would be the circumstances? Would there be anything special?"

"Good prenatal care, of course. I can supply you that, believe it or not." He gave a high, professional laugh. "I can also supply you a list of doctors in Calcutta if you wish. Max Taylor is a good man. You can go in to him for the last month."

"What about afterward? Raising him at York House?"

"No problem. I can give you a list for that too. Right sort of bottles, sterilizers, powders—have to avoid heat rash. And you'll want a certain sort of crib. Has to be equipped against mosquitoes."

"A net."

"Yes. And you'll have to set each leg in a cup of oil. The crib's legs, not your's." Again that high laugh.

"Why oil?"

"Ants. They like the smell of milk. Cockroaches too, of course, but they don't climb so well."

It went on like that, all very detailed and brisk. It was almost too brisk. Mary began to have a feeling that the doctor's mind was elsewhere, that there was something being evaded behind the terrible impersonality.

He showed her feeding charts, lists of baby clothes. Mary remembered that he himself had raised two children in India. The flow of information had ended and Mary was about to leave when the doctor leaned back in his chair, hands behind his head. His manner was no longer brisk.

"You know, Mrs. Goad, there is one matter that puzzles me about this. I'm interested that Edward Goad should consent to have a baby."

"Oh?"

"Have you spoken to him?"

"Of course."

"What did he say?"

"It was rather a surprise to him. He said he would consider it."

"Consider it." He repeated the words carefully.

"Is there any reason he wouldn't want a baby?"

"He's not young." He turned away, his eyes avoiding hers.

"He's not old either." She leaned forward. "Is there some reason? Edward did seem disturbed when I suggested a baby."

"I think you should ask him, Mrs. Goad. I'm a doctor."

"Exactly. You have a duty to tell me . . . a medical duty."

"It isn't medical." He looked at her and his eyes were suddenly compassionate. "I know you want this baby, Mrs. Goad. If he says no just leave it at that."

"That is all you will tell me?"

"That is all." He looked very tired.

"Good-bye, doctor, and thank you for the information. I shall see you again." She wanted there to be no doubt about it. She wanted a child. It was essential.

He called her back from the door. He had risen and came toward her. "Mrs. Goad, have you ever suggested to your husband that you both should live somewhere else?"

"Other than York House? He would never leave!"

"You're probably right. It would be useless. Good-bye, Mrs. Goad." He stood aside while she left. He looked as though he might soon be drinking from that whiskey bottle she had noticed among the bric-a-brac.

That night on the verandah Mary watched her husband. She wanted so much to tell Edward about her visit to Dr. MacDonough. It would be a proper and even wonderful thing to share with her husband, telling him about the feeding requirements and that Max Taylor might be their doctor. She might even repeat that silly remark of Dr. MacDonough's about putting her legs in a cup of oil.

She made herself be quiet. Her husband was so remote behind his newspaper. And she knew he would oppose her. He might well forbid her to see Dr. MacDonough again. She could not risk his anger now. First she would have to plan things, to be ready with answers to any objections.

So she sat silently, pondering. She could hear the faint evening sounds from beyond the verandah . . . the call of a crane from the marshes, the barking of pi-dogs from the coolie village, the everlasting, nightlong crowing of roosters, the tentative, distant music of coolie drum and flute.

She tried to sort things out. Childbirth at thirty-eight could be difficult. She had never tested her physical endurance, certainly not under the heat that would soon settle on York House.

And there really wasn't much time before beginning. To be born in the next cold weather, the baby must soon begin.

17

If she waited longer, the baby's earliest days would be smothered in daylong, nightlong heat. If she waited too long, of course, it could be too late for her entirely.

She was not unused to children; that would be an advantage. True, the Roecroft girls were older, entering school at ten, but their child would be ten someday and then she would be on firmer ground.

Meanwhile she must look over the house . . . must plan everything. If she could go to Edward with ideas and plans, he would see how much it meant to her. One night she would just go to him, take aside his newspaper, and lead him slowly into how it would be.

So Mary set about exploring the house. As a beginning, she would try to find a place for a nursery. Carrying a torch, she climbed to the dark upper floor of the house. It was dusty, shadowy. She paused once to peer from a turret window at the jute fields and river below, then followed the dim hall, opening doors, flashing her light into the unused and empty rooms.

One room gave Mary particular difficulty in entering. The door had been locked but the padlock had rusted. Mary leaned her strong body against the door and pushed into the room. She flicked her torch, probing the shadows.

Her eyes widened. The room was far from empty. It seemed almost a storage area. The first object she saw was a child's hobby horse.

Moving closer, Mary picked out a name on the saddle blanket. It had been stitched in gilt and the letters spelled "Julie."

She turned her light toward the walls. A reflected light flashed back at her and she saw that a mirrored door was returning her beam. She went closer.

It was a clothes armoire. A row of little dresses clustered behind the door. A child's parasol and two pair of small shoes rested beneath the dresses. Her light flicked to the side and picked out a blackboard. The name "Julie" had been scrawled in chalk.

Mary turned off her torch and backed toward the heavy door. She closed it, its hinges squeaking irritably, and went slowly down the hall toward the stairs.

One thought pounded in her head. Who was Julie? Was she Edward's child? Was she alive or dead? If Edward's child, that meant he had been married before . . . might still be married.

Mary felt her way down the dark stairway. She hardly knew how she reached the large hall. Her husband was in his office but Mary went quickly past. She couldn't face him about this. Not yet. She first wanted to calm herself.

But she had to know the answers . . . she had to! There was one person who might tell her. She would see Dr. Mac-Donough again.

26

DR. MacDONOUGH LEANED FORWARD IN HIS chair. "Wouldn't it be better just to give up the idea of having a baby?"

"I want to know, doctor. If there is a baby named 'Julie' and it is Edward's, I should know."

"There is no baby named Julie."

"What is it then? I found that room and all the child's things. I don't like mysteries, doctor."

"There's no mystery in this." He brushed his hand uncertainly across his eyes. Mary saw that they were bloodshot again. Perhaps his wife was back.

He hesitated. "There aren't many people who know this story. I heard it from one of my patients. I shan't tell you who. It explains many things about York House. Frankly I'm surprised he even married."

"What happened?"

"It's rather horrible." He looked at her carefully.

"If it affected my husband I should know."

"I'd best begin at the beginning." He leaned back, closed his eyes, and told the story as though he were recalling it from deep in his memory. Deep but still vivid to him.

"Edward Goad came to this area about nineteen-o-six. He

had been in India a year or two by then. He was single, about nineteen, and as assistant overseer he was a hard worker.

"He was obviously a man who was going to get somewhere. He didn't mix much at the estate, didn't go into Calcutta. He worked twelve to sixteen hours a day and saw to it that his coolies worked hard too. He was a hard man, even then, but just. My patient said that his workers liked him because he treated them fairly and more production meant more money in their pockets. Then, about nineteen-ten, Goad went to England and when he came back he had a wife with him."

"Edward has been married!"

"Yes. She was evidently a good enough sort but she probably never took to life on a jute estate, not as the wife of a coolie boss. Then, after three years, there was a little girl. Julie was her name. It doesn't sound particularly English but my patient thought she had been named after Juliana, the Dutch crown princess born about then."

He glanced at Mary who was sitting with her eyes down, her hands in her lap, folded as a pair of fists. "Goad worked harder than ever then. He'd been made an overseer right after his marriage, then assistant manager, and when Julie was about eight he was made manager. He was only in his thirties but he had been strict with himself and it had paid off."

"The trouble was that he was not only strict with himself. He was hard on his workers too. There was a new type of worker coming in then. Punjabi were being brought down and they weren't as easy to handle as the Bengali. There was one occasion when he banned a religious ceremony. It would have taken three days of the cutting time. The coolies were mutinous but he took a cane to a couple and that was that.

"It was his daughter who was his weak spot. Julie. My patient said you never saw one without the other. He had her on a pony when she was three . . . he'd had the pony shipped all the way from England . . . and when it wasn't too hot he took her into the fields with him and she'd trot along beside him. The only time he would go into Calcutta was when the governor gave his annual children's party and then Goad would take his family. He'd sit with Julie at the puppet show and he'd hold her on the little carousel the governor had set up on his grounds.

"He was good to his wife; there was no doubt of her importance to him. But it was Julie he hovered over. He was a rough man, tough in his stubborn Yorkshire way, but with Julie he was gentle. My patient said that to see that tough man bending down to listen to his little daughter was to know what father-love was.

"Then one day Julie disappeared. She'd been seen on her pony going out to meet her father and she didn't come home. My patient said it was terrible. Goad rushed through the fields like a crazy man. The Hooghly was in flood and he got out the whole coolie force at midnight, working by torch light, dragging the river bottom. There was no trace of Julie anywhere."

The doctor paused. His face was sweating. "Do you mind if I have a drink? I do drink, you know."

Mary shook her head. She didn't trust herself to speak. The doctor poured himself a quick drink and drank it, his hand shaking unsteadily. "Where was I?"

"They didn't find her."

"Yes." Pausing, he closed his eyes a moment. "On the third day there came the first trace. It was a finger. Goad had fallen asleep at his desk evidently . . . he'd gone without sleep for two days . . . and when he waked there on the desk by his head lay a small finger. There was no doubt what it was. It had been chopped off her right hand.

"This time the police were called up from Calcutta. For once Goad felt he couldn't cope with something himself. He didn't crack, mind you. His wife went into hysterics, but Goad just seemed to get a little more silent.

"The police were certain it was one of the coolie workers. But which? There were none missing. And there could be ten or a dozen who might hate him.

"Meanwhile, each day, another piece of his daughter was placed where it would be found. It was pieces of her fingers the first few days, then whole fingers, then toes, pieces of flesh. The house was watched, the fields were patrolled, yet each day . . . somehow . . . a piece of his daughter was put where Goad or her mother would find it. Houses were being searched, the whole countryside was organized. The workers continued peacefully in the fields but every day another horror was found.

"It was nearly two weeks before the ultimate was reached. That morning a small package was delivered. It was addressed to Goad and in the package was a single eye. It was his daughter's eye, no doubt of that, and it could only mean that, if she were not already dead, it was near the end. There could not be very much left of the child.

"And that day they caught Gujmal Singh. He was about eighteen and he was somehow identified as the boy who had mailed the package. He was brought out to the estate and identified as a cousin of one of the coolies.

"Goad asked to be left alone with him. He took Gujmal Singh into one of the sugar shacks. York House had a few acres in sugar then and there was always a vat of boiling sugar during the cutting season.

"Goad was alone in the shack with Singh for about an hour and when he came out he knew where his daughter was. My patient said it was hard to tell who looked the more frightening . . . Goad, grim and like an avenging angel . . . or Singh, half boiled and in shreds."

There was a groan from Mary. "My God."

"They found Julie but it was too late. She'd been dead five or six hours the doctors said. It was remarkable, they said, that she had lived so long.

"The terrible thing was that there were two women involved. They were the ones who guarded Julie while the coolies worked on the estate. There were six of them altogether, all workers, and they were all hanged. It was a sensational trial up here while it lasted but the war had recently ended, the men were coming back, and the public soon had other interests. My patient said no one talked about it anymore."

"How awful." Mary sat immobile.

"That is why he never leaves York House. And why, I suspect he doesn't want another child."

"Is Julie buried there?"

"In a way. He had her cremated and her ashes were scattered over the jute fields. He could have left York House since then; he has had offers at twice its value. He has resisted purchase, coolie troubles, hartals . . . he will never leave York House."

There was a silence. Flies droned in the corner, spiraling in and out of the patch of sun.

"What happened to the wife?"

"She went back to England. She'd stuck it a long time but this was too much. She wanted him to go but he wouldn't leave. She got her divorce. He didn't contest it. Now he owns York House. My patient said that in a way it was bought with Julie."

Mary roused herself. "I think I must leave."

"I'm sorry, Mrs. Goad. This is a terrible thing to tell you. I haven't said it easily."

"I wanted to know."

"Ahmed knows. He has been with Goad from the beginning. He is devoted to Goad sahib."

"I know."

"There is nothing simple out here, Mrs. Goad. Not even having a baby."

"I see that now. Good-bye." She put her hand out to him, almost to feel the reassuring touch of another human. He shook her hand. His palm was moist with sweat.

That night Mary sat opposite her husband on the verandah. She looked at him reading his paper, erect, disciplined, alert. It was almost, she thought, as though he were listening.

She watched him. That face was so broad and strong. Yet perhaps the hard mouth was too strong, too disciplined. And that yellowish skin reflected some inner fire. It was petrified lava.

Goad looked up and caught her eye. He nodded slightly, went back to his reading. Mary recognized that look as a defense. He was telling her to stay away.

She understood more now . . . why he stayed away from Calcutta, from the neighbors. He was guarding York House. It was not people who had rejected him; he had rejected them. York House was sacred ground. It was his trust.

Mary closed her eyes. Why had he asked her to marry him? What had made him choose her for York House, or choose any woman?

She looked again at her husband. She should probably get out of York House, out of the marriage entirely. India was a dark and frightening land, where a child could be cut to pieces, where the fields had known the last whimpering of a bewildered little girl.

Her husband looked up from his paper and smiled a little, carefully. Mary felt her heart catch. She couldn't run away now. He needed her. His marriage had been a cry for help.

The next morning, after her husband had gone into the fields, Mary went to the top floor. She again pushed aside the unlocked door and entered the dark and crowded room. She pulled back the closed windows and let in bright sunlight.

The things Mary had half seen the day before now showed clearly. She saw the saddle blanket with "Julie" stitched on it. She saw that the horse's eyes were blue calico, sewn haphazardly to each side of the head with pink thread. It gave the small horse a slightly red-rimmed set of eyes, not unlike those of Dr. MacDonough's.

Mary fingered the dresses hung from the racks. They were white or pink, quite long. Mary pictured the child in her ankle-length dresses, parading sedately with her father.

Mary now knew what she must do. It was monstrous to have Julie's room so dirty. What had seemed forlorn Mary now found unhealthy.

The next day Mary borrowed a broom, brush, and dustpan from the godown. She knew that her husband had gone to the fields and she planned a brisk several hours cleaning, dusting, tidying. She had tied a kerchief around her head and was determined.

Mary pushed aside the unlocked door, entered the dark room, and closed the door behind her. She opened the window and set to work. It was then that she saw her husband sitting quietly in a corner of the room.

"Edward."

"Ahmed said you would be here this morning. I am sorry to have deceived you about going into the fields but I thought I should be here to welcome you."

"How did Ahmed know I would be here."

"Ahmed knows most of what happens in this house. That is his responsibility."

"I see."

"He is my watchdog."

They stared at each other. Mary had stilled her fright at seeing him. How tired he looks, she thought. He must have known even yesterday that I had found this place. She felt a sudden sympathy for him and went in that familiar manner to sink on her knees in the dust before him.

"Edward, I wanted to clean up this room. I know about Julie."

"Dr. MacDonough." He nodded gravely.

"I made him tell me after I found this room! I want to help you forget what happened! To keep this place with her things in it is not good for you. Let me keep it clean for you."

"That won't bring Julie back."

"Does this? It's not fair to her. Let me fix it as she would want it. Sunlight, bright new curtains. A child's room."

"And put a child in it, I suppose. Your child."

"Our child. I want one more than ever now. You need one. A real child."

She knew immediately she had said the wrong thing. This room contained a real child. He gripped her arms, his face mottled with anger.

"There will not be another child in York House."

"Edward, my arm."

He thrust her away from him, fighting to control himself. When he spoke his voice rasped with the effort.

"You still don't know what it means to have a baby in India."

"Kitty Jolliffe has done it!" Mary was frightened but knew she now had to stand up to him—for his sake as well as hers.

"Kitty Jolliffe. You've seen her baby. Why do you think he sleeps so hard! He looks drugged, doesn't he?"

"He has a rash." Mary heard herself screaming the words.

"A rash—yes. And that rash disturbs that sensitive husband of hers. He can't work when the baby screams. So you know what she does? She gives the baby opium."

"No."

"Oh yes. It's common practice among the coolie women. Ian Jolliffe knew that. He insisted. What about you? Will you give our baby opium? It gets hot here. Babies scream with the rash."

He turned away but she went to him and gripped his shoulders desperately. "I don't care what the coolie mothers do, or Kitty either! We don't have to! The MacDonoughs didn't. Now their babies are healthy and safe in England."

"The MacDonoughs." He swung to her and she could see his face. She waited, knowing that whatever he said would be terrible. When he spoke his voice was tired, deeply sad. "The MacDonoughs have no children. They died long ago. Of dengue when they were small."

Mary shook her head desperately. "But she talks about them. She talks about seeing them next year on leave!"

"I know. She even keeps their room as it was, and keeps their photos on the verandah. But they're dead. That's why he drinks so much and why she's so bitter. She feels as a doctor he should have saved them. I think he does too."

"No."

"India's a forge, Mary! Realize it! People are hammered out on it. I won't bring another baby into this land."

"But we mustn't give up! I don't care what the Jolliffes do

or what happened to others. We need a baby, Edward! We must have a marriage!"

"There will be no more children here."

She drew a breath. "You hate India, don't you? Everything you do is to take revenge on it . . . the way you force the land and the coolies. It's not because you love York House . . . it's for revenge."

He said nothing but his hard face confirmed what she had said. She nodded slowly. "That is why you married me. It wasn't just for a memsahib or out of loneliness. I represented the Raj to you . . . the Empire. You found me quaint and old-fashioned. You used me as revenge. You were spitting at the Empire."

They stared at each other and she saw no denial in his face. It was almost as though he too were realizing it for the first time. He took a step toward her and she closed her eyes, expecting to be hit. There was no blow. She heard the old door wrenched open and slammed. She was alone.

An hour later Mary found herself at the dak bungalow. The ferryman at Duleep-chauraha had withdrawn from the midday sun. Two women, their cotton saris tucked between their legs, had been pounding laundry on the riverbank but they too had now gone.

It should have been a scene of peace for Mary. There was a harmony, a timelessness. She felt no peace. The real mistress of York House was a child, not even a real child.

Why *had* he married her? He had gone to Calcutta to find a wife. He had selected her and brought her to his home. Was it really because he hated the Raj and wanted revenge?

Mary pressed her hands convulsively to her eyes. He probably didn't know himself why he had married her. He had said he wanted a memsahib, someone to serve as a hostess for York House, and she had seemed a lady to him. Yet he never wanted a party when they had married, nor would he have guests.

Perhaps he had married out of loneliness and then, when he had married her, had hated his weakness and hated her. So he had punished her and punished himself.

Mary uttered a little cry of hopelessness. She was not used to judging people. Life had been simple for her, first at Cheltenham, then at Roecroft. Except for Tim, she had never had to test herself. She was too unprepared.

A crested lark in the tree above Mary lifted its head with

a sudden perky motion and floated down toward the river. Its fluted call drifted back before it sank out of sight in the marsh grass. A pair of crows alighted on the verandah of the bungalow, hopped vainly in search of food, then cawed angrily up toward the sky.

What now, Mary? There goes your latest effort. Your husband doesn't want a baby. You can add that to the list . . . no running the house, no being his hostess, now no family. It is really quite funny in a way. You took your place in the ranks and then found you were not even to be given a uniform. Nobody even knew you were present.

This was the worst. A baby would have made them a family. It would have been a link with her husband, and a link with other families in India. Nobody would stand alone.

But what would the future be now? She and her husband would probably build parallel lives, sharing little except place of residence. She would make a few friends of her own somehow, would probably go more to Calcutta. He couldn't keep her bound to the house. She would lead her own life, independent of his. It would be a poor sort of marriage, the sort her father had received.

Mary felt anger rising in her. She was a person, damn it. Not a sniveling petitioner. She had made her own way in the world and had something to bring to a marriage.

How much did she owe him? She had made every effort so far. It had been she who had tried to conciliate, to play the good wife. There must be a limit somewhere.

She pressed her hands angrily to her cheeks. Below her the drifting river murmured caution, reminding Mary of its long, patient search for the Bay. The shisham tree above her reached out a protective shade. The marsh grass waved in slow, soothing rhythm. The land was making tentative, almost apologetic advances.

Mary stood up. She would try once more. But only once. He was her husband but there was a limit.

Edward Goad held the piece of paper between the thumb and forefinger of his left hand and poured in the gray-green flakes of ganja. He poured evenly, up and down the length of paper.

He put down the tin container, smoothed the flaky crumbs with his right forefinger, licked the edge of the paper, and rolled the edges together.

His hands shook a little as he put the ganja in his mouth. He had come to a decision and had to tell Julie. It would be a farewell in a way. If ever there was a time for self-control it was now.

He lighted the end of the paper tube and stretched out on the bed. He knew the Punjabi woman would be sitting outside the bustee as usual, waiting to bring him another smoke if he called.

Sucking deeply, Goad held the smoke in a corner of his mouth, drawing only a fraction at a time into his lungs. He emptied his mouth slowly, then drew deeply on the paper for another supply. He could already feel the response in his bloodstream and knew it wouldn't be long.

Goad looked thoughtfully at the ceiling. He didn't regret the years of ganja. It had made livable a good many terrible years. Ganja had filled a void, had saved his sanity, probably life itself. But now it must go.

His eyes took in the long-familiar hut, the mud walls and single window. It was the only window in the coolie village with a glass pane. The Punjabi woman hadn't wanted that. She said it made their relationship too open. He wanted the pane of glass. He was afraid of mosquitoes and, if he were going to smoke ganja in her hut, he wanted to feel safe.

He sucked deeply, emptied his mouth into his lungs, then sucked again on the paper tube. Then it came—the release, the power.

The man on the bed groaned and the Punjabi woman entered. He groaned again and she caught the word "Julie." She knew then that it was his "daughter."

She watched. She knew what had to be done and knew that Ahmed would do his part.

In a way the woman felt sorry. She had nothing against the memsahib. But the mem should realize that Goad sahib was more Indian now than English, that the jute land had taken him over entirely.

She looked up toward the house. It shouldn't be long before the mem came. The sahib had always spent part of his afternoons this way and Ahmed had protected him, telling the mem he was in the fields. But now Ahmed would send her to the bustee. Ahmed loved the sahib and wanted him left alone with his Julie, wanted things to be the way they used to be. It was best for everyone.

The Punjabi woman looked at the man on the bed. Goad

was asleep now. His breathing told her he would be this way for several hours. Plenty of time for the memsahib to come and find him. And that should be the end of them. Englishwomen did not like it when their men used ganja. It was worse than a man's being ill in his brain. Ahmed had assured her that for this Englishwoman it would be especially bad.

The sweet, sickish aroma of ganja filled the room. The man on the bed snored heavily, his strong features relaxed and inert, his eyes lost.

The Punjabi woman lifted her head, listening. The sound of a motorcar reached her. It was the mem's auto coming toward the village from the great house. It had an impatient sound.

The Punjabi woman looked at the man on the bed, went to draw the curtain from the open doorway, then went outside to wait. The memsahib would arrive in a moment and she would then lead her into the bustee and show her the sahib.

27

IN THE JAIL AT POONA THE MAHATMA PATIENTLY turned his spinning wheel. The last of his visitors had gone and his thin face was contemplative.

His visitors had been fellow members of the Indian National Congress. He was not surprised at the news they had brought. He had simply refused to acknowledge it before this.

They had said that something must be done to revive the drive toward swaraj. The momentum had died since his hunger strike. In fact, the hunger strike, being directed toward the Untouchable problem, had set back swaraj.

The Mahatma reached out a weary hand to drink his lemon juice. He believed he had shown India the way to swaraj. His civil disobedience campaign had worked. The concessions by Britain in the Gandhi-Irwin Pact had testified to that. Then what had gone wrong?

The elderly prisoner paused in his spinning. He knew the causes. There had been a change of government in England for one thing. The Labour government of Ramsay MacDonald had been replaced by a coalition government. MacDonald was still Prime Minister but Stanley Baldwin and his Conservative Party held a majority in his Cabinet. In a way the Prime Minister was their prisoner. The Conservatives were less conciliatory than Labour toward India. Their choice for viceroy, this Willingdon, urbane and charming as he might be, was proving there was steel in him too.

But there was something else. The thought of it brought sadness to the ascetic face. There had been dissension among the Indians themselves. The Congress Party had been torn, Hindus wrangling with Muslims, the left wing shouting at the right. Indians had united behind him for the pact but now that it had been won, they wrangled over the concessions.

Gandhi turned the spinning wheel slowly. There was only one solution. There must be another civil disobedience campaign. The old selflessness must be brought back. It would not be easy. It had been some years since the last one and the machinery would be rusty.

But it had to be done. He needed to reassure himself that there was more to his people than rivalries. India must show him it deserved swaraj. Otherwise, the work of his life was for nothing.

Lord Willingdon stood at the window of his study at Vice-regal Palace and looked down at the marchers beyond the Peasant's gates. He had returned immediately to Delhi when the demonstrations had started.

It was impressive. Thousands marched by, men, women, and children, orderly and silent. Only occasionally did a loud shout of "swaraj" or "jai hind" reach his ears.

"Greatest demonstration I've ever seen in Delhi, sir." It was his secretary Jeffrey speaking, standing just behind.

"Can you read the signs?"

"Yes, sir. Those ranks are from the Kishan League. That's the Peasant's League from the United Provinces. That's the Textile Workers Union coming on. They're from Bombay. The Railway Federation passed some time ago."

"They're from Bengal?"

"Yes, sir. Patna. That's a long way, sir."

"Women and children too. One must give them credit, Jeffrey. When the Trade Union Federation and the Trade Union Congress finally do get together, they do very well. Close the window."

He turned away. He knew there would be no lack of those silent marchers. They would continue for several hours. "Do you have the reports?"

"Yes, sir." His secretary picked up a sheaf of telegrams. "From Dacca, sir. The Congress flag was hoisted over the Union Jack on two public buildings this morning. Taken down promptly with no difficulty." He glanced at another. "Barclay's Bank picketed in Madras, as well as the Imperial Tobacco office."

"Imperial Tobacco." The viceroy shook his head.

"Perhaps nonsmokers, sir." The secretary started to smile but at Lord Willingdon's expression he quickly continued. "District officer in Orissa reports land tax withholding has spread to four more districts."

"There's no doubt of it. It's another civil disobedience compaign. Lord Irwin had his turn, now it's mine."

"The Mahatma won over Lord Irwin, sir."

"I'm afraid I'm not such a good Christian as Lord Irwin. My reply will have to be a little less . . . conciliatory. We can start by abrogating the pact. We can revert then, start over." His face was grim.

"But it's been signed, sir. The Prime Minister himself approved."

"We can unsign it! It was his Labour government that agreed to that pact. We have a coalition now. Let them come to grips on this back in London—do they want to hold India or don't they?"

"It could mean a split, sir. Parliament might have to vote."

"Let them. That's their job."

"But Labour might win, sir. The pact is very popular in England. They are tired of hearing about India. The Conservatives might lose."

"If England wants to let the Empire go, let it say so. If it wants me to hold on, let it show me. Because my methods may need a strong back-up."

Lord Willingdon turned to the window. There were cries of swaraj. Louder and fiercer. The viceroy nodded. "Shout your heads off. They'll hear you all the way to London."

In London the debate was begun. The issue was simple, whether or not the Gandhi-Irwin Pact should be extended or allowed to lapse. The Conservatives favored an end to it. Labour, a minority in its own government, had chosen to fight.

A Labour speaker was addressing the House. He looked at the Conservative benches opposite and nodded grimly. "The issue is a simple question of morality. Britain has given its word. Home rule has been promised. It should not even be necessary to ask our colleagues to renew the pact. It should be assumed that Conservative honor is as dear to it as to all Englishmen."

He said the words gravely, nodding his massive head. He was a big man, seeming even larger in his rumpled clothes. His heavy body and bushy, unruly hair indicated only his coal-mining origin, not the intellect that had kept him in the forefront of his party.

The House of Commons listened. The Strangers Gallery, filled with London's Indian students, murmured approvingly. The debate had lasted three days so far. Labour was bringing up its biggest guns now. It was certain it was on firm ground. It was appealing to the morality of the British people, its sense of fair play. In swaraj it had an issue that would strengthen its position in the coalition.

The speaker shifted his feet ponderously, forcing the gallery to silence. He lowered his head momentarily to the dispatch box and continued.

"We owe India self-rule because we promised it them. Not only this government, long before that. By the Liberal government of the Great War. Thousands of Indian dead at Gallipoli, in Mesopotamia, and in German East Africa testified that they believed us. They died for a free Britain. We owe them their freedom as a debt of honor."

He spoke longer. He talked of "making a friend of India instead of a vassal," of the "need for friends in these somber times." He made his points heavily, with the massive patience of a man certain that his cause was both British and righteous.

That evening an invited few were gathered at the Conservative Club. They discussed the afternoon's debate and watched a silent man who sat to one side and thoughtfully smoked his pipe. He had a sturdy, broad face and was said to be the epitome of John Bull. He was their leader, twice

Prime Minister, now serving in a lesser post in the coalition but still, in his way, serving England and the Empire.

"This debate is dangerous, sir." It was the fretful voice of the secretary for India. "We had agreed to support the Prime Minister on foreign matters. It is only on domestic affairs we can disagree."

His Conservative leader eyed him. "I consider India a domestic matter. Not foreign."

"We could lose. Their speaker made an impression today. The press took down every word he said." The secretary clucked irritably. "Morality . . . always morality. You would think Labour had a monopoly on it."

The former Prime Minister glanced at his secretary. "How many votes do we have now?"

"A majority of perhaps fifteen, sir. Perhaps less after today's speech."

"Not very many. A close vote could mean another general election. We don't want that. The country couldn't afford it."

He closed his eyes. He knew very well what he might be doing, destroying the coalition which he had agreed to serve. "Stable," he had been called, and "trustworthy." These words had always been draped about his head like so many garlands. Now he was being called traitor, risking the government for his own ambitions.

Was it true? Was it really the Empire he wished to preserve or his own exalted position? He had always felt this government needed bucking up, that it was too intellectual, soft. If the coalition broke up over this, so be it. Better a government than the Empire.

The minister for home affairs spoke up in his precise voice. He was a small, thin man. "Extending the pact would help us with the Americans, sir. Gandhi is very popular there. It might put us in a firmer position to open financial talks." The minister cleared his throat. "I suggest we might concede a temporary extension, sir. If Labour wins, we may lose our majority in the coalition. If we concede we shall preserve our position."

"We should also be conceding India." The John Bull figure refilled his pipe, put a match to it, methodically drew in the flame. The others waited, almost fascinated while the tobacco caught in a puff of smoke, then settled to an aromatic glow.

He spoke slowly. "There is more at stake here than the

pact or even India." He turned in his chair to face them. "Did you notice the galleries today?"

"There were a good many Indians there, sir. Students mostly."

"It was not the Strangers Gallery I was watching. It was the Diplomatic Gallery. The Italian ambassador was there again. He has never before come to the House. Why should he come for a debate on India?"

"Probably sent by Il Duce."

"Exactly. And the German ambassador was there as well. Herr Hitler is sizing us up too. We are a new government, gentlemen. The question is whether this government can be a firm one or a government that concedes."

His advisers moved restlessly. The secretary for India shook his head. "We may have no government at all if we don't extend the pact. Labour will hammer us into a general election."

"We still have several days." He turned in his chair to the window and the wintry evening outside. "Tomorrow we'll bring up our own guns."

But the next afternoon Labour again went on the attack. Its speaker, this time one of the nation's intellectuals, was as gentle as his predecessor had been ponderous. He was tall, curiously elegant with his slender, waxed mustache and wavy black hair. He had spoken softly for some time, never looking toward the benches opposite, but now he raised his head and the irony grew sharper.

"I would remind the Honorable Members before me that General Clive and Lord Hastings have been dead for many years. So too has the illustrious Mr. Kipling. I'm quite certain this news has penetrated the Conservative Club. The British Square has been replaced by the tank; the Thin Red Line has given way to the bomber plane."

The speaker paused to eye the opposite benches. The occupants were no longer his fellow members; they were the enemy. He glared at them and his voice was a knife. "The world changes. One regrets the past but to embrace it as the present would be folly. England needs wisdom now, not the trumpet. Not the battlefield but conciliation." His voice was a snarl. "Clive has gone, so has Kipling. Let that world go with them. And good riddance."

He waited, switching his stare from one face before him to another, almost as though restraining himself from assault.

Then his face resumed its composed mask. He bowed briefly to the dais, then returned to his seat on the front bench.

There was a silence in the House disturbed only by the rustle of papers in the Press Gallery. The Labour member seated next to the last speaker touched him on the shoulder in quiet approval. The eyes of the House turned toward the first speaker for the Conservatives.

The speaker stood up and moved athletically to his position by the dispatch box. He bowed to the dais and turned to the benches stretching before him to the crowded galleries. Crowds were nothing new to him. He had been an athletic hero in his younger days, representing England at two Olympic Games, and was now one of the brighter young men in the party. His blond good looks, candid face, and quick grace belied a hardened and very tough competitor. He began his reply on a gentle note.

"The Honorable Member preceding has spoken of General Clive and Mr. Rudyard Kipling as though they were foreigners. These men, with whom he has been so . . . shall we simply say 'disrespectful' . . . were great Englishmen. Let us hope that his name is known in Britain half so long as theirs."

There were scattered murmurs of "hear, hear" from the Conservative benches, echoed with polite handclapping from supporters in the Strangers Gallery.

The speaker paused to stare calmly at his Labour opponent, was met by indifference, and turned again to his remarks. "The Honorable Member has spoken of England's not being left behind in this changing world. I submit that our first duty is not to the world but to England, specifically to our English out in India. They are thousands of miles from home, our brothers, sons, sisters. We have a duty to them."

He paused, went on more forcibly, gathering strength and power. He told the House that his party was not against swaraj; it had no intention of breaking a promise . . . though that promise had been contracted by the previous Labour Government.

He cried that India was not ready for swaraj; that was the Conservative position. As he said this, he turned full face toward the Indians in the gallery. He said that to cast India adrift at that time would be a crime far worse than nonfulfillment of a pledge. "It would be infanticide," he cried. "For India is the child of this Empire. It is from the imperial father that India has learned to walk, to take her first awkward steps. To push this child out of the home, still unsteady, would be to destroy the child." He pointed an accusing finger at the opposing benches. "Infanticide! Let the Labour Party carry that guilt, gentlemen, but not England!"

A storm broke loose in the staid House. Labour members were on their feet to cries of "Withdraw . . . withdraw!" There were shouts and whistles from the Indians in the gallery.

His party leader sat silently among his applauding followers, grimly nodded an approving head. Noting the approval, the speaker waited determinedly amid the uproar. There was no hurry.

In Yevrada Gaol the Mahatma received reports on the London debate. It was clear to him what was happening. If the new coalition government could repudiate the pact it would mean a reversion to the hard rule of the old days.

Gandhi bore no ill will against the British. For most of them India was a long way away. They had been buried in an economic slump for several years. This was no time to be giving up empire; quite the opposite.

He closed his eyes in brief prayer. The British must not vote down the pact. His people must be given another chance.

In Delhi Lord Willingdon read the cables in his study. Jeffrey stood nearby.

"When do you think they will vote, sir?"

"When the Conservative Party thinks it has the votes."

"It may not get the votes, sir, the way it's going."

"In which case our discussions are purely academic. There will be a new viceroy."

"I should hate to see that, sir."

"Thank you, Jeffrey. I shall recommend your services to my successor."

"Oh, I didn't mean that, sir."

"I know. Thank you." The viceroy put down the cables and rubbed his eyes; his slender, aristocratic face was tired. He found it hard to be patient with the democratic spectacle sometimes, even in the Mother of Parliaments.

"It seems so obvious, doesn't it?" he murmured.

"What's that, sir?"

"The correct policy in this case. Neither the pact nor force but both."

"I don't understand, sir."

"A dual policy. Keep the terrorists down with one hand and extend more power with the other. The stick and the carrot."

"A bit difficult to apply, sir. With both sides rocking the boat, so to speak." The secretary permitted a smile to disturb his usually careful face. He was aware he had mixed a few metaphors.

"As always, it's a question of timing. First the stick, beat them until they are willing to listen; then tell them what they wanted to hear in the first place. Only now on our terms."

"If Labour wins the vote I'm afraid it'll be the carrot, sir."

"If our former Prime Minister wins we shall want a very big stick. Because then we shall hear from Mr. Gupta."

"I certainly hope the Conservatives can win, sir."

"Spoken like a loyal civil servant, Jeffrey. Always stick with the commanding officer."

"Yes, sir." He was never quite certain he understood His Excellency. "Will there be any reply to the cables, sir?"

"Not for the moment. We might send along a copy of the Lord's Prayer, though we may be needing it ourselves."

"Yes, sir." Again that damned irony of His Lordship, very unsettling to a man used to the safe world of form letters and budget estimates. "Will that be all, sir?"

"Yes, thank you." The viceroy watched his secretary leave and shook his head. He really shouldn't be such a trial to Jeffrey; he had promised Her Ladyship.

He fingered the cables. It was really too bad about the pact; it might actually have worked, given more normal times. Now they were all in the same boat . . . he, Gandhi, even Gupta . . . caught up in some historical movement on which they could really have little influence. They were adrift on some vast ground swell, all in the same leaky lifeboat. The best they could do was bail for all they were worth.

A pity about revolutions but that was the way they were. They soon got out of hand. They started with the intellectuals and ended up with the apes. The French intellectuals were followed by Robespierre. Lenin was followed by this Stalin fellow. In America they were fortunate; the distances were too great. They couldn't get at each other.

The viceroy shrugged. At least he knew his role. He was a professional.

He put on his reading spectacles and eyed the cables. He looked like an aging but experienced actor getting up once more in a long-familiar role.

In Calcutta Gupta read the newspaper accounts of the debate with contempt. Each day the *Statesman* or the *Times of India* printed the names of the speakers in the House and gave a brief résumé of the debate.

Gupta would read the articles, then toss them aside with impatience. He knew that swaraj would not be decided in a debate. There must first be a disaster; there must be chaos. India must be made to appear a liability, then England might let go.

Meanwhile he waited. He wasn't interested in swaraj. He waited only for the best time to make the next move. For him to obtain the maximum attention from his move, India must be restless, in a surly mood. For that he hoped grimly that the vote would be against the pact, that Labour's helpful efforts to extend it would be defeated.

Besides, he was in no hurry. It amused him to watch the efforts of this Captain Flemyng to locate him. When the time came to act he would put an end to the captain's efforts as well.

The debate in Parliament had gone on for two weeks but was now drawing to a close. The issue would be put to a vote.

As the day arrived the attention of all England was on the House. The newspapers focused the issue. "Vote for the pact," exhorted the Labour dailies. "A vote for the pact is a vote for freedom."

"Vote against," urged the Conservative papers. "Back up our British in India. Our true pact is with them."

The House galleries, increasingly crowded with Indians—students or government officials—watched the voting intently. One by one the members rose from their places to record their "ayes" or "nays," the ayes for extending the pact, the nays for its suspension.

The last member cast his vote and the galleries leaned forward to catch the voice of the tally clerk. He had picked up the tally sheet and now stepped forward to the dais.

"Voting in favor of extension of Bill Number Three Hundred Seventy-nine, the Gandhi-Lord Irwin Pact . . ." He paused to peer at his sheet of paper. "Two hundred forty-three."

There was a murmur of approval from the Labour benches, a note of hope from the gallery.

The tally clerk picked up the second sheet. "Voting against extension of the pact . . . two hundred fifty-eight."

There was an immediate uproar from the Conservatives, hand-clapping, shouts of "well done." The secretary of state for India held out his hands to the Conservative leader. "A victory, sir. Britain still wants India."

"Do you see the galleries?" The secretary followed the other's glance. The Indians were filing slowly out.

"They look angry, sir."

"I'm glad Willingdon can't see that."

"He'll hold India, sir. With God's help."

The other glanced at him. "More likely the other fellow's." He gestured downward.

28

NEWS OF THE ABROGATION OF THE GANDHI-IRWIN Pact reached Calcutta very promptly. It was the week of the Saturday Club masquerade and the two events competed for discussion that week.

There was some talk of canceling the masquerade. Several members considered that the theme "Durbar, 1877," might be pouring salt in India's wounds at the moment.

The question of canceling was overruled. Club members and their wives both agreed on this—the males because to cancel might be interpreted by the Indians as a show of weakness. It was decided there must be no doubt that Calcutta favored a firm hand. The ladies were against cancellation because the Slap party would be the last big party of the year, perhaps a last opportunity for those still-unattached fishing fleeters. The cold weather season must carry on as usual.

The night of the party was festive. Guests arrived at the Slap in a steady flow of autos, taxis, even a few sedate gharries or open carriages.

Little effort had been made to decorate the club; a few streamers hung from the rafters of the ballroom, a papier-mâché fountain had been placed on the verandah near the tennis courts. After all, in the more than half century since the Durbar the Slap had changed very little.

Bunty and Jamie arrived a little late and the party was well in progress. It was their first experience of the Slap masquerade and they halted at the entrance to the ballroom.

The dancers, crowded, costumed, delighted Bunty. "Jamie." She clutched his arm. "It looks as though it were fifty years ago."

She was right. There were sahibs of all sorts, 1877 planters in broad topis and high trousers, business "box wallahs" in frock coats and pleated pants. There were army officers with sashes, swords, and epaulettes. A half dozen Disraelis or Gladstones danced with replicas of the Empress herself.

Though no Indians were ever allowed in the Slap there were fakirs with stained skins, elephant drivers with hooks, rajahs in enormous turbans, and nautch girls with bangles on their arms and ankles. For one instant, at least, the clock had been turned backward to a time less precarious.

"It's beautiful." Bunty nudged Jamis. "You go ahead. I'm going to the powder room to see how I look."

"You look fine."

"I'll only be a moment. I'll find you."

"They've got a table near the verandah. Don't be long," he added worriedly. "The Walkers have been waiting an hour."

"Two minutes." She put her fingers affectionately on his mouth and went into the powder room. Jamie pushed into the ballroom to find his consul general's table.

Bunty sat herself in front of a mirror. She had dressed carefully for the meeting with the Walkers. She was wearing a long evening gown Lady Thornton had provided. It might well have belonged to Lady Thornton's mother.

Bunty wore no makeup beyond a light face powder and her hair was piled high. She had achieved just the effect she wanted . . . demure, ladylike, somewhat helpless . . . a young girl in an adult world.

There was no doubt that Bunty had marriage on her mind. She loved Jamie. It was a word she had bandied about fairly frequently in her time. It was expected of one.

But with Jamie it was different. She had molded Jamie into a whole person. She could say that she had made a man of him. And she wanted him. She had all the adoration of a mother for her child.

A few hours later, at the Ammon Walker table, Bunty had no reason to believe she had failed. It had been a moderately gay evening. Mr. Walker, a gray-haired, rather quiet American, had danced twice with her, each time with appropriate courtesy and solemnity.

Mrs. Walker, large-jawed, efficient-looking, had asked a great many questions of Bunty. It was clear that she was experienced at this sort of thing and was being protective of their new vice consul, a mother hen.

Bunty had been shrewd enough to be candid. She had made no bones about being a working girl, an ordinary typist at Withrow & Jenks, Ltd. She had made no effort to establish a family background. She had none. Mrs. Walker had evidently accepted her, because there was now a certain cordiality.

Now if only Jamie would perk up a bit. He had danced with her often enough, responding carefully to her closeness, but he was now sitting at the table face down, taking no part in anything.

Jamie was feeling increasingly desperate. He had by now heard of the fishing fleet and was aware of what might be facing him. This was not the legendary diplomatic fling, the affair with the beautiful foreign woman. He had been seduced, presented with sex in all its clutching, gasping tyranny. But there was a price on it. Marriage. He was under the ax.

Mrs. Walker was talking, addressing Bunty in the practical matter-of-fact way of two women. "A wife in our consular service has certain problems you don't have in the British Diplomatic. Your British consuls might stay eight or ten years in a post. We seldom stay more than three. That means pulling children out of school every three years, finding new friends for them, packing and moving all the furniture . . ."

The voice droned on. Jamie felt the ax touch his neck tentatively, exploring, testing the skin. He closed his eyes.

He remembered the first time he had seen animals in copulation. It had been two sheep near his father's mission near Foochow. He and his father had been walking—he was about nine at the time—and they had come on a ram and a ewe in a corner of a sheep pen. He remembered how he had stared and how his father had shouted at the sheep and thrown stones at them. Finally his father had grabbed him by the arm and pulled him back to the mission.

He also remembered the dinner the next night, his pleasure at the unexpected treat of roast meat on the frugal table. But he could still remember the awful taste of the meat in his mouth when his father had said it was lamb and left no doubt as to which lamb he had purchased. The expression on his father's face—righteous, triumphant—was a warning to his son. Copulation was a sin, to be punished by death.

"Did you hear, Jamie?" It was Bunty again.

"What?"

She laughed. "I said a chap might need a wife in your service just to help him move so often."

Jamie, shaking his head, mumbled. "A fellow shouldn't marry young in our service. It'd be a handicap."

"A handicap!" Bunty's face was startled.

"There'd be babies and babies would mean there'd be fewer posts where he could be sent. He'd be limited."

"I should think that would be an asset. He'd have only the best posts." Bunty tried to sound gay.

Jamie shook his head stubbornly. "We can't marry an alien anyway. You have to hand in your resignation."

Mrs. Walker shook her head. "That's just a formality. If the girl's all right the resignation's never accepted."

"They might accept it," said Jamie doggedly.

"But I'm British, not an alien!" said Bunty desperately.

"British is just as alien as any other foreigner," said Jamie. It was a brutal remark, said brutally. Jamie looked down at his hands. The contrast between his heavy, farmerlike hands and his horn-rimmed glasses always interested him.

"I see. Of course," Bunty said dully. She sat hunched forward. "I've never thought of us as aliens. Anywhere." Then she looked up, smiling. "I think I had best be excused a moment. I want to fix up my face a little. May I, Mrs. Walker?"

"Of course, child."

Jamie looked up. "If you want to dance, Bunty . . ."

"Perhaps when I come back." She looked down at him coolly, then left.

Mr. Walker yawned. "I think it's time we went home, Ethel. It's late. Please say good night to Bunty for us, Wilson."

"Stay on if you want. Have another dance." He eyed his new vice consul speculatively. It wasn't the most promising of looks. "I'll see you Monday morning."

"Good night, James," said Mrs. Walker. "She's a very nice young lady. Bring her to see us."

"Thank you. Good night." He watched the older couple as they left, then sat down. His face was bleak. He knew he had made a bad beginning.

Then his face hardened. It was Bunty. She thought she could trap him with all that talk about marriage and needing a wife in his career. Marriage. Damn her, that was all girls thought about.

In the powder room Bunty sat slumped before the mirror. She glanced at the old-fashioned gown she wore, at her hair piled up so carefully. Her lips moved. "He doesn't want you. And the trouble is you really care about this fool." The pretty face twisted helplessly. Her hands flew to cover it.

Margot Danvers looked about her. She was wearing a sari, flame-colored, that she hoped was suitable for a ranee of the last century. She felt conspicuous in its brilliant color, the folds worn over her stringy hair, but for once in her life she was enjoying feeling conspicuous. She had been accepting the rewards of her engagement announcement in the *Statesman*. Friends and acquaintances of the Bracebridges had paused at the table to wish her well, to meet and congratulate Frank.

She did wish Frank would dance with her but he was not in a festive mood. He was, in fact, in an odd, even sullen mood. At first, when people came to congratulate him, he had been solemn and respectful. He had become increasingly silent. He had danced once with Margot and once with Lydia Bracebridge but, for the past hour, he had been morose.

This was his first visit to the Slap and Frank felt a fish out of water. He didn't see any of his Rugby Club pals and he missed the all-male atmosphere of the club. The costume he wore . . . a borrowed cricketer's outfit, there being no organized rugby club in Calcutta in 1877 . . . made him feel a fool. He had always looked on crickets as a posh game, namby-pamby. Now he had to wear one of their outfits because he could find nothing else of which Margot approved.

Margot . . . Margot . . . it was all Margot now. He had been somebody at the Rugby Club. He was the best hooker in Calcutta, if not in all of India, and had been for twelve years. He was not used to being just the "somebody" Margot was marrying.

He even had to go to that oily little doctor with Margot. They took their treatments together at a doctor she had picked out. At least he had given her the trouble in the first place. She couldn't take that away from him.

He looked around the room. He wished he could find somebody to drink with. Old Bracebridge was practically a teetotaler. The missus was too busy chattering with all her old lady friends to drink. You would think she were Queen Victoria herself instead of just being gotten up to look like her.

There might be somebody in the men's bar. It sounded lively enough. There ought to be somebody there who'd talk rugger or gents' furnishings, or just have a drink with him.

He eyed Margot. He certainly couldn't go until he'd had another dance with her. He didn't like the idea. She in that ruddy red sari and he in his cricketer outfit stood out like a pair of blasted lampposts.

"Dance, Margot?"

"I would love it." She rose to her feet. At last, she thought. He isn't going to ignore me entirely.

A few hours later, the party over, Margot waited alone at the table. The Bracebridges had gone some time ago. Margot could hear Frank in the bar, his voice raised in noisy familiarity with other late drinkers. Frank was making the most of things. As he made the most of many things, Margot reflected.

"I think it is marvelous about your good news, Margot." Margot looked up to see the bulky Lady Thornton. "Sir John and I are so looking forward to the wedding. St. Paul's, isn't it?"

"Yes."

"Of course. My, it's been a wonderful party, hasn't it? Bunty came with the Ammon Walkers. Young James Wilson too, of course. He's mad about Bunty. But then Bunty has so many young men." She smiled broadly, the undefeated smile Margot had seen on so many of the hostesses lately.

Lady Thornton turned toward the bar. "It is a bit noisy in the men's bar. Well, boys will be boys. You might as well get used to it." She waved cheerfully at Margot and left.

Margot pulled her sari closer. Flame-colored, alone, she sat back. Frank's laugh boomed toward her.

Tiger Flemyng began the evening seated in a side room with the party of Sir Gerald and Lady Andrews. There were nearly twenty at table and Tiger was seated inconspicuously near the far end.

He had not been the gayest of table companions. The news of the abrogation of the Gandhi-Irwin Pact had been a jolt. He had believed the pact to have been the one constructive act taken by the Raj in many years. It had really been the first time ever that the Indians had been treated as equals by the Raj. Lord Irwin and the Mahatma had met face to face in the sight of all. Now this symbol had been kicked aside. The pact was dead. And not only the pact but the methods that had produced it: Ahimsà, the Mahatma's nonviolent methods. That too had been a casualty.

The viceroy had already taken steps. Returned to Delhi, he had moved quietly but firmly. Orders in council were issued. There would be no more public marches or demonstrations. Unpaid taxes would be collected from the villages as a whole. The Mahatma was permitted to receive no more visitors, not even his wife. Military leaves were canceled. Three additional battalions were brought up from Singapore. The viceroy was responding to the parliamentary vote. The Raj was putting on a demonstration of its own.

Tiger looked around him. He had to admire his fellow British. They knew as well as he that there might well be bloodshed now. He knew that many had bought guns, those who didn't already possess them for shikar. Others had quickly sent their children home to England or to the hill stations. But for the vast majority there was business as usual. This "Durbar" was a demonstration that the Raj was still the Raj.

Only he was out of step. He could admire his fellow British but they weren't the ones who would have to enforce the peace now. That very afternoon he had attended an unpleasant affair, the police questioning of a suspected terrorist. It had been a sullen youth, believed to be a follower of Gupta. The police had immediately sent a constable for Captain Flemyng.

It had not been pleasant. Several of the police could remember constables murdered by the terrorists. They knew they were soldiers in a war. Methods had been used not condoned by Blackstone or British courts.

Tiger could still remember the boy's screams, could smell the stench as the boy's bowels had given way. He had witnessed other "questionings" in the past year but this had been the worst.

He looked out toward the dance floor and his thoughts were on other bits of reprisal—acts in which he himself had participated. He remembered "interrogations" of rebellious tribesmen on the Frontier, burying them up to their heads in sand and then galloping horses among them. Those lucky enough to have their mouths intact afterward were quite anxious to talk.

There was no doubt of it, Tiger thought, "Empire" could be a brutal and bloody business, perhaps necessarily so. It was kill or be killed. One killed to maintain order. To maintain order, he thought bitterly, was essential for parties like this one—for the garden parties, for the security of the fishing fleet and their hostesses. But, he thought, the Raj was like this party too—gay and brilliant at first but behind those gay streamers were the old rafters with their termites.

The trouble was that he was one of the killers. It was on him and men like him that the Empire depended. And he was beginning to be sick of it. Sick to death . . . other men's deaths.

Tiger knew what he was going to do that night. Drink. He would be off duty in a few hours. Sir Gerald would be leaving and he could return alone to the Slap. Meanwhile he would go now and have a look around the dance floor and perhaps have a drink in the men's bar. The governor liked him to move about occasionally. It kept up the fiction that his was only a social function.

Tiger went out to the edge of the ballroom and stood watching. He saw Bunty Cranston dancing with that American of hers. They danced fairly close together for a Calcutta party but Tiger thought the lad had a rather constrained expression on his face. So, thought Tiger. He's afraid of what people might think. Enjoy yourself with her, man. The hell with who's watching.

He saw Margot Danvers. He recognized her even with the mask . . . that angular body and thin-boned face were unmistakable.

Tiger watched her and the bulky man holding her. He

recognized Willis and remembered she was supposed to be engaged to him. From all accounts it was going to be a bang-up wedding. God bless 'em, he thought.

He saw other girls and Tiger felt a quick anger. It was a damned slave market. They were offering themselves to whoever wanted them the most. "Go on home," he muttered. "Get out of here. While there's still time." It was then that he saw the woman in gray.

There was a grace and dignity in the long, gray costume and the small crown on her head could have been truly regal. But there was an abandon in the way she danced and the crown was recklessly askew.

Two men came off the floor, young and grinning as they passed Tiger. "What is she supposed to be?" said one.

"She says she's Queen Victoria on a spree."

"Do you know her?"

"No, but let's make the most of it. Let's have another drink first."

Tiger went nearer. There was something in the way she held her head. Her hair was shorter now, not gathered at the back of the neck, but there was no doubt. He went quickly onto the floor.

"Mary."

The dancers stopped and she turned to him. "Hello, Tiger." She touched him on his 1870 epaulettes. "Still a soldier of the Queen."

"What are you doing here?"

"I'm dancing with this gentleman. Captain Flemyng, this is Prime Minister Gladstone."

He ignored the other man, swaying slightly. "I want to talk to you."

"I am dancing."

"A few moments."

Mary hesitated, then turned solemnly to her partner. "Thank you, Mr. Prime Minister. Come, Tiger."

She led the way toward the verandah, Tiger noting there was still that long, unhesitating stride. On the verandah she waited, her eyes on the lawn and the tennis courts beyond.

He stopped behind her. "I've missed you. It's been two months."

"Has it?" She calmly removed her mask and he stared at her. The good, honest face was the same: the intelligent eyes, the wide, full mouth. But there was something more, a fatigue. Despite himself, Tiger was startled. Impulsively he reached out a hand.

"Mary."

"I'm all right. A little tired, that's all." He looks much the same, she thought. Perhaps the eyes are a little deeper, the scars a little more naked-looking. After all, his wasn't a face that could change much now. That had been done for him years before.

"Why are you here? Where is your husband?"

"Edward is at York House. I came tonight with the Beauchamps."

"But how long have you been in Calcutta? You should have rung me." She said nothing. "I've missed you, Mary. You will see me later, won't you? Where are you staying, the Beauchamps?"

"The Great Eastern."

"I must return to Sir Gerald's table now. When the party's done, I'm free. We can meet here and have a talk afterward."

He took her hand. She does look older, he thought. Those lines. Dear Mary.

She didn't reply to his suggestion but he gripped her hand firmly. "After the party then. Right here."

He walked away, feeling curiously jubilant. It was marvelous to see Mary again. He had truly missed his friend.

But where was her husband? It was inconceivable that Goad would allow Mary to come to Calcutta by herself. She was one of his possessions now, like York House. It didn't really matter. It was good to see her again.

Behind him on the verandah, Mary hadn't moved. Her eyes watched the ballroom, the dancers, the brave streamers from the sagging wooden rafters.

He had asked her why she was at the party. Why not? There was nowhere else to go. She had sat in her room at the Great Eastern for several days, not even phoning Denise. Somehow going out, being seen publicly without her husband, was something she could not yet do.

So she stayed in her room, listening to the bicycle bells on the Esplanade below or the distant trams on Chowringhi, their iron wheels strident as they swerved around the Maidan corner. Late one night she had heard a faint scratching on her door, gentle, suggesting, and she remembered the hotel bearer who sat in the hall—a handsome, delicate-featured boy. She remembered the way he had watched her when she had come to the room, thinking her a tourist perhaps, alone, not unwilling, any more than the others. For one terrible moment she had nearly gone to the door to open it, then retreated to lie on her bed. The next morning she had phoned Denise.

Now she had come to the party with them. She had probably drunk too much. She had certainly danced with the lads with a trifle too much abandon.

It had been partly because of the questions people asked. Too many had stopped by the table to say hello and ask where her husband was. She didn't lie very well and could not bring herself to say she had simply come on a shopping trip. Her personal problems were her own, not to be discussed even with Denise. So, finally, she had left that problem, had fled to the dance floor. Now Tiger had come back.

Mary leaned her head back against the high wicker chair. The rough edge picked at her neck, now unprotected by her long hair.

She closed her eyes. What was she anyway? She had always known who she was, what sort of person, but now she was adrift. She had no standard, no base on which to rest.

Mr. Janeway had a term for that . . . the Lydian Stone. He said the people of ancient Lydia used a touchstone to tell gold from dross. It had a property that to them was magic.

It came to pass, Mr. Janeway said, that the stone became more important to the Lydians than the powers it possessed. They set it on a pedestal to be worshiped and, in time, it lost its magic. The Lydians too passed away.

Perhaps that was what had happened to her. She had set the Raj too high. She had worshiped the form and not the substance. In the same way, she had entered into a marriage without love. Her Lydian Stones had no substance. Now she was shorn of both.

The party finally ended but Tiger could not find Mary. He searched the small rooms, the ballroom, even went out to the tennis courts. There was no trace. Nor did the Beauchamps know. She had not been seen for some time.

He drove quickly over to the Great Eastern Hotel but was told by the night babu that Goad Memsahib had not returned. Her key was still in the key rack.

Tiger drove slowly along Chowringhi, glancing at the few strollers under the arcade. His long fingers drummed impatiently on the steering wheel, his dark eyes searched the sidewalk. Only cows could be seen under the arcade, walking among the sleeping bodies of people or reclining nearby. The city had gone to sleep.

Where was Mary in this silent city? He was needed; he was sure of that. Needed or not, he wanted to be with her. The sight of Mary had stirred something he hadn't known existed.

Suddenly he stopped the car. The lofty Memorial to Queen Victoria had caught his eye. In a moment Tiger had driven his motorcar into the Maidan, left it, and was walking quickly through the clumps of palm trees. He finally came to the shadowy space where he and Mary had sat.

It was the sound of weeping that drew him to the bench. Mary was seated at one end, leaning against the arm. Above her the moon drew shadows across the granite face of the Empress.

"Mary."

"Let me alone! Go away!" She jumped up angrily, retreating into the shadows at the foot of the Memorial.

"Mary, what's the trouble?"

"You've come to gloat. I know."

"Gloat? Why?"

"My marriage. You must know I've failed. I wasn't strong enough. I'm too sheltered, Victorian." Her voice rose in the shadows. "Do you know why I went to the Slap tonight? To get drunk . . . to have affairs with as many young men as I could. But I'm a prude. I couldn't even begin. I didn't know how."

Tiger stared into the shadows toward her voice. There was a frenzy here, a desperation even worse than he had realized.

"Come here and sit with me."

"I won't let you see me. I'm ashamed."

"You have nothing to be ashamed of. You tried. You had too many hopes for that marriage."

"It wasn't just the marriage." There was a silence from the shadows, then he heard her again, almost as though she were speaking up to the face of the Queen, accusing. "I was such a fool about the Raj. I thought you were disloyal. See her up there. When she died my family went into mourning for three months. We worshiped her."

Tiger heard her voice break and moved quickly into the shadows. He sat beside her. "Don't, Mary."

He put his arm gently behind her and she slowly leaned

her head back. "It's just that things have gone so wrong from what I had hoped. I wanted to make a good marriage, be a good English wife. I was going to take my place in the ranks."

"I know."

"Now I see I was just silly. I'm tired, Tiger. I'm afraid I'm not so young as I had thought."

"It's late. It's time I took you to the hotel."

"No."

"You can't stay here. It'll be daylight soon."

"I'm not going back to York House."

"There's your hotel."

"That empty room. No."

She closed her eyes. "I want to go someplace new. Where I don't know anyone."

"Chandernagore."

"Chandernagore?"

He laughed. "Perfect. It's French. About thirty miles up river. One of the last bits of France left in India. We'll both go." He was suddenly alive, even gay.

"You couldn't go. It would be deserting."

"If you need to get away, so do I. Even more."

"I couldn't do this to you."

"I'll go by myself if you don't go. I'll swim." He gestured extravagantly.

"You and I." The words came softly.

"Yes. Why not?" His arms were quietly around her, gentle.

"No. Please." She was trying not to turn to him, trembling. "My God. No."

"Mary. It's been inevitable."

She couldn't move from him. She knew only that he had looked for her, had searched until he had found her there, that she needed him.

She turned to him then, suddenly gripping him, looking up into that scarred face. "Don't kiss me now. Come."

Behind them, as they left, shadows drew a curtain across the face of the Queen.

29

THE ROOM WAS DIM AND THE YOUNG MEN HAD difficulty in seeing Gupta. They saw that he was wearing European clothes and knew they had not been summoned for nothing. It was as though Gupta, to impress them with the importance of the meeting, were reaching back to his European days, the time of his dedication to Nechayev.

The soft cherubic little man looked up at them. "It is time to take action."

The young men glanced at each other. At last.

Gupta continued, his eyes thoughtful. "There must be a minor killing first. Something to bring on an emergency. Then when we have gathered them all together . . ." He pulled his hands toward him, as a poker player might rake in a pot of chips. "Then we shall have the real killing."

The young men shouted, their teeth white in their dark faces.

"Who shall it be?" asked one of the young men.

Gupta smiled. "The choice will be wide."

The men nodded fiercely. "The governor—the viceroy—all of them."

Gupta shook his head. "We must not be greedy. One will be enough." He pointed to two young men. "Shinji, you and Ayub will do the small killing."

There was an angry growl in the crowd and Rajid pushed forward. "I want the first killing. I have waited too long."

"You will have to wait," said Gupta. His eyes were fixed on the young man but were not yielding.

Rajid muttered but fell back. Gupta turned to the others. "First the minor killing, the bait." He nodded to the young men. "You will kill him tomorrow."

Duncan Saunders was a Scot who liked his sports. Tennis, shikar, riding . . . it didn't matter so long as he exercised some part of each day. It had been easy in Calcutta with the Slap for tennis or the Jodhpur for riding but now that he had been temporarily assigned to Midnapore, he had found no opportunities whatever.

It was largely because he couldn't move about freely in public. He had been assigned as district magistrate because the previous DM had been murdered by Gupta's crowd and security had to be observed. It was bad enough being separated from Phyllis and the kids for a few months without going soft in the bargain.

So when the opportunity to play football with the local club came up, he snapped at it. He would station his two constables about the field and have a go at it. One couldn't be much safer than on a football field.

On the day of the game Saunders trotted out with his team. He was muscular and a bit taller than the other chaps so that the uniform they had found for him fit quite snugly, particularly the shorts. With his uniform, his waxed mustache that Phyllis twitted him about, and being the only European on the field, he knew he must look pretty silly. He checked to see that his constables were on hand. They were watching dutifully, one on each side of the field.

It was an after-work match and his side was the local Bengal-Nagpur Railway Club, mostly Anglo-Indians. That meant they would tire in the second half and the defense would have a bit of work. He was a fullback, playing on the left side, and he prayed that the other side's forwards would not be in good shape either.

The other team was a local side call the "Kickers." They were all Indian, wore green shirts and white pants, and it was soon obvious that, like most Indian sides, their wings were very fast indeed.

Saunders' wing, a thin, bony Indian, looked nearly emaciated to Saunders, but in ten minutes he knew he would have a hell of a time with this one. He was young, perhaps nineteen, and he ran after the ball with a frenzy that was frightening. It was as though the ball were the head of some dead enemy and he went flapping after it like a hungry crow. He didn't score, however, being content evidently to harry the ball down to Saunders' end, then cross it into the center or to his opposite wing.

Fifteen minutes after the second half had begun Saunders knew he couldn't keep it up. His halfbacks up front were tiring and he himself was in worse shape than he had realized. His wings showed no sign of letting up. He and his inside right, a short, almost rotund young Muslim, seemed to be doubling up on him. They had no trouble eluding the left halfback and were keeping the ball more and more on his side of the field, forcing one corner kick after another on the tiring fullback.

It was becoming apparent to Saunders that this was no ordinary match. There was something in the ferocity with which they hounded him, the recklessness in his wing's face, that finally brought a twinge of fear to Saunders. He would clear the ball up to his halfback and, in a moment, the two Indians would bring the ball back. They weren't crossing the ball into the center now but always kicked ahead into his corner, then closed in, kicking at the ball, his legs, his knees, anything they could reach with their boots.

Saunders looked for the referee but he always seemed to be at the other side of the field. He looked for help from his right fullback or center half but they were nearly as exhausted as he. There was only one thing to do for the minutes that were left and that was to fight them back.

He forced his wobbly legs to run. He tried to make his clearing kicks sharp though his ankles were aching and his feet felt as though the boots were vises. He pushed back against the two Indians when they closed in and he kicked their ankles and cursed them, his chest and throat torn with dryness and his words hoarse.

Finally he knew. It was his turn to die. When for the tenth time they had run him into the corner, he knew they had him. He could see the grin on the bony wing's face and the smirk on his pudgy teammate as they harried him, jamming the ball into his crotch, knocking him onto the corner flag.

He climbed once more to his shaking legs. He knew it would be useless to call his guards. They were far down the field. If only he were the player he used to be. He'd have shown these bastards some football.

He saw a revolver in the wing's hand, pulled from his sock, Saunders thought idly. There was a flash, a terribly loud report and he knew this was the end of him, on a football field of all places. As he sank to his knees, the blood spreading out from his heart through his jersey, he tried to bite the boot standing over him. Then he lay still. His father had always said sport would be the death of him and father was always right.

The viceroy had returned to Delhi and it was there that he received news of the killing. The assassins had been killed by the police but had later been identified as members of the Gupta group. Lord Willingdon had dutifully informed London and the next day, in his garden, had received a reply. He read it out loud to his aide, Captain Graham.

"Imperative that terrorists be checked. Believe situation requires immediate imposition in Calcutta of martial law." It was signed the "PM" but the viceroy knew that it would have been framed by "old Freddy," Secretary of State for India.

He smiled up at his aide. "Well, now we have our instructions. Martial law, hmmm." He tapped the cable thoughtfully against his fingers.

"But it's impossible, sir. It would mean bottling up the entire city."

"The Prime Minister has signed this, Captain. It has his approval." Old Freddy, he thought to himself. He has finally taken a stand. Of course it wasn't really a stand. Old Freddy was a wily one. He knew he could do one of two things under the circumstances: he could either leave the matter entirely to the viceroy to solve or he could issue an instruction so drastic that it must be ignored. He had chosen the latter course. It relieved him of all responsibility. The problem now was what to do that would save Freddy's face and yet be possible.

Captain Graham was now more amenable. "Martial law would keep the lid on tight, sir."

"Yes."

"And it is certainly what Sir Gerald would want. I believe the entire city council has voted for it."

"Very intelligent men, Captain."

"Of course the Indian members of the council are really afraid of Hindu-Muslim rioting. They're afraid religious killings could begin."

"Gupta would like that."

"I guess martial law is the best thing after all."

"Good for you, Captain. Always stick with the Prime Minister."

"Yes, sir." He peered at His Excellency. He never knew

what the viceroy was thinking when he had that little smile on his face.

"I am afraid that in this case, Captain, I shall have to go contrary to instructions. I trust you will bear with me."

"No martial law? But what . . ."

"A show of force. We shall parade a few regiments through the city, establish patrols, bring out the militia. Let them have a little fun parading. It will be much less drastic than martial law . . . more flexible."

And more dangerous, he thought. Martial law would be firm, no nonsense. Merely a show of force would be riding a stallion with a loose rein. He could break your neck. But you must chance it. You could always make a gelding out of him.

"We'll have to go back to Calcutta, of course."

"But you've just come back, sir."

"You wouldn't want to miss the fun, would you? Just the thing for ending the cold weather. Besides, I fancy Sir Gerald may need a little support, with all those chaps pushing for martial law."

"Yes, sir." He knew very well the viceroy knew the responsibility for the next few weeks rested with him. "What about Her Ladyship?"

"Her Ladyship will stay here. A few bazaars she had best open." His aide knew then that His Excellency fully expected trouble in Calcutta.

The viceroy nodded. "Besides, Sir Gerald will need every available soldier for a show of force and that includes you and me." His eyes twinkled. "We'll leave tomorrow."

"Yes, sir." Captain Graham saluted and left.

Lord Willingdon walked to the window of his study and looked out over his well-kept lawn. It was the dry season and a few sprinklers were frugally doling out drops to the hungry lawn. The viceroy watched, his eyes taking comfort from the slowly whirling sprays.

In Calcutta Gupta put down the newspaper and sucked thoughtfully on a spiced lemon. He was feeling pleased. He had reason to exult a bit. Matters were developing as he had planned. Nechayev would have been proud of him.

He picked up the paper again. It was all there, the word of the gathering in Calcutta of the top British officials in India. Even the viceroy was coming back. It would be quite a party. There remained only to make a choice.

Gupta sat back. This was the part he liked best, the planning. Bakunin had written that this was the test that must bring out the artist. There must be a surprise in it somewhere.

What could it be? The victim must be surprised, of course. And the time and the place must supply the right touch. The true artist would combine all these things.

He would have one additional pleasure in this killing: the executioner. That would be the nicest touch of all. Rajid was hungry to be given this killing. It was what he had clamored for. Now he would be told the terms.

Gupta started to smile, his eyes closed and rapt. He was beginning to feel the exaltation, the holy dedication that Nechayev said was the mark of the true terrorist.

Sir Gerald Andrews, Governor of Bengal, always dreaded receiving cables from the viceroy. His grim Scottishness was offended by the damned humor with which the man clothed his meanings. Sir Gerald read the latest cable again. "Arrange immediate show of force Calcutta beginning six AM Tuesday February 28 continuing until canceled We have paraded the girls for ten weeks Now we parade the lads Signed Willingdon"

Sir Gerald's face was dour. A crisis was coming, no doubt of that. And they were meeting it only with a show of force . . . a damned lot of parades.

He threw down the cable. Where was that Tiger Flemyng! This was no time to take off somewhere. Now of all times. Every man was needed.

30

CHANDERNAGORE WAS A RUN-DOWN FRENCH river port thirty miles up the Hooghly from Calcutta. It had been important once, when the French ruled India, but Clive had changed all that a hundred and fifty years before. Pondicherry in the west and Chandernagore in Bengal were all that was left of the great French domain. Chandernagore, still living in the eighteenth century, had been left to its secluded and private dream.

It was only a few square miles in size, a fraction of France surrounded by enormous British India, but, roadless and cut off, it remained defiantly French. It had a small square, a single avenue, tree-lined, that led from the square to the river, and its single hotel was small, decrepit. In the rear of the hotel a few tables in a courtyard served as a café.

The hotel and the café provided the French officials—four among twenty thousand Indians—with the hub of their universe. There were two French "militaires," policemen really, who provided French order and security. A priest, young and ardent, attended the café only to rant against his superiors in far-off France, and to bemoan his small flock of native Catholics, lost in the cathedral built for a once larger congregation.

The fourth member of the small French group was Monsieur le Gouverneur himself. Monsieur was a personage, France incarnate to the local population. It was as though the French government in its infinite wisdom had decided that its governor, surrounded by four hundred million British subjects, must be equal in "presence" if not in power.

Hercule Réveillac was about fifty and a bulk of a man. He had the wisdom to know his shortcomings, a lack of intellect and an excess of poundage, but he was a career civil servant and had done his best to fit his bulk into his tiny post.

He attended his office regularly, always punctual, always hot. He performed his duties with remorseless energy, mostly signing his expansive signature to a shrinking pile of shipping invoices.

Outside his office he made weekly inspections of his "militaires," led church parades on Sunday, and was restrained only by a shortage of funds from stretching a chain barrier across the Hooghly. The curé pointed out that, since there was no longer any British traffic on this part of the river other than jute barges, it was doubtful that his defiance, magnificent as it might be, would even be noticed. Monsieur Réveillac was forced to content himself with extra-noisy fireworks on the fourteenth of July.

It was to this small community that Tiger took Mary. Since

there were no roads, they arrived by launch. The governor
was pleased to see his handsome visitors at the hotel. They
were lovers he was sure. There could be no other reason for
such people to visit Chandernagore. It made his town seem
almost like Paris. He welcomed them with dignity.

For Tiger and Mary it could have been wonderful. Calcutta and the Raj seemed far away. There was the river for
fishing or rowing. There was the hotel with a dining courtyard in the rear with two palms, a macaw, and the aroma of
hibiscus.

And they were lovers. There had been little hesitation about
that, perhaps a moment of consideration on his part. Was
she too tired? It was late.

A certain dazed fatigue on her part; it had been a long
launch journey. Then a tentative approach to the bed, a growing passion on his part, on hers a certain desperation. Finally
a sort of peace.

There could not really be any peace. Mary knew that she
had burnt her bridges. She had left her marriage. No matter
how much provocation she might have had, she had failed.

"I tried to be a good wife," she said. They were lying side
by side the next morning, her head on Tiger's shoulder.

"It was a mistake for Edward to marry me. He wanted a
fishing fleeter yet he wanted someone who could love him
too."

He moved impatiently. "Don't feel sorry for him. His jute
came first with Goad, then that house of his, then his wife.
You were third."

"He'd had a loss. It was horrible. He had a daughter who
was murdered by some of his coolies when she was a child.
Did you know that?"

"I didn't even know he'd been married before."

"It was a long time ago. That's why he's the way he is,
I believe. He drives himself and he drives the coolies. It's as
though he hated India and York House and it were sort of
a revenge. I've thought perhaps that's why he married me.
I was sort of ridiculous to him. Old-fashioned. Silly. It was a
joke on India and on me too."

"Nonsense. Don't think about it."

"It was difficult up there. Not only for me but for young
Kitty Jolliffe and that Mrs. MacDonough too." She shivered
a little. "I think empires must be hard on their women."

"Empire is a sort of narcotic. An escape from the ordinary life."

"It was dedication. I actually felt a little holy. Silly, I know. It sort of protected me from the realities of empire."

"You had an illusion you picked up in Cheltenham."

"In my father's office." She smiled. "At the knees of his nice old patients."

"Is it over now? Outgrown?"

"I hope so. Illusions die hard."

"It's over." He leaned down to kiss her. She put her arms up and they held each other.

They spent the first days taking long walks about the town, climbing the low hill behind the cathedral to watch the few riverboats pass or gaze across the river to the flat, swampy land beyond.

They spoke little on their walks. They were a shade too polite with each other. It was a delicate balance they were trying to preserve, an excessive consideration that was both intimate and impersonal.

Mary knew that this was no harmless jaunt with Mr. Janeway. This was very much a man she was living with. She knew that at the end of the day they would return to the hotel, that there would be an intimacy that night. She knew that this man would be battering against her, not only her body but also her emotions.

She saw that he too had reservations. She sensed the uncertainties, the doubts that he had done the right thing in running away with her. She felt obligated to relieve his mind of any sense of his own obligation to her. She would sit silently while he stared from the rise across the river.

One day he suddenly waved a hand. "Chandernagore . . . there it is, all that's left. In another fifty years the swamps will have it all."

"Don't think about it."

"Why not? I always feel that Calcutta is on loan from the rivers too. Old Kali may come to take back his city. Have you ever seen Kali?"

"I hear it's horrible."

"He . . . or she, whatever it is . . . is out at Kali Ghat. They worship him, all blood red and black. Two arms pointing up and two pointing down, like a busy tram conductor. I think now he may have collected all the fares and is going to put us off—end of the line."

Mary touched him. "Darling, please. Don't think about it. It's peaceful here. We've left all that. Haven't we?" Her eyes searched his.

"I suppose."

"We can go back any time."

"I doubt I ever want to go back."

She took his hand gently but his face was averted, still staring across the river.

On the fourth day Tiger rented a fishing pirogue. It was flat-bottomed, broad with a seat at each end. Tiger poled, punt-fashion, to a quiet corner of the river and there let slip a heavy anchor. The pirogue swung gently to the river, then settled beneath a willow.

Tiger had been more cheerful that day. Mary had sensed less bitterness. When they had discovered the boat and had planned the picnic, he had been nearly giddy with pleasure.

He lazily extended a fishing pole into the water, then settled himself in the bottom of the boat. His scarred, craggy face looked almost peaceful.

Mary trailed her hand uncertainly in the water. His new mood seemed to provide an opportunity. Her own uncertainties needed an answer.

"How long are we staying here, Alastair?"

"Here? In this boat? Indefinitely."

"No, I mean Chandernagore."

"Don't you like it?"

"I love it but we can't go on indefinitely."

"Why not?"

"Alastair." She left her end of the boat and moved to sit beside him. He lay in the bottom, one hand holding a fishing rod.

"Careful. You'll disturb the fish."

"There are no fish. You haven't caught a fish all day."

"I would if I put bait on it. I'm just too stingy."

"Tiger." She settled beside him. "Please be serious."

"Then don't ask me serious questions. I can only be serious about foolish ones."

"Tell me a few."

"Oh, will the fish bite? Shall we have a good bottle of wine tonight? Or have the British any future in India?"

"That's not foolish."

"Right now I consider it of much less importance than will the fish bite."

"Alastair, be serious. We came to Chandernagore on impulse. You had been drinking and I was . . . at loose ends shall we say."

"Very loose."

"What now? You have your work and I am still Edward's wife."

"Better than the other way around. You have my work . . ."

"Alastair." She pounded him. "You were so serious in Calcutta. So wise. What's happened to you?"

"Chandernagore has happened to me. It's what every Empire wallah should see at least once." He dangled the fishing rod up and down without moving from the bottom of the boat. "If Sir Gerald could spend a week or two here I guarantee you he would cable Mr. Gandhi to come and get it. The whole lot, G-House, Belvedere, and all."

"But Sir Gerald isn't here. You are here and so am I."

"Are you bored?"

"Of course not."

"Are you in love with that husband of yours? York of Goad House or whatever he calls himself."

"He is my husband, Alastair."

He hesitated only a moment, glancing out at the end of his fishing pole. "Then you should get yourself a new husband."

"Who?"

"Me. Why not? I'm single. I'd make a very good husband if your standards weren't very high."

She turned her face away. "You don't know what you're saying."

"Mind the rod, damn it. There may be a fish out there. Of course I don't know what I'm saying. If half the men in this world knew what they were saying when they said it, they wouldn't say it."

"But I am married. To Edward."

"Divorce him. Or let him divorce you. We'll give him the grounds."

"You'd have to resign if we married. Aides have to be bachelors."

"There are other jobs."

"Not in the army. You convinced me of that. Your first wife couldn't stand it."

"Outside the army. How would you like that?"

"You'd resign?"

"I might. For a sufficient inducement."

"I'm not rich. In fact I have practically no money at all."

"Pity, but perhaps we could make out."

"It won't be easy. You aren't trained for anything but the army. And there's a slump."

"Damn it, do you want to marry me or not?"

"You might regret it and I couldn't stand it. If we were poor, you'd be restless. Every time a band went by I'd be afraid you'd fall in behind."

"I've had enough of bands."

"I've made so many mistakes. I couldn't stand another."

"Well, I like that. Here I am offering to marry you."

"Are you sure this isn't just conscience on your part?"

"I've no conscience about women. You're much too successful as it is."

"There is one other thing." She hesitated. "I'm older than you."

He shrugged. "I love you."

"I need you, God knows." She didn't resist now and let his hands touch her face, her shoulders. "Oh, God." She was making a last effort.

"Shall I go?" He moved closer to her in the bottom of the boat.

"No."

He kissed her, suddenly gentle. The boat drifted, the fishing pole dangling untended over the water. There was only silence as the boat rested in the eddy, the slender branches of the willow sheltering overhead. Then the boat rocked gently as though a weight were being shifted.

The marsh birds sailed high over the tree, placid, uncurious. Mary, looking up, comforting, knew faintly only the dim, unhurried sky.

They were happier now in Chandernagore. Mary became almost silly with happiness, singing childhood tunes in her low, strong voice, playing with facial makeup to Tiger's amusement.

One day in their bedroom she decided she would be an Indian woman, painting her toenails for Tiger's entertainment, flaunting bangles on her ankles. She had even found a cheap jewel in the bazaar and tried to paste it to her abdomen as a navel. When Tiger found it, he broke into hilarious, harsh laughter.

They discovered things about each other. Mary told him

about Roecroft and Mr. Janeway and their trips to England's historical treasures. She told him about her father and her mother and that she hadn't seen her mother in ten years.

She even told him finally about Tim, though that came slowly, with difficulty. Mary felt better afterward. It was as though she had mixed up Tiger and Tim before but now each was finally separate . . . the one very much alive and her own and the other at last at peace in his French grave.

Sometimes they made plans . . . uncertain, half-plans. They would live on an island or a houseboat in Kashmir. They would return to Europe or go to America. Tiger would find other work somehow. He spoke once of having his face mended. He said there were marvelous new things being done in face surgery. He would have his nose altered and the scars smoothed away.

Sometimes, when Mary was alone, she would stare at herself in the mirror. How young did she really look? Much older than Alastair? Her skin seemed already a bit toughened in the Indian sun, less English "peaches and cream." It was possible that she had already begun that aging process the ship's doctor had warned of. She might soon look years older than Tiger.

She made one decision. She would let her hair grow again. She knew it would be a long time before it regained its former, pre-York House length but she was determined. She would also put away the jodhpurs and cloth jackets she had worn on the estate and resume her long skirts, turtlenecks, and blouses. It might make her look older than Tiger but she wouldn't cheat him. She was determined to be what she really was.

The truth, of course, was that each was trying to restore some order to their lives, some familiar pattern. They had been used to discipline, Tiger in the army and Mary in the equally rigid attitudes and rules of Roecroft.

They had breached these disciplines. Tiger might reject the Raj but there must be something put in its place. Mary might have rejected her marriage but there must be something in which she could trust. She needed a Lydian Stone.

Tiger's emotions in proposing were only half sensed by him. He cared about Mary and he wanted her, no doubt of that. And as with her, marriage would re-establish a basis for his life. It would be a discipline, replacing the army and his loyalty to the Raj.

And in marrying Mary he might absolve himself. He had deserted the Raj but here, at least, he was doing the right thing.

So their happiness was not without its somber side. Their gaiety was perhaps a shade too gay, their lovemaking too dedicated. The days passed but they made no move to leave Chandernagore. The town had become their refuge.

One afternoon, when they returned to the hotel, they found the governor and the curé bent over the local two-page newspaper.

"Have you seen it?" The governor waved the paper. "Terrible."

"Someone has been killed," said the curé.

Tiger quickly took the newspaper. "Magistrat anglais assassiné," he read, then glanced at Mary. "Here. You can read French."

"Duncan Saunders," she read. "British magistrate to Midnapore, was murdered . . . that's assassinated . . . on Tuesday while playing football for the Bengal-Nagpur Railway team. The assassins were members of the équipe . . . that's team . . . opposing."

"That's Gupta all right. Just the right touch. Playing in a football match." Tiger nodded grimly.

"There's more," she said. "It has been announced by Sir Gerald Andrews, Governor of Bengal, that 'démarches de crise' . . . that is emergency measures . . . will be instituted." She shook her head. "A very elegant way of putting it."

"Never mind the humor." Tiger was walking intently up and down. Even the governor and the curé were silent.

"The emergency measures will include an immediate 'défilé de force.' I don't know what that means. Couldn't be a parade."

"Means a 'show of force.' " said Tiger. He stopped. "So they've done it."

"What does it mean?"

"It means Gupta and his killers have murdered another magistrate."

"This poor man, at a football game. Why would they do it like that?"

"To show us we're not safe anywhere. They think they can terrorize us out of India. And, of course, because they're mad."

"You will show them who is the Raj, eh?" said the governor.

"What?" Tiger glanced sharply at him but the Frenchman's expression was bland. "Come, Mary. Thanks for the paper, Monsieur."

"I am sorry about this news."

"Thank you. Come, Mary." He led her up the stairs toward their room.

Monsieur and le curé glanced at each other.

"C'est terrible," said le curé, shaking the newspaper.

"Oui." Monsieur spread his hands. "Au moins, nous en avons fini de tels problèmes."

"Grâce à Dieu." The curé raised his eyes thankfully.

Tiger said little as they went up to their room. When he went out to sit alone on the verandah, Mary watched him. She sat silently nearby, waiting. He seemed to sense her anxiety because he stood up. "I'm going for a walk."

It was several hours before he returned and his face was taut. Mary then knew. He spread his hands helplessly.

"I don't want to go. It'll only be for a little while."

"I know."

"There will be more from Gupta, I am sure. If I'm missing at this time, it will make matters worse for us."

"We shall need a good record for you if you resign."

"It shouldn't be more than a week."

"Of course. You must go."

"It's that damned Gupta." His voice was harsh. "I could almost lose the Raj to Gandhi but not Gupta."

"I'll help you pack. Here are your pajamas. I was going to have them laundered." Oh God, she thought. She would not look at him. She was afraid she would go to him, touch his face, the fierce eyes. He was like a painting now that had hung on their living room wall in Cheltenham—a British soldier awaiting the charge of the French cavalry at Waterloo. He had the same warrior look.

Then his face softened as he looked around the room. "It's been so simple here. Peaceful. It's the happiest I've been in a long while."

"I know."

"I should be back in a week. It will end before then."

"Here's your kit." She put his shaving kit in his bag and spoke without turning. "You will be careful."

"I'll be safe. Most of the time I'll just be following Sir Gerald about."

"Then tell him to be careful."

He took her in his arms. "I am sorry about this."

"Can't be helped. You must get an honorable discharge."

"I have asked you to marry me, you know."

"I remember." She put his small valise in his hand. "You had best go. You must find a launch somehow."

"The governor will manage that."

"You want me to come to the river with you?"

"Stay here." He kissed her, held her a moment, then picked up his valise. His eyes made a quick, methodical check of the room, then he left.

Mary sat on the bed. It had all happened so quickly. A few hours ago they were on the ridge above the river. Now, so suddenly, he was gone. And there was nothing of him left in the room, not even the shaving kit.

That night Mary sat down to write her husband. She wanted to clear the decks, as her Royal Navy uncle would have said. She wanted to feel clean now, waiting for Alastair.

But she was unable to begin the letter. The thought of adding another loss to that lonely man held her back. He had been hard with her, even brutal at times, yet there had been tragedy in his life. In his marriage to her he had found a brief escape from that tragedy. She sensed what she would now be taking from him.

Finally Mary set it down in a few simple words. "Dear Edward, I would like a divorce. Alastair Flemyng has asked me to marry him and I have accepted. I am sorry that our marriage must end in this manner. I know you did your best, as I did."

She hesitated. It was hard to write the next words. Three months ago it would have been unthinkable. "There has never been a divorce in my family. The least I can offer in return for the divorce is to have you divorce me. I shan't contest. Alastair and I shall be leaving India."

Mary held the signature. It seemed ridiculous to write "good luck" in view of what she might be doing to him. She simply added "Mary." She posted it that day. She was now free for Alastair.

In the days after Mary left York House, Edward Goad maintained his customary schedule. He went into the fields in the morning and ate tiffin wherever Ahmed happened to find him. In the evenings, eyeglasses low on his nose, he worked doggedly in his office. He never went to the Punjabi woman's bustee or to the coolie village.

In the late evenings Goad could be seen sitting alone on his bedroom verandah. Ahmed told the Punjabi woman that the sahib sat there sometimes until late at night, not drinking or reading but simply staring out over his jute fields. Ahmed said he could see the sahib's shadow on the balcony long after he himself had gone to bed. The next morning the sahib would be hard at work on his usual routine.

Once while watching the ditch coolies swirling the retted jute stalks through the water, he started to shout at them, then plunged fully dressed into the ditch, pulled a stalk from a frightened coolie, and began to slash it angrily up and down the ditch. For five minutes he continued to drive himself, shouting and whirling the stalk through the water, until the overseers jumped in to stop him. He was finally led exhausted to the bank.

The mem's name was not mentioned in the house. Goad never tried to explain Mary's absence. Ahmed went about his business carefully and in silence.

The killing of Duncan Saunders shook York House deeply. Word was brought to Goad when he was working in his office. That night he stayed an extra-long time on his verandah. He knew he would be called into Calcutta. He was a member of the Calcutta Light Horse, as were all the other Europeans in the area.

Two days later all members of the Light Horse were ordered to report to Calcutta. They gathered at York House for departure. There were the overseers, Dr. MacDonough and Joliffe, Brittingham and Robertshaw from up the river. They would all ride their own horses into Calcutta and were already in uniform.

But when Goad came down to meet them, they saw that he still wore the tan shorts and loose shirt in which they all worked.

They said nothing. They knew what was keeping him at York House. It was common knowledge that the memsahib had left. He was waiting for her. It would do no good to argue. He was a hard man.

Dr. MacDonough nodded. "You're staying."

"Aye."

"Come when you can." The men nodded and followed the doctor as he led them down the road.

Goad continued at York House. Three days after the men had left he was working late in the baling shed. There had been complaints from customers that the jute had been baled while still damp and that the heart of the fiber had become overheated and had rotted.

Goad was trying to determine why the damp jute had been baled and which worker might have been responsible. He was examining one of the bales when Ahmed entered and silently handed the sahib the letter from Mary.

Ahmed told the Punjabi woman later that it was a terrible and strange thing to see. He said the sahib took the letter, then walked to a corner of the baling shed before opening it. He said he saw the sahib read the mem's words. It seemed the sahib must have read them twice, even three times, because he stood so long in the corner of the baling shed. Then, Ahmed told the Punjabi woman, he heard a laugh from the sahib.

And, he said, this was the strange thing. When the sahib came from the corner, still holding the mem's letter, he said the sahib was no longer the grim man who had sat all night on the verandah. He was calm, as when a storm has passed.

And, Ahmed said, the sahib rode straightway back to the house and put on his Light Horse uniform. That very night he started for Calcutta.

31

EACH DAY MARY WALKED TO THE RISE WHERE she and Tiger had sat and peered down the river toward Calcutta. The climb seemed warmer now but she would sit nearly all day, moving only at midday into the shade of a lofty palm.

She tried to distract herself and sometimes found that she was murmuring, "Sister Anne, Sister Anne, do you see anyone coming?" But at this she closed her eyes tightly. The terror she had felt as a child at the tale of Bluebeard's wife was no stronger than she now felt. The days passed, but there was no boat on the river.

On the sixth day Monsieur le Gouverneur asked Mary to dine with him. He was a very good host, gracious and in his element.

Mary tried to be the attentive guest. She listened carefully to his tales of life in Hanoi and in Nouméa. He seemed to have served as a minor civil servant in many colonial posts.

After dinner the governor sat back with his small cognac, lit a cheroot, and glanced at her. His manner was sympathetic.

"What now are your plans, mademoiselle, if I may ask?"

Mary said nothing. She had noticed that for the first time since Alastair's departure, he had not addressed her as "madame."

"To remain here," she finally said. "I am waiting for Captain Flemyng."

"To remain here," he repeated. He looked at his cheroot. Its slenderness seemed to interest him. "To remain here one must have permission of the governor, of course."

"Yes, but you are the governor."

"Very true . . . true. But one is bound by the Code Nationale. The Code is very awkward. Chandernagore is very small. One must be careful."

"But surely I am not doing any harm here." Mary felt a growing bewilderment.

The governor patted her hand. "It is a pleasure to have mademoiselle in Chandernagore. Believe me, we do not have many ladies such as mademoiselle." He sighed. "But these are difficult times in India. One does not wish to become conspicuous at such a time."

"But Captain Flemyng will be here any day. Then we will go."

"I know. I have no doubt. But this Captain Flemyng . . . he is a very important man in Calcutta, I think. If it is known that he has used our little Chandernagore at a time like this for . . . for something of which his superior might not approve, it could make me difficulties."

Mary found herself becoming angry. "You didn't talk this way when we arrived. You were very hospitable."

He spread his hands. "When you came the British magistrate had not been murdered. Now matters are not normal."

"But I must wait for him! Please, Monsieur le Gouverneur."

"Of course, mademoiselle. I am not an ogre. Shall we say a few days more? Perhaps three."

"But he may not be back in three days. There is trouble in Calcutta."

"All the more reason not to have trouble in Chandernagore." He smiled. "One of the blessings of being unimportant. Our troubles are very small."

"Such as my being here. I see." She found she was able to laugh. "You are really wasted in such a minor post, Monsieur. You should have an embassy at least."

"I have often thought so. But, faute-de-mieux, this is my embassy."

"Thank you for a very nice dinner." Mary stood up, dignity itself. "Four days?"

"Three, mademoiselle." He bowed.

Mary spent the next few days with as much pride as she could manage. She refused to let herself go to the rise above the river again, knowing that the governor might well have been observing these trips. She strolled calmly through the town, returning for a leisurely tiffin, a rest, then, in the evening, made a promenade in her best finery.

She encountered Monsieur once or twice in the hotel but permitted no mention of Captain Flemyng to escape her. Each, by unspoken agreement, confined his quiet remarks to the condition of the weather or the few happenings of her daily walks.

On her last night Mary told Kim Dok, the little Annamese who ran the hotel, that she would be departing the next day. She said she required a launch to take her down the river. Kim Dok replied that the governor himself would supply the launch. She would have to leave it at the outskirts of Calcutta and find a taxi somehow. The governor was deeply regretful but he could not permit his launch to enter Calcutta.

The next morning when Mary left, Monsieur le Gouverneur and his entire staff stood at the hotel exit to bid Mary good-bye. There was Monsieur le curé, the two militaires, even Kim Dok, his wife, and two children. Monsieur le Gouverneur stepped forward to present Mary with a small bouquet. She accepted it and he kissed her hand with equal dignity.

Mary looked back as she was driven away and saw the little group still standing in front of the hotel, waving their good-byes. The governor seemed the most desolate of all. Mary pulled out her handkerchief and waved it. Each was following the rules.

Rajid left Gupta's presence and stumbled uncertainly down the steps toward the street. His young face was pale beneath the dark skin, his eyes wide with horror. He made a shambling way down the street toward the tramline.

He was still unclear as to how it had happened. Gupta had sent for him and he had hurried to the interview. He knew the next assignment to kill an Englishman would be his.

It had not turned out as he had expected. Gupta had been gentle with him, even paternal, but he had made it clear. He could not assign a man to such a killing who had not first proven his self-discipline, his dedication to killing beyond all else.

This would be no ordinary killing, he had said. No one could kill this personage in the place and manner selected and not die as well. Gupta regretted that Rajid might not be up to it.

Rajid had exploded with anger but Gupta had not yielded. He had been regretful but firm. He said he could not give such a deed to a man so mixed up he wore English-style clothes and even had a sweetheart who was half English. He would have to give this killing to one of the other young men, to Amiji or Sental. They were true Indians.

Rajid had shouted that this killing was his by rights; he had waited longest, worked hardest. He cursed Gupta and might have struck him if the guard had not held him.

"But your Dolly . . . you love her," Gupta said.

"I hate her!" Rajid had screamed. "I will kill her! I will show you!"

Gupta had tried to soothe the young man. "I will kill her," Rajid screamed again.

Then Gupta had done a curious thing. He had given Rajid two hundred rupees and told him he could spend it all on Dolly. He said that amount should satisfy Magda for several days. But, he said, unless Rajid could prove that the girl meant nothing to him, make good his boast about her, he would have to give the assignment to Amiji. Rajid had snatched the money, had shouted that he would prove he had no "Englishness"—he hated the English—and had then run from the house.

At Magda's Dolly waited for Rajid. She had just received his message and had arranged with Magda for his visit. Magda was pleased to find such a good customer just now. Her house had been about to reopen when this show of force nonsense had been announced.

Now there were patrols in all the streets. Her business was nil. Except for the Mr. Windendorp–Vera arrangements, plus Vera's chums, she had little income. She would kick out this Indian lover of Dolly's, however, in two days. She had her good name to consider.

Dolly was happy. She was seeing Rajid and they would have at least two days together, two days with no other man in her arms.

She was also happy because she had come to a decision. She was going to give up being an Anglo-Indian and be all Indian. It had not been an easy decision. Being partly English, wearing English clothes, having an English grandfather had been her one claim to pride. Even though she was a prostitute and knew she was not very well educated, there was always the chance of marrying a Tommy or a sailor and perhaps leaving India for good.

Now she would give up all this for Rajid as he had given up so much for her. She knew he was an educated man, had attended the university, and she knew that he might be able to obtain a large money payment from the parents of any Indian girl. Such educated youths could demand nearly anything. Yet he had turned his back on all that for her.

She knew a little of his revolutionary life. She knew that he had been in trouble at the university and was still hiding from the police. But this made him all the more dear to her. She sensed dimly that it must be lonely for him to be a revolutionary. He followed his terrible beliefs, isolated from a proper life, not even appreciated by the very people for whom he wanted to make a revolution.

Dolly knew she would have to go slowly in telling Rajid. She would begin by telling him she was leaving Magda's. She would then begin to wear Indian clothing, to cook Indian for him, to lapse into Bengali instead of always speaking English. Gradually he would see that he had an Indian woman instead of an "eight anna rupee" as he had once called her . . . half value.

Two days later at Magda's, Rajid lay in the darkened room beside Dolly and smoked a cigarette. Dolly was still sleeping heavily. He listened to the sound of the cavalry patrol in the narrow street. They had been going back and forth most of the day.

Rajid knew it was for him they were making their demonstration. The British didn't know it but it was. He was the killer who would light the spark that would finally set all India alight.

He looked down at the sleeping girl and he thought of what she had told him. She was leaving Acre Lane, leaving Magda to find her own place. She would support them both.

He touched her. She didn't know that he would be dead long before she left Magda's. She knew little of that side of his life. And when he was gone she would be alone.

It was really best that she go first. It would be so terrible for her when he had gone. It was difficult enough for an Anglo-Indian girl, even a smart one. And Dolly was not educated or smart. With him gone, she would be alone again. There was nothing worse than being alone and stupid.

Rajid's slender face was curiously relaxed, almost dreamy, as he looked down at the sleeping Dolly. She looked so young, so like a child as she lay with one pale arm stretched out toward him. She looked so white in that dark room. He wondered for a crazy moment whether he could just kill the white half and let the Indian half live.

No, he would have to kill it all. He had to cut out this cancer in himself. He had to show Gupta. He bent to kiss Dolly and she moved contentedly at his side.

Magda and her ayah were tidying their reception room, gossiping in Bengali, when a sudden screaming came from the room on the third floor. It was not a woman's scream. It was thin, high, like an Indian's, and there was a craziness in it, and an anguish.

"God," said Magda. "Hear dat. Dat is Dolly's room." She stared at the ayah. "Ao," she said and hurried briskly up the stairs, the ayah waddling after her.

Magda knew she shouldn't have let that crazy Indian in the house. Now there was this screaming. She reached the third floor and hurried down the hall. Dolly's door was closed.

"Dolly . . . Dolly," she called and pounded on the door. "It is Magda, child. You all right?"

There was an end to the screaming and then what sounded

like the slam of a window from Dolly's bathroom. Magda pulled a large key from her pocket, unlocked the door, and swung it wide. The ayah puffed up the stairs to stand beside her. Except for a pale streak of moonlight from the bathroom window, the room was dark.

Magda could see a figure on the bed and went inside. "Dolly?" The figure didn't answer and she went nearer. "Dolly, wake up. It's Magda, child."

She put out her hand to touch the girl's shoulder. The head rolled loosely against her fingers.

The ayah screamed and pointed to the girl's throat. Blood was still pumping out in thin, spurting trickles. The young girl's eyes were opening and closing in the shadowy room like the eyes of a child's doll. As they watched, the breath ended in a final, bubbling gasp and the eyes remained open and fixed.

"Murder! Police!" screamed the ayah and fled ponderously into the hall. Magda stared at the girl. She was not unused to violence and was a woman of action. She went quickly into the bathroom and saw the open window.

"Rajid," she called. There was no answer and she spat out the window. She went back into the room and looked down at Dolly.

It was really a mess. She would have to change the mattress and the sheets; there was even blood on the carpet. Besides this she was losing one of her best girls. Magda clucked irritably.

In the street outside Rajid leaned gasping against the house opposite. He stared up at Dolly's window, his lips opening and closing convulsively though no sound came. The window of the room suddenly whitened into light and the figure of a policeman appeared.

Rajid shrank back. The policeman seemed to know he was there. He flashed his torch into the dark, a long bony finger. Then the head and the light were withdrawn. Whistles sounded from inside the house and were answered from a street nearby.

Rajid glanced quickly toward the nearby corner. The pounding of heavy boots, hurrying toward the corner, pressed him back against the wall.

He turned then and ran desperately, with hiccupping spasms, up the alley and away from the crunching boots.

A warm wind minced its way after him, mocking Rajid's

feet with tiny whirlpools of dust. Booted feet rounded the
corner behind him. There was silence. The alley was empty.

32

AS MARY'S AUTO DREW NEAR CALCUTTA SHE SAW
a truckload of British soldiers heading for the city. She passed
the truck and a few miles further she was stopped at a road-
block. The British sergeant peered into her car, saw that she
was not Indian, and waved her on.

As she entered the city streets she saw a company of British
infantry. They were DLIs, the Durham Light Infantry, and
they marched quickly at route step, their rifles held hori-
zontally at the length of their arms.

She passed another company near Dalhousie Square and,
as her car entered the Maidan, she saw a troop of the Calcutta Light Horse.

Mary sat back in the auto. She knew her husband was in
the Horse and she didn't want him to see her. Not before she
was ready.

Mary went to her old room at the Great Eastern and soon
sat by the telephone. She had only to pick it up and in a few
moments she might be speaking with Alastair. She gave the
number of his flat.

Only a hoarse clicking sounded at the other end.

"The telephone doesn't answer, madam," said the hotel
operator.

"Please ring again." Mary forced her voice to be calm.
Her whole body was reaching out through that rasping click.

"I'm sorry. The number doesn't reply."

Mary hung up slowly and sat staring at the phone. She
knew she could ring Government House but he didn't want
her to phone him there. Now, of all times, he wouldn't like

it. One thing she could not do and that was wait in this room. He was too near.

She reached again for the telephone and gave the number of Denise Beauchamp.

She waited. "Damn those servants." She knew that Indian servants frequently let telephone rings go unanswered, particularly if the servants were "jungly," unused to city ways. Finally she heard Denise's voice.

"Denise, it's Mary. Mary deGive. I mean Mary Goad." She brushed her hair back from her forehead. She was so mixed up.

"Mary, what are you doing in Calcutta?"

"I'm at the Great Eastern." That seemed to be answer enough for now. Then Mary hesitated. She didn't want to say anything that might harm Edward, not yet, but she wanted to find Alastair.

"Denise, I'm trying to locate Edward. He's in the Light Horse. Where would they be?"

"He's out patrolling the streets probably, just as everyone else is."

"I can't very well search the streets for him."

"You might try the Slap. They all turn up there sooner or later. They've fixed up a canteen."

"The Slap!"

"Oh, they're having a lark. No office work. Just a holiday riding horses. Tom too." She sounded bitter.

"Thanks, Denise. I might look in there later."

"If you see Tom say hello for me. I haven't seen much of him since this started."

"I will. Good-bye." Mary hung up. She wondered briefly from Denise's tone whether Big Boy had arrived yet. Mary put it out of her mind. She had her own problems.

She went quickly to the mirror and eyed herself. She looked tired, no doubt of that, but probably everyone looked a little tired just then. It was not a time for beauty.

She would go to the Slap later and look for Tiger. Meanwhile she would try to remain in her room as long as possible. She was in the same city with him at least. That was better than remaining at Chandernagore. She would bathe and drink a cup of tea and then, if ever in her whole life she had tried to fix herself up, it would be this day.

And perhaps the phone would ring. Somehow he might know she was in Calcutta . . . from Denise perhaps. Denise might run into him. Or he might just sense that she was there waiting, as she was certain she would know if he were near.

Yes, she would wait in that room until he called. And when he did, she would be at her most delicious, most womanly best.

In the ten days since leaving Chandernagore Tiger Flemyng had literally lived, eaten, and slept at the Kidderpore police station. He had been welcomed back by Sir Gerald and for the moment was asked no questions. Any man of Flemyng's experience was invaluable just now.

Kidderpore was where Rajid had last been seen. Tiger had drawn up a grid of the sprawling city, had pored over it with Inspector Hanrahan at the Central Police Depot, and gradually narrowed the search for Gupta to Kidderpore.

Now Tiger drove the police. He had full backing from Sir Gerald and the police knew it. He introduced his Northwest Frontier methods—two duties on and one off. There was no time for the men to go home. They could sleep in their respective depots as he did.

The city was divided into districts and each morning Tiger allotted one squad to a district. He read their reports each time their first duty was finished, then planned their next duty. He drove them, cajoled, cursed—he had reverted to type, not the social aide-de-camp type he had been for nearly two years but the type who had won two DSMs and a citation.

Even his face seemed to take part. In anger the scars stood out redly. In thought, as he pored over the city maps, the twisted nose prodded and jabbed at the table before him.

Then came the first break. It was an informer who gave a hint. Pictures of Rajid had been distributed and a man, a Muslim who lived near a mosque in Garden Reach, said that he had frequently seen Rajid in that area—Rajid and other men. He didn't know the exact location but he was certain it was within a half mile of the mosque.

That was all Tiger needed. He moved his headquarters to the Garden Reach police depot. It was there, after two days, that the local police sergeant waked him one afternoon in the cell in which Tiger had been dozing. The sergeant shook him.

"We have somebody, sir. Sir."

"What? Sorry. What is it?"

"We've nabbed somebody, sir. He was buying food in the bazaar. The mosque man says he's one of the Gupta crowd."

"Where is he?"

"In my office. He won't say anything."

Tiger went quickly into the corridor, then to the police sergeant's office. There he found a young man. Gupta's bodyguard had been picked up while buying ghee for his master's monkey.

The young man was sitting on a chair. Two Indian constables stood nearby. The bodyguard's face was blank, his eyes fixed on the floor.

"He'll tell us nothing, sir. We'll have to release him in two hours. Prayer time. The Muslims'll raise holy hell if we keep him with no charge."

"We may not need two hours. One may be enough." He turned to one of the constables. "Do you know the Zoo?"

"Zoo?" The constable stared at him uncomprehending.

"The Zoological Gardens, man."

"Ah, hussoor." The Indian wagged his head affirmatively.

"How long will it take you to get there?"

"Twenty minutes. Motorbike."

"Take my car. The syce will drive you. I want you to bring something back. Here . . . take this." Tiger pulled a card from his pocket, his official aide-de-camp greeting card. He scribbled a sentence on it and handed it to the constable.

"Take that to McClure Sahib. Don't ask any questions. Just bring back what he gives you. Understand?"

"Hum juntha, sahib." Again the affirmation.

"Don't shake what he gives you. Hold it steady."

The eyes of the young constable grew round. It was plain he didn't like this assignment for the white hussoor. But he also knew that the hussoor was no man to be denied.

"Ah, sahib," he said resolutely.

Tiger shoved him. "Jeldi karo. Bahut jeldi. And hold it steady."

The constable left. Tiger turned back to the young man, who was watching the performance with some interest in his eyes. He now relapsed, eyes on the ground.

Tiger stood over him. "You'll have forty minutes in which to make up your mind. After that, we shall see. You may not get to prayers at all this sundown. More likely they will be praying for you."

He turned to the constable. "Let me know when your man is back. I want to ring McClure."

He went into the depot hall and the sergeant could hear

him speaking on the phone. The voice was emphatic but low. It was obvious that he was preparing the Zoo curator for the police constable's mission. It must have been a successful phone call because Captain Flemyng reappeared in a moment and eyed the prisoner. There was a certain grim anticipation in his look that made even the sergeant uneasy. He was glad he was not the prisoner.

Tiger went back to his cell and lit a cigarette. His hand shook a trifle but he knew it must be fatigue. One could not drive himself and others as he had for the past ten days and not have a hand shake.

He contemplated what must be done. It was not something he would enjoy doing and he was certain it was not legal. But if that young man knew the address of Gupta, he would get it out of him or the boy would die. It was as simple as that. If he got the address, there would be no questions asked. He would have Gupta.

If the boy died without talking—well, there was no point in thinking about that. It would be hushed up somehow. Unfortunately, he would be no nearer finding Gupta.

Tiger walked out into the corridor and examined the cells carefully. The right place would be needed for this. Someplace which was airtight; it would muffle any screams for one thing. For another—well, it was simply essential.

He examined each cell in the corridor, trying the bars, pulling at the doors. Finally he stopped before a locked and closed door and rattled the knob. He knew what it was, a toilet. It could be just the thing. With the doors and windows closed, even a hornet couldn't get out.

Hornet. It sounded innocuous enough but Tiger knew the deadliness of the biggest, most savage hornets in the world. He had seen English Tommies bitten to death by United Provinces hornets. He had seen the bodies of two others who had dived into a tank of water to escape them. They had drowned but not before the fury of the hornets had been bitten deep into their faces.

Tiger went back to sit thoughtfully in his cell. He was not absolutely certain this would work in the jail, nor that the hornets would be savage enough after special care in the Zoo. Nor was he certain the boy knew anything.

It was a chance he must take. Did he truly want to? He was no longer a believer in the Raj. Yet he would torture a boy horribly, risk his life. Why? He would be more damned than anyone for what might happen.

But he knew he would try. There were just the three of them in this . . . the hornets, the boy, and himself. There was almost a mystical feeling in it . . . a holy trinity. The boy would have been bewildered to see the hard face of the English captain. The scars and busted face wore a nearly kind expression. It was not a face of hatred but of love.

Nearly two hours later it was over. The task had not been done quickly. It had taken a half hour to ensure the privacy of the water closet and another twenty minutes to demonstrate to the boy what angry hornets from the UP could do to a pair of mice Tiger had commanded from the Zoo. He had forced the boy to watch through the water-closet window.

The bodyguard had listened to the fearful sound—the droning, quiet at first, then rising angrily as the box was shaken. Next he heard the frightened squeals of the mice as the hornets had knifed and stabbed, then the scurrying, the whimpering, and finally a thrashing on the floor and silence.

Quickly Tiger had shoved the boy inside. A second box of hornets had been brought up, shaken, then released. Tiger had watched through the door slit as the boy backed away, retreating to the corner.

But the boy had not given in. He had covered his face, screamed and cursed defiantly, had even thrown his cell stool toward the window slit.

Then the hornets descended and Tiger watched. It was curious. The expression on his hard face was not cruel or even determined. It was rapt, almost mystical. It was not unlike the face of Gupta.

Screaming now, the boy pawed at the air. He tore off his shirt and flailed at his attackers but this exposed his thin and naked body.

The hornets now descended with fury. The boy screamed no longer but fought silently, gasping, stumbling desperately from one side to the other.

It was useless. The hornets closed in. The boy fell to his knees, then Tiger saw him crawling slowly to the door. His face appeared before him in the slit, eyes already closing, the mouth puffed.

"Where is Gupta?" Tiger's voice was soft, even friendly but there was no answer.

"Where is Gupta?" Tiger's voice was sharper.

The boy's lips opened slightly and Tiger leaned closer to the window slit. The words came faintly.

"Rajid . . . Rajid must kill someone. He has been . . . he has been ordered."

Then the voice fell away. There was a terrible scream as more hornets appeared on the head and the face slipped down from the slit.

"Where is Gupta?" Tiger was shouting now, leaning forward to yell the question down into the cell. There was no answer.

"Shall we open, sir?" It was the police constable, already muffled with the net he had obtained from the Zoo.

Tiger was silent, staring toward the window as though waiting for the face to reappear. There was no face, only a low, hungry drone from the floor below.

"Sir?" It was the constable again.

"Bring him out! He'll talk to us here." Tiger's face was grim. He took his position beside the door.

It took the two police a good minute to unlock and open the cell door. Each wore protective nets and one carried a canister of some sort.

The door was finally opened and the police entered. The sound of gas being squirted was heard and Tiger saw wisps float from the half-opened cell. The men reappeared, dragging the young bodyguard. The door was slammed behind.

Tiger dropped to his knees beside the boy. He stared down into the swollen face. "Where is Gupta?" He shook the boy. "Tell me! I'll put you back in there!"

"I'm afraid he's dead, sir."

Tiger stared down. The mouth, or the place where he knew the mouth must be, sagged sideways. The eyes, tiny white dots in a swelling mound of brown, were without sight.

He pushed at the boy's chest. It was still, the skin puffy to the touch. It felt as though the bony body were covered at last with fat, an obscene and swelling fat.

Somewhere in the jail a typewriter was being pounded, erratic, halting under thick fingers. A cell door clanged in a nearby wing. Tin supper plates were scraped of their remains.

The eyes beneath Tiger slowly disappeared. The face, puffing, mud-brown, closed in.

33

A FEW HOURS LATER TIGER STOOD SILENTLY BE-
fore a somber Sir Gerald and a frowning Lord Willingdon.
He had gone straight to Government House from the Kidderpore police station to report his information, and Sir Gerald
had sent for the viceroy. They now knew as much as he did.
He waited.

The viceroy nodded toward Tiger. "I shan't ask you how
you got this information. You know there are rules on these
matters."

"Yes, sir."

"Was this all you found out? That this Rajid has been
ordered to kill someone? You didn't locate Gupta?"

"No, sir."

"Did you find out who was to be killed?"

"No, sir. Simply that Rajid has been ordered to kill someone."

"Speak up, man. I can't hear you."

Tiger pulled himself together. He knew he must be mum-
bling. He was tired, more tired than he could remember.

"He didn't say who, sir. It would be an Englishman."

Sir Gerald moved. "Don't worry about that, Your Excellency. We have a photo of this Rajid. It was found in the
possessions of the mistress he murdered. An Anglo-Indian
prostitute." He tossed a photo on the table.

The viceroy glanced at it, then tossed it back. Sir Gerald
picked up the photo. "He'll never get near you, sir. We have
had copies made of this and distributed to all police depots.
He will be picked up the moment he appears."

Tiger hesitated only a moment. Now, he thought. "I would
let him go, Your Excellency."

"Go?" For once the viceroy seemed startled.

"I would not pick him up. Gupta is the man we want. Rajid may yet lead us to him."

Sir Gerald exploded. "But he may kill someone! This man has orders!"

The viceroy put up a hand. "Just a moment." He was thoughtful, on the scent of something. "It isn't Rajid we care about. It isn't even Gupta . . . not he alone. Perhaps we can use this Rajid."

"But, Your Excellency . . ." Sir Gerald was plainly astonished.

"Why not? We used Gandhi to keep Gupta quiet. We let him fast. It succeeded, didn't it?"

"Of course, but . . ."

"We might now use Gupta to defeat Gandhi. Another killing would shake the Mahatma badly. It might cause him to withdraw entirely from the swaraj fight. Gandhi is our most dangerous enemy because he has India behind him."

"But this Rajid may kill someone. It might well be you, sir."

"It might also be you." The viceroy smiled. "Would you mind? If it set back swaraj?"

"It's not a question I should like to answer."

The viceroy glanced at Tiger, his eyes appraising. "You have made a very dangerous suggestion, Captain, letting Rajid loose. One that no sensible person could possibly approve."

"I know it, sir."

"You would risk my life and that of Sir Gerald . . . your own too, of course, as well as nameless others."

"Yes, sir."

"Wait outside. Sir Gerald and I will consider this."

Tiger went back to the anteroom. Captain Graham sprawled in a chair, waiting. Tiger went straight to a window looking out on the rear garden.

Down below the malis went about their careful tasks, squatting as they clipped the edges of the flower beds, moving slowly on bended knees. The marigolds, the asters, and the poppies had been freshly watered, and the Government House trees—the shisham, the bitter orange—reflected the solitude of the imperial garden.

The tranquillity before his eyes was not even seen. The fatigue in his bony face had deepened the furrows. If he had been a man in conflict before, he was now approaching the eye of the storm.

It was the face of the young boy that came to his mind. He remembered that face pressed against the cell window, then on the floor of the cell corridor, puffed, dying, still turned toward his English killer.

Tiger had seen other faces dying, turned toward him. Why should he remember this one?

This was different. He had killed for the Raj before with a certain frenzy, a cleansing ruthlessness that had later horrified him. He had felt a loathing for what he had done, nearly a despair.

This killing had come at a certain time in his life; he had broken the bonds in going to Chandernagore. He had made a choice, rejecting the Raj and choosing Mary.

But with this boy it had been different. He had known a sense of power. He had almost loved what he did and loved the object he destroyed.

He had been happy that the boy hadn't given in. He wanted to prolong the boy's resistance. Without resistance there could be no death at the end. No love.

Tiger turned wearily from the window. He was a true member of the Raj now. He had offered up his sacrifices. There was blood on the moon as in all ancient sacrifices.

Could he really marry Mary now? True, there was sanity with Mary. With her he might yet break away from India.

There was physical satisfaction as well. Their union had been good. He had sensed years of patience and self-denial in her. He had felt a desperation there too . . . once she had even cried out the name "Tim." But there had been acceptance finally and a certain wonder.

Yet he couldn't marry her and bring her into his army life. It would be damned hard to find another job in India. Men were being discharged, not hired. They would have to leave India.

Tiger glanced down toward the garden but again a face came to mind. Puffed, eyes bloated, it floated before him. A voice seemed to whisper, the boy's voice. "Stay. You belong to me now. To me."

Tiger leaned his head against the window. "Mary." The whisper was almost a plea.

But the boy's voice was louder. "You belong to India now."

Tiger groaned. His eyes closed against the agony.

Sir Gerald entered from the council chamber, his face grave. Captain Graham, snorting awake, scrambled to his feet.

The governor of Bengal faced his aide. "His Excellency likes your idea, Flemyng. He says it has just the right touch. The terrorists will lose, whatever happens. If they don't make a kill their campaign is over with Gupta gone. If they do, it will probably mean the withdrawal of Gandhi. Yes, it has a nice touch."

"Yes, sir." Oh God, he thought. Now I'm in for it.

"Now we shall see what Gupta had in store for us."

"It is taking a chance, sir. I should remind you."

"We all are. Every Englishman in India takes a chance. Empires aren't held without chances." He nodded grimly.

"Yes, sir." But it's seldom the generals or viceroys who take the chances, Tiger thought. This chance will be unique.

"We're going to the Slap now. His Excellency wants to drop in at the canteen for morale purposes. You have nothing planned, I trust."

"No, sir."

"No horse upcountry you want to inspect again? Or any other animal?" The mouth smiled but the eyes were sharp.

Tiger hesitated. "No, sir."

Sir Gerald did a surprising thing then. He punched his aide lightly on the shoulder, not without a certain respect.

"Damned fool. Come on."

Mary had waited long enough at the hotel. She had passed an afternoon and night in her room. She had phoned Tiger's flat twice but there had been no answer. She didn't phone Government House. She was afraid she might disturb him and he would be angry. Nor would it have been discreet of her. Nothing must prevent an honorable discharge so that they could be married honorably.

But she could wait no longer. She would go to the Slap and look for him. She could always pretend it was her husband or Tom Beauchamp for whom she searched.

Mary fixed herself carefully, putting on an extra touch of lipstick. She had never mastered the art of makeup. She had never used it at Roecroft and three months in India had proved too little time.

Mary donned her smartest new frock and high-heeled shoes. She knew it was a time for uniforms, a time of crisis, but she also knew that the wives and girls at the Slap would probably be younger. She was learning, she reflected, that when one was engaged to a younger man, it put certain pressures on a woman.

At the last moment Mary considered a parasol. It would undoubtedly make her conspicuous but it might also lend her an air.

She paraded before the mirror, then stopped. Her fingernails carried too much pink nail polish. The hand holding the parasol seemed suddenly ugly, a long bony claw. To call attention to her hands could be fatal. She would not take the parasol. It was too late to take off the nail polish. She was too impatient.

Mary's fingers trembled as she put on a hat. She would want a long rest when all this was settled. She and Alastair would have a long trip together. You might say, in fact, for the rest of their lives.

When Mary reached the Slap she was startled. She had remembered the club under normal circumstances, its gates wide, groups of tennis players and other members going and coming. Now there were troop lorries in the side street. Her taxi was stopped at the closed gates by a gurkha sentry with rifle and bayonet. A squad of gurkhas was drawn up inside the compound wall. Through the gates she saw members of the club, now wearing the tan uniform of the Light Horse, passing in and out.

Mary was permitted to alight from the taxi and enter but the auto was sent away. Inside the club she sensed an air of purpose, even of excitement. Yet there was also a touch of conviviality, of respite from the patrols.

Groups of the Light Horse stood together on the dance floor or took tea from a canteen set up at one end. The balcony was dotted with young men in tan uniforms and with them she saw many girls she knew to be fishing fleeters. The last time she had seen that ballroom it had been "Durbar 1877." It seemed long ago.

Mary moved slowly through the crowded halls. She searched only for one person, one tall figure, one beloved face.

She was aware that there were stares as she passed. Amid the uniforms, the serious activity of the canteen women, the general air of fatigue mixed with defiant purpose, she knew she must be conspicuous. Her very presence touched the frivolous.

She didn't care. She ignored the curious looks, the few half-giggles. She moved among the crowd with a purpose of her own, no less serious than theirs. It was only her uniform that was different.

It was near the verandah that she saw him, tall in his uniform among other soldiers. She stopped, sensing the fatigue in the beloved body, the lowered head. Then she moved closer, slowly, till she stood obediently beside him.

"Alastair."

He looked quickly down at her. There was a sudden jerky movement of his mouth, his face paled, then he glanced around.

"Come out to the verandah."

"Yes." She followed mechanically, seeing only the back in front of her.

They reached a quiet place on the verandah and he stopped. She moved toward him. "Darling."

"Why are you here? Why did you leave Chandernagore?"

"I couldn't wait. You were so long. Alastair . . . please." She moved again to be close to him but he held her off.

"Mary. No."

"Hold me. Alastair."

"There are people about. I'm with Sir Gerald and the vice-roy."

"I don't care." She clung to him a moment, then looked up. "I've asked Edward for a divorce."

"A divorce?" He repeated it as though he had never heard the word.

"It's been so awful without you. I tried to stay in Chandernagore but I had to come. I wrote Edward before I left."

"Mary, I want to tell you something." He didn't look at her. "I may be staying in the army. I'm needed just now."

"Of course. I'll do my best."

"You know how I feel about taking a wife into the army. I couldn't do it to you."

She looked up at him, puzzled. "What are you trying to say?"

He shook his head. "It's been awful. I'm such a confused person sometimes. It's the Irish in me." He tried to smile. Then, taking her hands firmly, he pulled himself together.

"Mary, these days the Raj is in trouble. It simply wouldn't be right to talk about marriage now."

"We could wait. This will be over."

"No. It will never be over."

"Don't you want to marry me?" The words were a question but there was disbelief. He hesitated. "Tell me."

"Hush, Mary."

"Tell me!" The cry was wrenched from her.

He shook his head, his face hard. "The army means something to me after all."

"That's no reason we can't marry."

"It isn't good for an officer to marry a divorced woman, especially one who was the wife of a sahib as important as Goad."

"I see. It's your career. Forget your career. You'll have another one. In Europe. We'll make one somehow."

"It's not just my career. It's . . . it's difficult to explain. I hardly know myself."

She saw for the first time how moved he was, saw the depths of his effort. "Tell me." Her voice was quiet.

"It's India. It's funny. It isn't as though India belonged to us but as though we belonged to India." He rushed on. "I've killed so many for the Raj. Just now a boy. Just yesterday."

"Tiger."

"I owe something. It's conscience perhaps but it's more than that. As though I were the prisoner. I'll never leave India. And there'll be no room for anyone else in my life."

He sounded weary, as though he could see the future, the long, dead future. He threw this feeling off, straightening up. "I'm sorry but I must return to the governor." He looked down at her, his deep eyes already withdrawing, closing her away. "Good-bye."

"Alastair. Wait. You can't go like this. My God."

"I must."

"But what have I done. In Chandernagore you loved me. I know you did."

"That was just a hope. An impulse."

"The whole thing? It wasn't!"

"Mary, there are people here. Lower your voice."

"I won't lower my voice."

He looked at her and his face hardened. He was already assuming the armor he must wear. The protection.

"Next time I shall choose someone my own age. I advise you to do the same."

He saw her face whiten, saw the lines around her mouth pinch as the lips tried to speak. He hesitated. He knew what he must be doing to her. He wasn't that callous. But there was also inevitability, a sense of what had to be.

"I'm sorry. I must go." He bowed and walked quickly away.

"Alastair." It was a cry of hopelessness. But he was gone.

Mary closed her eyes. It was like a child's game. She would count ten slowly, then she would open her eyes and go look for him. He was only hiding. Only she knew it was not a child's game. When she opened her eyes he would be truly gone.

For a moment she felt a wild sense of amusement. She had lost Tim twice. She had given two men to the Empire. It was such a shoddy old Empire really yet it had beaten her, not once but twice.

Mary walked from the verandah to sit by the tennis court. It was quiet there. The soft wind touched one of the courts, lifting a swirl of dust. It twirled daintily in a circle to collapse emptily against a baseline. Mary's eyes followed it only dimly.

It was over. She and Tiger had finished, almost as soon as they had begun. And it had all happened so quickly. She had entered the club looking for him just ten minutes ago.

The sun moved and the shadows stretched lazily on the tennis court. Small lizards rustled thirstily among dry leaves in the drains.

She had been jilted . . . this thought rustled through her consciousness. Alastair . . . Tiger . . . had jilted her. It was funny. She had never even been able to get his name straight. Alastair . . . Tiger . . . Tiger . . . Alastair . . . they had both jilted her. First Mr. Janeway, even Mr. Janeway, and now Tiger-Alastair.

What was the American expression? "It." She didn't have "it," that was the trouble. She was just a respectable lady of thirty-eight with a fondness for the British Empire. She should never have ventured away from Roecroft. She had been safe there. Perhaps she didn't belong in the adult world.

If only it didn't hurt so. She was getting on, that was the trouble. She was feeling what a German teacher at Roecroft had called "Türschlusspanik," the panic of the closing door. It was said to happen to all unmarried ladies at a certain age. She had certainly reached that certain age and she was as good as unmarried. She could feel the door swinging gently, inexorably shut.

Mary closed her eyes. She would stay there, safe behind

her eyelids. It was dark but out there in the light one found only pain.

The moments passed. The shadows reached tentatively toward her feet. Mary finally rose and walked slowly back toward the verandah. It was then that she saw her husband.

Edward Goad was sitting in a verandah corner with a group of older people, senior officers in the militia and their quiet, unfashionable wives. Goad wore the single crown of a captain on his shoulders. It occurred to Mary how out of place he looked, even now, with his yellow-brown skin and leathery face. He was always out of place . . . except at York House. She started to go back to the tennis court, to walk around the club somehow. Then she knew that he had seen her because he got to his feet and was walking toward her.

She moved quickly away. She couldn't bear to see him now. She stopped. The way around the clubhouse from the courts had been blocked by barbed wire and a sentry. She was trapped. She turned to find that he had caught up with her.

He said nothing but his hands shook a little as he stopped to light a cigarette.

She found herself chattering. "I wrote you a letter, Edward. I mailed it days ago. You must have received it by now. It explains everything."

"I received it." He spoke calmly, as though it were every day he received requests from his wife for a divorce. "I saw you with him just now."

"I loved him, Edward. And he did ask me to marry him. He did!"

"He's turned you down."

"Yes." Then suddenly she was sitting on a bench and weeping in great, hopeless sobs. Her hands pressed to cover her contorted face. Her hair twisted through her fingers.

Goad looked at her. "What are you going to do?"

"I don't know." She shook her head hopelessly.

"You have no money, have you? Of your own I mean."

"No."

"Will you go back to England?"

"I don't know."

He still stared down at her, his face contemplative. "Would you go back to York House?"

"What?" She looked up uncomprehendingly.

He took her hands, his grip strong. "I needed a wife when I married you. I still need one."

"But you know about Tiger now."

"You didn't tell me anything I hadn't thought was possible."

"Edward, I loved him."

He gripped her arms angrily. "You've loved before, haven't you? You lived through it. You will this time. If I can try, so can you."

She shook her head. "India . . . it frightens me."

"It frightens me. It frightens most of us." He grew almost jocular. "We don't always have to stay in India. Do you know I've never seen a great English school? We can make a tour. You can show me Roecroft."

"Don't patronize me."

"I'm not. I want to help and I want you to help me. We're not young, Mary, either of us. We may need each other." He took a breath. "Ours was a fishing fleet marriage. Without love. That's why I wouldn't give up the old ways. They were a defense against loving you."

"The ganja too?"

"That was the last day, the day you found me. I had decided to take a chance on us. I was cutting loose."

"From Julie too?"

"No. Julie will always be there. I can't deny my daughter. That is something we will have to live with, just as I will have to live now with your Tiger Flemyng. Someday we may put them both to rest."

He touched her. "I want you back. I'd be proud of you because I know it won't be easy for you now. When this trouble is done here I'll go back to York House to wait for you. You'll be welcome."

He started to go, then stopped. "We are what we are, Mary. If we don't accept ourselves, who will? Come home now."

He smiled at her, the first really personal look she had seen on that grim face. Then he walked away.

Mary sank back onto the bench. The familiar tennis court seemed alien, bewildering. Another pool of dust was teetering about the court.

He wanted her back. "We are what we are." That meant he wanted no apologies. She had betrayed him with Alastair but **he too had made mistakes.**

She could have another chance. His cause for despair had been infinitely greater than hers. He was willing to throw off bitterness, jealousy of Tiger, to try again.

Mary rose slowly to her feet. There was no one left outside the clubhouse beside herself. She stopped at the verandah. She could see the older officers and their wives still sitting where she had seen Edward. She saw the tiredness in the faces of the men and the patience in their plain wives. A few lines from Kipling, half-remembered from her schooldays, came to her. "The tumult and the shouting dies; the captains and the kings depart."

These were the "captains," these tired men and their wives. She felt a sudden appreciation of them. India wasn't all decay and ganja and giving babies opium. There were patience and loyalty and average people with average ambitions and lives. They had built something.

Mary shook her head. She knew that she should be impatient with these people. They were fools. They were finished in India and wouldn't face it. They wouldn't give up. Any more than Edward would give up with her.

And suddenly she wanted to be a part of these people. She would help Edward as he would help her. She would have as real a husband this time as she would be a wife. One thing was very clear to her; her husband was very much a man.

She went up on the verandah. She would tell Edward where she was staying. Then, if he really wanted to take her back, he would know where she could be found.

She then saw that where Edward had been sitting there was a vacant place. She knew he must have come in his motorcar and assumed he had gone for it to return to patrol duty. It was then that she heard the sharp sound of pistol shots.

Rajid had put his taxi in the rank opposite the main gate of the club. He could easily see into the compound and could spot anyone coming out of the club door.

It had amused Gupta to put Rajid into a Sikh taxi wallah outfit. A blue puggree was wound around his head and his face was covered with a scraggly beard. Disguising him had been very entertaining.

There was another factor in Gupta's prank. No one was less likely to be stopped for eccentric behavior in driving a taxi than a Sikh. One chided them at one's peril. They made up the bulk of Calcutta taxi wallahs and, sitting high in their front seats, their long, bony knees thrust heavenward, beards flowing, they were the scourge of the streets.

Rajid waited. If only he could remember better what he was supposed to do and whom he was supposed to kill. He knew it was someone in the clubhouse. Gupta had told him the name of the person and he had just been told, while waiting in rank in front of Firpo's, that he would find this person at the Saturday Club. But now he had forgotten.

He also knew there was some reason he had been put in a taxi. It was something about driving straight into the compound bawling "taxi" and then, when quite close to the person, killing him. The usual precautions around a personage such as this would be relaxed at sight of a mere taxi. The worst he could expect at first would be a cuffing for leaving his taxi rank.

He would kill the first person through the door, that was the solution. It didn't really matter, Gupta had said once, who was killed so much as the fact that someone was killed. He would really be following Gupta's orders.

Besides, he wasn't certain he wanted to kill the person Gupta had selected. He wasn't a slave, a nobody. He would kill whomever he pleased. Gupta had selected Dolly too, for that matter. That was why he had given him the money for Dolly. Now she was gone, killed by Gupta.

If only his head didn't hurt so much. Dolly used to rub the back of his neck when his head hurt like this. He used to laugh at her, rubbing his neck when it was his head that hurt. But now Dolly was gone, killed by Gupta.

His eyes narrowed as he peered through the compound gate. There was some activity there. The Indian doorkeeper had come out to whistle up a sahib's syce and motorcar. Rajid put his hand to the ignition. This was the one to kill. The first person through the door.

He tried to start his motor but it wouldn't catch. It was the ignition—he hadn't turned the key. His hands were shaking, then he turned the key and the motor started. He saw the doorkeeper step respectfully back as the sahib came out.

"Now," thought Rajid. He let in his gear and drove straight up the slight incline through the gate, past the startled gurka and into the compound. "Taxi!" he bawled and headed straight for the sahib.

A British sergeant turned a startled glance toward this

crazy Sikh. "Get him out of here," he yelled. "Hi! Taxi wallah!" He came running toward the clubhouse door.

But Rajid had his pistol out and was not three feet from the sahib. He leaned out as though to open his taxi door, left arm reaching back, meanwhile bawling, "Taxi, sahib!" and, as the sahib stood immobile on the doorstep, he shot him full in the chest.

Goad staggered back but didn't fall. He seemed to brace himself against the wall behind him, then, as Rajid fired twice more, he came lurching and snarling at him.

Rajid felt a brief fear. This man was incredible—hard, tough. He saw blood already appearing from the mouth before him. The yellow-brown skin was mottled with blood. Hysterically, Rajid fired two more shots into the face before him, then turned the gun backward and shot himself in the head.

The only sound for a moment was the whirr of wings as the pigeons flew up from the trees in the compound. There were shouts, angry commands, the harsh sound of hobnail boots running in the compound and from the street outside. The two bodies, Goad's hand still fastened to Rajid's shoulder, were freed from the taxi and laid at the foot of the steps.

A woman rushed out through the club door, stared at the bodies, and dropped on her knees. Mary touched her husband's shoulder just as he seemed to open his eyes once more. She said "Edward!" The eyes closed and that was all.

Men in uniform had pushed from the clubhouse. "It's Edward Goad," someone said. There was shock and puzzlement as though he were the last person one would expect to find in such a condition. More people gathered; the British sergeant and his gurkhas took up positions.

A police officer asked Mary a few brief questions. Could she identify the body? Did she know why he had been shot? She said "my husband" to the first. To the second she shook her head.

That was all. She stood aside as the bodies were taken away. She started to go back into the clubhouse but was pushed to one side as an important-looking group was leaving. She saw the viceroy come out first, surrounded by his security police and his aide-de-camp. The viceroy glanced once at Goad's body, shook his head, and climbed into his auto.

Then she saw Alastair. He came with the governor and

more police. She stood back as the official autos were driven up and the party, surrounded by police on motorcycles, drove quickly out of the compound gate toward the street.

Mary felt very tired. She did so want to sit down. But she didn't want to go back into the clubhouse now. She would try to reach her hotel.

She walked slowly out of the compound gate and into the street. Motor lorries filled with police hurtled past her. Squads of gurkha infantrymen jammed nearby. She walked alone unheeding. She knew dimly as she walked that it was warm. The rouge on her cheeks was dotted with drops of perspiration. The mascara on her lashes was slowly trickling to the skin and streaking her face. The few natives in the gardens she passed worked stripped to the waist.

Then she understood. The cold weather had passed. The season was over.

34

IT WAS A LARGE WEDDING, PROBABLY THE MOST impressive and fashionable in the cathedral that season. It had been postponed a week after Goad's death. Government had not relaxed control. In fact, it had even brought over another regiment from Burma. Margot had then decided that the wedding should be held anyway. It would be like a wartime wedding, being married within sound of the guns. Besides, she had waited long enough.

The cathedral was by no means full but the front half was occupied. Frank's Rugby Club had turned out en masse, many of them in the uniform of the Light Horse. Frank's side of the cathedral aisle seemed to be filled with wiry little scrum halves or brawny hookers and scrum forwards. The *Statesman* had made a great thing of the groom's rugger history in Calcutta and had sent its sportswriter to attend the wedding as well as its society editor.

Frank waited by the altar. Gordie Purvis, in Light Horse uniform, stood beside him as best man. Frank had spent a good bit of money on his wedding suit. He had wanted one from his own shop but he didn't carry cutaways and had been forced to have a suit made up by a durzi. He had managed to have one of his shop labels attached.

He perspired. The cathedral was a sea of waving fans. Frank always suffered more than most during the hot weather. He had never become used to India's heat. Now that he had given up rugger he would find himself putting on more weight and sweating more. He could feel his armpits already becoming damp.

He was not unhappy, however. He felt a sense of well-being as he looked out over the faces before him. He saw his old pals from the club; even the Haberdashers' Guild had sent a representative. He liked crowds, always had. He wasn't just a hooker now, lost in the pack, head down. He was right there in the open, a regular scrum half.

He was also moving up in the world a bit. He and Rufus Bracebridge had already made plans for moving him out of retail into something larger.

He looked at the rear of the church and saw the waiting Margot and her bridesmaids. He arranged his features appropriately. Yes, he had a very good thing ahead. Now if only the heat hadn't stirred up that tickling.

Margot had a few thoughts as she waited. She couldn't remember whether she had put into her traveling case that little medicine kit the Indian doctor had given her. She had put it in her jewel case but couldn't remember whether she'd put the jewel case in her valise.

She glanced ahead into the cathedral. She could see all the Bracebridge connections on her side of the aisle. The Thorntons were there and Sir Gerald Andrews, the governor. The viceroy had even sent a representative. Her father was not Sir Charles Danvers for nothing. She saw Tiger Flemyng with Sir Gerald.

She thought briefly of Mary Goad. It was really she who was responsible for this wedding. It was she who had persuaded Tiger Flemyng to second Frank for the Saturday Club.

It was too bad about Mary. She had heard that Mary hadn't left York House since her husband's death. Someone had said that he had been cremated and his ashes scattered over the jute fields.

The first notes of the organ sounded and Margot adjusted her white gown and veil and gripped her prayer book. She took the arm of Rufus Bracebridge and moved down the aisle. She kept her head high on her thin neck. She knew that this might be the only time in her life when people might look at her and say, "How lovely she looks."

The rows of pews drifted by. Margot was aware there were other girls watching her, girls she had known on the *Strathnaver* or had seen at Firpo's and the Slap. She knew she walked before them as one who had succeeded.

She saw Frank waiting by the altar and her thoughts swiftly clicked into place. He was such a fool really but, with her guidance, they would build a very satisfactory life in Calcutta. He would prosper, might even become a burra sahib. He would also grow portly, probably lose his hair, and he would likely bore the members at the Slap and newcomers at the Rugby Club with windy tales of his own playing days. She wouldn't permit too much of that. After all, she did have a weapon now, their common treatment. She could always remind him.

The organ swelled the familiar chords and Margot approached the altar. The benign features of good Bishop Anson waited above his robe. Margot looked at Frank and for one awful instant knew what she too might become— dominating, like her father, thin, shrewish. She wanted to cry out, "Help me, Frank. Don't let me dominate you. I want to love you."

She stopped before the altar. Rufus Bracebridge stepped aside and Frank Willis was beside her. The church was suddenly hushed. The bishop opened his Bible and Frank and Margot raised solemn eyes. They were about to be joined in the holy bonds.

A day later a group gathered at Howrah railway station to see Bunty off. Sir John and Lady Thornton were there as well as Tom and Denise Beauchamp.

The platform was crowded but Bunty glanced toward the far end. She knew he would not be coming. There would be none of this last-moment dashing onto the station platform. It was finished. He hadn't even come to say good-bye.

"Well, won't be long now," said Tom.

"They're all getting on," said Lady Thornton. She looked worried. No matter how many times she had been through this, she always expected the train might not leave.

Bunty could see the carriage doors banging shut. The last of the other girls were saying good-byes to their hosts and hostesses. The Indians, those who had not been able to squeeze onto the train, were squatting patiently on the platform until the next train appeared.

Bunty glanced down the platform. She could see the other girls getting on the train now. There seemed to be a general exodus of girls from Calcutta. It was probably the continuing political crisis as well as the end of the season. Some girls might have stayed on if it hadn't been for the murder of Mr. Goad.

No, she thought. It wasn't either of these things. Girls would stay, no matter what, if things were going well. Girls were just going out of style. It was partly the slump, a lack of jobs. Or perhaps boys were just developing a resistance. You inoculate them with a little sex and they become immune to it. Like Jamie.

"Are your bags all in?" It was Denise speaking.

"Yes."

"Here's a magazine," said Tom. "It's *The New Yorker*. It's very funny, particularly the cartoons. There's one by Peter Arno that's a riot." He handed her his well-used copy.

"Thank you," said Bunty mechanically.

"Now don't forget you will have five hours in Bombay before the boat sails." Bunty turned dutifully toward Lady Thornton's voice. "Go to the Gymkhana Club and have a good cup of tea. They know Sir John there."

"Thank you," said Bunty. She glanced down the platform. He wasn't coming. Oddly, she found she didn't care very much now. He really wasn't very much of a person after all. What was it Sir John had mentioned to her yesterday? He had heard that young Wilson and that South African fellow, Windendorp, had broken up their chummery. Sir John said he had heard that young Palmer-Martin had invited Wilson into his chummery again and that the Yank might accept. She had felt sick at the news and thankful she hadn't married him, even if he had asked her.

What should she do now? She could go back and marry Harry Mullins from the office. At least she would know where she stood with Harry. He was all male, no doubt of that.

Or she could work at Withrow & Jenks for a bit, save her money, then make another trip, perhaps to Canada or Australia. Only this time . . . this time she wouldn't rely only on her body. It had always served her well up to now but after Jamie . . . well, it was time she grew up a bit. There was more to caring about a man that just giving your body.

"Time to go, Bunty." Lady Thornton kissed her young visitor's cheek. She had grown somewhat fond of this unpredictable young thing. She would almost like to have asked her back but she knew how Sir John felt. Bunty was to be her last fishing fleeter. He had made that clear.

"Good-bye, Lady Thornton. Thank you very much." She kissed the older woman impulsively. "Good-bye, Sir John."

He patted her gruffly and the sight of his lined and crinkled skin made her think suddenly of Mary Goad. She knew Sir John had been spending long days at York House, trying to straighten out matters, initiating the estate settling. He had been Goad's legal counsel and Lady Thornton said he was acting on behalf of the government. The viceroy wanted everything possible done for Mrs. Goad.

Bunty made a resolution. She would write Mrs. Goad a note of sympathy. It would be her first effort toward thinking of someone else's problems rather than her own. She fancied she already felt a new and worthier Bunty Cranston.

"Have a good trip," said Tom Beauchamp. "Don't take any wooden rupees."

Bunty climbed aboard and the train slowly pulled away. Its last grateful flutterings withdrew westward into the dusk.

The people on the platform hesitated a proper time, then walked toward the exits to the street. There was a sudden gaiety in the step of some. Others walked more slowly, accommodating themselves to the fact that their visitors had actually gone.

Sir John hesitated as he came out of the station. The air seemed suddenly hot. He had thought he was long past noting the change of season, especially since it really changed so damned little.

"Henrietta, I didn't expect to see you here." It was Lydia Bracebridge squeaking up at Lady Thornton. Rufus Bracebridge stood morosely nearby.

His wife continued. "We've just been seeing Margot and her Frank off on their wedding trip. They're going up to Kashmir. It will be so lovely for them."

"Kashmir is cold this time of year," grunted Lady Thornton.

"Oh well, you know true love notices no weather." Lydia Bracebridge giggled, then she looked solemn. "I'm so sorry about your little Bunty. I saw that she was leaving."

Lady Thornton drew herself up belligerently. "She could have married the young Yank. She just decided she didn't want to. Come Johnnie. Good-bye, Rufus . . . Lydia." She took her husband's arm and marched him toward their auto. Lydia Bracebridge watched, a reluctant admiration on her face. It was the grudging tribute of one hostess to another.

Tom and Denise climbed into his roadster, Tom still in his Light Horse uniform. He had been able to obtain a few hours off duty to accompany Denise but he would not be out of uniform until the crisis was declared finished.

He drove the motorcar across Howrah bridge and turned up Strand Road.

Denise found herself thinking about Mary. She had written her a note of shocked sympathy, offering to come out to York House to stay if it would help. There had been no reply. She didn't like to think of Mary alone in York House with that damned cavernous entrance hall, those colored shadows and tinkling bells.

Sir John never talked about his visits to York House, of course. He was not a retired chief justice for nothing. But Lady Thornton had said that Mary seemed to him very remote and withdrawn, that she gave only the essential answers to his questions.

Denise was aware that Tom was speaking to her, looking straight ahead as he drove. "Big Boy is in town. I saw him at the Bengal Club. He's staying at the Great Eastern."

"Oh." Denise sank deeper into her corner of the car.

"He said he had heard I was trying to raise money for a Brazilian scheme. He had heard it from one of his agents."

"When do you want me to see him?" Denise spoke dully. She wanted only to get home.

"There's no hurry." Tom blew his horn angrily. "Look at that damned bullock cart. They're always in the way."

"But won't he be leaving?"

"Don't rush me, damn it. Anybody might think you wanted to see the guy." He banged on the horn, cursing. "Suihke buchha. I'll be glad to get out of this damned country."

Gupta sat quietly in his room. His few possessions had already been gathered together and he was prepared to leave. He knew that Goad's death had brought in more troops and that this viceroy had not loosened his grip. He also knew that his young bodyguard had been taken by the police and hadn't returned. The boy would not willingly betray him but the police, particularly Captain Flemyng, were resourceful. It was time he left.

He tarried only to enjoy a moment of satisfaction. He sat on the cot, his short legs stretched comfortably before him, his round face contented, and let his thoughts drift.

There was no need to stay longer in Calcutta, even in India. He would simply disappear, having left one more killing behind. The nice part was that the British would not know he had gone until he turned up on some distant day in another part of the world. They would meanwhile be waiting, on edge, afraid of a shadow.

Nothing might come of this killing politically. The British were keeping a tight control on Bengal. They were also seeing to it that the newspapers were full of the news. They wanted the Mahatma to be confronted with this latest killing at every turn. This viceroy was clever.

It didn't matter. Swaraj was never really his object. It was necessary that people be reminded from time to time of what they were. It was the duty of every terrorist to demonstrate to men the destruction of which they were capable. They must see their image and be horrified. It reduced them to a more malleable clay.

Gupta stretched contentedly. What now? He could stay in India and have more British killed but that would lend the acts a political purpose. By disappearing, by letting the terrorist campaign die away, he was emphasizing its very lack of purpose. The only purpose was the killing itself. This Rajid and the others had never understood. They were young and killed for a cause. Now most, including Rajid, were dead.

Gupta got to his feet. It was really time that he left. That persistent Captain Flemyng would be swooping down on him some day. He was tempted to leave a note for him, telling him where the tea was kept and to make himself at home.

But where should he now go? It really didn't matter much. Another part of India or Switzerland, even Latin America. Anyplace where he could read Nechayev, wait, and when the time came, involve himself in creating anarchy. Which revo-

lution or whose cause didn't matter, so long as there could
be violence.

Gupta took a last look around the little room. He had
enjoyed its peaceful quality. It had provided just the ascetic
atmosphere he most appreciated in which to plan his killings.

Gupta locked the outer door meticulously and went down
the stairs. He knew he was quite safe; it was only a few yards
to the river, the launch, and his long-arranged disappearance.
That evening there would simply be one more freighter carrying one more lascar on its crew list. He had been an Indian
seaman too long not to know the role perfectly.

Gupta didn't look back. He knew there would be another
tranquil room somewhere, more killings to arrange. He faced
the future with contentment.

35

IN GANDHI'S QUARTERS IN YEVRADA GAOL, IT
was a day of activity. There had been a hammering of crates
in the courtyard and a folding of bedding and cooking pots
in the small rooms. The Mahatma's wife and his secretary
worked happily. On that day Bapu would be a free man. He
was being released on order of the viceroy.

The Mahatma sat alone in his small chamber, bony knees
under him as he stared thoughtfully at his spinning wheel.
The cheerful bustling outside did not find a response in him.

He knew why he was being released. He knew of the killing
in Calcutta, the murder of that important jute planter. It had
been reported to him weeks before, the moment it had happened. It seemed to him that everyone since then had mentioned it.

The viceroy knew that the word of his release would cause
great rejoicing throughout India. People's happiness and

gratitude would soon quench the small terrorist flame. The viceroy was very astute.

Yet Lord Willingdon must know that he could resume his swaraj agitation. He could be much more dangerous now. The civil disobedience campaign had been a failure without his guidance. He could make his own terms. And he would now have the added status of another imprisonment behind him.

He pondered. He had had many opportunities to reflect in the past eight months. He had been shaken by the wranglings in the Congress Party, by the stories of Hindu-Muslim riots, by the killings. He wasn't certain now that he wished swaraj for his people. And he must be certain.

He wondered whether he might not, for the time being at least, turn his attention more fully to the plight of the Untouchables. He had made a beginning there. He could leave swaraj in the hands of Jawaharlal Nehru and the Congress Party. He could devote his remaining years to awakening the moral conscience of India. That had always been foremost in his mind. Swaraj had really been a moral issue with him. Now he could bring his moral authority to the aid of the harijans. Their freedom was as important as India's.

His secretary came solemnly from the courtyard. "It is not long now, Bapu. Perhaps twenty minutes."

"I am ready."

"The spinning wheel? We will need to pack it. You will have much use for that outside." He reached out his hands solicitously.

"Leave it here."

"But you will need it."

The thin little man shook his head. "It belongs here. Help me." He put out his frail hand to rise.

The secretary extended his arm and the great Indian climbed wearily to his naked feet. He glanced down only once at the wheel, then turned toward the courtyard.

In Delhi the slender figure of Lord Willingdon was bent over his wife's vegetables when Captain Graham appeared.

"Sir, a message from Poona. The Mahatma has just been released."

The viceroy squinted up at him. "I trust he was examined first."

"Yes, sir. By Dr. Mehta."

"He was in good health?"

"As good as might be expected. There was one thing, sir. The superintendent reports that the Mahatma left his spinning wheel behind."

"Is that so?"

"Do you think we should send it to him? That's been rather a symbol of swaraj for him."

"The Mahatma is not a forgetful man, Graham. If he left it, he meant to leave it." He was thoughtful a moment. "I wonder. Yes, it could be." He looked at his aide, an unaccustomed emotion struggling in his ascetic face.

"Graham, do you know what this might mean! He may be giving up. First Gupta, now Gandhi."

"It would be a great triumph for you, sir. The Raj will be safe."

"For now perhaps."

"But if they've withdrawn, you've beaten them."

"It's not that simple." The viceroy shook his head. There was almost a puzzled expression on his face. "There's been something bothering me ever since I've been here, what it is about India. Have you ever seen a dying ground?"

"A what, sir?"

"It's where old elephants go when they're about to die. They seem to know when their time has come and they make their way there to die. I saw one in Africa once. It was full of remains, the tusks, their bones."

"I don't understand, sir."

"Empires are like elephants, Graham. Hasn't it ever struck you? We look everlasting. Powerful, enormous, even majestic. But each elephant has its dying ground. I think that's what India may be for us. There'll be only the bones." The viceroy roused himself. "Well, it looks as though this old elephant isn't going to die yet. We still have our tusks."

Captain Graham grinned. "You're quite a mahout, sir. If I may say so."

"That's the naked fellow sits on the elephant's neck. Gives directions with his hook."

"Yes, sir."

"Elephants outlive their mahouts many times over. They have many mahouts but there's only one elephant. Let that be our motto. It may teach us modesty."

"Yes, sir."

The viceroy was thoughtful a moment. "If we have won

out, we shall have to let it be known. We might make one last use of the Mahatma and Gupta. Something that will reassure the world that the Raj still lives."

"What is that, sir?"

"I don't know. A ceremony perhaps. An awarding of medals and honors. A peaceful scene, the very peace of it should be reassuring. The crisis over. Britannia still Paxes. That sort of thing."

"But whom should you honor, sir?"

"It doesn't matter. The ceremony is the thing. There could be Sir Evan Roberts, Commander-in-Chief, Army in India. We might have that police chief in Calcutta, Franklin. We'd let Sir Gerald Andrews pick somebody. And what about Edward Goad?"

"Goad's dead, sir."

"That's just the reason. We could make a martyr of him."

"Goad wasn't exactly the martyr type, sir."

"All the more reason. The Raj covers a multitude of sinners. We'll present it to his widow."

"I understand Mrs. Goad may be leaving India."

"She might stay for this. I should say in about two weeks' time, if all goes well. It could be a very interesting ceremony. In a corner of Government House garden, Calcutta. Very peaceful. Oh, we'll hide plenty of troops about. It wouldn't do to have Gupta turn up and blow us sky-high. Very embarrassing. But so far as the world will see it, it must be a tranquil and reassuring scene."

"Shall I cable Sir Gerald, sir?"

"I'll draft something. We might as well have some fun with this. We'll send it in code. That's it. He'll be very testy about it, just a social ceremony in all those code words."

And the viceroy's slender, priestly face wore an almost mischievous look.

It was, as planned, a very peaceful ceremony held in a shady corner of the Government House garden. A towering flame-of-the-forest tree formed the perfect background for the award presentation and the little group of invited spectators thought they had never seen a more tranquil or touching ceremony.

Photographers from the *Statesman* and the *Bombay Mail*, the *Delhi Times,* and the *Times of India* were allowed suitable freedom and there could be no doubt of worldwide distribution. The two companies of gurkha rifle troops could barely be seen in the nearby streets. They would certainly not appear in the news photos.

The ceremony itself was brief. Mary was the only person present unused to a Calcutta April and she was aware that her short hair was clamped damply to her scalp, that it itched, that moisture was trickling along her body. She also knew that Tiger, rigid in new scarlet and black, stood nearby.

"I wish your husband were here, Mrs. Goad, with all my heart." The viceregal voice was gentle. There was no mocking quality at all in his face. It was a simple phrase, decently said.

"I want you to accept this honor on his behalf. It is rather a belated recognition of his steadfastness and his courage. It isn't a very big medal but it is given with gratitude."

He then hung the medallion about Mary's neck. She bowed and the medal touched her throat. "Rex Imperator," it said. And there was an engraved portrait, very small, of the Rex Imperator himself, King George the Fifth.

The viceroy then moved along to the others in line: Sir Gerald Andrews, small but wiry; Mr. Lewellyn Franklin, the Welsh chief of police, Calcutta; Sir Evan Roberts, tall Commander-in-Chief, Indian Army; and lastly the scarred, heroic figure of Major Alastair Flemyng.

And a medal for Tiger, Mary mused. The Mighty Warrior. She wondered whether it were awarded to him for Cowardice in the Face of a Woman.

She listened as the viceroy read the citation. "Persistence in the face of adversity . . . his doggedness in the best tradition of the army . . . assisted in effort to rid India of a brutal terrorist leader . . ."

Mary closed her eyes. It's a mockery, she thought. Tiger has rid India only of me.

Then the ceremony was finished and the photographers respectfully took their last photos. The occasion would now announce to the world that the situation was under control. The Raj was stable.

Mary made her farewells, curtsying deeply to Lord Willingdon and Sir Gerald. She wondered momentarily as she bent before the governor whether he remembered their meeting at his Garden Party, so long before. She then turned toward the gate.

"Major Flemyng." The governor nodded to his aide. "See that Mrs. Goad obtains her transportation."

Mary walked slowly toward Government House gates, aware of the bemedaled man beside her, the single crown of a new major in the Indian Army on his shoulder.

Tiger called. "Subidar."

"Hussoor." An Indian sergeant trotted up and saluted.

"Humara auto syce bulao."

"No," said Mary. "I don't need your auto. I have my own car." She pointed to the estate auto.

"You came in that from York House?"

"It is rather battered but it's the only one I like to drive."

He glanced toward the garden behind him. Lord Willingdon and the others had moved into the marquee. The Indian subidar had gone back to his post outside the gate.

"I hear you're going back to England."

"Yes."

"Are you selling York House?"

She nodded. "Sir John has a very good offer."

He hesitated. "I'm not going to apologize for what I did, Mary. I had to decide and I chose the army."

"I understand."

"I would like to see you again."

"I am leaving India."

"There must be some time. Perhaps next week."

She stared up at him, surprised at her calmness. Then she nodded toward the lawn and marquee. "There is Sir Gerald. I think he wants you."

"Mary."

"Good-bye, Tiger. Thank you for seeing me to my car." She touched him briefly, then climbed into the estate auto.

He watched her as she drove away, then turned toward the marquee. He walked buoyantly, confident, befitting a new major. He had spoken to Mary and she hadn't said no. There would be none of this marriage proposal again. He had learned his lesson. He was a man and a soldier.

A few weeks later at York House Sir John Thornton bowed over Mary's hand. "Good-bye, Mrs. Goad. I shall write you as soon as everything is arranged."

"Thank you."

"It should take four or five months to complete probate. Meanwhile, I shall press Andrew Yule and Company toward a contract. You will be quite a rich woman."

"Do things as quickly as possible."

"You should receive your papers by autumn. I envy you your voyage. You are leaving just in time. I am used to it, of course, but May can be damned hot in India."

"So I believe."

He fumbled with the papers. "Let me see . . . power of attorney, probate request . . . yes, I have everything." He bowed over her hand again, eyeing her sympathetically. She looked very tired. May was damned hot for outsiders.

"Good-bye, Sir John. And thank you."

He grunted something and turned for the verandah steps.

Mary watched his auto chug down the driveway toward the river road, then strolled down to the terrace. She took a letter from her pocket and read it again. It had arrived several weeks before but she had read it only once. It was from Denise.

"Dear Mary, this will be brief. I do want to apologize for not coming down to stay with you. The truth is Tom and I have been so happy this past month that I haven't wanted to leave him, not even to see you.

"You remember that old friend of mine who was going to visit? Big Boy as Tom called him. He arrived and I fully expected I should have to see him to raise the money Tom needed. Wonder of wonders, Tom said no, we would go along as we were.

"I don't know why Tom changed but he doesn't want to leave India. It may have been Edward's being killed. That made Tom mad and he simply may not have wanted to give up on the Raj. Even his accent has become less American.

"It may be, of course, that my husband simply loves me. I have wanted many times in the past to quit on Tom. Sometimes I have wanted to leave India too, perhaps more than he. Now I'm glad I stuck it out.

"That's all, darling. I just wanted you to know. I do hope you can stand this heat. Never mind, it shouldn't be long now, from what I hear, that you'll be heading back to Blighty."

There was a postscript. "Do you remember that little green box we kept on the verandah with Tom's pet snake inside? We found it smashed the other day. Tom says he must have dropped a pot on it by mistake. The poor snake was simply nowhere. It was harmless, of course, with no fangs. Tom said not to worry.

"Cheerio, darling. D."

Mary put the letter in her pocket. That dear, frumpy little woman. She had the heart of a lioness. Now came the reward, the wages of loyalty. She hadn't quit.

Mary moved further down the terrace. Below her lay the jute fields and the heavy-winding river.

She watched a motorcar on the river road and recognized the MacDonough auto. It was either the doctor, sober these days, going to inspect another village or it was his wife and young Kitty Jolliffe going about their nursing duties. Kitty had told Mary that Mrs. MacDonough was feeling better now and was particularly helpful with the coolie children. Kitty said, however, that she never really liked to leave her alone with them for very long.

Mary brushed her hand across her hair. She had cut it very short with the coming of the hot weather. It had been more comfortable and, in a way, a sort of mourning.

She looked down at the sloping fields, at the place where Edward had shot the tiger. So long ago it seemed. She could see the river road turn right around the bend to the dak bungalow where she and Edward had given their first party. Their first and last.

Now she would be free of York House, free of jute and ganja and Julie. It had been a very good offer Andrew Yule and Company had made. Sir John had said that she would be solvent the rest of her life.

Then why didn't she give Sir John the signature he wanted? What on earth could make her hesitate to leave this terrible land?

Mary reviewed the months since Edward's death. It had been a busy time. She had not wasted her time sitting in the cavernous entrance hall but had tried to keep the estate running. It was what Edward would have wanted.

She had ridden each day across the estate, checking with the overseers, watching the retting. It had been a hot and unfamiliar ordeal but she would not stop. The alternative was to mourn in silence and apathy. Edward would have thought that weak, a betrayal.

But now the work could be stopped. Andrew Yule and Company would take over. She was free to leave matters with Sir John and escape to England.

But Andrew Yule might be wrong for the estate; they might ruin what had taken Edward so long to build. If she stayed she could run the estate as Edward would have, bring-

ng in technicians, building laboratories, finding new uses
for jute.

The overseers and the coolies would stay. There really was
not much else for them in Bengal.

Could she do it? It wouldn't be easy. It would be lonely.
There would be the heat and the fatigue. There could always
be Tiger for company, of course. He had made it plain he
would like to see her again.

At the thought of Tiger, Mary's face changed, grew somber.
It became not unlike the face of Mrs. MacDonough. It might
really be a pleasure to have a little fun with Tiger. He was
a major and more vulnerable now. He might need a little
money to keep up with his new rank. He was ambitious and
his ambition could be used against him. And, if swaraj did
come to India one day and the Raj were finished, he would
be out on the end of a long limb, very vulnerable indeed.
Mary contemplated the thought of Tiger.

No. That was finished. There would be no room for men
like Tiger in her life. She would remember him as an unhappy
man, doubly flawed because he was more aware than lesser
men.

Nor would she seek any other marriage. There could be
other things. There was so much to learn in India, the jute
business, the religions, the language. She might even open a
school some day, a proper school, not just for English children
but Indians as well.

She could make a place for herself in the neighborhood.
She would throw open York House, make it a welcoming
place. In the cold weather she might invite a few fishing
fleeters herself. Bunty Cranston for one. It had been good
of Bunty to write her a note after Edward's death.

Most of all, there would always be Edward. It was really
the least she could do for him now. There would be no Julie.
Julie would be laid to rest at last. There would be York House
and Edward and herself.

Mary's face was bright. She felt suddenly alive, free. She
had really been freed of so much in India, money worries,
childhood fancies of the Raj, even of Tim.

She would stay. She would tell Sir John to tell the Andrew
Yule people that the sale was canceled. Goad Memsahib was
not leaving India.

Mary looked down toward the river. Below her the jute
plants seemed to wave gently, nodding a welcome. Below the

fields the river wound its long, patient way toward the Bay
   Mary glanced down at the letter in her hand. She must
write Denise in the morning.

That spring there was a slight earthquake in Bengal. In
Patna the bridge across the Ganges fell down and the Jesuit
mission outside the town lost its clock tower and one of its
children's dormitories. The town of Chittagong, near the
mouth of the Brahmaputra, was also shaken. The earthquake
appeared to be centered in the area between the two rivers.
   Calcutta was not hurt. The few people in Firpo's staying
late over Friday tiffin noticed the ceiling punkahs swaying
and a few native bustees were damaged but no lives were lost.
Everyone congratulated themselves. Calcutta was built on a
swamp, they said, and that was what had saved them. The
city had ridden up and down like a boat.
   But in the delta the snipe flew up from the marshes and
scattered from the city. Crocodiles in the Sundarbans were
seen to slither into the water and swim downriver toward the
Bay. In the city pieces of the Hooghly docks fell in the river
and, when their foundations were examined, it was found that
the pilings had sunk, sucked down into the delta mud.
   The rivers that had built the city were slowly, patiently
eating their way underneath.